Advanced Dungeons&Dragons®

Accessories

ENCYCLOPEDIA MAGICA™ Volume One

This is the first in a series of four accessories detailing every magic item printed by TSR in every publication and game product that we could find. This volume details items from *abacus of calculation* to *dust of blending*.

ENCYCLOPEDIA MAGICA™ Volume Two

This is the second release of TSR's greatest undertaking: listing every magic item it's ever printed. This 416-page volume details *dust of decoy* through *phylactery of righteousness*. Some of the more popular items included herein are figurines, gems, lamps, maces, oils, and orbs.

ENCYCLOPEDIA MAGICA™ Volume Three

This 416-page accessory details magic items from the *pick of earth parting* to the spellbook, *Thesis of Conditional Ruptures*. This volume includes potions, rings, robes, rods, scrolls, and shields—some of the most popular magic items.

ENCYCLOPEDIA MAGICA™ Volume Four

The last of the series, this 416-page volume details magic items from the Spellbook, *Theories on Converging Transitions*, through *Zwieback of Zymurgy*. This accessory features staves, swords, and wands. Also included are Magic Item Random Determination Tables and an extensive index.

FOR DUNGEON MASTERS

Fundamentals

DUNGEON MASTER® Guide

The single most important reference for any DM, this volume gives you the lowdown on how to create and run your own AD&D game campaign. From world-making to treasure-sorting, from role-playing to adventure generation, the *DMG* has it all.

MONSTROUS MANUAL™ Accessory

Where else can you find over 600 monsters of every sort, each with full game statistics and a full-color illustration of the beast in action? This is a fundamental reference for every DM.

DUNGEON MASTER® Screen & Master Index

This self-standing cardboard screen puts vital combat and encounter tables right before your eyes. It also hides your maps, die rolls, and secret information from players.

Accessories

DUNGEON MASTER® Guide Supplements

Add depth to your fantasy campaign and bring your adventures to greater life with these vital and comprehensive handbooks!

- Arms and Equipment Guide (handy for players, too!)
- Monster Mythology (nonhuman deities)
- The Complete Book of Villains (the best NPC book ever!)
- The Complete Book of Necromancers (the ultimate bad guys)

MONSTROUS COMPENDIUM® Annuals

One manual of monsters is not enough! Each year, a new compendium of bizarre horrors and startling creations is assembled, guaranteed to astonish the players, enliven the campaign, and please the DM.

Accessories

Book of Artifacts

This coveted collection of phenomenal devices features long-buried favorites from the original AD&D game tomes, as well as many new relics and devices native to certain TSR campaign worlds, all greatly expanded for AD&D 2nd Edition game players. You'll even learn how to create artifacts and other magical devices for your own campaign!

Adventures

The ultimate DMs' fantasies have been put together in these deluxe adventures, which can be set in any campaign world against almost any type of heroic group.

- DRAGON MOUNTAIN® Adventure
- Night Below: An UNDERDARK™ Campaign
- Temple, Tower, & Tomb
- The Rod of Seven Parts
- Labyrinth of Madness

The Rod of Seven Parts

The Rod of Seven Parts is one of the most powerful artifacts in the AD&D® game. The heroes face the incredible challenge of finding and piecing together all seven parts and harnessing the power of the Rod to defeat the Queen of Chaos and Miska the Wolf-Spider. Designed for character levels 10 to 12.

Night Below

The largest dungeon ever published! A full "generic" campaign setting for raising characters from 1st to 16th level, with hundreds of miles of underground caves, tunnels, and dungeons–even an ocean! New skills, monsters, magical items, and more will flesh out the fantasy underworld and cultures for which the AD&D game is justly famous.

m.A

Advanced Dungeons & Dragons®

Official Game Accessory

Tome
of
Magic

New spells and magical items for priest and wizard classes!

TSR, Inc.
201 Sheridan Springs Rd.
Lake Geneva,
WI 53147
U.S.A.

TSR Ltd.
120 Church End
Cherry Hinton
Cambridge CB1 3LB
United Kingdom

1-56076-107-5

Forward

Whew, another big project behind me! Never did I realize when I started work on the *Tome of Magic* that it would become such an undertaking. After all, it seemed so simple. At that point, I should have known better.

It all started with a seemingly innocent comment, something like, "There are a lot of gaps in the spell lists for wizards and priests. Maybe we should do something about it." I don't know if I said that, or if it was someone else's idea, but whoever said it was right. I knew they were right because I could see them clearly by the time the AD&D® 2nd Edition *Player's Handbook* was finished.

These gaps were not yawning chasms in the game system. They were little things, like, "Gee, it would be nice to have a spell that did X—or Y, or Z, or whatever." Sometimes they were things to help explain the weirdness people were always putting in adventures or little touches that would smooth things out for players and DMs alike. The *Tome of Magic* could be just the place to get some of these ideas into the AD&D® game system. Months later (because months always pass between the idea and actually doing the work), it was time to make all this real.

That's when I discovered the warts on the great idea—two in particular. First, filling a book with a mismatched collection of spells was not enough. How many variations on *fireball, lightning bolt,* and *confusion* did you really need? Second, a book of odds and ends didn't sound exciting for either a game designer or for the players. The *Tome of Magic* needed something—a hook—to make it interesting.

As a result, the *Tome of Magic* is much more than just a collection of spells. There are many new ideas about the types and uses of magic in these pages—wild magic, cooperative magic, focuses, elementalists, and more. In the end, the Tome of Magic offers more than just spells—it gives breadth and range to wizards and priests. In many ways, it is a peek inside the Pandora's box of magic.

On top of these concerns was a problem of mental health. If I alone had to fill all these pages with spells and magical items, I'd be writing from the nut-house by now. There was no way I could create all these new spells and remain sane. That's why there is a host of designers listed in the credits. Taking often the barest of my ideas and suggestions, these creative conspirators produced a wide variety of spells and items. After weeding out spells too similar in form and function, I can offer you the cleverness and diversity of six different designers, not just one!

For myself and the other designers, we hope you find the *Tome of Magic* both entertaining and useful. Let it be your guide to just how much further wizards and priests can go in the AD&D game.

David Cook
February, 1991

Table of Contents

Credits

Design: David Cook (Wild Magic, Faith Magic)
   Nigel Findley (Numbers, Thought, War)
   Anthony Herring (Elementalists, additional spells)
   Christopher Kubasik (Chaos, Law)
   Carl Sargent (Quest Spells, Metamagic)
   Rick Swan (Time, Travel, Wards)

Supervision and Development: David Cook

Editing and Additional Development: Anne Brown

Proofreading: Anne Brown, Rob King, Dori Watry

Cover Art: Jeff Easley

Black and White Art: Stephen Fabian

Color Art: Brom, Clyde Caldwell, Carol Heyer, John & Laura Lakey, Roger Loveless

Icons: Stephen Sullivan

Graphic Design: Stephanie Tabat

Typesetting: Gaye O'Keefe, Angelika Lokotz

Production: Sarah Feggestad

Seventh Printing: March, 1996

An apprentice stands in the laboratory of his ancient wizard master. The youth's eyes stray across tables cluttered with alembics, retorts, beakers, bat wings, and phials, and beyond to shelves of scrolls and books. A musty old volume, bound in cracked green leather with glittering silver hinges, catches his attention. His master is elsewhere, so the curious student pulls the heavy volume from the shelf and, with a puff of breath, blows away a thick layer of dust. "Tome of Magic" it reads, spelled out in silver leaf on the brittle cover.

The apprentice can't believe his discovery. He's never seen this book before. What secrets has his master been keeping from him? What secrets will he discover inside? With trembling fingers, the apprentice opens the creaking cover.

"Ahem, O callow youth! Perhaps you are dissatisfied with my training and would like to seek another master!" booms the master's voice from behind the apprentice. The youth startles and guiltily slams the cover shut. Turning, he smiles sheepishly at his master.

The old wizard, bald and portly, takes the book from his apprentice's hands. "Before you can learn secrets like these, you must first master the basics, which I sometimes doubt you ever will. Now tell me, what are the three Greater Gesticulations used· in casting a light spell?" The wizard deftly slides the tome back into place on the shelf as he speaks.

Flustered, the apprentice stammers out what feels like an elementary reply. But in his heart, he knows that someday he will read the secrets of that tome.

Someday is now!

How to Use This Book

With over two hundred new spells for wizards and priests and a host of new magical items, the question of how to use this book may seem fairly obvious to most players. It appears to be a simple matter of opening the pages, selecting spells and magical items, and tossing these into a campaign.

Of course, it can be done that way, but players and DMs who take this route will miss many of the new possibilities and expansions the *Tome of Magic* has to offer. On the surface, the *Tome of Magic* may appear to be just a collection of spells and magical items. But it contains new game rules and information that goes much deeper.

This volume introduces a new type of wizard magic, expanded specializations, new priest spheres, and new variations on priest magic. These rules have the potential to impact a campaign in a way greater than a first glance might suggest. To benefit the most from these expansions, the DM should carefully consider how to introduce and use the new rules.

Who Is It For?

The *Tome of Magic* is written with both the DM and ·player in mind. Dungeon Masters who keep this book out the hands of their players are doing their game a disservice. Likewise, players who want this book only to learn about the new magical items are missing the point. Both player and DM can use this book to improve and expand the game.

Wizards

In the game world of wizards, there are two significant additions—wild magic and elementalists. Wild magic is a strange, new type of magical power, just being explored and discovered for the first time. Wild mages are rare and exotic. Long before encountering such a wizard, characters may hear tell of a new type of magic in reports from travelers to distant lands. Of course, every adventurer knows that these reports tend to be exaggerated—more fiction than fact.

The first appearance of a wild mage is best presented by the DM as a mysterious NPC. The wild mage may join the party briefly or may be the springboard for an adventure. He should not be a henchman or hireling, but someone who is the characters' equal or superior. This gives players the opportunity to experience the wonders (and terrors) of wild magic before immersing themselves in this new art. After the characters have learned something of this strange magic, wild mage player characters may be introduced, perhaps as apprentices of the same NPC. Gradually, these new mages will become accepted members of the campaign world.

Elementalists can be introduced in a similar fashion, although their arrival is likely to be less mysterious. The first appearance of the specialization could be a small school or guild in a nearby town, established by an elementalist from distant lands (where such magic is common). The newly established wizard is likely to be looking for an apprentice; new characters are eligible to join the school. Of course, established mages may take an interest (both positive and negative) in his activities.

Priests

The introduction of new priest spheres can pose a logical problem in some campaigns—if an existing Power has influence in a certain sphere, why did his priests never have these spells before? Why do they wake up one morning and suddenly have access to spells never before seen?

The DM can use several solutions to this question. The first is most effective for such esoteric spheres as Thought and Numbers. In this case, few (if any) existing Powers have access to these spheres. Instead, priests arrive (as did wild mages) from distant lands, spreading the word of their god. These NPC priests have strange powers never before seen. In some locations, they may be accepted, while in others, they may be driven out with vengeance. As new player characters are created, this "new" faith with all its advantages and disadvantages becomes an option.

Another explanation, particularly useful for the spheres of War and Wards, is that the Power always had access to these spells, but never had the need to grant them. A deity of war could reasonably withhold spells of the War sphere until the threat of war exists. To introduce the War sphere into the campaign, the DM need only create a little border tension and massing of troops—the perfect background for many adventures.

Certain deities may be too aloof or remote to become involved in the affairs of men until the need arises. This is particularly appropriate for the spheres of Law and Chaos. A shift in the "harmony of the universe" might warrant the attention of these Powers to "set things right."

The introduction of subdivisions in the elemental sphere can be effected in a similar manner. Foreign priests may enter the campaign region and introduce the concept, or existing priests might discover their own deities suddenly taking a more active interest in their spells. Conflict or rivalry on the elemental planes can be used to justify rigid adherence to a particular element. A fire god, feeling the rising power of a sea god, may enforce strict elemental selection to bolster the devotion of his priests.

Of all the new priest material, quest spells are the easiest to introduce. These are given by the DM only when special conditions warrant. It is easy to justify that conditions have never yet warranted the need for quest spells.

Magical Items

Of all the new material in this book, magical items require the least effort to introduce. Many are simply treasures that can be discovered in a newly-won hoard. In this case, DMs are encouraged not to reveal all the powers of a newly-found item. Rather, the player should be forced to puzzle out an item's powers. For example, the characters find a magical quill. What does it do? How is it used? Answering these questions is a goal that players can set for their characters. After spending time, spells, and money on research and possibly more adventures, the characters may discover that they own a *quill of law*.

Another effective and logical method for introducing never-before-seen magical items is for NPCs to possess these fascinating new devices. Thus, a wild mage might own a *rod of disruption* or an elementalist a *wand of corridors*.

Patience, Patience, Patience

An important thing for both the DM and players to remember is that the existence of *Tome of Magic* does not mean that everything in it needs to be rushed into play. If the need for a particular spell does not exist right away, don't worry. Sooner or later, a player or DM will discover that it suits his needs perfectly. Properly used, the *Tome of Magic* will become a source of surprises and inspiration for many adventures to come.

New Rules for Wizards

Mages and magic, great and small, are a key element of a fantasy campaign. While endowed with considerable powers, there are still vast horizons for mages to explore. Just a small portion of these possibilities is explored in the *Tome of Magic*—wild magic, elemental specialists, and metamagic.

Wild Magic

One of the newest discoveries from the great lands of the Forgotten Realms is wild magic. Originally considered little more than the unfortunate by-product of an epic struggle among the gods of that world, the strange effects of the wild lands (as those areas affected by wild magic are known) have attracted the attention of many a curious or scholarly wizard.

In general, two types of wizards are drawn to these strange areas. The first are the researchers:

wizards devoted to the study of the theoretical underpinnings of magic. For them, the wild areas expose long-hidden secrets of the magical universe and give new insights into how magical energy functions. From their work have evolved the beginnings of a theory of random magic—one that defies the traditional schools.

The second type of wizard drawn to the wild lands is far less rigorous and methodical. These spellcasters are attracted by the sheer randomness and uncertainty of the wild lands. Such mages seek to incorporate wild magic into their spells by combining traditional magic with the new theories of random magic, throwing in a dose of their own chaotic natures as an extra measure. These wizards are the true wild mages who have been seen recently in various lands.

Although initially discovered and researched on Toril, the FORGOTTEN REALMS® campaign world, the art of wild magic has quickly spread to other places. Wild mages, through teleporting, spelljamming, planar hopping, and even walking, have carried the precepts of wild magic to lands and worlds far removed from Toril.

Wild Mages

With the discovery of wild magic has come the appearance of wizards devoted to its study. Like their traditional specialist brethren, wild mages have thrown themselves into the intense study of a single aspect of magic. This has given them unique benefits and restrictions on their powers. Wild magic is so different from traditional magic that only those devoted to its study may cast wild magic; no wizard other than a wild mage may attempt to use the spells of wild magic.

Wild mages are by no means specialist wizards—at least not in the traditional sense. Wild mages do not study within the confines of schools. Instead, their research into new theories of wild magic carries them into all different fields. Wild magic has strengths in some areas (particularly divination and evocation), but it is not confined to any single school of magic. The proponents of wild magic proudly trumpet their art's broad base and flexibility as its great advantages.

Of course, these same advocates are quick to downplay wild magic's drawbacks. First and foremost, it is *wild* magic. On rare occasions, any spell can have dangerously unpredictable results, including backfiring or creating an entirely different effect from what was desired. More commonly, the magnitude of a spell—range, duration, area of effect, or even damage—may fluctuate

from casting to casting. Spells cast by wild mages are inherently unpredictable.

Only characters with Intelligence of 16 or greater are qualified to become wild mages. The theories of wild magic are breaking new ground, and only characters of high intelligence are able to decipher the arcane convolutions of its meta-mathematical theory. Although wild magic is chaotic on the surface, study in this field requires diligence and discipline.

There are no restrictions to the alignment of a wild mage. The race of a wild mage is limited to those races with competency at magic; thus, only humans, elves, and half-elves can be wild mages. Gnomes have some magical talent, but lack the broad base of skills and knowledge necessary to master this new field.

Wild mages must abide by the normal restrictions for all wizards concerning weapons and armor. They use the same THAC0 and saving throw values of traditional wizards. They progress in level according to the Wizard Experience Levels and Wizard Spell Progression tables (Tables 20 and 21 in the *Player's Handbook*).

Wild mages have several abilities and restrictions. Like specialists, wild mages are able to memorize one extra spell per spell level. This spell must be a wild magic spell, although it can be from any school; wild mages have no opposition schools as do specialists.

Wild mages receive a bonus of +10% when learning new wild magic spells and a −5% penalty when learning other spells. Because wild magic is somewhat "fast and loose," wild mages can research new spells as if they were one level less difficult, decreasing the amount of time and money needed to create new spells.

Certain magical items behave differently in the hands of a wild mage. This is due to his understanding of the random processes that power them. Most notable of these is the *wand of wonder*. The wild mage has a 50% chance of controlling the wand, allowing him to use charges from the wand to cast any spell he already knows (but does not need to have memorized). The number of charges used by the wand is equal to the number of levels of the spell desired. If the attempt fails, only one charge is used and a random effect is generated.

The wild mage can control the following items 50% of the time, thereby allowing him to select the result or item instead of relying on chance: *amulet of the planes, bag of beans, bag of tricks, deck of illusions, deck of many things,* and the *well of many worlds.*

Level Variations

The most broad-reaching aspect of the wild mage's powers is his approach to spells. The wild mage's work with the principles of uncertainty affects all spells that have a level variable for range, duration, area of effect, or damage. Each time a wild mage uses a spell with a level variable, he randomly determines the resulting casting level of the spell. The spell may function at lesser, equal, or greater effect than normal. The degree of variation depends on the true level of the caster, as shown in Table 1: Level Variation.

To determine the level at which the spell is cast, the player must roll 1d20 at the moment the spell is cast. The variation from the caster's actual level is found at the point where the character's true level and the die roll intersect. (True level refers to the current experience level of the wild mage.) If the result is a positive number, that many levels are added to the caster's true level for purposes of casting the spell. If the result is a negative number, that many levels are subtracted from the caster's true level. If the result is 0, the spell is cast normally. The variation of a spell's power has no permanent effect on the mage's experience level or casting ability.

For example, Theos, a 7th-level wild mage, casts a *fireball*. He wishes it to take effect 70 yards away at the site of a band of advancing orcs. *Fireball* has level variables for range (10 yds. + 10 yds./level) and damage (1d6/level). A die roll is made on the Level Variation Table with a result of 19, indicating a level variation of +3. The *fireball* functions as if cast by a 10th-level wizard (7 + 3) and easily reaches its target, causing 10d6 points of damage. If the level variation had been −3 (die roll of 2), the spell would have operated as if it were 4th level. In this case, the *fireball* would have fallen short since its maximum range would have been 50 yards (10 yds + 10 yds × 4).

One additional effect can occur when casting level-variable spells. If the result from Table 1 is boldfaced, the caster has inadvertently created a *wild surge* in the spell in addition to the spell's effects. A wild surge briefly opens a doorway through which raw magical energy pours. The energy is incompletely controlled by the actions of the spellcaster. The result, often spectacular, is seldom what the caster intended and is sometimes a smaller or greater version of the desired spell. At other times, wildly improbable results occur. Songs may fill the air, people might appear out of nowhere, or the floor may become a pool of grease. Whatever happens, it is the essence of wildness.

When a wild surge occurs, the DM must roll on Table 2. Unlike many other instances in the AD&D® game in which the DM is encouraged to choose a suitable result, wild surges are best resolved by random chance. Actively choosing a result biases the nature of wild magic. DMs are encouraged to be random and have fun.

Table 1: LEVEL VARIATION

True Level	Die Roll (D20)																			
	1	2	3	4	5	6	7	8	9	10	11	12	13	14	15	16	17	18	19	20
1	−1	−1	−1	−1	−1	0	0	0	0	0	0	0	0	0	0	+1	+1	+1	+1	**+1**
2	−1	−1	−1	−1	−1	−1	0	0	0	0	0	0	**0**	0	+1	+1	+1	+1	+1	+1
3	−2	−1	−1	−1	−1	−1	−1	0	0	0	0	**0**	0	+1	+1	+1	+1	+1	+1	+2
4	−2	−2	−1	−1	−1	−1	−1	−1	0	0	0	0	+1	+1	+1	+1	+1	+1	**+2**	+2
5	−3	−2	−2	−1	−1	−1	−1	**−1**	−1	0	0	+1	+1	+1	+1	+1	+1	+2	+2	+3
6	−3	−3	−2	−2	**−1**	−1	−1	−1	−1	0	0	+1	+1	+1	+1	+1	+2	+2	+3	+3
7	−4	−3	−3	−2	−2	−1	−1	−1	−1	0	**0**	+1	+1	+1	+1	+2	+2	+3	+3	+4
8	−4	−4	−3	−3	−2	−2	−1	−1	−1	0	0	+1	+1	+1	**+2**	+2	+3	+3	+4	+4
9+	−5	−4	−4	−3	−3	−2	−2	−1	**−1**	0	0	+1	+1	+2	+2	+3	+3	+4	+4	+5

Boldface results indicate a *wild surge;* consult Table 2: Wild Surge Results.

Table 2: WILD SURGE RESULTS

D100

Roll	Result
01	*Wall of force* appears in front of caster
02	Caster smells like a skunk for spell duration
03	Caster shoots forth eight non-poisonous snakes from fingertips. Snakes do not attack.
04	Caster's clothes itch (+2 to initiative)
05	Caster glows as per a *light* spell
06	Spell effect has 60' radius centered on caster
07	Next phrase spoken by caster becomes true, lasting for 1 turn
08	Caster's hair grows one foot in length
09	Caster pivots 180 degrees
10	Caster's face is blackened by small explosion
11	Caster develops allergy to his magical items. Character cannot control sneezing until all magical items are removed. Allergy lasts 1d6 turns.
12	Caster's head enlarges for 1d3 turns
13	Caster *reduces* (reversed *enlarge*) for 1d3 turns
14	Caster falls madly in love with target until a *remove curse* is cast
15	Spell cannot be canceled at will by caster
16	Caster *polymorphs* randomly
17	Colorful bubbles come out of caster's mouth instead of words. Words are released when bubbles pop. Spells with verbal components cannot be cast for 1 turn.
18	Reversed *tongues* affects all within 60 feet of caster
19	*Wall of fire* encircles caster
20	Caster's feet enlarge, reducing movement to half normal and adding +4 to initiative rolls for 1d3 turns
21	Caster suffers same spell effect as target
22	Caster levitates 20' for 1d4 turns
23	*Cause fear* with 60' radius centered on caster. All within radius except the caster must make a saving throw.
24	Caster speaks in a squeaky voice for 1d6 days
25	Caster gains X-ray vision for 1d6 rounds
26	Caster ages 10 years
27	*Silence, 15' radius* centers on caster
28	10' × 10' pit appears immediately in front of caster, 5' deep per level of the caster
29	*Reverse gravity* beneath caster's feet for 1 round
30	Colored streamers pour from caster's fingertips
31	Spell effect rebounds on caster
32	Caster becomes *invisible*
33	*Color spray* from caster's fingertips
34	Stream of butterflies pours from caster's mouth
35	Caster leaves monster-shaped footprints instead of his own until a *dispel magic* is cast
36	3-30 gems shoot from caster's fingertips. Each gem is worth 1d6 × 10 gp.
37	Music fills the air
38	*Create food and water*
39	All normal fires within 60' of caster are extinguished
40	One magical item within 30' of caster (randomly chosen) is permanently drained
41	One normal item within 30' of caster (randomly chosen) becomes permanently magical
42	All magical weapons within 30' of caster are increased by +2 for 1 turn
43	Smoke trickles from the ears of all creatures within 60' of caster for 1 turn
44	*Dancing lights*
45	All creatures within 30' of caster begin to hiccup (+1 to casting times, −1 to THAC0)
46	All normal doors, secret doors, portcullises, etc. (including those locked or barred) within 60' of caster swing open
47	Caster and target exchange places
48	Spell affects random target within 60' of the caster
49	Spell fails but is not wiped from caster's mind
50	*Monster summoning II*
51	Sudden change in weather (temperature rise, snow, rain, etc.) lasting 1d6 turns
52	Deafening bang affects everyone within 60'. All those who can hear must save vs. spell or be stunned for 1d3 rounds.
53	Caster and target exchange voices until a *remove curse* is cast

D100

Roll	Result
54	*Gate* opens to randomly chosen outer plane; 50% chance for extra-planar creature to appear.
55	Spell functions but shrieks like a shrieker
56	Spell effectiveness (range, duration, area of effect, damage, etc.) decreases 50%
57	Spell reversed, if reverse is possible
58	Spell takes physical form of free-willed elemental and cannot be controlled by caster. Elemental remains for duration of spell. Touch of the elemental causes spell effect (THAC0 equal to caster's).
59	All weapons within 60' of caster glow for 1d4 rounds
60	Spell functions; any applicable saving throw is not allowed
61	Spell appears to fail when cast, but occurs 1-4 rounds later
62	All magical items within 60' of caster glow for 2d8 days
63	Caster and target switch personalities for 2d10 rounds
64	*Slow* spell centered on target
65	Target *deluded*
66	*Lightning bolt* shoots toward target
67	Target *enlarged*
68	*Darkness* centered on target
69	*Plant growth* centered on target
70	1,000 lbs. of non-living matter within 10' of target *vanishes*
71	*Fireball* centers on target
72	Target turns to stone
73	Spell is cast; material components and memory of spell are retained
74	Everyone within 10' of caster receives the benefits of a *heal*
75	Target becomes dizzy (−4 AC and THAC0, cannot cast spells) for 2d4 rounds
76	*Wall of fire* encircles target
77	Target levitates 20' for 1d3 turns
78	Target suffers *blindness*
79	Target is charmed as per *charm monster*
80	Target *forgets*
81	Target's feet enlarge, reducing movement to half normal and adding +4 to all initiative rolls for 1-3 turns
82	Rust monster appears in front of target
83	Target *polymorphs* randomly
84	Target falls madly in love with caster until a *dispel magic* is cast.
85	Target changes sex
86	Small, black raincloud forms over target
87	*Stinking cloud* centers on target
88	Heavy object (boulder, anvil, safe, etc.) appears over target and falls for 2d20 points of damage
89	Target begins sneezing. No spells can be cast until fit passes (1d6 rounds).
90	Spell effect has 60' radius centered on target (all within radius suffer the effect)
91	Target's clothes itch (+2 to initiative for 1d10 rounds)
92	Target's race randomly changes until canceled by *dispel magic*
93	Target turns ethereal for 2d4 rounds
94	Target *hastened*
95	All cloth on target crumbles to dust
96	Target sprouts leaves (no damage caused, can be pruned without harm)
97	Target sprouts new useless appendage (wings, arm, ear, etc.) which remains until *dispel magic* is cast
98	Target changes color (canceled by *dispel magic*)
99	Spell has a minimum duration of 1 turn (i.e., a *fireball* creates a ball of flame that remains for 1 turn, a *lightning bolt* bounces and continues, possibly rebounding, for 1 turn, etc.)
100	Spell effectiveness (range, duration, area of effect, damage, etc.) increases 200%

Unless otherwise noted, all spells created by a wild surge occur at the designated target point and function normally (appropriate saving throws are allowed). The caster's true level is used when calculating range, duration, area of effect, etc. of these spells.

The above list, while long, is only a small fraction of the possible results of a wild surge. The DM is free to create his own tables for wild surges.

Tables like the one above cannot take into account the situation at the instant of casting. It is not feasible to create tailored effects for every spell used in every possible way. Therefore, it is quite likely that some wild magic results will make no sense, be impossible, or have no visible effect. In these cases, the wild surge has no effect. For example, if a mage were casting a *wizard lock* on a door and triggered a wild surge with the result "Target changes sex," no effect would be visible, since doors do not have a sex (at least as far as we know). Likewise, a rock might be *hastened* or a snake might have its feet *enlarged.* In these cases, nothing happens—at least nothing that affects play. When determining the result of wild magic, the DM must use his best judgment.

Finally, not even the randomness of wild surges should be allowed to ruin the story of an adventure. As ultimate storyteller and arbiter of the game, the DM can overrule any wild surge he deems too destructive to the adventure. If this happens, reroll the dice to get a new result. In a case such as this, do not treat a wild surge as having no effect.

Clearly, wild mages are a risky proposition. Not every player will want to play a wild mage; not every party will want a wild mage. The DM should not add benefits to the wild mage, hoping to the make the class more "attractive" to his players. Players who like wild mages will play them without bribery. They will find the uncertainty and randomness of wild mages irresistible; these are the players for whom the wild mage was created.

Elemental Wizards

The elemental wizard is a new variety of specialist mage beginning to appear throughout the lands. These wizards scorn the "accepted" theories of magical classification (the rigid school structure) in favor of a holistic, natural understanding of magic. The result is elementalism.

Elementalism is not a school in itself; it is an area of specialization focusing on spells involving the four prime elements of air, earth, fire, and water. These spells may be from any of the nine schools of magic. The *fireball* spell, for example, belongs to the evocation school, but according to elementalists, it is also a spell of elemental fire.

Unlike other specialists, an elementalist does not specialize in a single school of magic, but may learn and cast spells belonging to any school. Although this may seem to be a great advantage, elementalists suffer considerable penalties when learning and casting spells that do not relate directly to the elements. The exception to this penalty is the spells of the school of lesser divination, which every wizard may learn.

Each element has a diametrical opposite: air opposes earth, fire opposes water, and vice versa.

Every elementalist must choose one element as his specialty. He may learn and cast any spells relating to his chosen element and gains advantages when doing so. He may also cast spells of the two elements which do not oppose his specialty, for which he receives no bonuses or penalties. Consequently, he may not learn or cast any spells associated with the element that opposes his element of specialty. For example, a fire elementalist may cast spells relating to fire, air, or earth, but may not cast spells of elemental water. A specialist is also prohibited from using magical items that duplicate spell effects of his oppositional element.

Fire

|

Air — opposes — Earth

|

Water

Although their repertoire of spells is small, elementalists are potent wizards, for they gain the following advantages when involved with spells of their chosen element:

- Elementalists receive a bonus of +25% when attempting to learn spells of their element and a bonus of +15% when learning other elemental spells. They suffer a penalty of −25% when trying to learn spells that do not relate to the elements.

- An elementalist may memorize one extra spell per level, providing that at least one of the memorized spells is from his element of specialty.

- Because elementalists have an enhanced understanding of spells within their element, they receive a +2 bonus when making saving throws against those spells. Other creatures suffer a −2 penalty when making saving throws against an elementalist casting spells from his specialty.

- Once per day, an elementalist may choose to cast one memorized spell from his element of specialty as if he were 1d4 levels higher. He must declare his decision to do this immediately prior to casting the spell. This affects range, duration, area of effect, and damage; it does not allow the wizard to cast a spell from a level which he normally could not use.

- When an elementalist attempts to create a new spell relating to his specialty element, the DM should count the new spell as one level less (for determining difficulty).

- Upon reaching 15th level, an elementalist does not need to concentrate when controlling elementals of his specialty element summoned by the 5th-level spell *conjure elemental*. The normal 5% chance of the elemental turning upon its summoner remains in effect.

• At 20th level, there is no chance of a summoned elemental turning upon an elementalist if the creature is of the wizard's specialty element.

A complete listing of elemental spells arranged by each element can be found in Appendix 1.

Metamagic

Metamagic is a special term used by erudite and educated wizards to describe a single class of spells and magical items—those powers that alter or affect other magical spells and items. Metamagic spells do not directly affect people, objects, or events. Instead, the powers of metamagic are used to alter the fabric of spells themselves. Through metamagic spells, such as *far reaching* or *squaring the circle*, the once inviolable limits of a spell can be altered. Range, duration, casting time, area of effect, and even sound and color can be tailored through the use of metamagical spells.

Although the concept of metamagic has existed since the beginning of magical study, it has generally been ignored by most wizards, who have been far more interested in spectacular effects and immediate results. However, a few independent researchers have continued to explore and expand this esoteric field of study.

New Rules for Priests

Priests are hardly the unglamorous and weak adventurers that they are sometimes portrayed to be. They are an important part of any society, serving as more than just handy doctors. Priests have great responsibilities for the defense, guidance, welfare, and protection of a community. Because of this, their spells reflect more diversity and application when compared with wizard spells. The *Tome of Magic* provides priests with more tools to help them achieve their goals.

Quest Spells

Priests and clerics are the servants of Powers—immortal entities with abilities far beyond those of mere mortals. Yet these servants do not wield magical forces equal to those of wizards; priests have nothing to compare with the *wish* spell, for example. Circumstances will arise when a priest should be able to call upon the magical energies controlled by his Power to achieve something extraordinary in serving a sacred duty. Quest spells are designed to satisfy these extremes and allow the priest to wield high-powered magic without drastically altering the scope of his magic.

Quest spells are a category of powerful spells without an assigned level. They should not be confused with the 5th-level spell *quest*, which is a specific single spell.

While quest spells are powerful, they are not as powerful as the energies used by Powers. If a god chose to flatten a mountain or raise an island, he could probably do so. Priests cannot achieve such huge effects; they are still mortal beings. But quest spells do provide a priest with magic more powerful than any other priestly magic; a quest spell could easily mean the difference between success or failure in a mission. Quest spells are capable of affecting large areas or numbers of creatures and allow the shaping of great energies; they are often difficult or impossible to resist or dispel.

Quest spells are not part of a priest's normal repertoire. These spells are granted powers, bestowed directly by one's deity to achieve special goals.

Why Quest Spells?

Two circumstances are most likely to warrant the granting of a quest spell to a priest. First, a Power may contact the priest in a dream or omen, or by sending a servant or avatar. In this case, the Power requests that the priest perform a vital service on behalf of the Power (the nature of such a request is discussed later). The priest is effectively commanded to go on a quest—hence, the generic title of quest spell.

A second case for the granting of a quest spell may occur if a priest were to discover something of fundamental importance to the faith which the Power must be appraised of (not all powers are omniscient). A priest contacting the Power (with a *commune* spell or by prayer) might beseech the Power to grant him some exceptional magic to address the situation. The request for a quest spell must never be motivated by selfish considerations on the priest's part (such hubris is grossly offensive to any Power), and circumstances must be truly exceptional. The Power then considers the priest's request and responds accordingly.

In game terms, the first condition translates to the DM using a quest spell as a plot device to spice up a quest for the priest and his party. The second condition translates to a player requesting exceptional aid for his priest PC followed by the DM's decision whether to allow this.

Conditions for Quest Spells

The circumstances which prompt a Power or priest to seek the use of a quest spell are usually related to a major sphere of concern of the Power. A god of druids is not likely to grant a quest spell to address a matter of warfare, commerce, politics, knightly virtue, or other irrelevance (as this Power would view them). However, destruction of a huge swathe of forest by fire is entirely different. To protect or regenerate a great natural resource, a druidic Power would surely consider dispatching his most powerful servants with awesome magic. A major challenge demands a major response.

A Power may choose to equip followers with a quest spell in preparation for a major conflict with servants of a hostile Power. This may be true for both sides in the conflict; the NPCs as well as the PCs might be equipped with quest spells. In this manner, two Powers avoid fighting each other directly; their servants carry out the warfare instead. This will be a major event in any campaign setting! Milder variations on this theme would include the razing of a major temple of the enemy Power or the destruction of a major resource belonging to the Power's servants.

This is a situation in which a DM must exercise caution. This kind of conflict can easily swerve out of control and threaten the destruction of the game world; no Power wants this. Only if a Power has stepped out of line is the retribution by a rival Power tolerable among the community of Powers. If an evil temple has stood in the capital of an evil land for centuries, it is unacceptable for a good deity to strike at it. If an evil temple is hidden in nonevil lands, it is reasonable for a good Power to strike it down. It is important that game balance and the status quo are maintained.

A Power is likely to grant a quest spell when there is a major threat to his followers, church, consecrated grounds, or territories. These situations may become considerably extended; a Power of healing may extend the use of quest magic to help his priests cure a virulent plague affecting ordinary folk. For such a Power, the welfare of the common man is important. In cases such as this, game balance must be maintained by granting quest spells only in true catastrophes.

Exceptional and unique circumstances will arise which will draw quest magic into the game. This may include racial interests (for elves, dwarves, etc.) such as defense of the homelands or protection of great fortresses, or it may include communities of exceptional artisans wishing to draw quest magic from Powers. The discovery of an intensely magical artifact or place important to the Power may necessitate the use of quest magic to secure it. Establishing and developing a major sacred location may justify the use of quest magic (especially with spheres such as Creation, Guardian, Protection, and Wards). Such cases will be individually determined by the DM as major elements of a campaign story line.

Situations Unworthy of Quest Spells

What types of requests do not warrant a Power granting a quest spell? Generally, a quest spell is not needed for events which affect only a minor sphere of interest for the deity and events that are part of normal Prime Material conflict; a senior priest being killed by an agent of an evil Power isn't enough to justify the use of a quest spell. Any problem that has limited scale or should resolve itself in time through the normal efforts of priests does not need quest magic.

The DM must consider whether a problem is out of the ordinary. Only under extraordinary circumstances should a quest spell be granted. If the DM is in doubt, a simple question may provide the answer: Could the problem have a fair chance of resolution through the use of upper-level priest spells if wisely used? Only if the answer is "no" should quest magic be considered.

Which Priests Receive Quest Spells?

Only true and faithful servants of a Power who have successfully used powerful magic are eligible for quest spells. This limits quest spells to priests; although a paladin may be true and faithful, his experience is not sufficient to command the magical energies of potent quest magic.

Level limitations are important. It is very rare for a priest of lower than 12th level to be granted quest magic. Priests of 9th level and lower cannot use quest magic; the strain of holding and shaping such magic is too great.

A priest must possess Wisdom of 17 or better in order to cast quest spells. It is quite possible that a priest could be granted a quest spell but not possess the wisdom to cast 7th-level clerical spells; Powers sometimes work in mysterious ways.

Under normal conditions, quest spells are granted to high-level priests rather than their junior counterparts (when such an option exists, such as in a large temple). If the hierarchy of a temple has been destroyed, then the best of the junior echelons may be granted quest spells.

Some cases may not offer as many options as to the recipient of a quest spell. If the nearest priest to the site of a mission is of a lower level than priests at a faraway temple, the chances are good that this priest will be granted a quest spell rather than awaiting the arrival of a faraway superior. Similarly, if the senior priests of a temple are too old to travel or are needed to maintain order at the temple, a priest of a lower level may be granted the quest spell.

In some situations, a Power will recognize an extremely devoted follower by granting him a quest spell, passing up older, more experienced colleagues. Age and experience do not indicate devotion or worthiness. Prodigies exist in all walks of life; clerics are no exception.

Faithfulness and piety of the priest are important but are difficult to judge. The priest must be unswerving in his alignment and have an exemplary record of service to the Power. It is reasonable to ignore an offense committed due to magical influence even if atonement was required (or voluntarily undergone) as a result.

Obviously, these criteria depend on DM judgment. The DM must remember that priests are mortals—and mortals have weaknesses. While a priest who has not been zealous in defense of the faith is a noncandidate for quest spells, a priest who is pure of heart but who has made a few errors might still be considered for quest magic. However, such a priest may be asked to undertake a preliminary quest to prove his worthiness to the Power. This is especially likely if there is no time pressure for the greater quest or if the priest has asked the Power for quest magic rather than the Power commanding the priest.

A preliminary quest is not a trivial affair; it should present a stiff challenge. In a campaign, it will be especially appropriate if such a quest doubles as a test of the priest's mettle and as an opportunity to acquire a new resource (magical items, henchmen, followers, NPC co-operation, etc.) which might assist the greater quest to come.

How Is the Quest Spell Granted?

A priest must undergo specific preparations to receive a quest spell. Isolated prayer and meditation for 24 hours are required (double this if he has Wisdom of only 17 or is below 12th level). If this period is interrupted, the priest must begin

anew. Following this period, the priest needs one hour to establish and maintain a direct mental link with his deity and receive the spell into his mind. During this communion, the priest is in a state of exultation and is oblivious to the outside world. He cannot be roused from this reverie. The DM may rule that specific ceremonies be carried out by the priest during the time of meditation and the time of the granting of the spell. These ceremonies should be determined in accordance with the nature of the religion. The priest may be required to be in a major church or temple for the ceremony. The presence of junior priests and acolytes, perhaps united in mass prayer, may also be needed. However, these are only suggestions and should not be rigidly enforced—a god of travelers would not require a quest spell to be granted in a temple, for example.

Introducing the Quest Spell

Bringing a quest spell into a campaign should be a major event. It should create a powerful atmosphere that includes elements of pageantry, solemnity, and ceremony to make the event come alive in the game. Such considerations of staging and flavor are left to DM discretion and the demands of the campaign.

The Cost of Quest Spells

Quest spells are not granted without a price. A priest receiving a quest spell is unable to memorize spells of the highest level which he is allowed. He loses any memorized spells of that level (e.g., a 13th-level cleric is unable to use 6th-level spells).

Once a cleric has been granted a quest spell, he does not gain the ability to automatically cast it again. Each time a priest wishes to use a quest spell, he must repeat the described procedures.

Adjudicating Quest Spells

The rules which follow apply to all quest spells. The DM should avoid altering these rules in order to use quest spells consistently and fairly.

Components: Material components are never needed for a quest spell. All quest spells use verbal and somatic components. Since this is invariant, components are therefore not included in the spell descriptions.

Duration: In the spell descriptions, the term "day" is often used. Day means "until the next dawn" if the spellcaster casts the spell during daylight hours and "until the next dusk" if he casts the spell during nighttime hours.

Countering Quest Spells: Most quest spells cannot be dispelled. Because of their semidivine origin, mortal *dispel magic* spells simply do not affect them. In most cases, only other quest magic will directly counter quest magic.

This also applies to attempts to counter specific elements of quest spells. For example, certain quest spells include the effect of a *prayer* spell in the area of effect of the quest spell. Such a *prayer* effect cannot be countered by the use of a mortal *prayer* spell. The quest *prayer* overrides the ordinary *prayer* spell.

Saving Throws: Target creatures at whom quest spells are cast are usually allowed no saving throws. Magical items which would normally protect them against the type of effect (e.g., a *ring of free action* against a hold/paralysis effect) allow a weakened saving throw of 18. Magic resistance functions, but at only one-half normal. If a quest spell has multiple magical effects, magic resistance checks must be made for each effect.

Faith Magic

A unique feature of clerical magic is faith magic. Using this special category of priest spells, clerics can create semipermanent wards, sanctify ground, ensure good harvests, or even improve the health of followers. In short, this amplified magic allows certain clerical spells to be increased and intensified through the combined efforts of priests and worshipers. Range, area of effect, duration, and even damage can be altered through devotion and combined spellcasting.

To gain this ability, priests and their worshipers form groups to create faith magic. Clerics of nearly all religions seek out worshipers, establish temples, retire to monasteries, and establish seminaries. While there are many mundane reasons to form such groups, priests' attitudes are also shaped by this important difference between clerical and wizardly magic—the ability to combine magical power. Wizard spells lack this property—even a large number of wizards cannot combine their spells into a whole. Thus, wizards gain no magical benefits from founding monasteries or attracting followers.

Devotional Power

The core of faith magic is devotional power. This power comes from the dedication of ardent followers and priests. It is not something that can be manipulated directly (like a spell), although it is the source of power for spells. Unlike magical energy, devotional energy is not tied to a particular character class. Ordinary people are as much a source of this power as are adventurers. Only priests are significantly different, their lifelong dedication to their god being the wellspring for even greater power.

Not everyone is a source of devotional energy. Almost every character generates a small amount of power, but only those persons dedicated in their beliefs provide the amounts needed for faith magic. Even at this level, the total energy provided by each person is very small. Thus, faith magic can be used only when large numbers of sincere worshipers gather, such as particularly devout congregations, monasteries, seminaries, and universities operated by a religious order. Sincere belief is the most important factor. While persons attending a service may be numerous, casual followers do not contribute to the effect.

Before its power can be harnessed, the devotional energy of a group must be gathered and concentrated toward a single effect. This is known as focusing the effect. Once focused, the devotional energy provides power needed to maintain a spell effect, increase its area of effect, or create a number of other different results. A focus is created by means of the spell *focus.*

Once the devotional energy has been focused, the cleric or clerics can cast the spell to be amplified. Using the devotional energy gathered by the *focus,* the spell's effect is increased in area of effect and duration. The exact increase depends on the level of the priest who casts the *focus.* Such amplified spells typically affect a building (such as a church or hospital), group of buildings, or even an estate.

The spell remains in effect as long as the *focus* exists. This requires a minimum number of worshipers and periodic renewals of the spell. Since the duration of a *focus* is long, these renewals often coincide with important festivals of the religion, when numerous worshipers are present to provide devotional energy.

Cooperative Magic

Cooperative spells are unique to priests. These spells allow several priests to combine their abilities to create a greater effect. *Combine* is one type of cooperative spell.

Cooperative spells do not require a focus or devotional energy; all that is required are two or more clerics of sufficient level to cast any cooperative spell. Casting times for cooperative spells are not excessive and their results are spectacular, making cooperative magic practical and useful to adventuring priests.

All priests who attempt cooperative magic must know the spell to be cast and must be of the same ethos. Generally, only priests of the same religion can use cooperative magic. However, priests of deities known to work in close harmony are sometimes able to use cooperative magic with each other. The decision lies with the DM, since the relations between different deities vary greatly from campaign to campaign.

New Spheres

In addition to the new types of clerical magic, a number of new spheres are introduced in *Tome of Magic*. These spheres help to round out and complete the priest class.

Chaos

Most of the spells in the Sphere of Chaos give the spellcaster the ability to add randomness and confusion to the world around him. Some of the spells change the probability of the outcomes of events, while others offer protection against Lawful influences.

Many of the spells of this sphere are tricky; while they usually help the spellcaster, there are times when the spell might harm the priest. Such is the way of Chaos—anyone who draws upon chaotic energy knows that nothing is certain, not even the influences of his god.

Powers that operate in this sphere are deities of mischief, trickery, ill luck, and those gods devoted to the power of the individual.

Law

The Sphere of Law is based on two principles. The first is that the group is more powerful than the sum of the individuals who make up the group. The second is that the individual must obey established rules whether or not he personally thinks they are good rules. In both cases, the idea of order is exploited, sometimes beneficially, sometimes harmfully.

The beneficial spells of the Sphere of Law draw upon the first principle. Such spells coordinate the power of a group of characters. By using spells of this sphere, individuals who work closely together can become focused into a strong, united force.

The harmful spells of the sphere draw upon the second principle; they take the concept of law one step too far and prevent the individual from operating with a free will. These spells limit a person's choices and obliterate spontaneity and indi-

vidual thought and action. Whereas beneficial spells draw a group together, harmful spells isolate the individual or even subjugate him to the commands of another person.

Deities of rulership, kingship, community, and culture are likely to act in this sphere.

Numbers

The Sphere of Numbers revolves around the concept that numbers and mathematical relationships between numbers represent the "core truths" of reality or the "secrets of the universe." By studying numbers and their relationships, some scholars believe they can learn truths otherwise inaccessible; by manipulating numbers, they believe they can actually alter the fabric of reality.

This sphere uses spells that allow a priest to comprehend and use the mysteries of numbers. Since many of these spells are incredibly intricate and depend on very esoteric concepts in mathematics and hypermathematics, only priests with relatively high intelligence (13 or higher) are allowed access to these spells.

Spells from this sphere are most likely to be granted by deities of knowledge (particularly arcane or hidden knowledge).

Many of the philosophies central to this sphere sound unusual, illogical, or even insane—things one might expect to hear from the lips of a senile "prophet" who has discovered the "truth of All" in the pseudomathematical scratchings he makes in his notebooks. There are many cranks and charlatans claiming to predict the future who are often mistaken for true practitioners of this sphere and vice versa. A priest who is granted spells from the Sphere of Numbers may sound like a crank when he claims the birthdates of kings predict the date of Doomsday, but there is one fundamental difference between him and the charlatan: The priest's spells *work*.

Thought

The Sphere of Thought is rooted in the philosophy of mentation and the effects of mental acts and structures on reality. Priests of this sphere believe that the common conception of the thought (i.e., a more-or-less objective analysis of sensory input which is in turn an objective perception of reality) is fallacious and misleading. These philosophers maintain that thought is and must be tied closely to reality. In effect, they believe that the thinker, the thought, and the subject of that thought somehow interact. Thus, thinking about an object or condition can sometimes cause a physical change in that object or condition.

Philosophers of this sphere also believe that once a thought has been created ("once a thought is thought"), it exists as a "freestanding mental object." This "thought object" can sometimes be detected and manipulated.

This sphere uses spells related to these philosophical beliefs. Like the Sphere of Numbers, these spells are intricate and are based on some esoteric concepts of philosophy. It is suggested that only priests with relatively high intelligence (13 or higher) be allowed access to these spells.

Spells of this sphere are most likely to be granted by deities of thought or knowledge (especially arcane or hidden knowledge). This sphere might have as its patrons certain deities who rule and exist in the abstract realms of thought. Certain isolated philosophers discuss the existence of a deity of solipsism (the philosophical belief that only the self exists). Since such a deity would believe that it exists alone in the universe, it would have no worshipers.

Time

The spells of the Sphere of Time explore ways in which time can be altered and perceived. These spells manipulate the effects of the passage of time on objects and creatures and can also affect the passage of time itself. Such spells are often the province of deities associated with nature, philosophy, divination, and trickery.

Travelers

Spells of this sphere provide aid and comfort to travelers, making their journeys safer, easier, and more enjoyable. Deities sympathetic to the well-being of explorers, nomads, and other wayfarers often allow access to this sphere.

War

The Sphere of War involves magic specifically for use on the battlefield—in mass combat between large units. Usually, these spells are granted by deities of war: those Powers who believe that victory and courage in battle are the ultimate goals for mortals.

Priests who follow these gods are sometimes generals or leaders of armies. For these priests, tactical and strategic brilliance are as important as personal skill in combat.

There are significant differences between the spheres of War and Combat. Combat spells are those the priest can use in personal altercations. These spells inflict physical damage on an opponent or improve the combat abilities of the priest and several comrades. War spells, on the other hand, are concerned with aspects of large-scale battles other than direct infliction of damage: observation, identification, movement, morale, and the like. Few spells of this sphere inflict physical damage on the enemy.

Unlike spells of other spheres, most War spells can be cast only on a single military "unit." The definition of a "unit" is that which is used in the BATTLESYSTEM® rules; however, the DM may rule that any large group of troops accompanied by PCs may qualify as a unit. Units can be infantry or cavalry (ground or airborne), human or non-human, of regular or irregular formation. In general, they must be organized as a single unit and must be at least five individuals in number. These spells are generally useless in individual combat.

Spells from the Sphere of War are designed to be used in large-scale battles like those played using BATTLESYSTEM® rules; thus, these spells refer to concepts from this game system. Distances are referred to in linear inches (not game inches) and times are referred to in BATTLESYSTEM turns, but the DM is free to modify these statistics to suit combat outside the BATTLESYSTEM rules.

The deities who preside over the Sphere of War are careful when granting these spells to their priests. They will generally grant such spells *only* when a priest is about to enter battle. In the case of the more militant war gods, a priest who petitions for these spells inappropriately or misuses them may suffer dire consequences.

Wards

This sphere includes spells that provide protection of clearly defined areas, ranging from small objects to entire villages. The magical boundaries established by these spells prevent entry or negate the effects of specific creatures, energies, or conditions. Many of the spells take advantage of cooperative magic, involving the casting of a spell by a number of assembled priests to enchant exceptionally large areas (refer to specific spells and the sections in this book on Faith Magic, Devotional Power, and Cooperative Magic for more information). Deities of war and protection, as well as those associated with benevolence and mercy, might bestow these spells.

Chapter 2: Wizard Spells

Wizard Spells

1st Level

Conjure Spell Component
Fire Burst
Fist of Stone
Hornung's Guess*
Lasting Breath
Metamorphose Liquids
Murdock's Feathery Flyer
Nahal's Reckless Dweomer*
Patternweave*

2nd Level

Chaos Shield*
Hornung's Baneful Deflector*
Insatiable Thirst
Maximilian's Earthen Grasp
Nahal's Nonsensical Nullifier*
Past Life
Protection From Paralysis
Ride the Wind
Sense Shifting

3rd Level

Alacrity
Alamir's Fundamental Breakdown
Alternate Reality*
Augmentation I
Far Reaching I
Fireflow*
Fool's Speech*
Lorloveim's Creeping Shadow
Maximilian's Stony Grasp
Minor Malison
Spirit Armor
Squaring the Circle
Watery Double
Wizard Sight

4th Level

Dilation I
Divination Enhancement
Far Reaching II
Greater Malison
Locate Creature
Mask of Death
Minor Spell Turning
Mordenkainen's Celerity
Summon Lycanthrope
There/Not There*
Thunder Staff
Turn Pebble to Boulder
Unluck*

5th Level

Far Reaching III
Khazid's Procurement
Lower Resistance
Magic Staff
Mind Fog
Safeguarding
Von Gasik's Refusal
Vortex*
Waveform*

6th Level

Augmentation II
Bloodstone's Spectral Steed
Claws of the Umber Hulk
Dilation II
Forest's Fiery Constrictor
Lorloveim's Shadowy Transforma
Wildshield*
Wildstrike*

7th Level

Acid Storm
Bloodstone's Frightful Joining
Hatch the Stone From the Egg
Hornung's Surge Selector*
Intensify Summoning
Malec-Keth's Flame Fist
Shadowcat
Spell Shape*
Steal Enchantment
Suffocate

8th Level

Abi-Dalzim's Horrid Wilting
Airboat
Gunther's Kaleidoscopic Strike
Homunculus Shield
Hornung's Random Dispatcher*
Wildzone*

9th Level

Chain Contingency
Elemental Aura
Estate Transference
Glorious Transmutation
Stabilize*
Wail of the Banshee
Wildfire*
Wildwind*

Italicized spell is reversible.
An asterisk (*) indicates a wild magic spell.

Wild magic spells are indicated by an asterisk (*) after the spell name.

First-Level Spells

Conjure Spell Component
(Conjuration/Summoning)

Range: 1 mile/level
Components: V, S
Duration: 1 round
Casting Time: 1
Area of Effect: 3 components/level
Saving Throw: None

When this spell is cast, the wizard teleports desired items directly to his hand. The objects must be naturally occurring components for spells the wizard knows and they must be within spell range. The components must be items commonly found in the area, such as a twig, feather, firefly, or bit of beeswax in a forest.

If the components lie underground or underwater at a depth greater than 10 feet, they cannot be conjured, even if the caster is at a similar depth (such as in a cavern or at the bottom of a lake).

The spell will not cause the appearance of components whose value exceeds 1 gp. Thus, it is impossible to summon gemstones, crystals, metals, pearls, etc. Additionally, components cannot be manmade or altered from their natural state (coins, jewelry, cut or crushed gems, mirrors, etc.), nor can they be taken from someone else's possession.

A single *conjure spell component* spell will summon three components per level of the caster. They may be three different components or multiples of a single component.

Attempts to conjure an animal's body parts (such as bat fur) produce unpredictable results. The DM should roll on the table below.

D4

Roll	Result
1	Desired component appears.
2	Component does not appear.
3	Creature is teleported to the caster.
4	Caster is teleported to the creature.

Only animals with Intelligence scores of 1-4 can be affected by this spell. Humanoids and fantastic animals (dragons, bugbears, unicorns, etc.) cannot be affected.

In all cases, the DM must use common sense to determine the likelihood of the component being located within spell range.

Fire Burst (Alteration, Evocation)

Range: 5 yards/level
Components: V, S
Duration: Instantaneous
Casting Time: 1
Area of Effect: One 10'-radius circle
Saving Throw: Neg.

When this spell is cast upon a nonmagical fire (such as a campfire, lantern, or candle), it causes the fire to flash and shoot arrows of flame. All creatures within 10 feet of the fire source suffer 1 point of damage per level of the caster (maximum of 10 points). Victims who roll a saving throw successfully suffer no damage.

Fist of Stone (Alteration)

Range: 0
Components: V, S
Duration: 1 round/level
Casting Time: 1
Area of Effect: The caster's hand
Saving Throw: None

Upon completion of this spell, one of the caster's hands (his choice) turns to stone. It is flexible and can be used to punch, smash, or crush objects and opponents as if the wizard had Strength of 18/00. Combat bonuses for Strength do not apply if the caster uses any weapon other than his fist.

While the spell is in effect, the wizard cannot cast spells requiring somatic components.

Hornung's Guess* (Divination)

Range: 300 yards
Component: V
Duration: Instantaneous
Casting Time: 2
Area of Effect: Special
Saving Throw: None

Hornung, one of the leading wizards in the field of wild magic (before his untimely disappearance while experimenting with *wildwind*), developed this spell to improve the accuracy of his estimates. The spell provides a wizard with an instant and highly accurate estimate of the number of persons or objects in a group.

The spell's area of effect is one group of a general class of objects. All objects of the group must be within spell range and the group as a whole must be visible to the caster. The wizard need not see every individual in the group, merely the general limits of the group's size and area. For example, a wizard on a hill could look down on a

forest and estimate the number of trees in all or part of it. He could not get an estimate of the number of goblins within the forest, however, since the group as a whole (the goblins) is concealed from sight.

The estimate generated is accurate to the largest factor of ten (rounded up). For example, if *Hornung's guess* were cast on a group of 439 horsemen, the estimate would be 400. If there were 2,670 horsemen, the spell would estimate 3,000. If there were 37 horsemen, the answer would be 40. Clearly, using the spell on small groups (especially those with fewer than 10 members) is pointless.

Hornung's guess can be used to quickly estimate the size of treasure hoards and army units. It is particularly popular with moneylenders and generals.

Lasting Breath (Alteration)

Range: 5 yards/level
Components: V, S
Duration: 1d4 rounds +1 round/level
Casting Time: 1
Area of Effect: One creature/level
Saving Throw: None

This spell increases the amount of time a character can hold his breath. As described in the *Player's Handbook*, a character can hold his breath for a number of rounds equal to one-third his Constitution score. The effect of this spell is added to that figure.

The duration of the spell is always unknown to the recipient; the DM secretly rolls 1d4 to determine the exact duration. At the end of this time, the character must succeed a Constitution check or be forced to take a breath as per the rules.

Metamorphose Liquids (Alteration)

Range: Touch
Components: V, S, M
Duration: Permanent
Casting Time: 1 round
Area of Effect: 1'-cube/level
Saving Throw: Special

This spell transmutes one type of liquid into an equal amount of a different, nonmagical fluid (water, wine, blood, oil, apple cider, etc.). The caster must touch the fluid itself (not simply its container) for the spell to take effect.

Magical liquids (such as potions) receive a saving throw vs. disintegration with a +3 bonus to avoid the spell's effect. Fluids can be transmuted

only into nonmagical liquids; it is not possible to change a magical liquid into another type of magical liquid. Poisons may be rendered harmless through use of this spell, but the spell has no effect on poisons already consumed.

Living creatures are unaffected by the spell, excluding those from the elemental plane of water. Such creatures are allowed a saving throw vs. spell. Failure results in 1d4 points of damage per level of the caster, while success indicates half damage. Only one creature can be affected by a single casting of this spell, regardless of the creature's size.

The material component is a drop of the liquid that the caster intends to create, which must be placed on the wizard's tongue and consumed. Creating poisons through use of this spell is especially dangerous.

Murdock's Feathery Flyer (Alteration)

Range: 0
Components: V, S, M
Duration: 1 round/level
Casting Time: 1
Area of Effect: The caster
Saving Throw: None

Upon casting this spell, a feathery membrane grows under the wizard's arms, extending along his sides all the way to his feet. The membrane appears to merge with the caster's skin and clothing.

If the caster spreads his arms and jumps from a height, he may glide through the air. For each foot of elevation, the wizard can glide five feet horizontally. Thus, a wizard jumping from a 10-foot wall could glide up to 50 feet. Gliding characters have a movement rate of 12 and Maneuverability Class E.

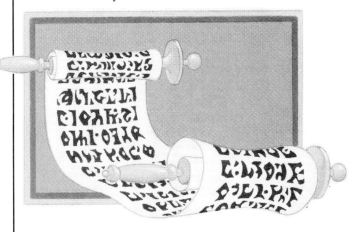

A wizard attempting to carry more than his normal weight allowance plummets to the earth upon takeoff.

When the spell expires, the feathers instantly disappear. If the wizard is airborne, he immediately plummets toward the ground.

The material component is an eagle's feather.

Nahal's Reckless Dweomer* (Invocation/Evocation)

Range: Special
Components: V, S
Duration: Special
Casting Time: 5
Area of Effect: Special
Saving Throw: Special

This spell is the wild mage's ultimate last-resort spell. When cast, the mage releases a sudden flood of wild magical energy in the hope of seizing and shaping that energy into a desired spell effect. The attempt usually fails, but something almost always occurs in the process.

Before casting the spell, the mage announces the spell effect he is trying to create. The mage must be able to cast the spell (i.e., have it in his spell books), but need not have it memorized. After announcing the spell (along with the target and any other conditions required by the spell), the wild mage casts *Nahal's reckless dweomer*. A burst of magical energy is released, which the wild mage tries to manipulate into the desired form. The actual effect of the spell is rolled randomly on Table 2: Wild Surge Results.

Because the release of energy is planned by the mage, his level is added to the dice roll. If the result indicates success, the mage has shaped the magical energy into the desired effect. More often than not, the effect is completely unexpected. The result may be beneficial to the mage or it may be completely disastrous; this is the risk the mage takes in casting *Nahal's reckless dweomer*.

Patternweave* (Divination)

Range: 10 yards
Components: V, S, M
Duration: 1 round
Casting Time: 3
Area of Effect: 10-foot square
Saving Throw: Special

Patternweave allows the caster to make sense of apparent chaos. The caster can see such things as pottery shards reformed into a whole pot, shreds of paper formed into a page, scattered parts as a working machine, or specific trails appearing out of overlapping footprints.

After casting the spell, the mage studies seemingly random elements—broken bits of glass, shreds of paper, intermingled trails, etc. The items to be studied must be tangible—coded flashing lights, garbled speech, or thoughts of any kind cannot be studied.

The wizard must study the random elements for one round, after which the DM secretly makes a saving throw vs. spell for the wizard. If the saving throw is failed, the spell fails. However, if the saving throw is successful, the caster sees in his mind the pattern these objects form. If the items studied are truly random, no information is gained.

After the caster has visualized the pattern, he can attempt to reassemble the parts into their original form. This requires another saving throw vs. spell to determine whether the mage remembers sufficient details to accomplish the task. The amount of time required and the quality of restoration vary according to the complexity of the pattern. Reassembling a shredded map may be easy; reassembling a broken clock is significantly more difficult; rebuilding a shattered mosaic is extremely difficult. In any case, the wizard can make only a reasonable copy of the item. He can use this spell to restore works of art, but they will be worth only a small percentage of their original value.

The material component is a small hand lens through which the caster studies the objects. The lens is not consumed in the casting.

Second-Level Spells

Chaos Shield* (Abjuration)

Range: 0
Components: V, S
Duration: 1d10 rounds + 2 rounds/level
Casting Time: 2
Area of Effect: The caster
Saving Throw: Special

Following the discovery of wild magic came the discovery of wild surges and the personal danger such surges create. After several wild mages destroyed themselves by rather spectacular means (or suffered very odd side effects), the *chaos shield* was created as protection from these surges.

This spell imbues the wild mage with special protection against the effects of wild surges. It protects only against wild surges caused by the caster's own spells, not from the effects of another mage's wild surges.

When a wild surge affects a caster protected by *chaos shield*, he is allowed a saving throw vs. magic. If the saving throw is successful, the effect of the surge on the caster is negated. If the saving throw is failed, the caster is affected normally by the surge. The spell does not protect against wild surges that might be caused by its own casting.

The *chaos shield* protects only the caster and does not negate the effects of a wild surge for other characters who might be in the area of effect. The caster cannot voluntarily cancel the protection once he has learned the nature of a wild surge; the *chaos shield* protects from both good and harmful effects. Thus, if a wild surge resulted in a *heal* spell for all characters within 10 feet of the caster, the protected caster might not benefit, while all others in the radius would be *healed*.

The spell remains in effect until it negates a wild surge or the spell duration expires.

Hornung's Baneful Deflector* (Evocation)

Range: Touch
Components: V, S, M
Duration: 2 rounds/level
Casting Time: 2
Area of Effect: One creature
Saving Throw: None

This spell partially surrounds the recipient in a shimmering, hemispherical field of force. The field is transparent and moves with the subject, forming a shell about one foot away from his body. The shell serves as a shield against all forms of individually targeted missile attacks (including *magic missiles* and other spells). The caster designates the position of the shell (protecting the front, rear, side, or top of the recipient). The spell does not protect against area effect spells or other attacks that strike several creatures at once.

Whenever an individual missile attack is directed at a protected creature, the *baneful deflector* activates. Instead of striking the target creature, the missile's target is determined randomly among all creatures within a 15-foot hemisphere of the protected creature, *including* the protected creature. The missile then changes course toward its new target with normal chances to hit. If the new target is beyond the range of the missile, no target is hit. If the protected creature is struck, the spell immediately fails. If several people are protected by *baneful deflector*, a missile will change course several times before reaching its target.

The material component is a small prism that shatters when the spell is cast.

Insatiable Thirst (Enchantment/Charm)

Range: 5 yards/level
Components: V, S
Duration: 1 round/level
Casting Time: 2
Area of Effect: One creature
Saving Throw: Neg.

This spell instills in the victim an uncontrollable desire to drink. The victim is allowed a saving throw to avoid the effect. If the roll is failed, the creature must consume any potable liquids it can find (including magical potions, which might result in strange effects if potions are mixed). Although poisons are not considered potable, a victim may not realize that a liquid is poisonous. The victim will not consume a liquid he knows to be poisonous.

No matter how much the creature drinks, its magical thirst is not quenched until the spell ends. During this time, the creature can do nothing but drink or look for liquids to drink. Victims of this spell believe they are dying of thirst and (depending upon their nature) may be willing to kill for drinkable fluids.

Maximilian's Earthen Grasp (Alteration)

Range: 10 yards + 10 yards/level
Components: V, S, M
Duration: 3 rounds + 1 round/level
Casting Time: 2
Area of Effect: One creature
Saving Throw: Special

This spell causes an arm made of compacted soil to rise from the ground. The spell must be cast on open turf, such as a grassy field or a dirt floor.

The earthen arm and hand (which are about the same size as a normal human limb) arise from the ground beneath one creature targeted by the caster. The hand attempts to grasp the creature's leg. The victim must attempt a saving throw; if successful, the hand sinks into the ground. Each round thereafter (until the spell ends or the target moves out of spell range), the hand has a 5% chance per level of the caster of reappearing beneath the targeted creature, at which time another saving throw is required.

If a saving throw is missed, the earthen limb firmly grasps and holds the creature in place. An individual held by the hand suffers a movement rate of 0, Armor Class penalty of −2, and attack penalty of −2. All Dexterity combat bonuses are negated. The hand causes no physical damage to the victim.

The arm may be attacked by any creature, including the arm's victim. The arm has AC 5 and hit points equal to double the caster's maximum hit points. For example, a caster who normally has 15 hit points can create an earthen hand with 30 hit points. The maximum number of hit points that an earthen hand may have is 40. When the arm's hit points are reduced to zero or when the spell duration ends, the hand crumbles.

The material component is a miniature hand sculpted from clay, which crumbles to dust when the spell is cast.

Nahal's Nonsensical Nullifier* (Abjuration)

Range: Touch
Components: V, S, M
Duration: 1d6 rounds + 1 round/level
Casting Time: 2
Area of Effect: Creature touched
Saving Throw: None

This spell scrambles the aura of the affected creature, giving random results to *know alignment*, *detect evil*, and *detect lie* spells cast on that creature.

When a protected creature is the focus of one of these divinations, the information gained is randomly determined. Thus, if *know alignment* is used against a chaotic evil creature protected by the *nonsensical nullifier,* the response could be any alignment combination. If two characters both use the same divination on the same target, two random results are generated.

A new random result is generated each round; thus, continued observation of a protected creature usually results in different answers. The table below should be used to determine the random alignment.

D10

Roll	Alignment
1	Lawful Good
2	Lawful Neutral
3	Lawful Evil
4	Neutral Good
5	Neutral
6	Neutral Evil
7	Chaotic Good
8	Chaotic Evil
9	Chaotic Neutral
10	No alignment

The material component is a small amount of egg yolk smeared into the hair of the recipient.

Past Life (Divination)

Range: Touch
Components: V, S
Duration: Special
Casting Time: 1 round
Area of Effect: One creature
Saving Throw: None

By touching the remains of a dead creature, this spell allows a caster to gain a mental image of the deceased's former appearance. The remains can be of any age and only a tiny fragment is required, such as a bone splinter or a strand of hair.

When cast by a wizard of at least 7th level, he is able to view the final minute of the subject's life from the subject's point of view.

When cast by a wizard of at least 9th level, a personal possession (a ring, a favorite walking stick, etc.) may be substituted for bodily remains.

Protection From Paralysis (**Abjuration**)

Range: Touch
Components: V, S, M
Duration: 1 turn/level
Casting Time: 2
Area of Effect: One creature
Saving Throw: None

The recipient of this spell receives total immunity to magical paralysis. Spells such as *hold person* and *slow* have no effect on the individual. This spell also provides protection against the paralysis attacks of monsters (a ghoul's touch, for example). This spell offers no protection against physical damage.

The material component is a bit of cloth taken from a priest's robes.

Ride the Wind (**Alteration**)

Range: 5 yards/level
Components: V, S, M
Duration: 1 turn/level
Casting Time: 2
Area of Effect: One creature/level
Saving Throw: Neg.

This spell allows creatures targeted by the caster to become virtually weightless and be lifted upon the wind. Affected creatures can control their altitude by rising or descending at a movement rate of 12, but are at the mercy of the wind for speed and direction. Recipients can stop forward movement only by grasping something to anchor them in place. If no wind is present, this spell has no effect.

Unwilling targets are allowed a saving throw to resist the effect.

Each subject and his equipment must weigh less than 100 pounds per level of the caster. Thus, a 6th-level wizard could affect six creatures each weighing 600 lbs. or less. This spell may be cast only on living creatures.

The material components are a small handful of straw and a dry leaf.

Sense Shifting (**Alteration**)

Range: 0
Components: V, S, M
Duration: 3 turns
Casting Time: 2
Area of Effect: The caster
Saving Throw: None

Sense shifting allows the wizard to affect all spells of levels 1 through 3 that he casts within the duration of the spell. For each spell, he can modify one of three sensory features pertaining to the spell: color, sound, or patterned visual appearance of the spell effect. The changes produced by this spell do not affect the functions of the affected spell nor any saving throws that apply against their effects.

Sense shifting might be used to produce green *fireballs*, *magic missiles* that streak through the air with a scream, colored *continual light* globes, customized designs for a *hypnotic pattern*, or a *spectral hand* that makes scrabbling sounds as it attempts to grasp a target.

Sense shifting cannot create any form of invisibility. It cannot completely silence a spell effect (thus, a *fireball's* blast might be muted, but not wholly eliminated).

The material component is a twist of multicolored ribbon with a small silver bell fastened to its end.

Third-Level Spells

Alacrity (Alteration)

Range: 0
Components: V, S, M
Duration: 1 turn + 1 round/level
Casting Time: 1
Area of Effect: The caster
Saving Throw: None

The use of an *alacrity* spell allows the wizard to speed up the casting of spells of 5th level and lower. Only spells that are cast within the *alacrity* spell's duration are affected.

Casting times of 2-5 are reduced by 1; casting times of 6-9 are reduced by 2; and a casting time of one round is reduced to a casting time of 8. Casting times for spells which require more than 1 round are reduced by 20% (e.g., an *animate dead* spell affected by *alacrity* could be cast in only 4 rounds). Spells which have a casting time of 1 are not affected by this spell.

The material component is a miniature hourglass which is destroyed when the spell is cast.

Alamir's Fundamental Breakdown (Divination)

Range: Touch
Components: V, S, M
Duration: Special
Casting Time: 1 round
Area of Effect: One item
Saving Throw: Special

By casting this spell, the wizard learns what ingredients and formulas were used to create a chemical mixture or magical item.

The information instantly appears in the caster's mind but may be lost if the wizard cannot comprehend it. The caster must roll an Intelligence check; if successful, the wizard understands the formula and retains it in his memory. If the roll is missed, the caster cannot comprehend what he has learned and the information is immediately forgotten. If the spell is cast a second time on the same substance, the spell automatically fails unless the wizard has advanced to the next experience level.

The caster's level determines the type of information gleaned:

5th Level: The type and quantity of ingredients and the preparation process required to produce a non-magical mixture are learned. For example, the wizard could learn how to produce Greek fire or gunpowder, or could learn the recipe for something simple, like chocolate cake.

9th Level: The wizard may learn the proper ingredients and formula for making a magical liquid (potion, scroll ink, etc.).

14th Level: The caster may learn the formula for creating any type of magical object, excluding unique items and objects of extreme power (artifacts and relics).

In all cases, simply knowing the proper formula does not mean the wizard can successfully create the item or material. The construction of alchemical mixtures and magical items is a time-consuming and expensive undertaking.

This spell has detrimental effects on the magical item analyzed. Single-use items (potions, oils, etc.) are automatically destroyed; the spell consumes the item in the process of analyzing it. Reusable magical items must make a saving throw vs. disintegration. If the saving throw is failed, *Alamir's fundamental breakdown* releases the magic of the item in an explosive blast, rendering it permanently nonmagical. The caster suffers 4d8 points of damage from the explosion.

The material component is a wand cut from a 100-year-old oak tree. The wand is used to touch the item in question, and vanishes in a puff of smoke when the spell is complete.

Alternate Reality* (Alteration)

Range: 0
Components: V, S, M
Duration: Instantaneous
Casting Time: 3
Area of Effect: Creature touched
Saving Throw: None

With this spell, the caster creates a small variation in probabilities. This variation lasts only a moment, but creates alternate results for one recent event. When the spell is cast, any one event attempted by the recipient during the previous round is recalculated, essentially allowing (or forcing) the creature to make new die rolls.

Only events that begin and end in a single round can be affected. Only one die roll can be rerolled. If the creature touched is a willing recipient, the player can choose which roll (the original or the new roll) affects him, more than likely picking the most successful. If the creature is unwilling, he must redo the action. The second result, whatever its outcome, cannot be changed.

Typical uses of this spell include allowing a fighter to reroll an attack, forcing an opponent to reroll a saving throw, or allowing a wizard to reroll the damage caused by a *fireball*.

The material component is a small, unmarked die.

Augmentation I (Invocation/Evocation)

Range: 0
Components: V, S, M
Duration: Special
Casting Time: 2
Area of Effect: Special
Saving Throw: None

This spell augments the damage inflicted by any spell of levels 1-3. For each die of damage rolled, the caster adds one point to the damage total.

The *augmentation I* spell affects only one spell cast on the round immediately following the *augmentation*. If an entire round or more elapses, the *augmentation* is wasted.

Only spells which cause direct physical damage are affected by *augmentation*; for example, monsters gained through *monster summoning I* gain no bonuses to their damage.

The material component is a pair of concentric circles of bronze or silver.

Far Reaching I (Alteration)

Range: 0
Component: V
Duration: Special
Casting Time: 2
Area of Effect: Special
Saving Throw: None

This spell allows the wizard to extend the range of any one 1st- or 2nd-level spell by 50% or any one 3rd-level spell by 25%. The spell to be affected must be cast on the round immediately following the *far reaching I* spell. If a complete round or more elapses, the *far reaching I* is wasted.

Far reaching I affects only a spell cast by the same wizard. *Far reaching I* does not affect spells that have range of 0 or touch.

Fireflow* (Alteration)

Range: 30 yards
Components: V, S, M
Duration: 1 round/level
Casting Time: 3
Area of Effect: One fire source
Saving Throw: None

This spell allows a wizard to control natural fires by manipulating randomness and adjusting probabilities to cause them to spread and take shape in any direction he desires. Once cast, the wizard points at any fire within range. He can then cause that fire to move in any direction desired within spell range, as long as the flames contact a solid surface (the fire may not be raised in the air).

The caster must maintain concentration or the spell fails. The flames can be spread at the rate of 50 square feet per turn. Thus, if a caster affects a campfire, he could create a flaming line 1 foot wide and 50 feet long or fill a 5′ × 10′ square in a single round.

The flames are not limited by a lack of burnable material and can be directed to spread over water, snow, ice, and other nonflammable surfaces. The surface is not harmed, but objects and creatures caught in the flames suffer damage as if they had stepped into the original fire source. Thus, a character caught in flames created from a candle will suffer only minor damage, while a character caught in a blaze that originated from a huge bonfire will be severely burned.

The material components are a small paintbrush and a pot of pitch.

Fool's Speech* (Alteration)

Range: Touch
Components: V, S, M
Duration: 1 hour/level
Casting Time: 1 turn
Area of Effect: Caster +1 creature/level
Saving Throw: None

With this spell, the wizard empowers himself and others of his choosing with the ability to speak a secret language incomprehensible to others. Creatures designated to speak the language must be touching each other when the spell is cast.

Once cast, the characters can choose to speak normally or in their secret tongue. They can speak and understand this mysterious language fluently.

Fool's speech is not recognizable as any known language, nor does it remotely sound like any language. A *comprehend languages* or *tongues* spell will not translate it. It can be understood by a character wearing a *helm of comprehending languages and reading magic*, although the normal percentage chances apply.

The material component is a small whistle made of bone.

Lorloveim's Creeping Shadow (Illusion)

Range: 0
Components: V, S, M
Duration: 1 round/level
Casting Time: 7
Area of Effect: The caster's shadow
Saving Throw: None

This spell causes the wizard's shadow to elongate, stretching away from his body at a rate of 15 yards per round. It can elongate a maximum distance of 10 yards per level of the caster.

The shadow moves as an ordinary shadow, along floors and up walls. The caster may maneuver in any manner feasible to place the shadow where he desires. A caster might position his shadow over a high window in a tower in order to spy on the tower's occupants. The shadow makes no sound and is 90% undetectable in all but the brightest surroundings.

While the spell lasts, the illusionist can see, hear, and speak through his shadow. The shadow cannot physically touch, pick up, or attack creatures or objects. It can be struck only by spells, magical weapons of +1 or better, or other special attacks (such as a dragon's breath). The shadow has the same Armor Class as the caster. Hit points lost by the shadow are suffered by the caster.

To cast the spell, a light source of at least the brightness of a candle must be present.

The material component is a small statuette of the caster sculpted from a piece of obsidian worth at least 1,000 gp.

Maximilian's Stony Grasp (Alteration)

Range: 20 yards + 10 yards/level
Components: V, S, M
Duration: 5 rounds + 1 round/level
Casting Time: 3
Area of Effect: One creature
Saving Throw: Special

This spell must be cast on stony ground, such as a manmade stone floor, a natural cavern floor, or a boulder-strewn field. It is not possible to cast the spell on a stone wall or ceiling. The spell causes an arm made of stone (about the same size as a normal human limb) to rise from the ground beneath any creature targeted by the caster. The stony hand attempts to grasp the leg of the targeted creature, who is allowed a saving throw to avoid the effect; if the save is successful, the hand disappears. Each round thereafter, the hand has a 5% chance per level of the caster of reappearing and attacking.

Creatures grasped by the hand suffer a movement rate of 0, AC penalty of −2, and attack penalty of −2. Grasped characters lose any Dexterity bonuses. The hand causes no damage to its victim.

The stony limb has AC 2 and hit points equal to triple the caster's maximum hit points. The maximum number of hit points a stony hand may have is 60.

The material component is a miniature hand sculpted from stone, which crumbles to dust when the conjured hand is destroyed or the spell expires.

Minor Malison (Enchantment/Charm)

Range: 60 feet
Component: V
Duration: 2 rounds/level
Casting Time: 2
Area of Effect: 30-foot-radius sphere
Saving Throw: None

This spell allows a wizard to adversely affect all the saving throws of his enemies. Opponents under the influence of this spell make all saving throws at a penalty of −1.

Alternatively, the wizard may select any one school of magic and cause his enemies to make all saving throws against magic from that school at −2. This penalty is not cumulative with a saving throw penalty derived from the wizard being a specialist; the penalty is not increased to −3.

Spirit Armor (Necromancy)

Range: 0
Components: V, S
Duration: 2 rounds/level
Casting Time: 3
Area of Effect: The caster
Saving Throw: Special

This spell allows the wizard to surround himself with a portion of his own life essence, which takes the form of a shimmering aura. The *spirit armor* offers protection equivalent to splint mail (AC 4) and grants the wizard a +3 bonus to saving throws vs. magical attacks. The *spirit armor's* effects are not cumulative with other types of armor or magical protection, but Dexterity bonuses apply.

The *spirit armor* is effective against magical and nonmagical weapons and attacks. It does not hinder movement or add weight or encumbrance. It does not interfere with spellcasting.

When the spell ends, the aura dissipates and the caster temporarily loses a bit of his life essence, suffering 2d3 points of damage unless he succeeds at a saving throw vs. spell. No damage is sustained if the save is successful. The hit points lost can be regained only through magical healing.

Squaring the Circle (Alteration)

Range: 0
Components: V, S, M
Duration: 1 round/level
Casting Time: 2
Area of Effect: Special
Saving Throw: None

Squaring the circle allows a wizard to alter the shape of the area of effect of one spell of 1st-through 5th-level spells. The spell to be affected must be cast within the duration of the *squaring the circle* spell.

Square or cubic areas of effect can be transformed into circular or spherical areas of effect. Circular or spherical areas of effect can likewise be transformed into square or cubic areas of effect. In both cases, the length of a side of a square area is equated to the diameter of a circular or spherical area.

Alternatively, a square or cubic area can be transformed into a rectangle. The rectangle cannot cover more or less square footage than the standard square area of the spell.

Similarly, a circular or spherical area can be transformed into an oval or egg shape. The area covered by the oval or egg shape cannot cover more or less square footage than the original area of the spell.

The material component is a small pendant of any precious metal with a circle fashioned inside a square.

Watery Double
(Conjuration/Summoning, Enchantment)

Range: Touch
Components: V, S
Duration: Special; max. 10 rounds
Casting Time: 3
Area of Effect: One body of liquid
Saving Throw: Neg.

This spell may be cast on any body of liquid as large as an ocean or as small as a glass of wine. The first creature whose reflection is cast on the surface of the liquid releases the spell. When the spell is triggered, the liquid immediately forms an exact three-dimensional image of the reflected creature. If more than one creature casts a reflec-

tion simultaneously, only one *watery double* forms. Each creature has an equal chance of being the victim of the spell (roll randomly).

The size of the *watery double* is restricted by the volume of fluid available. If the spell were cast on a full mug of ale, the double would form from the ale, becoming a mug-sized duplicate of the victim. The *watery double* will never exceed the actual size of the victim regardless of the size of the body of liquid.

When the spell is cast on the liquid, its duration is considered permanent until the power is released by a creature's reflection. The liquid will not evaporate until the spell is triggered. When the *watery double* forms, it remains animated for 1 round per experience level of the caster, to a maximum of 10 rounds.

The *watery double* attempts to touch the creature it has duplicated. It can affect only the creature that it resembles. It has the same THAC0 and current hit points as the creature it duplicates, but cannot cast spells or use any of the creature's magical items or special abilities. The *watery double* is AC 6 and its movement rate is double that of the victim. It may seep under doors and through cracks.

If the *watery double* succeeds in touching the creature, it merges with the individual, covering his entire body in a skin of liquid. The victim must attempt a saving throw. If successful, the creature has resisted the spell's effect and the *watery double* "dies," becoming normal fluid (and soaking the creature in the process). If the saving throw is failed, the *watery double* begins forcing its way into the victim's body, inflicting 1d8 points of damage per round until it is destroyed.

The *watery double* dissipates if reduced to zero hit points or when the spell's duration expires. Striking the *watery double* while it is wrapped around its victim causes an equal amount of damage to the victim. *Part water, lower water,* and *transmute water to dust* spells instantly destroy a *watery double.*

Wizard Sight (Divination)

Range: 0
Components: V, S
Duration: 1 round/level
Casting Time: 3
Area of Effect: The caster
Saving Throw: None

Upon completion of this spell, the caster's eyes glow blue and he is able to see the magical auras of spellcasters and enchanted objects. Only the auras of those things normally visible to the caster are seen; this spell does not grant the wizard the ability to see invisible objects, nor does it give him X-ray vision. This spell does not reveal the presence of good or evil or reveal alignment.

While *wizard sight* is in effect, a wizard is able to see whether someone is a spellcaster and whether that person is a priest or a wizard (and what type of specialist, if any). He can sense if a nonspellcaster has the potential to learn and cast wizard spells (e.g., whether a fighter will some-day gain the ability to cast a spell).

Although a spellcaster's level cannot be discerned, the wizard can see the intensity of a spellcaster's aura and guess at the individual's magical power (dim, faint, moderate, strong, overwhelming). This can be extremely ambiguous even when a wizard has some method of comparison; the DM might announce that a subject's intensity is roughly equivalent to that of a companion, or he might announce that a subject's aura is the strongest the wizard has ever encountered.

An object's magical abilities cannot be discerned. The fact that it is magical and the type of magic (abjuration, alteration, etc.) are obvious. The wizard can see the intensity of an item's magical aura and guess at its power, but cannot tell whether a magical item is cursed.

Fourth-Level Spells

Dilation I (Alteration)

Range: 0
Component: V
Duration: Special
Casting Time: 4
Area of Effect: Special
Saving Throw: None

Dilation I allows a wizard to increase the area of effect of any one spell of levels 1-3. The area of effect is increased by 25%; thus, a *stinking cloud* would fill a 25-foot cube, while a *slow* spell would affect creatures in a 50-foot cube. Fractions of feet or yards (as appropriate to the spell) are dropped.

Dilation I must be cast immediately prior to the spell to be dilated; if a complete round or more elapses, the dilation is wasted. The dilation spell affects only spells which have areas of effect defined in feet or yards (numbers of creatures cannot be increased). The dilation affects only spells cast by the same wizard.

Divination Enhancement (Evocation)

Range: 0
Component: V
Duration: 2 turns + 2 rounds/level
Casting Time: 4
Area of Effect: The caster
Saving Throw: None

This spell allows a wizard to extend both the duration and range of the *wizard eye* spell and any divination spells of levels 1-4. Duration and range are both increased by 50% for the length of the *divination enhancement*.

All divination spells cast within the duration of the enhancement are increased. The expiration of the enhancement cancels all divination spells in effect.

Far Reaching II (Alteration)

Range: 0
Component: V
Duration: Special
Casting Time: 4
Area of Effect: Special
Saving Throw: None

This spell's function is identical to the 3rd-level *far reaching I* spell, except that a spell of 1st or 2nd level has its range doubled and a spell of 3rd level has its range increased by 50%. In addition, any spell of 4th level has its range extended by 25%.

Greater Malison (Enchantment/Charm)

Range: 60 feet
Component: V
Duration: 2 rounds/level
Casting Time: 4
Area of Effect: 30-foot-radius sphere
Saving Throw: None

This spell operates exactly like the 3rd-level *minor malison* spell except that the wizard places a −2 penalty on all saving throws of all hostile creatures within the area of effect. Optionally, the wizard may create a −3 penalty to saving throws against spells from one school of magic. This penalty is not cumulative with a saving throw penalty which derived from the wizard being a specialist; the penalty is not increased to −4.

Locate Creature (Divination)

Range: 50 yards/level
Components: V, S, M
Duration: 1 turn/level
Casting Time: 5
Area of Effect: One creature
Saving Throw: None

This spell is similar to the 2nd-level *locate object* spell. Instead of finding an inanimate object, however, it allows the wizard to find a creature. The wizard casts the spell, slowly turns, and is able to sense the direction of the person or creature, provided the subject is within range. The wizard learns how far away the creature is and in what direction it is moving (if at all).

This spell can locate a general species of creature (a horse or umber hulk, for instance) or can be used to find a specific individual. The wizard must have physically seen the individual or the type of creature at least once from a distance of no more than 10 yards.

Unlike *locate object*, this spell is not blocked by lead. It is blocked, however, by running water (such as a river or stream). Objects cannot be found through use of this spell.

The material component is a bit of a bloodhound's fur.

Mask of Death (Necromancy)

Range: Touch
Components: V, S, M
Duration: 1 hour/level
Casting Time: 1 round
Area of Effect: One creature
Saving Throw: None

By casting this spell, a wizard can change a corpse's features to make it appear to be someone else. The caster must possess an accurate portrait of the individual to be duplicated, or must have a clear mental image of the person based on personal experience.

If *animate dead* is cast on the body, it can be animated to become a zombie that looks exactly like the copied person. The double is a mindless automaton, however, having all the characteristics of a normal zombie.

This spell may be cast on a creature that has already become a zombie. The wizard must successfully touch the zombie in combat, unless the zombie is controlled by the caster.

The material component of this spell is a drop of doppleganger's blood.

Minor Spell Turning (Abjuration)

Range: 0
Components: V, S, M
Duration: 3 rounds/level
Casting Time: 4
Area of Effect: The caster
Saving Throw: None

This spell is similar to the 7th-level *spell turning*, which causes spells cast against the wizard to rebound on the original caster. This includes spells cast from scrolls and innate spell-like abilities, but excludes the following: area effects that are not centered directly upon the protected wizard, spell effects delivered by touch, and spell effects from devices such as wands, staves, and so forth. Thus, a *light* spell cast to blind the protected wizard could be turned back upon and possibly blind the caster, while the same spell would be unaffected if cast to light an area in which the protected wizard were standing.

One to four (1d4) spell levels may be turned. The exact number is secretly rolled by the DM; the player never knows how effective the spell is.

Unlike the 7th level version of this spell, *minor spell turning* is not capable of partially turning a spell. For example, if a wizard has three levels of spell turning, he can turn three 1st-level spells, one 1st and one 2nd, or one 3rd-level spell. He can in no way turn spells of 4th level or above. If the caster is the target of a spell of a higher level than he is capable of turning, the caster receives the full brunt of the spell.

If the protected wizard and a spellcasting attacker both have spell turning effects operating, a resonating field is created that has the following effects:

D100

Roll	Effect
01-70	Spell drains away without effect
71-80	Spell affects both equally at full damage
81-97	Both turning effects are rendered non-functional for 1d4 turns
98-00	Both casters are sucked through a rift into the Positive Material plane

The material component of this spell is a smoothly polished silver coin.

Mordenkainen's Celerity
(Alteration, Invocation)

Range: 0
Components: V, S, M
Duration: 1 turn
Casting Time: 4
Area of Effect: Special
Saving Throw: None

Mordenkainen's celerity affects spells of levels 1-3 which alter the movement of the wizard such as *feather fall, jump, spider climb, levitate, fly,* and *haste.* Spells to be affected must be cast within 1 turn of the casting of the celerity. Spells do not expire when the celerity expires.

Spells cast following the celerity receive a 25% bonus to duration. This effect may not be gained in conjunction with other means of magically extending a spell's duration. In addition, the caster's movement rate is increased by 25%. *Feather fall* is an exception; the rate of descent may be reduced by 25% at the caster's option.

The area of effect is always the caster, except in the case of the *haste* spell, for which the effects of the celerity will operate on 1d4 creatures in addition to the wizard. The celerity will not affect the other creatures in any other manner.

The celerity gives the wizard a +2 bonus to his saving throws against spells of levels 1-3 which directly affect his movement. This includes *web, hold person,* and *slow.* The wizard also gains a +2 bonus on all saving throws against magical paralysis attacks.

The material component is a small pouch or vessel containing centipede or millipede legs.

Summon Lycanthrope
(Conjuration/Summoning)

Range: Special
Components: V, S, M
Duration: Special
Casting Time: 1 turn
Area of Effect: One creature
Saving Throw: Neg.

This spell is effective only on the night of a full moon and one night immediately preceding and following it.

For the spell to be effective, the caster and the lycanthrope must be on the same plane of existence; there is no other range limitation. When the spell is cast, the nearest lycanthrope (as determined by the DM) of the chosen species must attempt a saving throw. If successful, the creature is unaffected. If it fails, the lycanthrope instantly appears near the caster.

Upon arrival, the creature can freely attack the wizard unless the caster has created a warding circle. If a circle is present, the lycanthrope appears in the circle; otherwise, it appears 1d10 feet away from the caster in a random direction (the DM should use the scatter diagram for grenade-like missiles found in the *DUNGEON MASTER® Guide* to determine direction).

A warding circle is a temporary prison drawn with specially prepared pigments laced with silver filings. These pigments cost 100 gp for each foot of diameter of the circle (thus, a circle 10 feet across costs 1,000 gp). A warding circle must be at least 5 feet in diameter; if smaller, the lycanthrope is automatically freed. Preparing the circle takes one turn per foot of diameter.

Even with such protection, the lycanthrope can break out of the circle and wreak vengeance upon the summoner. The creature's base chance of success is 20%, modified by the difference between its Hit Dice and the wizard's experience level. If the spellcaster is of a higher level, the difference is subtracted from the creature's chance of escaping the circle. If the lycanthrope is of higher Hit Dice than the wizard's level, the difference is added to its chance. Each creature is allowed only one attempt to escape.

Any break in the circle spoils the power of the spell and enables the lycanthrope to break free. Even a straw dropped across the line of a magic circle destroys its power. Fortunately, the creature cannot take any action against any portion of the ward, for the magic of the barrier absolutely prevents this.

Once safely ensnared, the lycanthrope can be

held for as long as the summoner dares. The creature cannot leave the circle, nor can any of its attacks or powers penetrate the magical barrier. When the full moon sets, the lycanthrope reverts to its human form. At this time, it is free of the spell and may leave the circle.

The material components are a drop of blood from any animal, a human hair, and a moonstone worth at least 150 gp. If the caster elects to create the warding circle, the components described above are also required.

There/Not There* (Evocation)

Range: 30 yards
Components: V, S, M
Duration: 1-6 turns
Casting Time: 1 round
Area of Effect: 10' cube
Saving Throw: None

This peculiar wild magic creates a random fluctuation in the probabilities of existence. The spell can be cast only upon nonliving objects and can affect only materials within a 10' × 10' × 10' cube.

Objects in the area of effect either remain normal and visible or they disappear (50% chance). The state of existence for any object is determined randomly and changes with each viewing and viewer. Thus, a single object could appear and disappear several times during the course of the spell. Furthermore, it might be "there" for one onlooker, but "not there" for another.

For example, a wild mage casts this spell on a doorway. The DM rolls percentile dice and determines the door is "there" for the wizard. The wizard's companion also looks at the door. The DM rolls and determines that the door is "not there" for the companion. The pair studies the door for several minutes, during which time the door does not change (this counts as a single viewing for each character).

The wizard and his companion then close their eyes. When they look at the door again, new checks for each character reveal the door is "not there" for both characters. The pair steps through the open archway and turns around to look at the door once again. This time it is "not there" for the wizard, but "there" for his companion. This random changing continues throughout the duration of the spell.

Objects that are "there" are normal in all respects. Doors can be opened, chests can be picked up and carried, and rocks can be used as barricades. Objects that are "not there" are gone, although their absence does not cause ceilings to collapse or other damage. A wizard could walk through a "not there" wall without difficulty.

When two parties perceive a *there/not there* object differently, the object functions for each party according to its own perceptions. For example, a wizard hides behind a rock that he sees as "there." Her enemy, a fighter, perceives the rock as "not there" and fires arrows at the wizard. The wizard would perceive the arrows as bouncing off the rock, while the fighter would perceive the arrows as missing their target or falling short. The fighter would be subject to a check before firing each arrow to determine whether his perception changes (assume that the fighter must look away from the rock every time he nocks an arrow; each time he takes aim, this counts as a new viewing).

After the spell is cast, any objects removed from the area of effect retain their uncertain existence for the duration of the spell. Thus, a pair of heroes could pick up a treasure chest, carry it down the hall, set it down, and discover it had vanished while their backs were turned. Worse still, one might see the chest and the other not!

The material component is a small piece of cat fur sealed inside a small box.

Thunder Staff (Invocation/Evocation)

Range: 0
Components: V, S, M
Duration: Instantaneous
Casting Time: 4
Area of Effect: 20' × 40' cone
Saving Throw: 1/2

Upon completion of this spell, the wizard raps his staff on the ground and produces a thundering cone of force 5' wide at the apex, 20' wide at the base, and 40' long. All creatures wholly or partially within this cone must roll a successful saving throw or be stunned for 1d3 rounds. Stunned creatures are unable to think coherently or act during this time and are deafened for 1d3+1 rounds. Additionally, those who fail the save are hurled 4d4+4 feet by the wave of force, suffering 1 point of damage per two feet thrown. Intervening surfaces (walls, doors, etc.) may restrict this distance, but damage remains the same (4d4+4).

If the save is successful, the victim is not stunned, but is deafened for 1d3+1 rounds and is hurled only half the distance.

Giant-sized or larger creatures who succeed at their saving throws are deafened but are not thrown, suffer no loss of hit points, and are not stunned. If the saving throw is failed, such creatures are hurled 2d4+2 feet, suffer one point of damage per two feet thrown, and are deafened and stunned.

The cone of force is considered to have a Strength of 19 for purposes of opening locked, barred, or magically held doors. This spell can move objects weighing up to 640 pounds a maximum distance of 4d4 + 4 feet. Fragile items must make a saving throw vs. crushing blow or be destroyed.

The material components are a vial of rain gathered during a thunderstorm and the wizard's staff, which must be made of oak. The staff is not destroyed during casting.

Turn Pebble to Boulder (Alteration) Reversible

Range: Touch
Components: V, S, M
Duration: Special
Casting Time: 4
Area of Effect: Special
Saving Throw: None

At the culmination of this spell, the caster hurls a pebble which grows and increases in speed, becoming a deadly boulder that inflicts 3d6 + 8 points of damage if it strikes the target. (The rules for boulders as missile weapons apply as described in the *DUNGEON MASTER Guide.*) The caster's THAC0 is used to determine success, and the caster is considered to be proficient with the thrown pebble and receives no penalty for range. The maximum range of attack is equal to 50 feet plus 10 feet per level of the caster. Only the caster may throw the pebble.

The wizard can enchant one stone at 7th level and gains one stone per three levels of experience thereafter (two stones at 10th level, three at 13th level, etc.). Only one pebble may be thrown per round, and pebbles must be hurled in consecutive rounds. The spell has a duration in rounds equal to the number of pebbles enchanted. Each pebble requires a separate attack roll. Pebbles may be thrown at different targets within range.

The material components are pebbles, which revert to normal size when the spell expires.

The reverse of this spell, *turn boulder to pebble*, shrinks a boulder to the size of a pebble. It affects only naturally occurring rocks and can not be used to shrink a statue or a cut gemstone.

The number of rocks that may be affected is equal to the number of experience levels of the caster. Boulders must not exceed one cubic foot per level of the caster. Thus, a 10th-level wizard could shrink 10 rocks, each of which is equal to or less than 10 cubic feet in size. All rocks are affected in the same round the spell is cast. Though they need not be touched, the boulders must be within 50 feet of the caster. Boulders that have been shrunk remain so until dispelled.

Unluck* (Evocation)

Range: 10 yards
Components: V, S, M
Duration: 2d10 rounds
Casting Time: 4
Area of Effect: One creature
Saving Throw: Neg.

With this spell, the wild mage creates a negative pattern in the random forces surrounding one creature. The creature is allowed a saving throw; if successful, the spell fails. If the saving throw is failed, random chance falls into an unlucky pattern. Any action involving random chance (i.e., any time a die roll affects the character) performed by the victim during the next 2-20 rounds requires two separate attempts; the worse result is always applied. (The victim rolls twice for attacks, damages, saving throws, etc., always using the worse die roll.)

A *luckstone* or similar magical device will negate *unluck*. Doing so, however, prevents the magical item from functioning for 2d10 rounds.

The material component is a piece of a broken mirror.

Fifth-Level Spells

Far Reaching III (Alteration)

Range: 0
Component: V
Duration: Special
Casting Time: 5
Area of Effect: Special
Saving Throw: None

This spell operates exactly like the 3rd-level *far reaching I* spell except that the range of any spell of levels 1-3 is increased by 150% and the range of any 4th- or 5th-level spell is increased by 50%.

Khazid's Procurement
(Divination, Summoning)

Range: Special
Components: V, S, M
Duration: 1 round/level
Casting Time: 1 turn
Area of Effect: Special
Saving Throw: None

This spell allows the caster to more easily access rare or dangerous spell components. The wizard casts this spell upon a silver mirror while concentrating on a mental image of the material he desires. The base chance of success is 50%, modified by the following factors:

- +1% per level of the caster
- +10% if the caster has seen the same type of substance or object before; this bonus is not cumulative with the following bonus
- +20% if the caster has a sample of the material or the same type of object in his possession; this bonus is not cumulative with the bonus above
- +30% if the wizard knows the location of the desired object
- −50% if the caster has never seen the same type of material or item before

If the percentile roll indicates failure, the caster is unable to locate the desired ingredient and the spell ends. If the roll indicates success, the wizard has located the object or substance and the mirror becomes a magical gate through which the caster can see the target. The size of the gate is determined by the size of the mirror, to a maximum size of 3 feet by 2 feet.

The gate always appears within arm's length of the target, allowing the wizard to reach through the mirror, grasp the object of his desire, and draw it back through the gate. The wizard must risk his own safety—the gate does not allow the use of probes, long-handled ladles, tongs, or other equipment to gather the material. The caster cannot move completely through the gate.

The gate vanishes when the spell's duration expires or when the target or the wizard moves more than 10' away from it.

The gate is visible from both sides, and other creatures can reach through the gate. Breath weapons, gaze attacks, missiles, spells, and similar attacks cannot be cast through the gate. Because creatures can pass their limbs through the gate, physical attacks and touch spells can be used.

The only limit to the range of this spell is that the caster and the target must be on the same plane of existence. Elemental forces (not creatures) will not pass through the gate. Thus, the wizard does not run the risk of flooding his laboratory by opening a gate beneath the sea, for example. However, the spell does not provide any sort of protection against a hostile environment.

The material components are an exquisite silver mirror of no less than 10,000 gp value and a black opal worth at least 1,000 gp which must be powdered and sprinkled on the mirror. The mirror is not lost after casting and may be used again, but the powdered opal is consumed in the casting.

Lower Resistance (Abjuration, Alteration)

Range: 60 yards
Components: V, S, M
Duration: 1 turn +1 round/level
Casting Time: 5
Area of Effect: One creature
Saving Throw: None

Using this spell, a wizard may attempt to reduce the magic resistance of a target creature. The magic resistance of the victim works against the *lower resistance* spell itself, but at only half its normal value. No saving throw is permitted in addition to magic resistance.

If the victim does not resist the effects of this spell, his magic resistance is reduced by a base 30% plus 1% per experience level of the wizard casting the spell.

This spell has no effect on creatures that have no magic resistance.

The material component is a broken iron rod.

Magic Staff (Enchantment/Charm)

Range: Touch
Components: V, S, M
Duration: Special
Casting Time: Special
Area of Effect: The wizard's staff
Saving Throw: None

This spell allows a wizard's staff to store one spell level for every three levels of the caster. Thus, a 9th-level wizard can store three spell levels (three 1st-level spells, one 1st and one 2nd, or one 3rd-level spell).

Spells that are to be stored in the staff must be memorized normally by the wizard. The spells are then cast as normal when charging the staff; casting requires the spell's normal casting time plus one round. The spell is wiped from memory and material components are consumed. All spells to be stored must be cast into the staff within 1 turn.

All stored spells have a casting time of 1.

Spells remain in the staff until cast or dispelled, or up to 1 hour per level of the caster. After this time, all stored spells fade away.

Only wizards who know the *magic staff* spell can cast spells from another wizard's staff. This applies to wizards who have never learned or could not normally cast the spells stored in a staff. It is common, however, for the staff's owner to implement a command word which must be known by anyone wishing to use the staff.

The material component for this spell is a staff cut from an ash tree. For each spell level the wizard intends to imbue into the staff, it must be inlaid with rubies worth at least 1,000 gp.

Mind Fog (Enchantment/Charm)

Range: 80 yards
Components: V, S
Duration: 3 turns
Casting Time: 3
Area of Effect: 20-foot cube
Saving Throw: Neg.

A *mind fog* is a physical block of fog that enables the wizard to weaken the mental resistance of his victims. Victims are allowed a saving throw at a −2 penalty to avoid the effects.

A creature who falls victim to the *mind fog* suffers −2 penalties to all saving throws against two categories of magic: all spells of the illusion/phantasm and enchantment/charm schools that affect the mind directly; and spells of 1st through 5th level which affect the mind directly. For ex-

ample, *phantasmal force* is a mind-affecting spell; *phantom steed* is not.

The penalty to saving throws operates cumulatively with any penalties that operate for other reasons. Affected creatures suffer the penalty as long as they remain in the fog and for 2d6 rounds thereafter.

Safeguarding (Abjuration)

Range: 0
Components: V, S, M
Duration: 1 turn +1 turn/level
Casting Time: 5
Area of Effect: 15-foot-radius sphere
Saving Throw: None

Use of this spell protects the wizard and anyone in the area of effect from damage caused by the rebounding of the wizard's spells. This includes damage from a *fireball* cast in an area too small for its effects, a reflected *lightning bolt*, or any other offensive area spell that overlaps the *safeguarding's* area of effect. The protection is effective against spells of 7th level and lower. The protection does not apply to damage from spells rebounded by any form of magical spell turning. This spell does not protect the wizard against damage from spells or attacks cast by enemies or other party members.

A wizard who has cast *safeguarding* is free to move and act normally. The spell's effect is always centered on him, regardless of his actions. Other creatures are free to enter and exit the area of effect.

An area spell cast by the wizard will take effect normally, but its effects will be negated within the area of the *safeguarding* spell. This applies *only* to area spells centered outside the radius of the *safeguarding* spell. If the wizard casts an offensive area spell within the area of the *safeguarding*, the *safeguarding* is immediately negated and those within the area suffer full damage from the spell. The wizard is free to cast non-offensive area spells and individually targeted spells within the area of the *safeguarding*.

The material component is a piece of preserved skin from any creature that possesses natural magic resistance.

Von Gasik's Refusal (Abjuration)

Range: 10 yards/level
Components: V, S, M
Duration: 1 hour/level
Casting Time: 5
Area of Effect: 20-foot-square/level
Saving Throw: None

This powerful spell is designed to prevent unauthorized spellcasters from entering a hallway, doorway, window, or other point of entry.

The spell creates an invisible barrier that blocks the targeted area. Any nonspellcasters and those spellcasters specifically named by the caster may pass freely. All other spellcasters collide with the invisible barrier. Members of classes with lesser spellcasting abilities (paladins, rangers, and bards) are blocked only if the character is of sufficient level to cast spells.

The wizard is able to ward one area up to 20'-square for each level of his experience. Thus, a 12th-level wizard may protect a square area 240 feet on a side. The area of effect may be divided among several smaller portals as long as the total area does not exceed the caster's limit. Each portal must be in range and sight of the caster at the time the spell is cast.

The barriers exist for one hour per level of the caster unless they are dismissed by the caster or dispelled by a *dispel magic* spell. A *disintegrate* spell immediately destroys a barrier, as does a *rod of cancellation* or a *sphere of annihilation*.

The invisible walls are not affected by physical blows, cold, heat, or electricity. Thrown and projected weapons (both magical and mundane) are not repelled by the barrier and may pass through the area normally. Spells can be cast through the barrier. *Dimension door, teleport,* and similar effects can bypass the barriers.

The material component is a pinch of dust from any wizard's tomb.

Vortex* (Evocation)

Range: 30 yards
Components: V, S, M
Duration: 1d4 rounds + 1 round/level
Casting Time: 5
Area of effect: 5-foot-diameter circle
Saving Throw: 1/2

A *vortex* is a swirling mass of magical energy, barely controllable by the caster. On the round of casting, a small sparkle of lights fills the air at the desired position. On the second round, a 7'-tall, multicolored tornado appears. From this moment on, the caster must maintain concentration in order for the *vortex* to remain.

Each round, the caster can move the *vortex* 60 feet. However, control of direction is not perfect. The caster has complete control over distance, but can only suggest the desired direction. The caster has a 50% chance of moving the *vortex* in the direction he desires; if the die roll indicates failure, the *vortex* moves according to the scatter diagram for grenade-like missiles. Thus, the *vortex* usually moves in the general direction desired, but on occasion, it may move to either side or directly toward the caster.

The *vortex* cannot pass through objects larger than its area of effect (it could move through a sapling but not an ancient oak tree) and will be redirected by these, rebounding along the general line of movement. For example, if cast in a narrow hallway, the *vortex* might ricochet down the hall, bouncing from side to side.

The *vortex* is composed of raw magical energy. Nonmagical creatures struck by the *vortex* suffer 1d4 points of damage per level of the caster. Magical creatures and spellcasters suffer 1d6 points of damage per level of the caster. Creatures struck are allowed a saving throw vs. magic to suffer only half damage.

Each time a creature is struck, there is a 5% chance that the *vortex* will explode in a wild surge. Use Table 2 to determine the results of any wild surge. If the *vortex* causes a wild surge, the spell ends immediately.

The material components are a silk streamer and a handful of straw.

Waveform* (Alteration)

Range: 40 yards
Components: S, M
Duration: 1d10 rounds
Casting Time: 5
Area of Effect: 10-foot-cube/level
Saving Throw: 1/2

By means of this spell, the wild mage is able to shape and direct the patterns of water currents, allowing him to mold liquids into a variety of forms. The spell affects a quantity of liquid no larger than the area of effect. If cast onto a larger body, such as an ocean or large lake, the spell affects only the water within the area of effect.

After casting *waveform*, the mage can form the water into any desired shape. The spell does not bind the liquid together in any fashion; it is still limited by its fluid properties and gravity. Thus, a mage could not use *waveform* to create a humanoid creature with arms and legs and direct it to walk across land. He could, however, create a roughly human shape with flowing arms that rises out of the water, crashes forward in a huge splash, then rises and repeats the process. Other possible shapes include gigantic waves, geysers, whirlpools, and troughs.

The shape takes one round to form, after which it can be maintained by concentration. The shape can be directed to move in any direction at the rate of 90 feet per round. If the *waveform* moves into or through a body of water, the form loses no intensity. However, if the wave is moved over dry ground, it loses one die of damage for every 10 feet crossed.

If propelled against a target, the *waveform* causes 1d4 points of damage per level of the caster to creatures in its path. The *waveform* can be directed against creatures on the surface or underwater. Those struck are allowed a saving throw; success indicates half damage.

If the victims are in or on a body of water, the shape will sweep them along. Creatures of small size are carried with the form, moving at its speed. Medium and large size creatures are swept along at half the water's speed. Creatures larger than this resist the movement. Those caught in the current can make a Strength check each round to swim free of the current.

Boats and ships are particularly vulnerable to the *waveform*. If the *waveform* is twice the size of the vessel or more, the ship must make a seaworthiness check (as described in Table 77 of the *DMG*). Vessels passing the check suffer damage as described above, reducing seaworthiness ratings for future checks by 2d6 points until repairs are made.

Alternatively, this spell can be cast directly at a single water-based creature—a water weird, water elemental, or other creature from the elemental plane of water. In this case, the spell causes 1d6 points of damage per level of the caster. The effect is instantaneous and the spell ends immediately after the attack is made.

The material component is a small, carved oar decorated with aquamarines worth at least 500 gp. The oar disintegrates when the spell is cast.

Sixth-Level Spells

Augmentation II (Evocation)

Range: 0
Components: V, S, M
Duration: 3 turns
Casting Time: 6
Area of Effect: Special
Saving Throw: None

This spell functions exactly like the 3rd-level *augmentation I* spell except that five spells of levels 1-3 may be affected. For each die of damage caused by augmented spells, one hit point is added to the damage total.

Augmentation II affects the first five spells which cause direct damage that are cast within the duration of the *augmentation II* spell. Only spells that cause direct physical damage are affected by this spell.

The material component is a pair of concentric circles of gold or platinum.

Bloodstone's Spectral Steed (Necromancy)

Range: 10 yards
Components: V, S, M
Duration: 1 hour/level
Casting Time: 1 round
Area of Effect: Special
Saving Throw: None

This spell allows a wizard to create a quasi-real, vulturelike creature. The flying steed can carry the caster and one other person per three levels of the wizard's experience (four at 12th level, five at 15th, etc.). All passengers must be specifically named during the casting.

The spectral steed looks like a huge, skeletal vulture with tattered wings. As it flies, it utters hideous screeches that echo through the sky. The spectral steed flies at a movement rate of 4 per level of the caster, to a maximum movement rate of 48. It appears with a bit and bridle, plus one saddle per passenger.

All normal animals shun the spectral steed and only monsters will attack it. The mount has AC 2 and 10 hit points plus 1 hit point per level of the caster. If it loses all of its hit points, the spectral steed disappears. It has no attack mode.

The material component is a hollow bone from a vulture's wing, which must be carved into a whistle and blown when the spell is cast.

Claws of the Umber Hulk (Alteration)

Range: Touch
Components: V, S, M
Duration: 1 turn/level
Casting Time: 1 round
Area of Effect: One creature
Saving Throw: None

When this spell is cast, the subject's hands widen and his fingernails thicken and grow, becoming equivalent in size and power to the iron-like claws of an umber hulk. The transformation takes one full round and is excruciatingly painful, requiring a system shock roll. A failed roll causes the subject to suffer 3d4 points of damage.

The subject can burrow as an umber hulk, cutting through 10 feet of solid stone or 60 feet of soil per turn. The only limitation to this is the subject's stamina; at the end of each turn of burrowing, the subject must succeed a Constitution check or be forced to rest for one turn.

Burrowing through soil does not necessarily create a passable tunnel. If the subject wishes to make a passage in which others can travel or that he can exit when the spell ends, he must dig at a rate of 30 feet per turn. Cutting a tunnel through solid rock does not require extra care or time.

The recipient of this spell can make two claw attacks per round, each inflicting 2d6 points of damage plus any Strength bonuses. Each attack is made with a −2 penalty to hit. This penalty applies until the subject has made two successful consecutive attacks (not necessarily in the same round), at which time he is accustomed to using the claws. The penalty is dropped for the remainder of the spell.

The material component is an umber hulk's claw.

Dilation II (Alteration)

Range: 0
Component: V
Duration: Special
Casting Time: 5
Area of Effect: Special
Saving Throw: None

This spell functions exactly like the 4th-level *dilation I* spell, except that the area of effect of a 1st-, 2nd-, or 3rd- level spell is extended by 50%. Alternatively, the wizard may extend the area of effect of one 4th- or 5th-level spell by 25%.

Forest's Fiery Constrictor (Conjuration/Summoning)

Range: 10 yards/level
Components: V, S, M
Duration: 1 round/level
Casting Time: 6
Area of Effect: One source of fire
Saving Throw: Special

This spell causes a tentacle of magical flame to snake forth from any existing source of natural or magical fire. The flaming tendril is 10 feet long, has AC 7, can be hit only by magical weapons of +2 or better, and has hit points equal to double the caster's level.

Any creature within 20 feet of the tentacle is subject to attack as directed by the caster. The victim must attempt a saving throw; if successful, the subject has avoided entanglement, but suffers 1d6 points of fire damage from contact with the tendril. If the saving throw is failed, the victim is entangled by the flaming serpent and suffers 3d6 points of fire damage each round until the tendril is destroyed or the spell expires.

If the fire source from which the tentacle emanates is extinguished, the remaining time that the fiery constrictor may exist is cut in half.

The material component is a red dragon's scale.

Lorloveim's Shadowy Transformation (Illusion)

Range: Touch
Components: V, S
Duration: 1d4 rounds + 1 round/level
Casting Time: 6
Area of Effect: Special
Saving Throw: Neg.

When this spell is cast, the illusionist transforms one creature or a specified amount of non-living material into shadow, making it insubstantial. Thus, a door could be turned to shadow and entered. The maximum amount of inanimate material that may be transformed is one cubic foot per level of the caster.

Unwilling creatures are allowed a saving throw to resist the *shadowy transformation*. Magical items and the magical effects of spells (such as *Bigby's forceful hand* or a *wall of stone*) cannot be affected.

A transformed creature and all its gear become insubstantial. The creature can pass through small holes, narrow openings, and the smallest cracks. The creature cannot fly without additional magic.

No form of attack is possible when in shadow form except against creatures that exist on the Ethereal plane. In this case, all attacks are normal; however, the shadowy creature may be harmed only by magical weapons of +1 or greater or by creatures able to affect those struck only by magical weapons. Spells and special attacks have normal effects.

Most undead creatures will ignore a creature in shadow form, believing it to be a wraith or spectre; however, liches and powerful undead may save vs. spell with a −4 penalty to recognize the spell. A successful *dispel magic* spell forces the creature in shadow form back to normal form.

Wildshield* (Alteration)

Range: 0
Components: V, S, M
Duration: Special
Casting Time: 1 round
Area of Effect: The caster
Saving Throw: None

This spell cloaks the caster in a whirling band of scintillating colors, completely concealing him. The caster is able to see normally within and outside the shield.

The *wildshield* protects the caster from the effects of spells and magical items. The shield can completely absorb 2d6 spell levels (i.e., if the roll of 2d6 results in 10, the shield could absorb ten 1st-level spells, two 5th-level spells, or any similar combination), thereby negating their effects on the caster. Both area effect spells and those individually targeted at the wild mage can be absorbed. In the case of area spells, the *wildshield* protects only the mage. All others in the area of effect suffer normal effects from the spell.

Wildshield also protects against wild surges, whether caused by the caster's magic or by an outside source. Each wild surge is considered equal to 1d6 spell levels.

The spell remains in effect until it is either canceled by the caster or it reaches its spell level capacity. If the capacity is met exactly, the *wildshield* simply ceases to function. However, if the *wildshield* is struck by more spell levels than it can absorb, it explodes in a wild surge. The spell that triggered the surge is completely negated, its energy instead transformed into a wild surge (see Table 2). Since the shield no longer functions, the formerly protected wizard is subject to full effects of this wild surge.

The material component is a small sponge.

Wildstrike* (Conjuration/Summoning)

Range: 30 yards
Components: V, S, M
Duration: 2d4 rounds
Casting Time: 6
Area of Effect: One creature
Saving Throw: Neg.

This spell is used primarily against hostile spellcasters. It distorts all attempts at spellcasting, converting spell energy into wild surges.

The victim of a *wildstrike* is allowed a saving throw; if successful, the spell has no effect. If the saving throw is failed, the target is enclosed within a field of wild magic. If the victim casts spells or uses a charge from a magical item, a wild surge is automatically created (refer to Table 2). When determining the effects of this surge, the true level of the wild mage who cast the *wildstrike* is subtracted from the die roll, making the effects of the wild surge more likely to affect the victim.

The material component is a small glass tube that is shattered in the casting.

Seventh-Level Spells

Acid Storm (Evocation)

Range: 10 yards/level
Components: V, S, M
Duration: 1 round/level
Casting Time: 7
Area of Effect: 40-foot-diameter circle
Saving Throw: ½

This deadly spell unleashes a downpour of magical, gelatinous acid droplets. All creatures within the area of effect are coated by globs of gooey acid. The acid can be washed off only with wine, vinegar, or by a successful *dispel magic* or similar spell. The acid remains present for 1 round per level of the caster, then vanishes.

Creatures coated by the acid suffer 1d4 hit points of damage each round during rounds 1-3, 1d6 points in each of rounds 4-6, and 1d8 points on each round thereafter. Characters who successfully save vs. spells during the first round suffer only half damage from the acid for the remaining rounds. When the spell expires, no further damage is inflicted.

Acid damage can be healed through any means except regeneration. The material component is a drop of acid.

Bloodstone's Frightful Joining (Necromancy)

Range: Touch
Components: V, S
Duration: 1 turn/level
Casting Time: 7
Area of Effect: One undead creature
Saving Throw: Special

When this powerful spell is employed, the wizard transfers his spirit to the body of an undead creature, totally dominating it. If the undead creature has intelligence, it is allowed a saving throw vs. spell to resist the joining. If the save is successful, the caster's spirit is forced back into his own body. The wizard must make a system shock roll; if the roll fails, the wizard suffers 5d6 points of damage. If the roll succeeds, the wizard suffers half this damage.

If the creature's save fails, the necromancer joins his life essence with that of the undead. While in the creature's body, the caster can use all of its special attacks and innate abilities, excluding spells memorized by the creature.

The wizard's body remains comatose, is subject to all regular attacks, and suffers damage normally. The wizard's spirit can travel an unlim-

ited distance from his physical body as long as they remain on the same plane of existence.

If intelligent, the possessed undead continually tries to purge the caster with mental threats that can be heard only by the wizard. The thoughts of the undead are ghastly. During the first minute of each hour of possession, the caster must succeed an Intelligence check in order to retain his sanity. The roll is modified by the difference between the creature's Intelligence and that of the spellcaster. If the undead has a higher score, the difference is added to the die roll. If the necromancer has a higher Intelligence, the difference is subtracted from the roll.

If the roll is successful, nothing happens and the caster may continue to possess the undead. If the Intelligence roll fails, the wizard's intellect degenerates, making him a raving, homicidal maniac. His spirit is immediately forced to return to his body, and he must attempt a system shock roll with damage occurring as outlined above. The caster remains dangerously insane until a *heal* or *wish* spell is used to restore his intellect.

This spell can be very useful when combined with the *mask of death* spell.

When the spell's duration expires, the necromancer's spirit immediately returns to his body.

Hatch the Stone from the Egg
(Alteration, Enchantment, Evocation)

Range: Touch
Components: V, S, M
Duration: Special
Casting Time: 1d4 + 4 hours
Area of Effect: One alchemical mixture
Saving Throw: None

When a wizard wishes to create the magical item known as the *philosopher's stone*, he must first discover its alchemical formula, which tells him the necessary ingredients and the method of preparing them. This information is not provided by this spell, and this spell is useless without the formula. (The exact ingredients and formula are decided by the Dungeon Master and must be discovered by the wizard by adventuring.)

When the formula has been discovered and the ingredients prepared, the wizard enchants the alchemical mixture with the *enchant an item* spell. *Hatch the stone from the egg* is then cast upon the mixture. This spell slowly transmutes the mixture into its final form as the philosopher's stone. The process is completed with a *permanency* spell.

The material component for this spell is a magical item known as the *philosopher's egg*, which is an enchanted retort used to hold the alchemical mixture. The egg is not destroyed upon completion of the spell and may be used again. (Further details about the *philosopher's egg* are found in Chapter 4 of this book.)

Hornung's Surge Selector* (**Alteration**)

Range: 0
Components: V, S, M
Duration: Special
Casting Time: 1 round
Area of Effect: The caster
Saving Throw: None

The great Hornung, having been blasted more than once by his own wild surges, devised a method of improving the results of wild magic and, not incidentally, his own chances of survival. The result was *Hornung's surge selector*. By casting this spell, the wild mage gains greater control over wild surges. When the caster's spell creates a wild surge, two separate results are determined from Table 2. The caster can then choose which of the two results will take effect. This spell can be used in conjunction with *Nahal's reckless dweomer*.

The spell's duration is a fixed number of surges or 12 hours, whichever comes first. The wild mage is able to shape one wild surge per five levels of his experience; thus, a 15th-level caster could shape three wild surges within a 12-hour period. At the end of 12 hours, the spell expires, regardless of the number of surges remaining.

The material component is a brass spinner.

Intensify Summoning
(Conjuration/Summoning, Necromancy)

Range: Special
Components: V, S, M
Duration: 1 turn
Casting Time: 6
Area of Effect: Special
Saving Throw: None

This spell enhances the strength of creatures summoned by the caster via 1st through 6th level conjuration/summoning spells. Only spells which bring summoned creatures to the wizard are affected.

The first two conjuration/summoning spells cast by the wizard within one turn following the *intensify summoning* spell are affected. Summoned creatures gain 2 hit points per hit die. The affected creatures retain their bonus hit points until

the normal expiration of the spell that summoned them.

The material components are a small leather pouch and a miniature silver candelabra.

Malec-Keth's Flame Fist (**Evocation**)

Range: 0
Components: V, S
Duration: 1 round/level
Casting Time: 1
Area of Effect: One creature or object
Saving Throw: Special

When this spell is completed, one of the caster's hands (his choice) bursts into light and is surrounded by an aura of flame. The caster suffers no damage from this effect. Illumination is equal to that of a torch.

If the wizard successfully touches an opponent, the subject must attempt a saving throw. If the roll is successful, the flame remains on the caster's hand (and he may use it to make further attacks until the spell's duration expires) and the touched creature suffers 1d4 + 2 points of fire damage. If the save is failed, the flame leaves the caster's hand to surround the victim's body in an aura of searing fire. The superheated aura burns for 1 round, inflicting 1d4 points of damage per level of the caster.

Instead of attacking a creature, the caster may choose to touch any single object, which is automatically surrounded by the searing aura for 1 round and must succeed at an item saving throw vs. magical fire or be destroyed. The aura can surround an object up to 5 cubic feet in volume per level of the caster.

Shadowcat (**Illusion**)

Range: 10 yards/level
Components: V, S, M
Duration: 1 turn/level
Casting Time: 3
Area of Effect: Special
Saving Throw: None

When this spell is cast, the wizard brings into being a cat made of shadow. The *shadowcat* is the size of a normal cat and may be either grey or black at the caster's option. The caster has complete telepathic control of the feline; he can see, hear, and even speak through it as long as it remains within range. At the moment it moves out of range, the *shadowcat* vanishes. The caster does not need to concentrate on the *shadowcat*.

The shadowy feline is insubstantial, making it

subject only to magical or special attacks, including those by weapons of +1 or better. It has AC 5, a movement rate of 18, and saving throws equal to those of the caster. The cat dissipates if it loses hit points equal to one-half the caster's total hit points. The *shadowcat* has no attacks of its own and cannot touch or carry objects. A successful *dispel magic* spell causes the cat to vanish.

A *shadowcat* makes no sound as it moves. It is 90% undetectable in all but the brightest conditions. It can pass through small holes or narrow openings.

The material components of this spell are a black pearl of at least 100 gp value and a claw from a grey or black cat.

Spell Shape* (Alteration)

Range: 0
Components: V, S, M
Duration: 1d4 +1 rounds
Casting Time: 1 round
Area of Effect: The caster
Saving Throw: Special

This spell gives the wild mage the ability to seize magical energy directed at him and reshape it as he desires. While it is in effect, the spell gives no visible sign of its existence. It offers no protection against area effect spells.

If a wild mage is the target of a spell or magical item, this spell automatically allows him a saving throw. If the saving throw is failed, the opponent's spell has normal effects. If the saving throw is successful, the *spell shape* absorbs the magical energy of the opponent's spell. The wild mage can then choose to let the energy dissipate or he can instantly use it to cast a spell back at the opposing mage. The return spell must be of an equal or lesser spell level than the original one and must be currently memorized by the mage. The act of returning the spell does not cost the wild mage any of his memorized spells. Spell energy cannot be saved; if not used immediately, it dissipates.

For example, Hamos, a wild mage, is protected by a *spell shape* and is struck by a *finger of death* (a 7th-level spell). He succeeds at his saving throw and is now able to cast a spell of 7th level or lower. Hamos currently has *feeblemind* memorized. Since it is only a 5th-level spell, he chooses to cast it back at his enemy. He makes his level variation check (and doesn't get a wild surge) and the *feeblemind* is sent hurtling back at his foe. Hamos still has his original *feeblemind* memorized. The remaining two spell levels are lost, since they were not used in the same round.

If a wild mage is struck by two spells at once, he may choose which spell to shape. He suffers all effects of the remaining spell.

The material component is a diamond worth no less than 2,000 gp. When the spell is cast, the diamond is transformed into a lump of coal.

Steal Enchantment (Enchantment)

Range: Touch
Components: V, S, M
Duration: Permanent
Casting Time: 1 hour
Area of Effect: One item
Saving Throw: Neg.

This spell "steals" the enchantment from a magical item and places it within another, nonmagical item (the material component). Both objects must be touched by the wizard during casting. The two items must be of the same category (blunt weapon, edged weapon, ring, amulet, shield, armor, wand, etc.).

The enchantment can be transferred only to a nonmagical item. Only the energy of one item can be transferred; it is not possible to combine two magical items into one item. The new item has all the properties of the original magical item (including the same number of charges, if any).

At the culmination of the spell, the original magical object is allowed an item saving throw vs. disintegration with all modifiers it is allowed as a magical item. Exceptionally powerful objects (such as artifacts) may be considered to automatically succeed the saving throw at the DM's discretion.

If the saving throw is successful, the magical object resists the effect and the spell ends in failure. If the roll is failed, the magical item loses all of its powers, which are transferred to the previously nonmagical object.

Even if the magical item fails its saving throw, the spell's success is not guaranteed. There is a chance that the enchantment might be lost. The base chance of this occurring is 100%, modified by −5% per level of the caster. Thus, a 20th-level wizard has no chance of losing the magic. If the enchantment is lost, both items become nonmagical.

The material component is the nonmagical item which is to receive the enchantment. It must be of equal or greater value than the object to be drained.

Suffocate (Alteration, Necromancy)

Range: 30 yards
Components: V, S, M
Duration: 1 round/level
Casting Time: 7
Area of Effect: 10-foot-radius circle
Saving Throw: Neg.

This spell draws the breath out of all creatures within the area of effect who fail a saving throw. Their breath is placed within a small silk bag held by the caster.

Each round, a victim of this spell must attempt a Constitution check. If failed, the creature suffers 2d4 points of damage. If successful, the subject has taken in enough air to reduce the damage to 1d4.

As they struggle and gasp for air, affected creatures move and attack at half their normal rates, have a −4 Armor Class penalty, an attack penalty of −4, and lose all Dexterity combat bonuses.

Effects of this spell continue each round regardless of whether the victims remain in the original area of effect. The damage accumulates until the spell expires, the silk bag is opened, or a successful *dispel magic* spell is cast upon the bag. The penalties to combat remain in effect for 1d3 rounds after the spell ends.

The material component is a small silk bag studded with black opals worth a total of no less than 5,000 gp. The bag is not destroyed during casting, but becomes useless for future castings if a successful *dispel magic* spell is used on it.

Eighth-Level Spells

Abi-Dalzim's Horrid Wilting
(Alteration, Necromancy)

Range: 20 yards/level
Components: V, S, M
Duration: Instantaneous
Casting Time: 8
Area of Effect: 30-foot cube
Saving Throw: 1/2

This spell evaporates moisture from the bodies of every living creature within the area of effect, inflicting 1d8 points of damage per level of the caster. Affected creatures are allowed a saving throw, with success indicating half damage.

This spell is especially devastating to water elementals and plant creatures, who receive a penalty of −2 to their saving throws.

The material component is a bit of sponge.

Airboat (Alteration, Enchantment)

Range: 1 mile
Components: V, S
Duration: 1 hour/level
Casting Time: 1 round
Area of Effect: Special
Saving Throw: None

This spell must be cast under a cloudy sky. The caster points at a cloud, which immediately descends toward him. As it comes closer, the cloud changes shape, becoming any sort of vessel imagined by the wizard (a dragon-shaped galley, a one-man dinghy, etc.).

Although the *airboat* is made of cloud, it feels solid and can support the weight of the caster plus one passenger per level of the wizard. It can move at a rate of 21 (MC:D).

The caster maintains total telepathic control over the airboat's speed and direction. While controlling the vessel, the wizard is able to perform other actions but may not cast other spells.

Gunther's Kaleidoscopic Strike
(Invocation/Evocation)

Range: 5 yards/level
Components: V, S
Duration: Instantaneous
Casting Time: 8
Area of Effect: One creature
Saving Throw: Neg.

When this spell is cast, a thin beam of shimmering, kaleidoscopic light shoots from the wizard's fingertips toward his target. The victim is allowed a saving throw to resist the beam.

This spell has no effect on nonspellcasters, causing them no harm whatsoever. Creatures with innate spell-like abilities are also unaffected. Against wizards and priests, this spell can be devastating. It "short-circuits" the arcane energy stored in a spellcaster's mind, wiping away a number of memorized spells. Lost spells must be rememorized.

The number of spells drained is equal to the caster's level minus 1d20. Thus, a 16th-level wizard drains a maximum of 15 spells, but could drain no spells depending on the die roll. After subtracting the die roll from the caster's level, any result of zero or a negative number indicates that the victim loses no spells.

Spells are drained from the wizard's memorized spells beginning with 1st-level spells and working up to higher level spells. Any decision regarding which spell should be drained from a specific level should be determined randomly.

Homunculus Shield (Evocation, Necromancy)

Range: 0
Components: V, S, M
Duration: 1 round/level
Casting Time: 3
Area of Effect: The caster
Saving Throw: None

By creating a *homunculus shield*, the wizard separates a portion of his mind in the form of an exteriorized magical homunculus. This creature is invisible to all but the caster and appears as a miniature version of the caster perched atop the wizard's head.

The wizard may move and act normally while this spell is in effect. The magical homunculus operates as an independent spellcaster. It may cast only *teleport*, *contingency*, and protective spells of 4th level and lower. It casts only spells from the wizard's memorized store of spells, but any spells cast by the homunculus are done so with a casting time of 1. The wizard selects which spells are cast by his homunculus; after they are cast, they are wiped from the caster's memory.

The homunculus has 1 hit point per two levels of the caster. These points are "borrowed" from the caster; while the homunculus is present, the wizard's hit points are reduced by this amount.

The homunculus cannot be struck by melee or missile weapons separately from the wizard. It can be damaged separately from the wizard (e.g., by a *magic missile* targeted at the homunculus or by area effect spells). The homunculus has the at-

tributes and saving throws of the wizard.

At the end of the spell's duration, the homunculus disappears and any hit points it had are restored to the wizard. Hit points lost by the homunculus can be regained only by magical healing.

If the wizard's hit points are reduced to zero at any time during the spell, the wizard is dead even if the homunculus had hit points remaining.

A wizard with an active *homunculus shield* suffers a −4 saving throw penalty against *magic jar* spells cast upon him due to the division of his mental energy.

The material component is a miniature sculpted bust of the spellcaster.

Hornung's Random Dispatcher* (Abjuration)

Range: 30 yards
Component: V
Duration: Instantaneous
Casting Time: 2
Area of Effect: One creature
Saving Throw: Neg.

With the utterance of a few words, this spell can hurl a creature to a random plane and leave him there. The target, if unwilling, is allowed a saving throw. If successful, the spell fails. If unsuccessful, the victim and all items carried by him are sent to a random plane. To determine the plane, roll on the table below.

D100

Roll	Plane
01-03	Abyss
04-06	Acheron
07-12	Alternate Prime Material Plane
13-17	Arcadia
18-23	Astral Plane
24-27	Beastlands (Happy Hunting Grounds)
28-30	Concordant Opposition
31-35	Elemental Plane (Air, Fire, Earth, or Water)
36-38	Elysium
39-44	Ethereal Plane
45-47	Gehenna
48-50	Gladsheim
51-53	Hades
54-58	Limbo
59-61	Negative Material Plane
62-64	Negative Quasi-Plane (Vacuum, Ash, Dust, or Salt)
65-67	Nine Hells
68-70	Nirvana
71-73	Olympus
74-76	Pandemonium

D100

Roll	Plane
77-79	Para-Elemental Plane (Smoke, Magma, Ooze, or Ice)
80-82	Positive Material Plane
83-85	Positive Quasi-Plane (Lightning, Radiance, Minerals, or Steam)
86-91	Prime Material Plane*
92-94	Seven Heavens
95-97	Tarterus
98-100	Twin Paradises

* Characters sent to the Prime Material plane are teleported elsewhere in the same world.

The caster has no control over the destination of the target. The conditions at the destination may kill the target (for example, arriving in the elemental plane of fire) or merely make life difficult. This determination is left to the DM.

Wildzone* (Conjuration/Summoning)

Range: 0
Components: V, S, M
Duration: 2d6 turns
Casting Time: 1d6 rounds
Area of Effect: 300′ × 300′ square
Saving Throw: None

This powerful spell creates a disruption in magical forces similar to the conditions found in wild magic regions (areas where the effects of magic have been permanently altered). This spell has only a temporary effect, although the effects of *wildzone* could possibly be rendered permanent.

The spell creates a wild magic region centered on the caster. The area of effect cannot be shaped in any way; it is *always* a square 300 feet long on each side (90,000 square feet).

Within the *wildzone*, wild magic reigns. Any spell cast in the area of effect is automatically treated as a wild surge (see Table 2). Effects from magical items that expend charges are also treated as wild surges when used in the area. Other magical items function normally.

Spells cast into the *wildzone* from outside the area of effect function normally, but spells cannot be cast out of the area of effect without triggering a wild surge.

The material components are several pots of paint which must be spilled across a sheet of hammered silver worth no less than 2,000 gp.

Ninth-Level Spells

Chain Contingency (Evocation)

Range: 0
Components: V, S, M
Duration: 1 day/level
Casting Time: 2 turns
Area of Effect: The caster
Saving Throw: None

This powerful spell is similar to the 6th-level *contingency* spell.

Chain contingency allows the caster to designate either two or three spells that will take effect automatically under a specific set of conditions. In other words, when a set of conditions is met, the designated spells are "cast" immediately without the caster's intervention.

Chain contingency must be cast together with the spells it is to trigger. The caster may choose either two spells to occur simultaneously or three spells to occur consecutively, one per round. Spells must be of 8th level or lower. Only the 6th-level *contingency* spell may not be included. The casting time of 2 turns includes the casting of the spells to be triggered.

Unlike the *contingency* spell, spells "stored" in *chain contingency* can affect creatures other than the caster. These instructions must be carefully worded; the spell obeys the letter of its instructions and not the caster's intentions.

In casting *chain contingency*, the wizard defines the conditions that will trigger the "stored" spells. This definition must be carefully worded, but may be as limiting or general as the caster desires. The caster also states the exact order, target, range, and manner in which the stored spells are to be cast.

The spell has several limitations in triggering its spells. It does not have any powers of discernment; thus, an instruction to "target the highest-level enemy" is not possible. Furthermore, the conditions cannot involve a delay; a spell cannot be ordered to trigger "three turns after I sneeze."

When the named conditions are met, the *chain contingency* is automatically triggered. If all specifics of casting a spell are not specified (e.g., target or area of effect), the effect is automatically centered on the caster.

Possible triggers might include a fall from a distance greater than the caster's height, the appearance of the first beholder within 30 feet of the caster, or the wizard pointing his finger and pronouncing a specified word.

Only one *chain contingency* can be placed on the spellcaster at any one time. If a second is cast, the first *chain contingency* is cancelled. It is possible to have both a *contingency* and a *chain contingency* operating at the same time, provided that there is no overlap in the conditions specified for triggering the two spells.

Spells triggered by the *chain contingency* have a casting time of 1. If the spell is triggered under conditions that are impossible to fulfill, it fails. If one of the spells in a series cannot be fulfilled, the remaining spells in the series are lost. Normal conditions, including line of sight to the target, must be fulfilled. All spells originate from the caster; thus, it is not possible for a caster to *teleport* and leave behind a series of *fireballs* to blast his enemies. In this case, the *fireballs* would either fail or destroy something at the caster's destination.

The material components are (in addition to those of the companion spells) 500 gp worth of quicksilver; a gem of at least 1,000 gp value; an eyelash from an ogre mage, ki-rin, or similar spell-using creature; and an ivory statuette of the wizard (which is not destroyed in the casting of the spell) which must be carried by the spellcaster in order for the *chain contingency* to perform its function when triggered.

Elemental Aura (Abjuration, Evocation)

Range: 0
Component: V
Duration: 1 hour/level
Casting Time: 1 round
Area of Effect: The caster
Saving Throw: None

This spell has four very different effects depending on the type (air, earth, fire, water) of *elemental aura* cast. Only the caster may receive an *elemental aura*, and it is not possible to benefit from more than one aura at one time.

Each aura is three inches thick and covers the caster's entire body. An aura of air is hazy white in color, an aura of earth is dull grey, an aura of fire is flickering red, and an aura of water is shimmering blue. The auras have these effects:

Air
- immunity to gas and air-based attacks
- total protection from physical attacks by creatures of the elemental plane of Air
- ability to cast *fly* and *protection from normal missiles* once each

Earth
- immunity to attacks from nonmagical weapons made of stone or metal
- immunity to physical attacks by creatures of the elemental plane of Earth
- ability to breathe and move at full movement rate within the element of earth
- ability to cast *wall of stone* once

Fire
- immunity to normal and magical fire
- total protection from physical attacks by creatures of the elemental plane of Fire
- ability to breathe and move at full movement rate within the element of fire
- total protection from hostile environmental effects while traveling plane of Fire
- ability to cast *wall of fire* once

Water
- immunity to water- and cold-based attacks
- total protection from physical attacks by creatures of the plane of Water
- ability to breathe and move at full movement rate within the element of water
- ability to cast *wall of ice* once

The auras do not restrict the caster in any way. He is free to move and act normally while under the influence of an aura.

Estate Transference (Alteration)

Range: 0
Components: V, S, M
Duration: Permanent
Casting Time: 10 turns
Area of Effect: 1 square mile/level
Saving Throw: None

This powerful spell allows a caster to transfer a large area of land in the Prime Material plane to any of the elemental planes. All buildings, people, and wildlife within the area of effect are also transported. The land forms a pocket of the Prime Material plane within the elemental plane. The pocket is a sphere with a diameter equal to the diameter of the land. The surface of the pocket allows creatures to enter or exit the pocket, but prevents the elements from entering the pocket.

Inside the pocket, the land is surrounded by air of a temperature matching that of the Prime Material plane at the moment the land was moved. In addition, a source of water is created within the pocket.

Before the spell is cast, the area to be moved must be surrounded by solid markers of material from the destination plane. Thus, if a wizard wants to move his castle to the Elemental Plane of Fire, he must first surround the area with solid blocks of matter from the Elemental Plane of Fire, such as hardened magma or magically-crystallized fire. The blocks must be spaced no more than five feet apart and may be placed above ground or under the surface (at a depth of no more than three feet).

The wizard must be within the area to be moved when he casts the spell. When the land moves, a hemispherical crater is left behind in the Prime Material plane. Inside its pocket on the desired plane, the land continues its existence as if nothing changed, with the exception of occasional visits from planar creatures.

Any land that is moved in this manner can never again be moved with this spell.

The material component (in addition to the markers) is the appropriate magical device to control elementals of the desired plane (*bowl commanding water elementals, brazier commanding fire elementals, censer controlling air elementals,* or *stone controlling earth elementals*). The item must be permanently placed at the heart of the area of effect and cannot be used for any other purpose. If the device is disturbed in any way, the spell immediately fails, allowing the energies of the elemental plane to flood into the protected area.

Glorious Transmutation (Alteration)

Range: Touch
Components: V, S, M
Duration: Permanent
Casting Time: 1 turn
Area of Effect: Special
Saving Throw: None

This spell turns iron into silver or lead into gold at the caster's option. The prime ingredient for this spell is a magical item called the *philosopher's stone,* which must be touched by the wizard and alchemically combined with the metal during casting. The formula for mixing the stone and the metal must be known by the caster; this information is not provided by this spell and the spell is useless without it. (The exact ingredients and formula are decided by the Dungeon Master and must be discovered by the wizard in the course of adventuring.)

Philosopher's stones vary in quality so much that each is capable of transmuting either 1d10×50 pounds of iron into an equal quantity of silver *or* 1d10×10 pounds of lead into the same amount of gold. It is not possible to know how much metal can be transmuted until the process is complete. If the caster has more iron or lead prepared than the spell is capable of changing, any excess is unchanged.

The entire transmutation must be made at one time. Only one stone may be used per casting of the spell. The entire *philosopher's stone* is consumed in the process.

Stabilize* (Abjuration)

Range: 0
Components: V, S
Duration: 1d4+1 turns
Casting Time: 1 turn
Area of Effect: 30-foot-radius circle
Saving Throw: None

This spell requires immense magical effort to cast, relegating it to the highest spell level. *Stabilize* negates the effects of wild magic regions, allowing the caster and all creatures in a 30-foot radius to cast spells and use magical items normally. The spell is centered on the caster and follows his movements.

The caster's own spells never cause wild surges when cast within the duration of a *stabilize* spell, nor do the effects of wild surges extend into the protected area. Furthermore, the wild mage's spells function at his true level; Table 2 is *not* used to determine level variation. The spell affects *wildstrike, wildzone,* and *wildwind.*

Wail of the Banshee (Necromancy)

Range: 0
Components: V, S, M
Duration: Instantaneous
Casting Time: 9
Area of Effect: 30-foot-radius sphere
Saving Throw: Neg.

At the culmination of this dreadful spell, the wizard screams like a banshee (a groaning spirit). For each level of the caster, one listener within 30 feet hears the wail. Those who fail a saving throw vs. death magic die instantly.

The wizard cannot be the victim of his own spell, nor can he choose who will be affected. If there are more potential victims than the level of the caster, the DM must randomly determine which creatures are affected. Creatures who cannot hear (due to ear plugs, deafness, etc.) can be targets, but cannot be affected and are considered to automatically make their saving throws.

The material component is a lock of hair from an evil female elf.

Wildfire* (Invocation/Evocation)

Range: 0
Component: V
Duration: Variable
Casting Time: 1
Area of Effect: Variable
Saving Throw: Variable

By means of this spell, the wild mage is able to channel raw magical energy through himself, shaping it into any form or effect he desires. The energy is similar in many ways to a *wish* spell, but has unique differences.

Wildfire allows the caster to create the effect of any wizard spell of 8th level or lower. He need only have general knowledge of the spell and its effects; the spell does not need to be in his own spellbooks.

Any normal saving throws vs. the spell effects are made at a −2 penalty.

Wildfire can also be used in the creation of magical items. The energy created by the spell may be used to generate effects that are not created by known spells.

Wildfire can also be used to create items out of nothing. The magical energy can be shaped and hardened to form solid objects. These objects have a greenish, glowing tinge and radiate magic. These objects are stronger than steel yet possess almost no weight. They are immune to fire, cold, electricity, and all forms of magical attack except *dispel magic* and *wish* spells. Even if they are subjected to these spells, a saving throw is allowed (equal to the creator's saving throw vs. spell).

When creating objects, the caster is limited only by his own skill and the dimensions of the object. Items larger than a 10-foot-radius sphere cannot be fashioned. Creating the object requires only one round, regardless of size. Thus, a wizard could make an impenetrable dome or a small boat with this spell.

Objects made of *wildfire* are neither stable nor permanent. Since the object is made of magic separated from the magical continuum, the material gradually deteriorates until the magical bonds become too weak to hold the *wildfire* in the chosen form. This decay takes 1d6 +4 hours.

Wildwind* (Conjuration/Summoning)

Range: 100 yards
Components: V, S
Duration: 1d3 turns
Casting Time: 8
Area of Effect: Special
Saving Throw: None

This spell is similar in effect to *wildstrike* and *wildzone*. When cast, a wall of faint, multi-colored lights springs into existence at the point indicated by the caster. These lights form a line 150 feet long. After the first round of the spell, the wizard can move the wall of lights. Each round, the caster can move the wall in the same direction or as much as 45 degrees to either side. Once the wall is set in motion, it cannot be stopped unless the spell is cancelled or dispelled. The lights can move 60 feet per round.

The *wildwind* has two significant effects. First, all creatures struck by the magical lights suffer 2d6 points of damage. Second, any spellcaster struck while attempting to cast a spell automatically triggers a wild surge (use Table 2). Magical items that expend charges that touch the wall of lights automatically release one charge, also resulting in a wild surge.

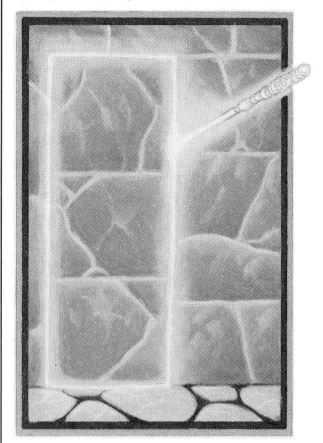

1st Level

Analyze Balance
Anti-Vermin Barrier
Call Upon Faith
Courage
Emotion Read
Know Age
Know Direction
Know Time
Log of Everburning
Mistaken Missive
Morale
Personal Reading
*Ring of Hands**
Sacred Guardian
Speak With Astral Traveler
Thought Capture
Weighty Chest

2nd Level

Aura of Comfort
Calm Chaos
Create Holy Symbol
Dissension's Feast
Draw Upon Holy Might
Emotion Perception
Frisky Chest
Hesitation
Idea
Lighten Load
Mind Read
Moment
Music of the Spheres
*Mystic Transfer**
Nap
Rally
*Sanctify**
Zone of Truth

3rd Level

Accelerate Healing
Adaptation
Astral Window
Caltrops
Choose Future
Create Campsite
Efficacious Monster Ward
Emotion Control
Extradimensional Detection
Helping Hand
Invisibility Purge
Know Customs
*Line of Protection**
Memory Read
Miscast Magic
Moment Reading
Random Causality
Rigid Thinking
Slow Rot
Squeaking Floors
Strength of One
Telepathy
Telethaumaturgy
Thief's Lament
*Unearthly Choir**
Zone of Sweet Air

4th Level

Addition
Age Plant
Blessed Warmth
Body Clock
Chaotic Combat
Chaotic Sleep
Circle of Privacy
Compulsive Order
Defensive Harmony
Dimensional Folding
Fire Purge
*Focus**
*Fortify**
Genius
Inverted Ethics
Join With Astral Traveler
Leadership
Mental Domination
Modify Memory
Probability Control
Rapport
Solipsism
Tanglefoot
Thought Broadcast
Tree Steed
*Uplift**
Weather Stasis

5th Level

Age Object
Barrier of Retention
Blessed Abundance
Champion's Strength
Chaotic Commands
Clear Path
Cloud of Purification
Consequence
Disguise
Easy March
Elemental Forbiddance
Extradimensional
   Manipulation
Extradimensional Pocket
Grounding
Illusory Artillery
Impeding Permission
Meld*
Memory Wrack
Mindshatter
Repeat Action
Shrieking Walls
Thoughtwave*
Time Pool
Unceasing Vigilance of
   the Holy
   Sentinel
Undead Ward

6th Level

Age Creature
Crushing Walls
Disbelief
Dragonbane
Gravity Variation
*The Great Circle**
Group Mind
Land of Stability
Legal Thoughts
Monster Mount
Physical Mirror
Reverse Time
Seclusion
Skip Day
Sol's Searing Orb
*Spiritual Wrath**

7th Level

Age Dragon
Breath of Life
Divine Inspiration
Hovering Road
Illusory Fortification
Mind Tracker
Shadow Engines
Spaceworp
*Spirit of Power**
Tentacle Walls
Timelessness
Uncontrolled Weather

Quest Spells

Abundance
Animal Horde
Circle of Sunmotes
Conformance
Elemental Swarm
Etherwalk
Fear Contagion
Health Blessing
Highway
Imago Interrogation
Implosion/Inversion
Interdiction
Mindnet
Planar Quest
Preservation
Revelation
Reversion
Robe of Healing
Siege Wall
Shooting Stars
Sphere of Security
Spiral of Degeneration
Stalker
Storm of Vengeance
Transformation
Undead Plague
Warband Quest
Ward Matrix
Wolf Spirits

Italicized spells are reversible.
An asterisk (*) indicates a cooperative magic spell.

First-Level Spells

Analyze Balance (**Divination**)

Sphere: Numbers, Divination
Range: 80 yards
Components: V, S, M
Duration: 5 rounds + 1 round/level
Casting Time: 1 round
Area of Effect: One creature, object, or 10' square
Saving Throw: None

This spell allows a priest to sense how far a character, creature, object, or area is from a condition of balance—in other words, the degree to which its alignment is removed from true Neutral. The spell gives no indication of the "direction" in which the alignment is removed from true Neutral except under certain conditions which follow. The spell does, however, indicate along which axis or axes of alignment the variation lies.

For example, a priest uses this spell to analyze the balance of a Chaotic Neutral creature. The spell indicates that the creature is removed from Neutral by one grade, and the variation is along the Law/Chaos axis; thus, the creature must be either Chaotic Neutral or Lawful Neutral. If the creature were Chaotic Evil, the spell would indicate that it is removed from balance by two grades, one along each axis; thus, the creature must be Chaotic Evil, Chaotic Good, Lawful Evil, or Lawful Good.

A priest has a 5% chance per level of correctly determining the direction of variation along one randomly chosen axis. This means that a 10th-level priest evaluating the balance of a Chaotic Neutral creature would have a 50% chance of learning that the creature is Chaotic (and hence Chaotic Neutral, since it is only one step away from balance).

Similar to spells such as *detect evil*, this spell will not yield a result on a hidden trap. If cast on a creature with an intelligence level of "animal" or "non-," it will always read true Neutral (i.e., zero steps removed from balance).

The material components are four iron coins which the priest tosses in his hand while concentrating on the spell. The coins are not consumed in the casting.

Anti-Vermin Barrier (**Abjuration**)

Sphere: Wards
Range: 30 yards
Components: V, S, M
Duration: 1 hour/level
Casting Time: 1
Area of Effect: 10-foot cube/level
Saving Throw: None

With this spell, the caster creates an invisible force field that repels nonmagical insects, rodents, spiders, snakes, worms, and similar vermin of less than 1 Hit Die. The spell has no effect on giant-sized versions of these creatures unless they are less than 1 Hit Die. The barrier affects summoned creatures, such as those called by a *summon insects* spell.

Any vermin within the area of effect when the spell is cast are not affected; however, when these creatures exit the area, they cannot return.

The spell affects a cubic area whose sides are 10 feet times the caster's level (for instance, a 2nd-level priest could affect a 20' × 20' × 20' cube.

The material components are the caster's holy symbol and a rodent's whisker.

Call Upon Faith (**Invocation**)

Sphere: Summoning
Range: 0
Components: V, S, M
Duration: 1 round
Casting Time: 1
Area of Effect: The caster
Saving Throw: None

Before attempting a difficult task, the priest may cast *call upon faith* to aid his performance. If the priest has been true to his faith (as determined by the DM), the priest gains a +3 (or +15%) bonus to one die roll (his choice) needed to complete the task. The bonus may be used to affect a saving throw, attack roll, ability check, etc. For example, if a priest were about to cross a narrow log high above a chasm, he could cast this spell and gain a +3 bonus to his Dexterity ability check.

The material component is the priest's holy symbol.

Courage (Enchantment/Charm)

Sphere: War
Range: 240 yards
Components: V, S, M
Duration: Special
Casting Time: 1 turn
Area of Effect: One unit up to 200 individuals
Saving Throw: None

This spell imbues the target unit with a temporary burst of courage. To cast this spell, the priest must have an uninterrupted line of sight to the target unit.

A *courage* spell enables a unit to automatically pass its first morale check following the casting of this spell. When circumstances arise that would necessitate a morale check, no die roll is made and the unit is assumed to have passed the check. After this occurs, the spell ends and the unit must make all future morale checks normally.

If a unit under the influence of a *courage* spell is not forced to make any morale checks, the spell expires at the first sunset.

When several different events simultaneously trigger morale checks, the BATTLESYSTEM rules apply penalties to a single morale check. If this occurs to a unit under the influence of a *courage* spell, the player commanding the unit selects one such event and its modifier is ignored.

No more than one *courage* spell can affect a unit at one time. Once the spell has expired, a priest can cast the spell again on the same unit.

The material component is a cube of cast iron.

Emotion Read (Divination)

Sphere: Thought
Range: 5 yards/level
Components: V, S, M
Duration: Instantaneous
Casting Time: 3
Area of Effect: One creature
Saving Throw: Neg.

This spell allows the priest to perform an instantaneous reading of a single subject's emotional state. It can be used on any subject possessing Intelligence of 3 or better. This reading is neither deep nor specific and cannot pick out mixed emotions or intricate details. For example, it might tell the priest that the subject is fearful, but the spell cannot reveal what the subject is afraid of or why he is afraid.

Emotion read does not reveal individual thoughts or the subject's motivation. Thus, the spell might reveal that the subject is coldly unemotional at the moment, but not the fact that the subject is contemplating the cold-blooded murder of the priest.

Note that this reading is instantaneous. It reveals only the emotion that is strongest at the instant the spell is used. While this will usually be related to the subject's overall emotional state, it is always possible that the subject might be distracted for a moment or remember and respond to past events.

The subject is allowed a normal saving throw vs. spells to resist this spell. If the saving throw is successful, the priest receives no reading at all. If the subject's roll exceeds the necessary number by six or more, the priest perceives an emotion diametrically opposite to the subject's true emotion.

The material component is a square of unmarked white wax.

Know Age (Divination)

Sphere: Time
Range: 0
Components: V, S, M
Duration: Instantaneous
Casting Time: 1
Area of Effect: One object or creature
Saving Throw: None

This spell enables the caster to instantly know the age of any single person, creature, or object on which he concentrates. The age is accurate to the nearest year.

The material component is a calendar page.

Know Direction (Divination)

Sphere: Travelers
Range: 0
Components: V, S, M
Duration: Instantaneous
Casting Time: 1
Area of Effect: Special
Saving Throw: None

Know direction allows the caster to instantly know the direction of north. The spell is effective in any environment, whether underwater, underground, or in darkness (including magical darkness).

The material component is a small scrap of a parchment map that is at least 100 years old.

Know Time (Divination)

Sphere: Time
Range: 0
Components: V, S
Duration: Instantaneous
Casting Time: 1
Area of Effect: The caster
Saving Throw: None

Know time is particularly useful when the caster has been unconscious. This spell enables the caster to know the precise time of day to the nearest minute, including the current hour, day, month, and year.

Log of Everburning (Enchantment)

Sphere: Elemental Fire, Plant
Range: Touch
Components: V, S
Duration: 1 hour/level
Casting Time: 1
Area of Effect: Special
Saving Throw: None

This spell increases the amount of time that a wooden object will burn before being consumed. Wood that is enchanted in this manner burns brightly without being consumed for the duration of the spell. When the spell ends, the wooden object crumbles to ash.

This spell does not cause the wood to catch fire; it must be ignited normally. While it burns, the wood gives off twice the normal amount of heat; thus, a single log can make a cozy fire.

The affected wood radiates magic. The priest may enchant up to 1 cubic foot of wood per level of experience. The spell is effective on torches.

Mistaken Missive (Alteration)

Sphere: Chaos
Range: Touch
Components: V, S, M
Duration: Permanent
Casting Time: 1
Area of Effect: One page/level
Saving Throw: None

This spell alters the appearance of words written in ink. When the spell is cast upon a written page, the ink imperceptibly begins to move. Over the next few days, the message becomes progressively more illegible. If the page is left undisturbed for six days, an entirely new message forms on the page. The new message is completely legible and is recognizable as the handwriting of the original author, but is contrary in content to the original message.

After the spell is cast, the message will appear different every day. The DM decides the message that the page will carry after the sixth day has passed. Following is a sample of the changes that could take place in a message.

Day One: The words of the letter appear faint, as if the author of the letter was running out of ink as he wrote.

Day Two: The words have moved slightly from their original positions, as if the person writing the letter were shaking or in a moving carriage when the letter was written.

Days Three and Four: The message is gibberish. Although the ink forms groups of letters arranged in lines with punctuation, nearly all the words are meaningless. This may appear to be some sort of code, but it means nothing.

Day Five: The ink has formed real words. However, the sentence construction is still meaningless (e.g., Egg west worse green!).

Day Six (and beyond): The message is coherent, but the opposite intent of the original message has been created. If the original letter read, "Send troops quickly," the new letter reads, "All is fine. Keep your men in reserve."

If *mistaken missive* is cast on the pages of a spellbook or a scroll, the ink on the page reforms into a new spell of the same level as the original spell. Thus, a *darkness* spell might become a *maze* spell. However, the spell formula will be wrong. Although it will look like a proper spell, it will not function when cast.

A coded message that is subjected to *mistaken missive* will appear as a coded message on the sixth day but will hold a different meaning than the original message.

A *glass of preserved words* will allow the original message to be read correctly. *Dispel magic* will restore the message to its original form.

The material component is three drops of ink.

Morale (Enchantment/Charm)

Sphere: War
Range: Special
Components: V, S, M
Duration: Special
Casting Time: Special
Area of Effect: One unit up to 200 individuals
Saving Throw: None

This spell can be used in two distinct ways. The first is appropriate for battlefield use. The priest can cast this spell on any unit within 240 yards in an uninterrupted line of sight. The casting time for this use is one turn and the material component is a gem of at least 100 gp value which is consumed during the casting.

At the conclusion of this use of the spell, the target unit's morale is modified by 1, either positively or negatively, as the caster desires. This modification remains in effect for 1d4 + 2 turns.

The second and more powerful use of the spell requires lengthy preparations. Casting must take place inside or within 100 yards of a place of worship dedicated to the casting priest's deity. Both the priest and the unit to be affected must be present. The casting time for this use is 5 turns. The material component is the priest's holy symbol.

At the conclusion of this use of the spell, the unit's morale is raised by 3 (maximum of 19). This morale increase lasts until the next sunset. Only priests of 10th level or higher can cast this version of the spell.

Personal Reading (Divination)

Sphere: Numbers
Range: 0
Components: V, S, M
Duration: Special
Casting Time: 2 turns
Area of Effect: One creature
Saving Throw: None

This spell allows the priest to mathematically analyze personal information about one human or demihuman character and learn valuable facts about that character. To cast this spell, the priest must know the subject's real name (the name the subject was given as a child) or the date and place of the character's birth. The priest analyzes this information and is able to build a rough picture of the character's life history and personal specifics.

The "historical" information discovered through this spell is generally vague. For example, the priest might learn that the subject was born in the woods and moved to the city only after hardship made his life untenable. Specific information is up to the DM. The DM might provide some or all of the following information.

- The subject's character class or career
- The subject's approximate level (stated in terms such as "novice," "highly skilled," "moderately competent," etc.)

- The subject's standing in the community ("highly respected," "mistrusted," "considered an enigma," etc.)
- The subject's success or failure in his profession
- The subject's prevailing character traits or mannerisms

If the priest casts the spell based on an alias or incorrect birth information, the reading will be inaccurate. The DM should develop a history and personality at odds with the truth. This might allow the priest to determine whether the name of the subject is correct—a reading giving information that conflicts with what the priest already knows should be a clue that the name is incorrect.

The subject need not be present during the casting. The priest can cast the spell without ever having met the subject.

The material component is a small book of numerological formulae and notes (different from the book used in *telethaumaturgy*). The book is not consumed in the casting.

A DM may rule that this spell can be cast on humanoids or monstrous creatures. The information available will be similar (considering that words like "profession" will mean something different when applied to an ogre). This spell will categorically fail on creatures that have no concept of a personal name.

Ring of Hands (Abjuration)
Reversible

Sphere: Protection
Range: 0
Components: V, S
Duration: 2d10 rounds
Casting Time: 5
Area of Effect: Special
Saving Throw: None

This is a cooperative magic spell. It requires a minimum of two priests and can accommodate a maximum of ten. Each priest must cast *ring of hands* on the same round. At the end of the casting, the priests involved join hands, thus completing the spell. If any priest breaks the circle, the spell immediately ceases. The priests may not move from their locations but are free to speak. They may not cast spells requiring a somatic or material component while the ring is formed.

The *ring of hands* forms a protective barrier around the priests and everything within their circle. For each priest, assume a five-foot circumference of the circle; thus, three priests would create a circle of 15-foot circumference. For easy calculation, assume that for each priest, the circle can accommodate four persons.

The barrier functions as a *protection from evil* spell. Attacks by evil creatures suffer a −1 penalty for every priest forming the circle. Saving throws made by the priests or anyone in the circle against attacks from such creatures receive a +1 bonus for every priest in the circle.

Attempts at mental control over protected creatures are blocked. Extraplanar and conjured creatures are unable to touch the priests and those within the circle, although melee attacks against such creatures by those within the ring break the barrier.

Because the priests casting the spell cannot move and must hold hands, they do not receive any Dexterity bonuses to Armor Class. Furthermore, opponents gain a +2 bonus on attack rolls against the priests, since there is little they can do to avoid a blow. Creatures within the ring are free to act as they wish. Melee attacks by those within the ring are limited to piercing weapons and suffer a −1 penalty to attack rolls since the priests intervene.

The reverse of this spell, *ring of woe*, functions as detailed above except the effect applies to good creatures as would a *protection from good* spell.

Sacred Guardian (Enchantment/Charm)

Sphere: Guardian
Range: Touch
Components: V, S, M
Duration: 1 day/level
Casting Time: 1
Area of Effect: Creature touched
Saving Throw: None

By use of this spell, a priest becomes instantly aware when the recipient of the spell is in danger, regardless of the distance between the the priest and the recipient. The recipient may be on a different plane of existence than the priest.

When this spell is cast by a priest of at least 3rd level, he receives a mental image of the endangered person's situation. At no time, however, does the priest know the person's location through the use of this spell.

The material component is a rose petal that has been kissed by the spell recipient.

Speak With Astral Traveler (Alteration)

Sphere: Astral
Range: Touch
Components: V, S
Duration: 1 round/level
Casting Time: 1 round
Area of Effect: One creature
Saving Throw: None

When a priest casts the 7th-level *astral spell*, he leaves his physical body in suspended animation while his astral body travels. By touching the comatose body and casting *speak with astral traveler*, a priest can mentally communicate with the projected individual. Although communication is mental, it takes the same amount of time as a normal, verbal dialogue. The spell ends abruptly when its duration expires.

Thought Capture (Divination)

Sphere: Thought
Range: 0
Components: V, S
Duration: Instantaneous
Casting Time: 3
Area of Effect: 10 yards
Saving Throw: None

One of the more bizarre contentions held by priests of the School of Thought is generally scoffed at by outsiders. The theory states that once a thought has occurred in someone's brain, it exists as a "freestanding mental object." This "thought object" usually remains inside the brain of the creature that created it, but sometimes it escapes (this supposedly explains why people forget things). When this happens, the thought object stays in the geographical area where it was lost. Any receptive brain (usually the brain of the creature that initially created the thought) can pick it up again simply by bumping into the invisible, free-floating thought. According to the theory, this is the reason that people can regain a lost thought by going back to the location where the thought was lost. This supposedly works because the free-floating thought is recaptured, not because the locale reminds them of of the thought. Unfortunately for philosophers who disagree with this, *thought capture* seems to be extremely strong evidence for this theory.

This spell makes the priest's brain something of a magnet that attracts thought objects in close proximity. The priest can sense strong thoughts and emotions and can sometimes even see momentary visions of creatures who died or suffered some powerful emotion in the immediate vicinity. Thought objects are always attracted to the priest in the order of the strongest (those attached to powerful emotions or significant events) to the weakest. Thus, if several thought objects share the same vicinity, the priest will perceive information about the most interesting or significant event. The priest might pick up images of a battle from the point of view of a warrior who died there, or he might gain information about the victor of the battle.

The DM dictates the information provided to the priest, and thus can use this spell to provide players with important background information or can add texture to a campaign world. The information provided might be highly cryptic or symbolic, perhaps in the form of a rhyme or riddle.

The priest gains one thought object per casting of the spell. The spell may be cast a number of times in the same locale, with the priest gaining a different thought object with each casting. A locale contains a finite number of thoughts, however, and once the priest has gained all of them (per the DM), the spell will fail in that locale.

Weighty Chest (Alteration)

Sphere: Wards
Range: Touch
Components: V, S, M
Duration: 1 day/level
Casting Time: 1
Area of Effect: 5-foot cube
Saving Throw: None

This spell enables the caster to enchant a chest, book, package, or any other nonliving object no larger than a 5′ × 5′ × 5′ cube. When the enchanted object is touched by anyone other than the caster, the apparent weight of the object increases, becoming 2-5 (1d4 + 1) times the weight of the person or persons touching it. This condition makes the object extremely difficult to move for anyone but the caster. The caster can move the object normally throughout the duration of the spell.

The material component is a lead ball.

Second-Level Spells

Aura of Comfort (Evocation)

Sphere: Travelers
Range: Touch
Components: V, S
Duration: 1 hour/level
Casting Time: 2
Area of Effect: Creature touched
Saving Throw: None

When this spell is cast, a faintly shimmering aura surrounds the recipient. The aura insulates the recipient from the effects of nonmagical heat and cold in a range of −20° F. to 140° F. Any time a traveler encounters temperatures in this range, he maintains a comfortable temperature of 70° F., regardless of prevailing weather conditions. Additionally, the spell acts as a shield against rain, snow, and hail, which are blocked by the aura.

If a recipient encounters a temperature above or below the stated range, the temperature within the aura is altered by an equal number of degrees. For example, a recipient who encounters a temperature of 150° will actually experience a temperature of 80°F.

All physical objects other than rain, snow, and hail can pass through the aura. The recipient can cast spells normally while the *aura of comfort* is in effect. The spell offers no protection against magically generated weather, such as that caused by *weather summoning* and *ice storm*. It does not protect against fire, nor does it shield against fire- or cold-based attacks.

Calm Chaos (Enchantment/Charm)

Sphere: Law
Range: 20 yards
Components: V, S
Duration: Special
Casting Time: 1
Area of Effect: 1d6 creatures/level
Saving Throw: Special

This spell temporarily calms a chaotic situation involving a group of people. The situation may involve any range of emotions from violence (as in a barroom brawl) to joy and merrymaking (as in a festival or carnival).

Unlike the *emotion* spell, *calm chaos* does not cause a change in the emotions of affected creatures—anger, fear, or intense joy remain in each individual. The emotion is simply restrained rather than released. Thus, an angry character intent on attacking someone will still feel the desire to do so, but he will withhold his action as long as the spell remains in effect.

Creatures to be affected are allowed a saving throw vs. spell at a −4 penalty to avoid the effects. If more creatures are present than can be affected, creatures nearest the caster are affected first.

After casting the spell, the priest makes a Charisma check. If successful, all characters affected by the spell are compelled to stop what they are doing. They are filled with the sensation that something important is about to occur. At this time, the priest or a character of his choosing must gain the attention of the affected creatures by giving a speech, performing for the crowd, or casting spells with intriguing visual effects (such as *dancing lights*). The attention of the crowd is then held for as long as the distraction continues. A character could filibuster and maintain control over the affected characters for hours or days.

Two conditions will cause the group to resume its original actions. In the first, the method of entertaining the crowd ceases for one round—the speech ends or the spell expires. If this action is not replaced with another distraction within one round, the crowd is freed of the spell.

In the second condition, if an event occurs that is more immediate than the distraction, the crowd will divert its attention to that event. Thus, if the spell were used to stop a barroom brawl and the building caught fire or was attacked, the crowd's attention would be diverted and the individuals could act freely.

Creatures whose attention is held by the spell cannot be instructed to attack or perform any action. Such creatures will ignore suggestions of this nature. Depending on the nature of the request, the DM may deem that the suggestion causes a distraction that ends the spell.

Create Holy Symbol (Conjuration)

Sphere: Creation
Range: 0
Component: V
Duration: Permanent
Casting Time: 2
Area of Effect: The caster
Saving Throw: None

When the words of this spell are uttered, a holy symbol appropriate to the priest's deity appears out of thin air. The item appears in the priest's hands. It may be used as a component for spells or for any other purpose for which the priest would normally use his holy symbol (such as turning undead). He may also opt to give it to a lower level priest of the same deity. The holy symbol is a permanent object.

Dissension's Feast
(Enchantment/Charm, Alteration)

Sphere: Chaos
Range: Touch
Components: V, S
Duration: 5 turns +2 turns/level
Casting Time: 2 turns
Area of Effect: Special
Saving Throw: Neg.

This spell must be cast by a priest during the preparation of food for a meal. The spell is cast on any one quantity of food; thus, the priest could cast the spell on the batter of a wedding cake, or he could cast the spell on a quantity of onions as they are diced for both a salad and a stew. The spell affects 10 pounds of food per level of the caster. Anyone who eats the affected food (even a character who eats the salad but not the stew) is subject to the effects of the spell.

The effects of the spell begin five rounds after the food has been eaten. At that time, creatures who have eaten the affected food are allowed a saving throw; success indicates that a creature is not affected.

Affected creatures quickly become agitated. Petty events ranging from poor table manners to loud talking bother everyone. After five minutes, tempers flare, characters feel compelled to shout at and insult one another, and threats are hurled. Even normally calm characters will feel compelled to vent their frustrations violently.

Creatures maintain no alliances while under the effect of *dissension's feast*. A king and his wife who are normally madly in love will find themselves bickering with each other in a matter of minutes. Members of a diplomatic delegation might come to blows with each other within minutes of eating the food.

At the end of the spell duration, characters undergo the sensation of waking up. All are free to behave as they wish. Characters at the meal will still be angry, although they will have no idea why they became angry.

Draw Upon Holy Might (Invocation)

Sphere: Summoning
Range: 0
Components: V, S, M
Duration: 1 round/level
Casting Time: 2
Area of Effect: The caster
Saving Throw: None

When this spell is cast, the priest's body shudders and glows with a shimmering aura as it becomes a vessel for the power of his god. As a result, the caster may choose to increase one ability score (only Strength, Dexterity, Constitution, and Charisma are eligible) by +1 per three levels of his experience (+1 at 3rd level, +2 at 6th, etc.).

Only one attribute may be increased. The effect lasts for the duration of the spell. Attributes may be increased above the normal restrictions due to race and class, to a maximum of +6. All benefits for exceptional attributes listed in the *Player's Handbook* apply; however, the divine abilities found in the *Legends & Lore* book cannot be gained by use of this spell.

For example, an 18th-level priest with Strength 15 could increase his Strength to 21 for 18 rounds, granting him a +4 attack bonus, a +9 damage adjustment, etc.

When the spell ends, the energy abruptly leaves the priest's body, leaving him physically and mentally drained. He is nearly comatose and can do nothing but rest for the next 4d6 turns. A successful Constitution check (at the priest's normal attribute score) reduces this time by 50%.

The material components are the priest's holy symbol and a vial of holy water that has been blessed by the high priest of the character's faith.

Emotion Perception (Divination)

Sphere: War
Range: 300 yards
Components: V, S, M
Duration: Instantaneous
Casting Time: 1 turn
Area of Effect: One unit/five levels
Saving Throw: None

This spell allows the caster to sense the emotional state and the level of determination of one or more military units. The priest must have an uninterrupted line of sight to the entire target unit. When this spell is cast, the priest instantly learns the current morale rating and morale status of the target unit. The DM describes morale using the appropriate term; for example, steady, elite, etc.

The material component is the priest's holy symbol.

Frisky Chest (Enchantment/Charm)

Sphere: Wards
Range: Touch
Components: V, S, M
Duration: Permanent
Casting Time: 2
Area of Effect: 10-foot cube
Saving Throw: None

With this spell, the caster can enchant a chest, book, or any other nonliving object no larger than a 10' × 10' × 10' cube. When any creature other than the caster comes within three feet of the enchanted object, it instantly sprouts appendages and moves away from the creature as quickly as possible. The enchanted object continues to move until it is at least 10 feet away from the nearest creatures in the area.

After the enchanted object has moved a satisfactory distance from the nearest creature, the appendages disappear. When a creature again comes within three feet of the enchanted object, the enchanted object sprouts appendages and flees. This process continues until the enchantment is negated (through a *dispel magic* or similar spell) or the enchanted object is subdued or destroyed.

The enchanted object can sprout feet (MV 24), wings (Fl 24, maneuverability class B), or fins (Sw 24), whichever is most advantageous. Thus, a book on a shelf might sprout wings and fly away, while a table might gallop around a room. The enchanted object can freely and instantly trade appendages as necessary.

The enchanted object will move only through open spaces. It will not crash through windows, shatter a closed door, or dig through the earth. It cannot attack or take any actions other than movement. If surrounded or cornered, the enchanted object moves in random directions until it is restrained or destroyed.

The enchantment ends if the caster voluntarily negates it, if the enchanted object is destroyed (the object has the same vulnerabilities as it has in its normal state), or if the enchanted object is restrained for 2-5 (1d4 + 1) consecutive rounds. Restraint means that the object is prevented from fleeing; if a creature is able to grapple, lift, or sit on the object, it is considered restrained. A creature capable of lifting the object in its normal state is considered strong enough to restrain it (for instance, a person capable of lifting a 50-pound box is also capable of restraining such a box enchanted by *frisky chest*). The object may also be restrained by tossing a net or heavy blanket over it or by surrounding it with several characters.

The material components are a dried frog's leg, a feather, and a fish scale.

Hesitation (Enchantment/Charm)

Sphere: Time
Range: 30 yards
Components: V, S, M
Duration: 1 round/level
Casting Time: 2
Area of Effect: 20-foot-radius circle
Saving Throw: Neg.

Creatures affected by this spell hesitate before executing their intended actions. This causes them to modify their initiative rolls by +4. The initiative modifier occurs in the round following the round in which *hesitation* is cast.

The spell affects 2-8 Hit Dice or levels of creatures, although only one creature of 4 or more Hit Dice can be affected regardless of the number rolled. All possible victims are allowed saving throws vs. spells; those failing their saving throws modify their initiative rolls by +4 for a number of rounds equal to the caster's level.

The material component is a fragment of a turtle's shell.

Idea (Divination)

Sphere: Thought
Range: 0
Components: V, S, M
Duration: Instantaneous
Casting Time: 4
Area of Effect: The caster
Saving Throw: None

This spell stimulates the priest's mind to experience a flash of insight. In game terms, the DM reminds the priest's player of a fact or event that has been forgotten, overlooked, or discounted. Thus, the DM might remind the player about an important clue that the priest discovered but the player did not consider significant.

If there are no forgotten facts, the DM may, at his discretion, tell the player of new information relevant to the condition at hand.

The DM must be careful in adjudicating use of this spell. The reminder or information should always be relevant and useful but should not be unbalancing to the situation. The reminder can be cryptic, depending on the DM's campaign.

The material component is a gold coin. This spell can be cast only once in any six hour period.

Lighten Load (Alteration)

Sphere: Travelers
Range: 30 yards
Components: V, S, M
Duration: 1 hour/level
Casting Time: 2
Area of Effect: 10-foot cube
Saving Throw: None

This spell reduces the weight of equipment, supplies, and other objects by 50%. Weapons, supplies, and even disabled characters can all be made more portable by use of a *lighten load* spell.

This spell affects one pile of objects whose volume is equivalent to a 10-foot cube; after the spell has been cast, the affected objects can be divided among several characters or mounts. The spell has no effect on magical items.

An object affected by *lighten load* can be used normally; the spell has no effect on an object's mass, texture, size, strength, or other physical features.

The material components are a feather and a slip of paper moistened by a soap bubble.

Mind Read (Divination)

Sphere: Thought
Range: 5 yards/level
Components: V, S
Duration: 1 round/level
Casting Time: 2
Area of Effect: Special
Saving Throw: None

This spell is a sensitive version of the wizard spell *ESP*. In addition to detecting the surface thoughts of any creatures in range, the priest is able to probe deeper into the mind of a single creature. *Mind read* will always reveal the kind of creature being probed, although this identity may be couched in the creature's own language or in a (possibly distorted) body image. The spell has a 20% chance of revealing the character class of an individual.

The details and the usefulness of the creature's thoughts will depend on the intelligence of the subject. While a priest could read the thoughts of an animal, he would probably receive only a confused jumble of emotions and instincts. Reading the mind of a highly intelligent wizard, however, would be much more illuminating; the priest might be amazed by the crystal clarity and deep insight of the wizard's mental processes.

If *mind read* is used as part of an interrogation, an intelligent and wary subject receives a saving throw at a −2 penalty. If successful, the creature resists the spell's effects and the priest learns no information. If the saving throw is failed, the priest may learn additional information according to the DM's ruling.

Moment (Divination)

Sphere: Numbers
Range: 0
Components: V, S, M
Duration: 1 round/level
Casting Time: 1 round
Area of Effect: 50-foot radius
Saving Throw: None

Theoretically, every action has a particular moment at which it will have its greatest possible effect. Using the arcane mathematics of this spell, the priest can determine the "ideal moment" for any single action in each round that the spell is in effect. This action must be performed by a character other than the priest.

In practice, another character informs the priest of an action he wants to undertake in a round. The priest concentrates on the action, then informs the character when the "correct moment" has come. The character then gains a bonus of 20% (+4 on a d20) to the success of his action. The spell can affect only a single action in a given round. When used in combat, the priest can advise the best moment to initiate an action (affecting initiative) or what moment offers the greatest success in striking (affecting the chance to hit).

If the character seeks advice concerning initiative, he gains a −2 modifier to the initiative roll, but only at the cost of −2 on his chance to hit. Characters who seek the best attack frequently delay their actions. These characters suffer a +1 on their initiative roll but gain a +4 on their chance to hit. The spell cannot affect the amount of damage caused, since the act (striking) has already succeeded at that point.

Characters are not obliged to wait for the moment specified by the priest. For example, a fight-er might decide that striking first is more important than gaining +4 to hit. The character can act normally, based on his or her unmodified initiative. The character gains no bonus from the *moment* spell, and the priest can affect no other action in that round.

Noncombat actions can also benefit from the *moment* spell. For example, a thief planning to climb a wall may wait to start her climb until the priest informs her that the moment is right. If she waits, she gains a bonus of 20% to her Climb Walls roll (in this case, the bonus is *subtracted* from her roll).

While concentrating on this spell, the priest can take no other action. A break in the priest's concentration—taking damage in combat, for example—terminates the spell instantly.

The material component is a set of three silver dice, which the priest tosses in his hand while concentrating on the spell. The dice are not consumed in the casting.

Music of the Spheres (Enchantment/Charm)

Sphere: Numbers, Charm
Range: 50 yards
Components: V, S, M
Duration: 1 turn + 1 round/level
Casting Time: 4
Area of Effect: 20-foot-diameter circle
Saving Throw: Neg.

With this spell, the priest creates tones and harmonies of such unearthly beauty and complexity that they entrance the listener, making it difficult for the listener to attack or otherwise harm the priest. The listener receives a normal saving throw against this effect. Failure means that the listener is entranced and is unable to attack the priest for the duration of the spell.

In addition, the music makes the subject gullible and more susceptible to charm magics such as *charm person, suggestion,* and *hypnotism*. While the music spell is in effect, the subject saves against charm spells with a −3 penalty.

This spell does not protect other characters in company with the priest; listeners who have fallen prey to the music are free to attack anyone else. The spell effect ends instantly if the priest takes any hostile action against a creature under the influence of the spell.

Music of the spheres can affect one creature per three levels of the priest (one subject at 3rd level, two at 6th level, etc.). Subjects must be within a 20-foot-diameter circle.

Potential victims must have Intelligence of at least 1 (necessary to understand the concept of music) and must be able to hear the music (i.e., they cannot be deaf and there can be nothing obstructing the victim's ears). This also means that the level of background noise must be low enough for the music to be audible. The DM should assume that the music is the same volume as an average human's normal speaking voice. If the potential subject could not hear speech at the appropriate range under prevailing conditions, the spell cannot affect that subject. The spell would be virtually useless in the midst of a full-scale battle or during a hurricane.

The material component comprises a set of three small bows made from fine silver, each costing 100 gp. The lengths of the bows must be in the ratio of 1 to 4 to 9. The priest strokes these bows together in an intricate sequence while casting the spell. The bows are not consumed in the casting.

Mystic Transfer (Invocation)

Sphere: Charm
Range: 0
Components: V, S
Duration: 9 rounds
Casting Time: 1 round
Area of Effect: The caster
Saving Throw: None

This spell is one of the few cooperative spells that requires one priest to cast the transfer spell, but another priest to use its effect. On one round, a priest (or priests) casts the *mystic transfer*. The spell is then active for the remaining nine rounds of the turn.

Mystic transfer allows a priest to receive spells from another priest of the same ethos. Any priest of the same religion can cast a spell and transfer it to a second priest within that spell's maximum range. The spell does not take effect; instead, it is channelled through the *mystic transfer* into the receiving priest. This priest must immediately cast the spell or pass it to another priest cloaked in a *mystic transfer* within the spell's range. Any number of transfers can be made in the same round, provided each new recipient is within spell range of the previous recipient. If the spell is not transferred, the spell takes effect.

For example, a 3rd-level priest casts a *mystic transfer*. On the following round, a 10th-level priest "passes" a *flame strike* to the 3rd-level priest. The two priests could be 60 yards apart (the maximum range of the *flame strike*). The

3rd-level priest could then use the *flame strike* to attack any target within 60 yards, or could pass the spell on to another priest who has an active *mystic transfer*.

The spell passed by the *mystic transfer* has the range, area of effect, damage, and other effects equal to the level of the original caster. In the example above, the *flame strike* would function as if cast by a 10th-level priest.

The *mystic transfer* does not require concentration. However, on any round in which a priest is receiving and/or transferring a spell, the caster cannot take any other significant action.

A priest can receive spells only from priests who worship the same deity and who specifically target spells to him. Area effect spells may be passed. A priest can never use *mystic transfer* to pluck an opponent's spells out of the air.

Nap (Alteration)

Sphere: Time
Range: Touch
Components: V, S, M
Duration: Special
Casting Time: 2
Area of Effect: One creature/level
Saving Throw: None

Creatures affected by this spell are put to sleep for one hour. Upon awakening, the creature is as refreshed as if he had slept for eight hours. The affected person recovers lost hit points as if he rested for a full night. Wizards can memorize spells as if real time had passed.

Because the rest is so complete and rejuvenating, a character does not feel fatigued after waking. Attempts to use *nap* more than once in an 18-hour period are ineffective (the character simply is not sleepy). Only willing subjects can be affected by *nap*.

The material components are a scrap of pillow ticking, a feather, and a pebble that the caster has kept in his pocket for seven nights.

Rally (Enchantment/Charm)

Sphere: War
Range: 240 yards
Components: V, S, M
Duration: Instantaneous
Casting Time: 1 turn
Area of Effect: One unit of up to 300 individuals
Saving Throw: None

This spell allows the subject unit to make an immediate rally check. It allows the check during the Magic Phase, rather than forcing the unit to wait for the Rally Phase in the BATTLESYSTEM rules. If the priest casting the spell is of 12th level or higher, the subject unit receives a +1 bonus to its rally check die roll. The priest must have an uninterrupted line of sight to the unit.

The material component is a miniature duplicate of a pennant or standard that represents the cause for which the unit is fighting (such as a national flag or the blazon of the unit's liege lord). The pennant is consumed in the casting.

Sanctify (Conjuration/Summoning)
Reversible

Sphere: All
Range: 10 yards
Components: V, S, M
Duration: Special
Casting Time: 1 turn
Area of Effect: 10 yard × 10 yard square/priest
Saving Throw: None

This cooperative spell allows the priests to create a beneficial atmosphere within a specified area. Companions of similar alignment to the casters will feel fortified and encouraged while in the sanctified area. The spell can be cast by a single priest or a group of priests.

After casting *sanctify*, the affected area is imbued with the deity's majesty. For followers of that deity, the area radiates a holy aura. These followers gain a +2 bonus to saving throws against all fear- and charm-based powers (a +2 to morale for BATTLESYSTEM rules units). Persons of the same alignment as the caster but of different faiths gain a +1 to saving throws (+1 in BATTLESYSTEM rules). The effect applies only as long as the characters remain in the sanctified area.

Creatures intent on harming the priest or his followers suffer a −1 on saving throws vs. fear and charm (−1 to morale for BATTLESYSTEM rules units) when on sanctified ground.

Undead creatures within the area are easier to turn; any priest standing on sanctified ground turns undead as if he were one level higher.

Although this spell can be cast by a single priest, it is most effective when cast by several priests at once. The duration of the spell is equal to one round per level of the caster. When several priests cast the spell, the level of the most powerful priest is used, with two rounds added for every contributing priest. Thus, one 8th-level and three 6th-level priests would give the spell a duration of 14 rounds (8 + 2 + 2 + 2).

Sanctify is often used in conjunction with *focus* to protect the grounds of a temple or encourage men defending a castle.

The material components are the priest's holy symbol and a handful of dirt from the grounds of an existing temple of the same faith.

The reverse of this spell, *defile*, functions in an identical manner with respect to saving throws for charm and fear. However, priests standing on defiled ground who attempt to turn undead do so at one level lower than their current level.

The material components for the reverse are the priest's holy symbol and a handful of earth from a grave.

Zone of Truth (Enchantment/Charm)

Sphere: Wards
Range: 30 yards
Components: V, S, M
Duration: 1 round/level
Casting Time: 2
Area of Effect: 5-foot square/level
Saving Throw: Neg.

This spell prevents creatures within the area of effect (or those who enter it) from speaking any deliberate and knowing lies. Creatures are allowed a saving throw to avoid the effects; those who fail the save are affected fully. Affected characters are aware of this enchantment; therefore, they may avoid answering questions to which they would normally respond with a lie or they may be evasive as long as they remain within the boundaries of the truth. When a character leaves the area, he is free to speak as he chooses.

The spell affects a square whose sides are five feet long per level of the caster; thus, a 4th-level priest could affect a 20 foot by 20 foot square.

The material components are the priest's holy symbol and a phony emerald, ruby, or diamond.

Third-Level Spells

Accelerate Healing (Alteration)

Sphere: Time
Range: Touch
Components: V, S
Duration: 1-4 days
Casting Time: 1 turn
Area of Effect: One creature
Saving Throw: None

This spell enables the affected creature to experience natural healing at twice the normal rate for 1-4 days. In other words, a person affected by *accelerate healing* regains 2 hit points per day of normal rest or 6 hit points per day spent resting in bed. The spell has no effect on *potions of healing* or other magical forms of healing.

Adaptation (Enchantment/Charm, Alteration)

Sphere: War
Range: Special
Components: V, S, M
Duration: Special
Casting Time: Special
Area of Effect: One unit of up to 200 individuals
Saving Throw: None

This spell can be cast in two different ways. The first, appropriate for battlefield use, has a range of 180 yards, a casting time of one turn, and duration of 1d4 + 2 turns. During this period, the affected unit can fight in one specific type of terrain (specified by the caster) as if it were the favored terrain (per BATTLESYSTEM rules) for that unit. While this spell is in effect, the unit gains no benefit when fighting in their actual favored terrain; the magically-enforced favored terrain takes precedence. The priest can cancel the spell before the duration expires if desired.

The material component is a pinch of clay dust.

The second effect requires preparation in advance. The priest and unit must be within 100 yards of a place of worship dedicated to the casting priest's deity. The casting time is 5 turns.

At the conclusion of the casting, the unit gains the benefit described above, with two main differences. First, the unit does not lose the benefit of fighting in its own actual favored terrain (the unit effectively has two favored terrains). Second, the spell endures until the next sunset. Only priests of 12th level and higher can cast this variation.

The material component is the priest's holy symbol.

Astral Window (Divination)

Sphere: Astral
Range: 5 yards
Components: V, S
Duration: 2 rounds/level
Casting Time: 3
Area of Effect: 10' × 10' area
Saving Throw: None

When this spell is cast, a "window" appears in the air before the priest, through which he (and any others present) can see into the Astral plane. The astral window ranges in size from one square foot up to a 10' × 10' square, at the caster's choosing. The window is not mobile, and if the priest moves more than 5 yards away from it, it immediately vanishes and the spell ends.

By stating a subject's name, the priest may view a specific creature or object in the window. More than one subject may be viewed during the spell's duration. Each time a new subject is chosen, the window becomes streaked with grey as the Astral plane flies past. This continues for 1d4 rounds, until the window finally focuses upon the chosen subject. If the person is not in the Astral plane, the window instead chooses a random location.

The window operates from both sides; creatures in the Astral plane can see the priest as easily as he can see them. Verbal communication is not possible, however.

Normally, creatures cannot pass through the window. If an attempt is made, there is a base 5% chance of success. This is modified by +1% per level or Hit Dice of the individual. In order to pass through, the creature or object must be small enough to fit through the window; otherwise, only a portion of the subject may reach through (such as a monster's arm or searching tongue).

By casting the *astral window* spell, a character who subsequently casts the 7th-level *astral spell* may choose to arrive in the Astral plane at the place shown in the window.

Caltrops (Evocation)

Sphere: War
Range: 20 yards/level
Components: V, S, M
Duration: 1 turn/level
Casting Time: 1 turn
Area of Effect: Special
Saving Throw: None

This spell allows a priest to plant a section of ground with magically created caltrops.

The spell can create two kinds of caltrops: infantry and cavalry. The first are of small size and are designed to harm foot soldiers. The latter are larger and cause serious damage to cavalry or units composed of size L or larger creatures. Cavalry caltrops are so large that size M or smaller creatures can easily step around them. This prevents damage to infantry units.

Each time a unit moves into a planted area, the unit suffers an attack of AD = 4 (for infantry caltrops) or AD = 6 (for cavalry caltrops). Units charging through a planted area suffer double damage. If a unit ends its movement in a caltrop-sown region, it suffers another attack when it moves out of the area.

This spell can create a rectangular field of infantry caltrops up to 160 square yards in area (e.g., 4 yards × 40 yards, 2 yards × 80 yards, etc.), or a field of cavalry caltrops up to 90 square yards in area (e.g., 3 yards × 30 yards, 2 yards × 45 yards, etc.).

Ordinary caltrops make no distinction between friend or foe; all creatures entering a caltrop-sown area suffer the same consequences. The same is true of magical caltrops, with one exception: the casting priest can terminate the spell at any time, causing the caltrops to vanish and leaving the terrain clear.

Unlike normal caltrops, a region sown with magical caltrops cannot be "swept" clear; the magical caltrops remain in place until the spell terminates.

The material component is a golden caltrop.

Choose Future (Divination)

Sphere: Time
Range: Touch
Components: V, S, M
Duration: 1 round
Casting Time: 3
Area of Effect: One creature
Saving Throw: None

In the round immediately following the casting of this spell, the affected creature is allowed two rolls for any normal attack roll, initiative roll, or saving throw. The affected creature can then choose the roll he prefers.

For example, a priest casts *choose future* on a warrior companion. In the next round, the warrior attacks an enemy with his sword. The warrior makes two attack rolls instead of one, then chooses which roll will determine the outcome of his attack.

The material components are two grains of sand and a rose petal.

Create Campsite
(Conjuration/Summoning)
Reversible

Sphere: Travelers
Range: 0
Components: V, S, M
Duration: Special
Casting Time: 3
Area of Effect: 50-foot radius
Saving Throw: None

With this spell, the caster generates a squadron of tiny invisible servants who create a campsite for the caster and his companions. The caster indicates the desired area for the campsite (an area of 50-foot radius or less) and the number of persons the campsite is to accommodate (a number of persons equal to three times the level of the caster).

The servants clear the area of debris, set up tents and bedrolls, start a campfire, fetch water, and prepare a bland meal. The campsite is so skillfully prepared that it blends with the surrounding terrain, reducing the chance that the camp could be noticed by 50%. Campfires, loud noises, and other activities can negate this.

The entire process takes 4-16 (4d4) rounds to complete.

The servants make camp with the gear and equipment provided for them; otherwise, the servants will improvise with materials available in the immediate area (50 yards of the designated campsite). For instance, if the party has no tents or beds, the servants will construct crude but comfortable beds of weeds and grass and temporary shelters of leaves and branches. If no materials are available, such as in the desert or similarly barren terrain, the servants will do their best to make the party as comfortable as possible within the environmental limitations.

The servants cannot fight for the party, deliver messages, or take any other actions other than creating the campsite.

The material components are a piece of string, a bit of wood, and a drop of water.

The reverse, *break camp*, causes the invisible servants to strike a campsite (an area of 50-foot radius or less). The servants extinguish fires, dispose of debris, and pack gear for a number of people equal to three times the level of the caster. The entire process takes 4-16 (4d4) rounds to complete. When completed, all traces of the campsite are eliminated. The material components are the same as those for *create campsite*.

Efficacious Monster Ward (Abjuration)

Sphere: Wards
Range: 30 yards
Components: V, S, M
Duration: 1 round/level
Casting Time: 3
Area of Effect: 10-foot cube/level
Saving Throw: Neg.

This spell prevents monsters of 2 or fewer Hit Dice from entering the area of effect. Such creatures are allowed a saving throw; success indicates that they avoid the spell's effects and are able to enter the area of effect.

The spell affects a cubic area whose sides equal the caster's level times 10 feet (for example, a 9th-level caster could affect an area equal to a 90' × 90' × 90' cube).

Monsters within the area of effect when the spell is cast are not affected; however, when they leave the area of effect, they cannot return. Monsters outside the area of effect can hurl rocks, spears, and other missile weapons at targets inside and can also cast spells into the warded area.

The material components are the priest's holy symbol and a pinch of salt.

Emotion Control
(Alteration, Enchantment/Charm)

Sphere: Thought, Charm
Range: 10 yards
Components: V, S, M
Duration: 1 round/level
Casting Time: 5
Area of Effect: One creature/5 levels of the caster within a 20' cube
Saving Throw: Special

This spell can be cast in one of two ways: in a manner that affects the priest, or in a manner that affects a subject other than the priest.

The first method affects only the priest and allows him to shield his true emotions from magical examination. Thus, it can block wizard spells such as *ESP* or priest spells such as *emotion read*. While *emotion control* is in effect, anyone using one of these spells will sense the emotion designated by the priest rather than his true emotions. When the priest casts *emotion control*, he designates the false emotion he wishes to be revealed.

This use of *emotion control* also gives the priest a +2 bonus to saving throws against the following spells: *spook, taunt, irritation, know alignment, scare, emotion, fear,* and *phantasmal killer.* When any of these spells are cast on the priest, he is immediately aware of the attempt, although he does not learn the source of the spell.

If another character casts *emotion read, ESP,* or a similar spell on the priest, the priest must make a saving throw vs. spells with a +1 bonus for each 5 levels of the priest. If the priest successfully saves, the other spellcaster reads the false emotion; if the priest fails the saving throw, the spellcaster reads the priest's true emotion.

The second use of this spell allows the priest to create a single emotional reaction in the subject(s) (similar to the wizard spell *emotion*). Some typical emotions follow, but the DM may allow other similar effects.

Courage: The subject becomes berserk, gaining +1 to attack rolls and +3 to damage, and temporarily gaining 4 hit points (damage against the subject is deducted from these temporary points first). The subject need never check morale, and receives a +5 bonus to saving throws against the various forms of *fear.* Courage counters (and is countered by) *fear.*

Fear: The subject flees from the priest for the duration of the spell, even if this takes him out of spell range. Fear counters (and is countered by) courage.

Friendship: The subject reacts positively to any encounter; in game terms, any result of a roll on the Encounter Reactions table (Table 59 in the *DMG*) is moved one column to the left. Thus, a threatening PC becomes cautious, an indifferent PC becomes friendly, etc. Friendship counters (and is countered by) hate.

Happiness: The subject experiences feelings of warmth, well-being, and confidence, modifying all reaction rolls by +3. The subject is unlikely to attack unless provoked. Happiness counters (and is countered by) sadness.

Hate: The subject reacts negatively to any encounter; in game terms, any result of a roll on the Encounter Reactions table is moved one column to the right (i.e., a friendly PC becomes indifferent, a cautious PC becomes threatening, etc.). Hate counters (and is countered by) friendship.

Hope: The subject's morale is improved by +2. His saving throw rolls, attack, and damage rolls are all improved by +1 while this emotion is in effect. Hope counters (and is countered by) hopelessness.

Hopelessness: The subject's morale suffers a −10 penalty. In addition, in the round in which the emotion is initially established, all subjects must immediately make a morale check. Hopelessness counters (and is countered by) hope.

Sadness: The subject feels uncontrollably glum and is prone to fits of morose introspection. All attack rolls suffer a −1 penalty and initiative rolls suffer a +1 penalty. The subject's chance of being surprised is increased by −2. Sadness counters (and is countered by) happiness.

All subjects of the second version, even willing targets, must save vs. spell to resist the emotion. In addition to all other modifiers, the saving throw is modified by −1 for every three levels of the priest casting the spell.

The material component for both versions of the spell is a small bunch of fleece or uncarded wool that is consumed in the casting.

Extradimensional Detection (Divination)

Sphere: Numbers, Divination
Range: 0
Components: V, S
Duration: 1 round/level
Casting Time: 3
Area of Effect: One 10'-wide path, 60 feet long
Saving Throw: None

When *extradimensional detection* is cast, the priest detects the existence of any extradimensional spaces or pockets in a path 10 feet wide and 60 feet long in the direction he is facing. The priest may turn, scanning a 60° arc each round, or may move slowly while the spell is in effect to change the sweep of the detection.

Extradimensional spaces include those created by spells such as *rope trick* and those contained within such items as *bags of holding* and *portable holes*. The priest does not automatically know the size of the space or its source.

This spell detects interplanar gates and the "gate" opened by the spell *extradimensional folding.*

The spell can be blocked by a stone wall of one foot thickness or more, a one-inch thickness of solid metal, or one yard or more of solid wood.

Helping Hand (Evocation)

Sphere: Travelers
Range: Special
Components: V, S, M
Duration: 1 hour/level
Casting Time: 1 round
Area of Effect: Special
Saving Throw: None

When a priest is trapped or otherwise endangered, this spell can summon help. The spell creates a hovering, ghostly image of a hand about one foot high. The caster can command it to locate a character or creature of the caster's choice based on a physical description. The caster can specify race, sex, and appearance, but not ambiguous factors such as level, alignment, or class.

After the hand receives its orders, it begins to search for the indicated creature, flying at a movement rate of 48. The hand can search within a 5-mile radius of the caster.

If the hand is unable to locate the indicated creature, it returns to the caster (provided he is still within the area of effect). The hand displays an outstretched palm, indicating that no such character or creature could be found. The hand then disappears.

If the hand locates the indicated subject, the hand beckons the subject to follow it. If the subject follows, the hand points in the direction of the caster, leading the subject in the most direct, feasible route. The hand hovers 10 feet in front of the subject, moving before him. Once the hand leads the subject to the caster, it disappears.

The subject is not compelled to follow the hand or help the caster. If the subject chooses not to follow the hand, the hand continues to beckon for the duration of the spell, then disappears. If the spell expires while the subject is en route to the caster, the hand disappears; the subject will have to rely on his own devices to locate the caster.

If there is more than one subject within a 5-mile radius that meets the caster's description, the hand locates the closest creature. If that creature refuses to follow the hand, the hand will not seek out a second subject.

The ghostly hand has no physical form. The hand can be seen only by the caster and potential targets. It cannot engage in combat or execute any other task aside from locating the subject and leading him back to the caster. The hand will not pass through solid objects, but can pass through small cracks and slits.

The material component is a black silk glove.

Invisibility Purge (**Abjuration**)

Sphere: Wards
Range: 30 yards
Components: V, S, M
Duration: 1 turn/level
Casting Time: 1 turn
Area of Effect: 10-foot square/priest
Saving Throw: None

All invisible creatures who enter an area enchanted with *invisiblity purge* instantly become visible. *Invisibility*-related spells do not take effect within the boundaries of the enchanted area, and magical devices such as *potions of invisibility* do not function. Creatures with the natural ability to become invisible are unable to use this ability within the area of effect. Invisible objects carried into the warded area also become visible.

Invisible creatures or persons within the area of effect when *invisibility purge* is cast remain invisible; however, if such creatures exit the area of effect and later re-enter, they instantly become visible. Such creatures also lose any natural ability to turn invisible as long as they remain within the area of effect.

A creature who consumes a *potion of invisibility* outside the warded area becomes invisible normally, but becomes visible when he enters the area of effect; if the duration of the *potion of invisibility* has not yet expired when he exits the area of effect, he becomes invisible again outside the area.

Creatures who are invisible in their natural state or have no visible form (such as invisible stalkers) are not affected by this spell.

The material components are the priest's holy symbol and a silver mirror no more than three inches in diameter.

The *invisibility purge* can be cast as a cooperative magic spell. The potency of this spell can be increased if several priests cast it at the same time. The duration of the spell is then equal to one turn per level of the most powerful priest, plus one turn for every contributing priest. Each priest also increases the area of effect by one 10′ × 10′ square (these areas must be contiguous). Thus, a 9th-level priest and two 5th-level priests could create a 30′ × 10′ *invisibility purge* area having a duration of 11 turns.

Know Customs (**Divination**)

Sphere: Travelers
Range: Special
Components: V, S
Duration: Special
Casting Time: 3
Area of Effect: The caster
Saving Throw: Neg.

This spell allows a caster to gain general knowledge of the customs, laws, and social etiquette of a tribe or village. The caster must be within 30 yards of a member of the tribe or village for the spell to have effect. The selected villager must possess the knowledge sought by the caster; for instance, he cannot be an infant, nor can he be mentally unstable or dead (although he can be asleep or unconscious).

The selected villager is allowed a saving throw; if he succeeds, the spell fails.

If the saving throw fails, the caster gains a general knowledge of the villager's local laws and customs, including those that apply to relevant tribal or clan types (such as customs observed by all giants). Typical information revealed by *know customs* includes common courtesies (outsiders must avert their eyes when addressing local officials), local restrictions (no animals or unaccompanied elves within the city limits), important festivals, and common passwords that are known by the majority of citizens (such as a phrase necessary to pass the guards at the main gate). Additionally, the spell gives the caster a +1 reaction adjustment to encounters with members of the relevant tribe or village.

Knowing the local laws and customs does not guarantee that the caster will conduct himself properly. *Know customs* is to be used as a guide; the DM is free to adjust the quality of information provided by a villager.

Line of Protection (**Abjuration**)
Reversible

Sphere: Protection
Range: 0
Components: V, S, M
Duration: 1 round/level
Casting Time: 1 round
Area of Effect: 30-yard line
Saving Throw: Neg.

This cooperative spell requires at least two priests to cast the spell simultaneously. During the casting, the priests determine whether the line will be stationary or portable.

If the spell is stationary, each priest must inscribe a magical sigil on parallel facing surfaces, such as facing walls of a gatehouse or two tree trunks. If the spell is portable, the priests must stand at each end of the line, thereby anchoring it.

After the spell is cast, a shimmering field of force appears between the two anchors (the sigils or priests). The field is 10 feet high and sparkles with energy. Objects on the opposite side of the translucent field, while recognizable, are hazy and indistinct.

The field causes 1d3 points of damage to all creatures passing through it; evil creatures and undead suffer 1d8 points of damage from the field. Creatures that roll a successful saving throw suffer no damage. Creatures that can fly over the field, burrow under it, or *teleport* to the other side are immune to damage.

If the spell is cast in its portable form, the priests can move at half their movement rates (limited to the rate of the slower priest). The priests can take no other action, since all their energy is spent in walking and maintaining the field.

Once created, the field cannot be increased or decreased in length and must remain straight. The priests could maneuver by pivoting, but could not walk toward each other or bend the field around a corner. If the line of sight between the two priests is blocked by any object of greater than 5' diameter, the spell immediately fails. Thus, creatures, low walls, young trees, pillars, and similar objects will not disrupt the spell.

As a cooperative spell, several priests can link together to create a longer field. Each priest (or sigil) forms the end of one field and the beginning of another, much like fenceposts. Each section of the spell must extend in a straight line, but the field can be bent at each junction. Four priests could form a long line, a square, or a Z pattern. The restrictions on moving the fields apply as outlined above. The DM may apply movement penalties depending on the complexity of the pattern.

The material components are the priests' croziers, staves, or religious standards, held aloft by each caster.

The reverse of this spell, *line of destruction*, causes 1d3 damage to all creatures passing through it. It causes 1d8 damage to paladins and creatures of good alignment who pass through it. Creatures that roll a successful saving throw suffer no damage.

Memory Read (Divination)

Sphere: Thought
Range: 5 yards
Components: V, S, M
Duration: 1 round/level
Casting Time: 1 round
Area of Effect: One creature
Saving Throw: Neg.

This spell allows the priest to read the memory of a single subject. The priest experiences the memory with the same intensity as the subject. The time required to view a memory is one-fiftieth of the time that the actual event lasted. Thus, a priest can view the memory of an event that lasted for one hour in a little more than one round. The subject experiences the memory at the same time the caster reads it.

The subject must have an Intelligence score of 5 or more and must remain within range of the priest throughout the time it takes to read the desired memory. Priests can cast this spell on unconscious, sleeping, *held*, or *paralyzed* creatures.

The subject receives a saving throw when the priest casts the spell (this saving throw is allowed even if the subject is asleep or otherwise unaware of the attempt). In addition, if the memory that the priest wants to view concerns something the subject wants to keep secret, or is something that the subject is trying to suppress, the subject receives a +5 bonus to the saving throw. If the memory the priest wishes to view is more than six months old, the subject receives a second saving throw, with bonuses depending on the age of the memory as follows:

Age of Memory	Bonus
6-12 months	0
1 to 4 years	+1
5 years or more	+3

If the subject succeeds either of these saving throws, the spell fails.

This spell creates a mental drain on the priest, causing him to temporarily lose 1-3 points of Constitution. These can be regained only after eight hours of rest. The spell cannot be cast again until the priest's constitution is restored.

The material component is a small piece of linen cloth with threads of gold interspersed throughout its weave. This is consumed during the casting.

Miscast Magic (Invocation/Evocation)

Sphere: Chaos
Range: 40 yards + 10 yards/level
Components: V, S
Duration: Special
Casting Time: 2
Area of Effect: One creature
Saving Throw: Neg.

Miscast magic can be cast only on a wizard. It causes the next spell cast by the affected wizard to be chosen randomly from his memorized spells of the same or lower level. Thus, if a wizard affected by *miscast magic* had four 1st-level spells memorized (*armor, feather fall, jump,* and *sleep*) and he attempted to cast the *sleep* spell, the DM would determine the resulting spell randomly from the wizard's four memorized spells. The wizard has only a 25% chance of casting the *sleep* spell.

Only spells currently memorized are eligible to be exchanged with the desired spell. If a wizard had only one spell memorized, the *miscast magic* would have no effect and the wizard's spell would be cast normally.

The miscast spell operates normally. If a wizard tried to *levitate* a companion but a *web* spell resulted, the companion would be trapped by the webs and subject to all resulting effects. If the target of the spell were in range of the *levitate* spell but not in range of the *web*, the spell would be lost in a fizzle of energy and the *web* spell would be wiped from the caster's memory.

The wizard who casts the spell performs the proper verbal and somatic components of the spell he wishes to cast; he does not discover the altered results until the wrong spell takes effect. The wizard will also discover that the material component for the resulting spell has vanished (in addition to the material component for the desired spell).

Wizards who are targets of *miscast magic* are allowed a saving throw vs. spell to avoid the effect.

Moment Reading (Divination)

Sphere: Numbers
Range: 0
Components: V, S, M
Duration: Instantaneous
Casting Time: 1 round
Area of Effect: Special
Saving Throw: None

This spell allows the priest to determine the "tenor of the now"—in other words, to learn the "force" that is most dominant at the time. To cast the spell, the priest generates a series of random numbers and then studies the pattern contained in that string of numbers. This pattern contains information about current conditions.

In game terms, when this spell is cast, the DM communicates to the priest's player a single word or short phrase (no more than five words) describing the "tone" of the situation. Examples of suitable "tones" are "imminent danger" (the DM knows a dragon is approaching the area); "peace and tranquility" (the woods in which the PCs camp may look threatening, but the area is actually free of evil influence); or "betrayal" (one of the PCs' hirelings is actually a spy of their enemy). The DM can make this comment cryptic, but it should always be accurate and contain some useful information.

This spell has no specified area of effect. The result of *moment reading* will always concern the priest and anyone else in his immediate vicinity, but the definition of "vicinity" will vary depending on the circumstances. For example, the tenor of the moment might be "severe danger" if the priest is entering the territory of a dragon who attacks interlopers on sight.

The tenor of the moment is always personally applicable to the priest. For example, even if the priest is in a nation dangerously close to war with its neighbor, this condition will not appear in the tenor of the moment unless the priest is personally involved (if he's currently in the direct path of an invading army, for instance).

One casting of this spell tends to "taint" subsequent castings of the same spell unless they are separated by a minimum length of time. If a priest casts this spell twice within 12 hours, the second reading gives the same result as the first, regardless of the actual situation. If a second priest casts the spell within 12 hours of another priest's use of the spell, he receives an accurate reading.

The material component is a set of 36 small disks made of polished bone engraved with runes that represent numbers. These disks are not consumed in the casting.

Random Causality (Alteration)

Sphere: Chaos
Range: 10 yards
Components: V, S, M
Duration: Special
Casting Time: 3 rounds + 1 round/level
Area of Effect: One weapon
Saving Throw: Neg.

This spell creates a rift in the nature of cause and effect. The spell is cast upon an opponent's weapon. When the weapon is used, it hits and causes damage normally, but the damage is not applied to the creature struck by the weapon. Instead, the person wielding the weapon or one of his companions suffers the damage. If the weapon misses its target on any round, no damage is caused in that round.

Using a die roll, the DM randomly determines the victim of the damage. The DM selects a die with a value nearest the number of eligible creatures (the wielder of the weapon and his companions). If the number of creatures does not equate to highest value of a die, the wielder of the enchanted weapon takes the extra chances to be hit. For example, if a goblin wields a sword affected by this spell, he and his six companions are eligible to receive the damage. The DM rolls 1d8. On a roll of 1-6, one of the goblin's companions suffers the damage; on a roll of 7 or 8, the goblin with the affected weapon suffers the damage.

The weapon is affected for 3 rounds + 1 round/level of the spell caster. If the wielder of the weapon changes weapons while the spell is in effect, the discarded weapon remains enchanted.

The material component is a bronze die.

Rigid Thinking (Enchantment/Charm)

Sphere: Law
Range: 60 yards
Components: V, S
Duration: 1 round/level
Casting Time: 1 turn
Area of Effect: One creature
Saving Throw: Neg.

Rigid thinking can be cast only upon a creature with Intelligence of 3 or greater. The creature is allowed a saving throw to avoid the effects.

The creature affected by *rigid thinking* is incapable of performing any action other than the activity he is involved in when the spell takes effect. The creature's mind simply cannot decide on another course of action—it becomes frozen into a single thought and cannot change even if new circumstances would suggest otherwise. Thus, a warrior fighting a kobold will ignore the arrival of a beholder, and a thief picking a lock will pay no heed to the arrival of three guards.

The affected creature does not mechanically repeat the action; he is not an automaton. He will not continue to fire his bow at a dragon if he runs out of arrows, but will choose another means of attacking the dragon to the exclusion of all other activities.

A spellcaster in the process of casting a spell when *rigid thinking* takes effect will not attempt to repeat the spell (unless the spell has been memorized more than once). The spellcaster will, however, devote his attention to the target of that spell until his goal is met (e.g., if the caster were attacking a creature, he would continue to direct attacks at that creature; if the caster were trying to open a door, he would continue to work on the door until it opens).

The spell expires when the creature accomplishes his goal (i.e., the kobold is killed or the lock is opened) or when the duration of the spell has ended.

Slow Rot (Abjuration)

Sphere: Plant
Range: Touch
Components: V, S, M
Duration: 1 week/level
Casting Time: 1 round
Area of Effect: Special
Saving Throw: None

This spell increases the amount of time that fruits, vegetables, and grains remain wholesome and ripe. The spell will not take effect upon meat of any kind.

The caster can affect as much as 100 cubic feet of plant material per level. Thus, even a low level priest could effectively keep a farmer's grain from rotting while in storage or keep the fruit on the trees in his orchard ripe until they are harvested. This spell does not prevent pests (such as rats) from eating the food.

The material component is a pinch of sugar.

Squeaking Floors (Evocation)

Sphere: Wards
Range: 30 yards
Components: V, S, M
Duration: 1 hour/level
Casting Time: 3
Area of Effect: 10-foot square/level
Saving Throw: None

A surface affected by *squeaking floors* squeaks loudly when any creature larger than a normal rat (larger than one-half cubic foot or weighing more than three pounds) steps on it or touches it. The spell affects a square whose sides equal the caster's level times 10 feet (a 9th-level priest could affect a square whose sides are 90 feet long).

The squeaks can be heard in a 100-foot radius, regardless of interposing barriers such as walls and doors. The squeaks occur regardless of the surface, whether wood, stone, dirt, or any other solid material. Listeners automatically know the direction of the sounds.

Characters who successfully move silently reduce the radius of the noise to 50 feet. Those able to *fly* or otherwise avoid direct contact with the affected surface will not activate the *squeaking floor*.

The material component is a rusty iron hinge that squeaks when moved.

Strength of One (Alteration)

Sphere: Law
Range: 10 yards
Components: V, S
Duration: 2d6 rounds
Casting Time: 3
Area of Effect: One creature + 1creature/2 levels
Saving Throw: None

By casting this spell on a group of lawful creatures, the priest imbues each creature with a Strength bonus equal to that of the strongest creature in the group. To be affected by the spell, all creatures must touch the hand of the priest at the time of casting. Only human, demihuman, and humanoid creatures of man-size or smaller may be affected. The characters can be a mixed group of Lawful Neutral, Lawful Good, or Lawful Evil alignments. The spell will not take effect if any creature of Neutral or Chaotic alignment is included in the group.

Prior to casting, one creature is designated the keystone. There may never be more than one keystone in a group, even if another creature has equal strength.

Upon completion of the spell, all affected characters gain a bonus to damage equal to the keystone's bonus to damage from Strength. Any magical bonuses belonging to the keystone are not added; only the keystone's natural strength is conferred on the group.

This bonus supersedes any bonus a character might normally receive. Thus, a warrior with 16 Strength (a +1 bonus to damage) who benefits from this spell with a keystone who has Strength 18/07 (a damage bonus of +3) gains a total bonus of +3 to damage (not +4 to damage). The keystone receives no bonus.

Affected creatures gain no improvements to THAC0, bend bars/lift gates, or other functions of Strength.

The spell ends if the keystone is killed before the duration expires. The bonus and duration are not affected if a member of the group is killed within the duration of the spell.

Telepathy (Divination, Alteration)

Sphere: Thought
Range: 30 yards
Components: V, S
Duration: 1 turn + 2 rounds/level
Casting Time: 5
Area of Effect: One creature
Saving Throw: Neg.

This spell establishes direct, two-way mental contact between the priest and a single subject. The subject must have Intelligence of at least 5 for the spell to take effect. While the spell is in effect, the two participants can communicate silently and rapidly, regardless of whether they share a common language.

Telepathy does not give either participant access to the other's thoughts, memories, or emotions. Participants can only "hear" the thoughts that the other participant actively "sends."

Mind-to-mind communication is approximately four times faster than verbal communication. The level of complexity that can be communicated is only that which can be expressed through language. Gestures, expressions, and body language cannot be conveyed.

A priest can establish separate "telepathic channels" to multiple individuals. Each linkage is established through a separate casting of the spell. There is no network between the channels. For example, Balfas the priest establishes *telepathy* with Alra the warrior and Zymor the thief by casting this spell twice. Balfas can communicate a single thought to both Alra and Zymor, but Alra and Zymor cannot communicate with each other. Balfas, however, can "target" a thought so that only one of the two participants receives it.

If the priest casts this spell on an unwilling subject (for example, if the priest wants to silently threaten or taunt the subject), the subject receives a saving throw vs. spell to resist the effect. Willing subjects need not make a saving throw.

Lead sheeting of more than ¹/₂″ thickness will totally block *telepathy*.

Telethaumaturgy (Enchantment/Charm)

Sphere: Numbers
Range: 0
Components: V, S, M
Duration: Special
Casting Time: 2 rounds
Area of Effect: One creature
Saving Throw: None

This spell requires the priest to perform a numerological analysis of a subject's correct name. The result is that the priest may cast another spell that affects the subject individual at a range much greater than normal. In other words, by gaining deep knowledge of the individual, the priest creates a "channel" to that individual that makes a subsequent spell easier to cast on that subject.

Only certain spells can benefit from *telethaumaturgy*:

*bless**
command
charm person or mammal
detect charm
hold person
know alignment
*remove curse**
probability control
quest
confusion (one creature only)
exaction

For spells marked with an asterisk (*), *telethaumaturgy* also increases the range of the reversed spell. Unless indicated, *telethaumaturgy* does not increase the range of the reversed spells.

The increase in range depends on the level of the priest casting *telethaumaturgy*:

Level	Range Multiplier
1-6	× 2
7-11	× 3
12-16	× 4
17+	× 5

Thus, a 12th-level priest who has cast *telethaumaturgy* on an individual could subsequently cast *charm person* on that individual at a range of 320 yards, rather than the normal range of 80 yards.

A spell to be enhanced by *telethaumaturgy* must be cast on the round immediately following the completion of *telethaumaturgy*. Spells that normally affect more than one individual (such as *confusion*) will affect only the selected subject when cast following *telethaumaturgy*.

When *telethaumaturgy* is cast by a priest of 11th level or higher, it has an additional effect. If the target is within the normal range of the subsequent spell (e.g., 80 yards for *charm person*), the subject's saving throw suffers a penalty of −2.

Like the *personal reading* spell, *telethaumaturgy* functions only if the priest knows the correct name of his subject. If the priest casts the spell using an alias, he will not know that *telethaumaturgy* has not taken effect until the subsequent spell fails. The priest does not automatically know why the subsequent spell failed (the subject might simply have made a successful saving throw).

The material component is a small book of numerological formulae and notes. This book is different from the book used in *personal reading*. The book is not consumed in the casting.

Thief's Lament (Alteration)

Sphere: Wards
Range: 10 yards/level
Components: V, S, M
Duration: 1 hour/level
Casting Time: 3
Area of Effect: 5-foot cube/level
Saving Throw: Neg.

A thief entering an area enchanted with *thief's lament* suffers a great reduction in his thieving skills. The thief is allowed a saving throw to resist the effects of the spell; failure indicates that he suffers the full effects of the lament. All attempts to pick pockets, open locks, find/remove traps, move silently, detect noise, climb walls, and hide in shadows are reduced by 25% (although a skill cannot be reduced below 5%, presuming the character has at least a score of 5% in any skill).

The spell affects a cube whose sides equal the caster's level times five feet (a 10th-level caster could affect a cube whose sides equal 50 feet).

The material components are the priest's holy symbol and a silver key.

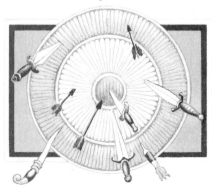

Unearthly Choir (Invocation)

Sphere: Combat
Range: 0
Component: V
Duration: Instantaneous
Casting Time: 5
Area of Effect: Special
Saving Throw: $1/2$

This cooperative spell requires at least three priests casting the spell simultaneously. At the time of casting, the priests must be within 10 feet of each other. Upon completion of the spell, the priests sing a single, dissonant chord. The result of the spell depends on the number of voices in the choir.

Trio. In this form, the spell projects a cone of sonic force 120 feet long and 40 feet wide at the base. All creatures within the area of effect must save vs. spells or suffer 2d4 points of damage. Those who successfully save suffer only 1d4 points. Undead suffer a −2 penalty to their saving throws.

Quartet. With four voices, the spell has the same area of effect as described above. However, all those who fail their saving throw suffer 2d4 points of damage and are deafened for one round. Those who successfully save suffer half damage and are not deafened. Undead creatures are not allowed a saving throw.

Quintet. Five singers produce a chord of major power. All within the area of effect suffer 3d4 points of damage (saving throw for half damage). Undead are not allowed a saving throw. All creatures are deafened for one round. Furthermore, pottery, glassware, crystal, and similar breakable goods must save vs. fall or be shattered.

Ensemble. An ensemble of singers consists of six to ten priests. In this case, the area of effect increases to a cone 180 feet long and 60 feet wide at the base. All creatures within this area suffer 1d4 points of damage per priest and are deafened for 1d4 rounds. A successful saving throw vs. spell reduces the damage and duration of deafness by half. Undead creatures of 3 hit dice or less are immediately destroyed. All other undead suffer normal damage, but are not allowed a saving throw. Glass, pottery, crystal, bone, and all wooden items that are the strength of a door or less (chests, tables, chairs, etc.) must save vs. crushing blow or be shattered.

Choir. The most powerful group, a choir, requires eleven or more priests. In this case, the area of effect expands to a cone 300 feet long and 100 feet wide at the base. All within the area of effect suffer 1d6 points of damage per priest to a maximum of 20d6. A saving throw vs. spells reduces the damage to half. Those who fail to save are deafened for 1d10 rounds; those who succeed are deafened only 1d6 rounds. Undead creatures of 5 hit dice or less are immediately destroyed. Undead with more hit dice are not allowed a saving throw. Structures within the area of effect are damaged as if they suffered a direct hit from a catapult (one hit per four priests in the choir). Doors, chests, and other breakable items are instantly shattered.

Zone of Sweet Air (Abjuration)

Sphere: Wards
Range: 10 yards/level
Components: V, S, M
Duration: 1 turn/level
Casting Time: 3
Area of Effect: 10-foot cube/level
Saving Throw: None

Zone of sweet air creates an invisible barrier around the area of effect that repels all noxious elements from poisonous vapors, including those created magically (such as a *stinking cloud*). The spell offers no protection against poisonous vapors created by a dragon's breath weapon (such as the chlorine gas of a green dragon). Noxious gases already within the area of effect when the spell is cast are not affected. Fresh air passes into the area normally.

If a poisonous vapor is expelled within the area of effect (for example, a *stinking cloud* is cast), the spell takes effect normally but dissipates in half the time normally required.

The spell affects a cube whose sides equal the caster's level times 10 feet (for instance, a 10th-level caster could affect a cube whose sides are 100 feet long).

The material components are the priest's holy symbol, a silk handkerchief, and a strand of spider web.

Fourth-Level Spells

Addition (Alteration)

Sphere: Numbers, Creation
Range: 30 yards
Components: V, S, M
Duration: Special
Casting Time: 1 round
Area of Effect: Special
Saving Throw: None

The philosophy of the Sphere of Numbers holds that the structure of reality—the "equation of the moment"—can be analyzed and modified by someone with sufficient knowledge and power. The *addition* spell allows a priest to add a new mathematical term to the equation of the moment. This effectively allows a new object or even a living creature to be brought into existence temporarily.

The effect of this spell varies depending on the level of the caster. At 10th level or lower, *addition* can create a single, inanimate object weighing up to 10 pounds. The spell gives the priest only rudimentary control over the creation process, so the object cannot be complex. The object must be described in a single word or short phrase (e.g., "a water pitcher" or "a block of stone"). The caster has no control over elements such as shape or color; thus, the water pitcher might be short, squat, and blue, or tall, slender, and red.

Objects created with this spell cannot be of any greater mechanical complexity or technological level than a crossbow. If the priest tries to create an object that breaks this prohibition, the spell fails and nothing is created. Thus, if the priest tried to create "a pistol," assuming he had heard the word somewhere, the spell would fail.

Objects cannot contain any information in an abstract form such as writing or diagrams. If the priest tries to create an object that breaks this prohibition, there are two possible results: the spell may fail, or the object may be created without the information. Thus, if the priest were to attempt to create "a spellbook," the result would be either a book similar to a spellbook with blank pages, or nothing at all.

The object appears at whatever location the caster wills, as long as it is within spell range. The object cannot appear in the same space occupied by another object or creature, or within a hollow object (for example, the priest cannot create an object blocking the trachea of an enemy).

The object created by *addition* remains in existence for 1 turn per level of the caster. During this time, it obeys all the laws of physics as if it were a "real" object. The object cannot be disbelieved and spells such as *true seeing* cannot distinguish it from a naturally-occurring object.

Priests of 11th to 15th level can create a single inanimate object of up to 20 pounds in mass or two identical objects, each of up to five pounds in mass. The object(s) so created remains in existence for two hours (12 turns) per level of the caster.

Priests of 16th to 19th level can create a single inanimate object of up to 50 pounds in mass or up to 10 identical objects, each of up to five pounds in mass. The object(s) is permanent unless destroyed. Since these objects are not magical constructs, but real additions to the "equation of the moment," *dispel magic* has no effect on them. Alternatively, the caster can create a single normal (nonmonstrous) living creature of up to 20 pounds in weight. The creature, once created, behaves as a normal member of its species; the caster has no control over its actions. This creature remains in existence for 5 rounds per level of the caster.

Priests of 20th level and above can create a single inanimate object of up to 100 pounds in mass or up to 10 identical objects, each of up to 10 pounds in mass. The object(s) are permanent. Alternatively, the caster can create a single normal (nonmonstrous) living creature of up to 100 pounds in weight and up to 2 hit dice. The creature, once created, behaves as a normal member of its species; the caster has no control over its actions. This creature remains in existence for 2 turns per level of the caster.

The material component is a small table of numerological formulae inscribed on an ivory plaque, plus a length of silken cord. During the casting, the priest ties the cord into a complex knot. As the magical energy is discharged, the cord vanishes in a flash of light. The plaque is not consumed in the casting.

Age Plant (Alteration)

Sphere: Time
Range: 30 yards
Components: V, S, M
Duration: Permanent
Casting Time: 1 round
Area of Effect: One plant, seed, or tree/level
Saving Throw: None

This spell enables the caster to affect the aging of any plant, seed, or tree. The process can operate either forward or backward, causing flowers to blossom, seeds to sprout and grow, and trees to bear fruit; or fruit to turn to blossoms, trees to become saplings, and new shoots to turn to seeds.

The change in age, either forward or backward, is chosen by the priest at the time of casting. The changes associated with normal or reversed growth occur instantaneously. Plants can be altered in age up to 10 years per level of the caster. The caster can stop the aging at any point within the limits imposed by his level; he could cause a tree to grow from a sapling until it withers and dies from old age or he could stop the tree's growth at a stage at which it would shelter his home.

The spell does not alter the appearance or characteristics of a plant except those that result from normal aging (or regression). *Age plant* has no effect on magically-generated plants or plant-type monsters.

The material components are the priest's holy symbol and the petal from an apple blossom.

Blessed Warmth (Alteration)

Sphere: Sun
Range: Touch
Components: V, S
Duration: 1 round/level
Casting Time: 4
Area of Effect: Special
Saving Throw: None

When this spell is cast, a narrow shaft of light shines down upon the priest, making him immune to the effects of natural cold (such as a blizzard) and granting him a +3 bonus to saving throws vs. magical cold (such as a white dragon's breath weapon).

For each level of the priest above 7th, an additional beam of light may be created to protect another creature, who must be standing within 3' of the priest. Thus, a 10th-level priest could protect four other creatures in a 3' radius.

Body Clock (Alteration)

Sphere: Time
Range: Touch
Components: V, S, M
Duration: 1 hour/level
Casting Time: 4
Area of Effect: One creature
Saving Throw: None

Body clock affects a subject in the following ways.

• The subject's need for sleep is reduced. For every hour that a subject sleeps, he is as refreshed as if he slept 10 hours. For every two hours that a subject sleeps during the spell (20 hours of rest), he regains hit points as if he spent a day of complete rest. However, wizards are not able to memorize spells; "real" time must pass for this to occur.

• The subject's need to breathe is reduced. He breathes only 10% as often as normal for the duration of the spell, enabling him to hold his breath 10 times longer than normal and use less air in enclosed situations.

• The subject can set an internal "alarm clock" to alert him when a specific amount of time has passed. The subject then hears a brief ringing in his ears, audible only to him. The ringing is loud enough to wake the subject. He can set as many internal alarm clocks as he wishes, as long as they all occur within the duration of the spell.

The spell has no effect on movement, spellcasting, or any other normal activities.

The material components are a kernel of corn, a drop of water, and a stoppered glass bottle.

Chaotic Combat (Invocation/Evocation)

Sphere: Chaos
Range: 30 yards
Components: V, S
Duration: 1 round/level
Casting Time: 3
Area of Effect: One creature
Saving Throw: None

When *chaotic combat* is cast on a fighter, he is inspired beyond his years of training and is suddenly struck with numerous insights for variations on the standard moves of attack and defense. The spell affects only warriors.

Unfortunately, these insights are helpful in only two-thirds of the warrior's attacks. In the remaining attacks, the spell actually impairs the warrior's standard performance. At the beginning of each round, after the player has declared his character's actions, 1d6 is rolled for the affected warrior. On a roll of 1, 2, 3, or 4, the warrior gains bonuses of +2 to attack rolls and +2 to armor class. On a roll of 5 or 6, the warrior suffers a −2 penalty to attack rolls and a −2 penalty to armor class. This must be determined at the beginning of the round so that both the warrior and his opponents can apply the necessary changes.

The insight imparted by this spell is lost after the spell expires. The insight is generated by chaos, which is nearly impossible to contain. After the spell expires, the warrior remembers the battle but not the specifics of his actions. He is unable to duplicate the maneuvers.

Chaotic Sleep (Alteration)

Sphere: Chaos
Range: Touch
Components: V, S, M
Duration: Permanent
Casting Time: 1 turn
Area of Effect: One creature
Saving Throw: Neg.

After casting this spell, the priest must successfully touch his victim. The victim is then allowed a saving throw to avoid the spell's effect. If the saving throw is failed, the spell takes effect at the next sunrise or sunset (whichever comes first).

From the time the spell takes effect until the spell is negated, the sleeping pattern of the victim is randomly disrupted. At sunset and sunrise of every day, a check is made to determine the effects of *chaotic sleep.* In the 12-hour period that follows the check, there is an equal chance that the character will be unable to sleep or unable to remain awake (roll 1d6; on a roll of 1-3, the character is awake, on a roll of 4-6, he sleeps). This condition lasts until the next sunrise (or sunset) when the check is made again.

For example, a fighter fails to save against *chaotic sleep.* For the next few hours, the spell has no effect. At sundown, the first check is made, resulting in a 2. The fighter does not notice anything until he tries to sleep that night, at which time he is wide awake, fidgeting and restless. At sunrise, another die roll is made, resulting in a 6. The fighter is suddenly exhuasted and sleeps until sunset.

Characters who sleep as a result of this spell can be roused only by physical stimuli—a slap or a wound, for example. Once awake, the character remains conscious only as long as there are active stimuli around him, such as a fight. Walking through caves or riding a horse will not keep the character awake. Unlike a *sleep* spell, characters affected by *chaotic sleep* doze off as soon as they are left relatively undisturbed. Keeping an affected character awake is difficult at best.

Lack of sleep will eventually take a physical toll on any character under the influence of the spell. For every 12-hour period that a character remains awake beyond the first, he suffers a −1 penalty to THAC0. Such characters do not regain hit points as a result of normal healing. Spellcasters cannot memorize spells until they have had sufficient sleep.

Chaotic sleep can be removed with a *remove curse.*

The material components are a pinch of sand and three coffee beans.

Circle of Privacy (Alteration)

Sphere: Travelers
Range: Special
Components: V, S, M
Duration: 1 hour/level
Casting Time: 4
Area of Effect: 50-foot-diameter circle
Saving Throw: None

This spell helps to discourage predators and trespassers from disturbing a campsite. The caster sprinkles salt in a circle enclosing an area up to 50 feet in diameter. For the duration of the spell, all sounds and scents generated within the circle are muted, making the area less noticeable to those outside the circle. Therefore, the group's chance of encounter is reduced by 50% for the duration of the spell. The spell provides no protection against infravision or other forms of magical detection.

The material components are a hair from a skunk, a whisker from a mouse, and enough salt to make a 50-foot-diameter circle.

Compulsive Order (Enchantment/Charm)

Sphere: Law
Range: 10 yards
Components: V, S, M
Duration: Permanent
Casting Time: 5
Area of Effect: One creature
Saving Throw: Neg.

The victim of *compulsive order* is compelled to place everything he encounters into perfect order. If he discovers treasure, he divides it into tidy piles or containers of silver, gold, and copper. He is reluctant to enter a dungeon because it is a messy place, but once inside, he is obsessed with cleaning it. A character under the power of this spell will sweep dirt from dungeon corridors into neat piles, arrange the corpses of a defeated orc band according to size, dash forward to remove a bit of lint on clothing, and insist that the party organize themselves alphabetically, then by size, and then by age. While the spell does not affect a character's abilities, the overwhelming desire for order impairs the character's usefulness in most adventures.

When a character afflicted by this spell attempts to undertake a new event (begin a battle, haggle with the merchant, etc.), the player must rationalize the action on the basis of his compulsion for order. Thus, the character cannot simply attack a goblin; he must announce a condition such as attacking the tallest goblin and fighting his way down according to size. Once stated, the character must follow through with this plan.

If the player cannot conceive a rationale for his character's behavior, the character is forced to delay his actions for 1d6 rounds, with the time spent in preparation for the subsequent action. The character spends time arranging spell components artistically, deciding how to hold his sword, cleaning his weapon, etc.

Anyone affected by *compulsive order* may become violent if he is prevented from being neat. He will do what he must to make the world around him more orderly. If he is allowed to organize his surroundings, he will quickly calm down again. The victim will constantly petition the people around him to be neat and organized.

The victim is allowed a saving throw to avoid the effects of the spell. *Compulsive order* can be removed with a *dispel magic* spell.

The material component is a perfect cube made of metal.

Defensive Harmony (Enchantment/Charm)

Sphere: Law
Range: 5 yards
Components: V, S
Duration: 1 round + 2d4 rounds
Casting Time: 1
Area of Effect: One creature/two levels
Saving Throw: None

This spell must be cast on at least two creatures. The priest may affect one creature per two levels of his experience, and all creatures to be affected must be within three feet of each other at the time of casting. After the spell is completed, affected characters may move about freely.

Defensive harmony grants affected creatures a defensive bonus by bestowing an enhanced coordination of their attacks and defenses. The affected creatures must be involved in a single battle so that their efforts harmonize to the benefit of all

involved. For example, the affected creatures can attack one dragon or a group of orcs in a single area. They can also attack additional enemy forces that arrive in the same combat. If the enemy forces divide and flee, the affected creatures can follow, continue to attack, and benefit from the spell. If the affected group is split into two smaller groups when attacked, however, it gains no benefit from *defensive harmony*.

While the spell is in effect, each affected creature gains a +1 bonus to armor class for every other creature benefitting from the spell, to a maximum bonus of +5 (although more than five characters may be affected by the spell). Thus, if four creatures are affected by *defensive harmony*, each creature gains a +3 bonus to armor class.

This bonus represents a mystical coordination of effort on the part of all affected creatures. A fighter will naturally wage his attack to distract the troll attacking the thief. The ranger will instinctively block the swing of an orc, thereby protecting the wizard. Creatures affected by the spell are not consciously aware of these efforts, and they are unable to create specific strategies and tactics.

Dimensional Folding (Alteration)

Sphere: Numbers
Range: 5 feet
Components: V, S, M
Duration: 1 round
Casting Time: 1 round
Area of Effect: 10-foot circle
Saving Throw: None

This spell allows the caster to selectively warp the fabric of space, folding it into higher dimensions.

This effect can be best explained through an example. If an ant crawling along the west edge of a map decided to travel to the east edge of the map, it would have to crawl the full width of the map. But if the map were folded in two so that the east and west edges were touching, the ant would travel almost no distance at all. The ant's world (the map) would have been folded through the third dimension. The *dimensional folding* spell does something similar with the three-dimensional world: it folds it through a higher dimension (the fourth), allowing instantaneous travel between two locales on the same plane of existence.

Although this effect may seem similar to the wizard spell *teleport*, in practice, it is much different. The *dimensional folding* spell opens a gate that allows instantaneous, bidirectional access to a distant locale on the same plane. This gate is circular, of any size up to 10' in diameter, and remains in existence for up to 1 full round. The caster and any other creatures can pass through the gate in either direction while it remains open. Missile weapons and magic spells can also pass through the gate.

The gate appears as a shimmering ring, glowing with a faint light equivalent to starshine. Vision through the gate is clear and unobstructed in both directions, allowing the priest to "look before he leaps." However, anyone on the other side of the gate is able to see the priest and his point of origin.

The "near side" of the gate always appears within 5 feet of the priest. The location of the "far side" of the gate always opens within 5 feet of the place the priest desires. Thus, there is no chance of arriving at the wrong destination, as with the wizard spell *teleport*.

There is a risk involved in using *dimensional folding*, however. Many philosophers believe that what we know as time is simply another dimension, and the behavior of this spell seems to support this thesis. Unless the priest is extremely familiar with the destination, there is a significant chance that any creature passing through a *dimensional folding* gate will suffer instantaneous aging. Theorists believe that this is the same kind of "slippage" that can cause a *teleporting* wizard to land high or low, except that in this case, the slippage is in the time dimension.

The chance of this instantaneous aging occurring depends on how familiar the priest is with the destination. The table that follows outlines the conditions and effects of aging.

Destination is:	Chance of aging	Amount of aging
Very familiar*	2%	1 year
Studied carefully	5%	1d2 years
Seen casually	10%	1d3 years
Viewed once	15%	1d6 years
Never seen	25%	1d10 years

* Use this row if the desired location is within view of the priest.

If the die roll indicates that aging occurs, every creature that passes through the gate in either direction suffers the aging effect. Multiple creatures passing through the gate in the same direction all age by the same amount determined by a single die roll. Although the chance of aging is low and

the potential amount of aging is minimal for familiar destinations, the effects can add up and become significant over time.

Although the word "destination" is used to refer to the "far end" of the gate, the priest need not be the one doing the traveling. For example, a priest may open the gate near a distant ally so he may travel instantaneously to join the priest.

The material component is a sheet of platinum "tissue" worth at least 15 gp, which the priest folds intricately during the casting. The tissue is consumed when the gate closes.

Fire Purge (Abjuration)

Sphere: Wards
Range: 10 yards/level
Components: V, S, M
Duration: 1 turn/level
Casting Time: 1 turn
Area of Effect: 10-yard square/priest
Saving Throw: None

An area enchanted with *fire purge* is protected against all types of normal and magical fires. Normal fires (including camp fires, torches, and oil fires) cannot burn in the area of effect. Magical fires (including fiery dragon breath, other creature-generated fires, and spell-related fires such as *burning hands* and *fireball*) cause only 50% of their normal damage. Additionally, creatures within the area of effect receive a +4 bonus to saving throws made vs. fire attacks, regardless of whether the attacks originate inside or outside the warded area.

Fire purge has no effect on fires that are within the area of effect when the spell is cast, (i.e., it does not extinguish existing fires).

The material components are the priest's holy symbol and a scorched sliver of wood.

Fire purge can be cast as cooperative magic. If a number of priests cast this spell simultaneously, its effectiveness is significantly increased. The duration of the spell is then equal to 1 turn per level of the most powerful priest plus 1 turn for every other contributing priest. The area of effect is a square whose sides equal the number of priests times 10 yards (thus, six priests could create a 60-yard by 60-yard square of protection).

Focus (Invocation)

Sphere: All
Range: 10 feet
Components: V, S, M
Duration: Special
Casting Time: 1 day
Area of Effect: Special
Saving Throw: None

This spell creates the necessary conditions for devotional energy to be used. For faith magic to work, the priest must create a focus to harness the necessary devotional energy. This spell creates that focus. *A focus cannot function without a source of devotional energy.*

The focus gathers devotional energy and reshapes it in order to amplify other spells cast by the priest (or priests). The same energy keeps the focus in existence. If the spell is cast and there is no immediate source of devotional energy within 100 feet, the *focus* immediately fails.

Once created, most foci cannot be moved. This condition and the need for a constant supply of devotional energy tends to limit the use of foci to temples, churches, monasteries, shrines, and seminaries—permanent structures where followers of the religion gather on a regular basis. Sometimes a focus is created for a special gathering such as a holy day, conclave, grand wedding, or yearly festival.

Not all foci are identical. The particular form of the focus depends on the power and nature of the spell being amplified. All foci can be seen by *detect magic*. There are three basic types of foci: site, item, and living.

Site foci are connected to a place, whether a room, building, field, or forest. Once cast, the foci cannot be moved. It causes no disturbance in the surroundings; it is invisible and intangible.

Item foci are centered on a single object. Customarily, this object is large and immovable, such as an altar, but it is possible for the focus to be as small as is practical. The item can be as elaborate or plain as desired, but should have some significance to the religion.

Living foci are the rarest of all types. In this case, the focus is created on a living plant, animal, or person. *Detect charm* reveals the person is somehow enchanted, although not under the influence of a typical charm spell.

The type of focus created (site, item, or living) depends on the religion and nature of the spell amplified. These choices are listed in Table 3: Focused Spell Effects.

Casting the *focus* spell is a long and complicated process, accompanied by many ceremonies and rituals. During the day spent casting the spell, the priest will need the assistance of at least two other priests of the same faith. These aides need not memorize the spell (or even be capable of casting it). Their duty is to provide the extra hands and voices needed at specific points of the casting. A large number of worshipers must also be present since the focus requires their energy. Not surprisingly, the casting of this spell is often incorporated into important holy festivals or special occasions.

The duration of the focus is one year. If the devotional energy falls below a minimum level, the spell ends sooner. A focus requires the devotional energy of at least 100 devout worshipers. Lay monks (those dedicated to the religion but not priests) count as two worshipers, while priests (of any level) count as ten. A focus could be maintained by a congregation of 100, a monastery of fifty, or a seminary of as few as 10 priests (or any combination of the above). The focus must receive this energy for at least 10 hours out of every day. If these conditions are not met, the focus weakens. The area of effect of the amplified spell decreases by 20% each day until it fades away completely.

Once the focus is created, the priest or priests have 1 turn in which to cast the desired spell upon the focus. A focus can amplify only one spell, and each item, creature, or place can receive only one focus. Spells that can be cast upon a focus are listed on Table 3.

Table 3: FOCUSED SPELL EFFECTS

Spell	Possible Focus Type
Anti-animal shell	S/I/L
Anti-plant shell	S/I/L
Bless	S/I
Control temperature, 10' radius	S*
Control winds	S/I*
Cure disease	I/L
Cure blindness or deafness	I/L
Detect poison	S/I
Detect lie	I
Detect magic	I
Dispel evil	S/I
Endure cold/endure heat	S*
Know alignment	I/L
Negative plane protection	S/I
Protection from evil	S/I
Protection from lightning	S

Protections from fire	S
Purify food and drink	I
Remove fear	S/I/L
Remove curse	I
Repel insects	S/I
Resist fire/resist cold	S
Speak with animals	S/I/L
Tongues	S/I
True seeing	S

* The caster must state a desired range (temperature, wind strength, etc.) within the spell's normal limitations at the time it is cast.

Once the spell is cast, the normal duration and area of effect for that spell are ignored. The focus begins to increase these factors of the spell's power. After one day, the amplified spell reaches its full area of effect. Thereafter, it remains over that area until the focus fails.

The area affected by the focus (and its amplified spell) depends on the level of the caster. The spell expands in a radius from the focus, 20 feet per level of the caster, although it can deliberately be created smaller. Within that area of effect, the amplified spell exerts its normal effect. A 13th-level priest could create a focus up to 260 feet in diameter.

The material components are many, including special vestments, incense, oils, waters, and other equipment the DM deems appropriate. The cost of these materials is never less than 1,000 gp plus 100 gp per level of spell being amplified. These items are given up as offerings to the deity (perhaps to be distributed to the poor), and new ones must be obtained each time the spell is cast.

Fortify (Necromancy)

Sphere: Healing
Range: 0
Components: V, S, M
Duration: Special
Casting Time: 6
Area of Effect: Creature touched
Saving Throw: None

This is a simple cooperative magic spell. Only one priest can cast the spell, but like *mystic transfer*, another priest is required for the spell to have any effect. Through this spell, the priest improves the quality of another priest's healing spells.

For the *fortify* spell to work, it must be cast simultaneously with a *cure light wounds*, *cure serious wounds*, or *cure critical wounds*. The priest casting *fortify* must lay his hand on the priest attempting the cure. When both spells are cast, additional energy flows through the second priest and into the creature being healed. *Fortify* automatically causes the cure spell to function at maximum effect. Thus, a *cure serious wounds* would automatically heal 17 points of damage and a *cure critical wounds* would heal 27 points of damage.

The material component is the priest's holy symbol.

Genius (Divination)

Sphere: Thought
Range: 0
Components: V, S, M
Duration: Instantaneous
Casting Time: 5
Area of Effect: Caster
Saving Throw: None

This spell is similar to *idea*, except that the priest's player can ask the DM one question about any event occurring at the moment. The question must be somehow related to evaluation of the current situation, such as "What are these monsters?" Speculation about the future, such as "What's on the other side of the door?" is not permitted.

As with *idea*, the DM must be careful in adjudicating this spell. The answer to the question should always be relevant and correct, although not necessarily complete, and should not be unbalancing to the situation. The answer can also be cryptic, in the form of a riddle or rhyme, depending on the DM's assessment of the situation. In general, the answer will be a single word or a short phrase of no more than five words.

The material component is a gem of at least 50 gp value. This spell can be cast only once in any 12-hour period. Subsequent attempts to cast the spell result in no answer.

Inverted Ethics (Enchantment/Charm)

Sphere: Chaos
Range: 120 yards
Components: V, S, M
Duration: 1 turn
Casting Time: 1
Area of Effect: Special
Saving Throw: Neg.

This spell reverses the ethics of a person or group of people. While under the influence of this spell, a creature behaves in a manner opposite to the way he normally would behave. Thus, a shopkeeper influenced by *inverted ethics* will think it perfectly normal for someone to pick up an item from his shop and walk out the door without paying for it. If someone tried to pay for an item, he would be insulted. If the spell is cast on a shopper in a store, he would find it natural to steal the item, thinking that he is behaving in a proper way. If the spell is cast on a professed thief, he will no longer steal, choosing to pay for his goods instead.

Inverted ethics does not cause a creature to actively commit evil deeds (or good deeds). Thus, an affected creature will not go on a shoplifting rampage; he will steal only as the opportunity presents itself.

The spell affects one character per level of the caster within a 20' radius. Each target of the spell is allowed a saving throw vs. spell to avoid the effect.

The material component is a miniature golden balance (i.e., similar to the scales of justice).

Join With Astral Traveler (Alteration)

Sphere: Astral
Range: 0
Components: V, S
Duration: Special
Casting Time: 1 turn
Area of Effect: The caster
Saving Throw: None

When a priest casts the 7th-level *astral spell*, he leaves his physical body in suspended animation while his astral body travels. By touching the comatose body and casting *join with astral traveler*, a priest can cause his own astral body to leave his physical body in suspended animation. His astral body then travels along the silver cord of the originally projected priest. The caster joins the projected priest as if he were part of the original casting of the *astral spell*; i.e., his own silver cord is connected to the priest's silver cord, and he is dependent upon the originally projected priest.

A priest who casts the 7th-level *astral spell* can project as many as seven other creatures along with himself. However, priests casting *join with astral traveler* are an exception to this limit. Any number of priests may join another priest in the Astral plane by use of this spell.

Leadership (Enchantment/Charm, Alteration) Reversible

Sphere: War
Range: Special
Components: V, S, M
Duration: Special
Casting Time: Special
Area of Effect: One creature
Saving Throw: None

This spell can be cast in one of two variations. The first, appropriate for battlefield use, has a range of 240 yards, duration of 1d4 + 6 turns, and a casting time of 1 turn. The priest can cast the spell on any single individual (a commander or hero) within his line of sight.

While under the influence of this spell, the subject's command radius is increased by 50% (round fractions up).

The reverse of this variation, *doubt*, requires the target to make a saving throw vs. spell. If failed, *doubt* halves the command radius (round fractions down) of the targeted individual for 1d3 + 4 turns.

The material component for this variation is a pinch of steel dust.

The second variation must take place in or within 100' of a place of worship officially dedicated to the casting priest's deity. Both the priest and the individual to be affected must be present. The casting time is 5 turns and involves an intricate ritual and many prayers. At the conclusion of the spell, the subject's command radius is doubled. This effect lasts 2d12 hours.

The priest can cast either aspect (but not both at once) on himself. No individual can be the subject of more than one casting of this spell at one time, whether different aspects or cast by different priests. If more than one spell is attempted on the individual, only the most recent casting takes effect.

The material component for the second variation is the priest's holy symbol.

Mental Domination (Enchantment/Charm)

Sphere: Thought
Range: 50 yards
Components: V, S, M
Duration: 3 rounds/level
Casting Time: 4
Area of Effect: One creature
Saving Throw: Neg.

This spell is similar to the wizard spell *domination* in that it establishes a telepathic link between

the priest and the subject through which the priest can control the subject's bodily movements. There are some significant differences between the spells, however.

Elves and half-elves have no innate resistance to this spell. Priest and subject need not share a common language. The priest can force the subject into combat, but the subject's attack rolls suffer a −2 penalty. The priest cannot force the subject to cast spells or use any innate magical or magiclike abilities. The priest can force the subject to speak, although the priest cannot inject a full range of emotions into the subject's voice (everything said by the subject is in a monotone).

This spell gives the priest no access to the subject's thoughts, memory, or sensory apparatus. Thus, the priest cannot see through the subject's eyes. To control the subject, the priest must be within the range of the spell *and* must be able to see the subject. Breaking either of these conditions causes the spell to terminate immediately.

This spell requires a moderate level of concentration by the priest. While maintaining this spell, he can move or enter combat, but cannot cast another spell. If the priest is wounded, rendered unconscious, or killed, the spell immediately terminates.

If the priest is 10th level or lower, he or she cannot force the subject to perform particularly delicate actions, such as picking a lock. At 11th level or higher, however, this restriction is removed. The priest could thus force a thief to pick a lock. Any such delicate actions suffer a −15% penalty (or −3 on 1d20) to reflect the "remote control" nature of the action.

The material component is a mesh of fine threads that the priest loops around the fingertips of one hand and manipulates in the way that a puppeteer controls a puppet.

Modify Memory (Enchantment/Charm)

Sphere: Time
Range: 30 feet
Components: V, S
Duration: Permanent
Casting Time: Special
Area of Effect: One creature
Saving Throw: Neg.

This spell enables the caster to reach into the subject's mind and modify up to five minutes of his memory in one of the following ways:

• Eliminate all memory of an event the subject actually experienced. This spell cannot negate *charm, suggestion, geas, quest,* or similar spells.

• Allow the subject to recall with perfect clarity an event he actually experienced. For instance, he could recall every word from a five-minute conversation or every detail from a passage in a book.

• Change the details of an event the subject actually experienced.

• Implant a memory of an event the subject never experienced.

Casting the spell takes one round. If the subject fails to save vs. spell, the caster proceeds with the spell by spending up to five minutes visualizing the memory he wishes to modify in the subject. If the caster's concentration is disturbed before the visualization is complete, the spell is lost.

Modified memory will not necessarily affect the subject's actions, particularly if they contradict his natural inclinations. An illogical *modified memory,* such as the subject recalling how much he enjoyed drinking poison, will be dismissed by the subject as a bad dream or a memory muddied by too much wine. More useful applications of *modified memory* include implanting memories of friendly encounters with the caster (inclining the subject to act favorably toward the caster), changing the details of orders given to the subject by a superior, or causing the subject to forget that the caster cheated him in a card game. The DM reserves the right to decide whether a *modified memory* is too nonsensical to significantly affect the subject.

Probability Control (Alteration)

Sphere: Numbers
Range: 30 yards
Components: V, S, M
Duration: Special
Casting Time: 4
Area of Effect: One creature
Saving Throw: Neg.

This spell allows the priest to increase or decrease by a small margin the probability of success for one action. This action can be anything that requires a die roll—an attack, a saving throw, an attempt to use thieving skills, an ability check, or even an attempt to successfully *teleport* on target. The action *must* be something performed by a single creature.

The basic modification is 15% (15 on 1d100 or 3 on 1d20), plus an additional 5% per five levels of the caster. This modification can be either positive or negative, as deemed by the spellcaster. Thus, a 10th-level priest can modify a subject's saving throw or attack roll by +5 or −5, or a thief's "climb walls" roll by +25% or −25%. The priest may cast this spell on himself.

For a noncombat action such as an attempt to climb a wall, the priest simply casts the spell on the subject immediately before the action is attempted, informing the DM whether the modification is positive or negative. To use this spell in combat, the priest must specify the action to be affected (e.g., the target's next attack roll) and whether the modification will be positive or negative. The spell remains in effect until the subject attempts the specified action or until a number of rounds equal to the caster's level passes. If the latter occurs, the spell ends without effect.

Once the spell is cast, the priest does not need to maintain any level of concentration; the spell will function even if the casting priest is killed before the spell takes effect.

The subject of the spell has no way of knowing whether any modification made by this spell is positive or negative (or even whether he was the subject of the spell at all). Thus, a lying priest could claim to raise a thief's chance of climbing the wall, while actually lowering it. The thief would be none the wiser. However, an unwilling subject of this spell receives a normal saving throw to negate its effect.

The material components are a small cube of a thickened sugar-and-milk mixture and a cubic die of matching size. Both are consumed in the casting.

Rapport (**Divination, Alteration**)

Sphere: Thought
Range: 30 yards
Components: V, S
Duration: 1 turn +1 round/level
Casting Time: 1 round
Area of Effect: One creature
Saving Throw: None

This spell is a deeper and more intense version of *telepathy*. It allows the priest to communicate silently and instantly with a single willing subject. Participants may share deeper thoughts than with *telepathy*, including emotions and memories. Each participant sees, hears, and otherwise senses everything experienced by the other, although such vicarious experiences feel diluted and cannot be mistaken for direct sensations.

The participants can quickly share such personal concepts as plans, hopes, and fears, but they *cannot* share skills or spells. Thus, it is im-

possible to communicate the procedure for casting a particular spell or for picking a lock.

Communication through *rapport* is approximately 15 times faster than verbal communication. As with *telepathy*, the priest can establish separate "channels" to multiple individuals; each such linkage costs one casting of the spell. There is no "crosstalk" between the channels, however.

Rapport cannot be used on unwilling subjects.

Solipsism (**Alteration**)

Sphere: Thought
Range: 10 yards/level
Components: V, S, M
Duration: Special
Casting Time: 1 round
Area of Effect: 100 sq. ft. +100 sq. ft./level
Saving Throw: Special

This unusual spell is similar to *phantasmal force* and other illusion magic, except that the priest who casts the spell is the only creature who automatically believes the results of the spell. The spell creates the illusion of any object, creature, or force, as long as it is within the boundaries of the spell's area of effect. The illusion is visual and tactile (that is, it can be seen and felt), but no other sensory stimuli are created.

Solipsism is the opposite of normal illusions in that anyone other than the caster must make an active effort to *believe* (rather than *dis*believe) the illusion. Characters trying to believe the reality of a solipsistic illusion must make a saving throw vs. breath weapon, modified by the magical defense adjustment for Wisdom. A successful save means that the character believes the illusion and it is part of reality for him. A failed save means that the character cannot convince himself of the illusion's reality, and the illusion has no effect on him. A character can make a single attempt to believe each round.

Unlike true illusions, the image created by this spell does more than just duplicate reality. The image formed is *real* for those who believe in it. The illusion has all the normal properties that its form and function allow. Thus, a solipsistic bridge spanning a chasm could be crossed by the priest and those who believed. All others would see the priest apparently walking out onto nothingnesss. Likewise, a solipsistic giant would cause real damage to those who believed it.

The illusion remains in effect for as long as the priest continues to concentrate on it, until the priest is struck in combat, or until he is rendered unconscious. The level of concentration required is not extreme; the priest can move normally and may engage in combat, but is unable to cast any spell while maintaining a *solipsistic* illusion.

Solipsism can create only illusions that are external to the priest. Thus, the priest cannot create an illusion that he is the size of a giant, is unwounded, or has sprouted wings.

The material components are a lotus blossom that the priest must swallow and a bit of fleece.

Tanglefoot (Alteration, Abjuration)

Reversible

Sphere: War
Range: 240 yards
Components: V, S, M
Duration: 2 turns/level
Casting Time: 2 turns
Area of Effect: 100 sq. yards/level
Saving Throw: None

This spell temporarily doubles the movement cost of one region of ground. Units allied to the priest are unaffected and movement is made at normal cost; only enemy units suffer the penalty.

A variety of effects result from the spell depending on the terrain: grass twists hinderingly around troops' ankles, swamp becomes more viscous, rocks and gravel shift underfoot, etc.

The spell affects only units—that is, groups of soldiers moving in regular or irregular formation. The spell does not affect individuals or monsters moving and operating alone. (When using the BATTLESYSTEM rules, figures that represent individual heroes are not affected by this spell.)

When casting this spell, the priest must have an uninterrupted line of sight to the terrain to be affected. The priest can choose the shape of the area, up to the maximum area of effect. This spell can create only one continuous area of *tanglefoot*. There is no way of detecting that a particular area is under the influence of this spell simply by looking at the area. *Detect magic* will reveal that the area is magically affected.

The reverse of this spell, *selective passage*, cuts the movement cost of an area in half (round fractions up) for friendly units. Again, individual heroes and creatures are not affected by this spell (which means that advancing troops must be careful not to leave their leader behind!).

The material component is a drop of molasses for *tanglefoot*, and a pinch of powdered graphite for *selective passage*.

Thought Broadcast (Alteration)

Sphere: Thought
Range: 30 yards
Components: V, S, M
Duration: 1 turn + 3 rounds/level
Casting Time: 5
Area of Effect: One creature
Saving Throw: Neg.

This spell turns the subject into a "thought broadcaster." For the duration of the spell, everyone within 30 yards of the subject senses the subject's thoughts, making it impossible for him to lie, keep secrets, conceal motives, etc. The subject is not automatically aware that his thoughts are being sensed. Everyone who senses these thoughts, on the other hand, knows their source.

This spell causes the broadcast of only surface thoughts and motivations, not memories. There is no need for a common language between broadcaster and receivers; for this purpose, thoughts are considered to be symbolic, not dependent on language. The detail level of the thoughts is insufficient for others to learn specific skills from the subject. Thus, if the subject casts a spell, everyone within range knows what spell is being cast before it takes effect, but no one learns any knowledge about how the spell is cast.

If the broadcaster is *invisible* or hiding in shadows, the broadcast functions normally, and all receivers are aware that someone is in the vicinity whom they cannot see. While receivers cannot pinpoint the broadcaster's location, the broadcaster's thoughts will inevitably reveal his general position ("Oh no, he's looking right at me," etc.). A character hiding in shadows will be automatically detected, while attacks against an *invisible* broadcaster suffer a −2 penalty, rather than the normal −4. This spell totally negates the chance of surprise by the broadcaster.

The subject must have an Intelligence score of 1 or more to become a broadcaster, and must have a "normal" mind as understood by PCs. Thoughts that are broadcast can be received only by individuals with Intelligence scores of 3 or better. An unwilling subject receives a normal saving throw vs. spell to avoid the effects. A willing subject can waive this saving throw.

The material component is small balloon that the priest inflates upon casting. This balloon is consumed in the casting.

Tree Steed (Alteration, Enchantment/Charm)

Sphere: Travelers
Range: 10 yards
Components: V, S, M
Duration: 1 hour/level
Casting Time: 4
Area of Effect: One log or plank
Saving Throw: None

This spell enchants a log, plank, or similar piece of wood to become a temporary steed. The log or plank must be at least one foot wide, three inches thick, and three to ten feet long. Any type of wood is suitable.

When the spell is cast, the log sprouts four wooden, horselike legs. The *tree steed* may be ridden like a normal horse and may be used to carry equipment. The *tree steed* can carry up to 600 pounds of riders and gear before breaking. If the *tree steed* breaks under the weight of the riders or gear, the enchantment instantly ends and the *tree steed* again becomes a normal (although broken) log or plank.

The *tree steed* obeys all of the caster's verbal commands to move, slow, speed up, stop, and turn. It has a movement rate of 12 on land. It can move in the water (Sw 6), floating on the surface and paddling with its legs. The *tree steed* must remain within 10 yards of the caster in order to move; if the distance between the *tree steed* and the caster exceeds 10 yards, the *tree steed* stops until the caster is again within range.

The *tree steed* will not fight for the caster and is incapable of any action other than movement. The *tree steed* does not become fatigued and does not eat. It has all the vulnerabilities of normal wood, including fire, and can be damaged by both magical and physical attacks. It has AC 8 and 20 hit points.

The material components are a log or plank of suitable size and a horseshoe.

Uplift (Alteration)

Sphere: All
Range: 0
Components: V, M
Duration: 1 turn
Casting Time: 12 hours
Area of Effect: One priest
Saving Throw: None

Uplift bestows increased spellcasting ability on one priest, including additional spells per level and use of spells beyond the caster's normal level. This cooperative spell requires two priests who must spend the day casting this spell. During the casting, the priests must decide which additional spells (of all levels) are desired. Upon completion of the casting, the priests touch palms, and the priest of higher level receives a charge of magical energy. This charge temporarily boosts the level of the priest for spellcasting purposes. The amount of increase is one level per five levels of the lower level caster (fractions rounded up). If both priests are of equal level, the casters must decide who benefits from the spell.

The spell grants the priest the spellcasting ability of the new level. It does not improve hit points, attack rolls, or other abilities. If the increase allows more spells per level, the additional spells are instantly placed in the character's memory. A priest is also enabled to cast spells normally beyond his level. Range, duration, area of effect, and other variables are all based on the character's temporary level.

The increased effect lasts only 1 turn. At the end of the turn, all additional spells are lost and the character reverts to his normal level.

As an example, consider a party with a fallen comrade. The two priests in the party are 7th and 8th level, both unable to cast *raise dead*. After a night's rest, each priest adds *uplift* to his memorized spells. After casting the spell, the 8th-level priest suddenly gains the casting abilities of a 10th-level priest, including the ability to cast *raise dead*. At the end of one turn, the priest's abilities revert to 8th-level.

Casting this spell is an arduous task, causing a severe drain on the priests. When the spell expires, the uplifted character suffers 2d6 points of damage from mental exhaustion. This damage cannot be healed by any means until the character has had at least eight hours of rest.

The material components are the priests' holy symbols and an offering worth at least 500 gp from each priest.

Weather Stasis (Abjuration)

Sphere: Wards, Weather
Range: 30 yards
Components: V, S, M
Duration: 1 hour/level
Casting Time: 1 turn
Area of Effect: 10-foot cube/level
Saving Throw: None

Weather stasis maintains the weather conditions prevalent in the area of effect when the spell is cast. The spell affects a cube whose sides equal the caster's level times 10 feet (a 10th-level caster could affect a 100' × 100' × 100' cube).

An area protected by *weather stasis* is unaffected by temperature variations in the surrounding environment. The spell also acts as a shield against rain, snow, and hail, which cannot enter the protected area. If conditions of precipitation existed in the area of effect when the spell was cast, the identical weather will continue for the duration of the spell.

For example, *weather stasis* is cast in an area where the temperature is 75° F. and no precipitation is falling. Half an hour later, the temperature drops to 60 degrees and rain begins to fall. The protected area remains dry and the temperature stays at 75 degrees. If the spell had been cast while rain was falling in the area of effect, rain would continue to fall for the duration of the spell, even after it stopped raining in the surrounding area.

All physical objects other than rain, snow, and hail can pass into the protected area. All creatures and characters can move freely into and out of the area. The spell does not prevent water-based spells or water-based creatures (such as water elementals) from operating in the area.

The spell protects against both natural and magically generated weather. Night and day pass normally in the protected area, although temperature variations associated with night and day do not occur.

The material components are the priest's holy symbol and a drop of rain.

Fifth-Level Spells

Age Object (Alteration)
Reversible

Sphere: Time
Range: 10 yards
Components: V, S, M
Duration: Permanent
Casting Time: 1 round
Area of Effect: 1 cubic foot/level
Saving Throw: None

With this spell, the caster can cause an amount of nonliving, nonmagical matter to age dramatically. Matter can be aged up to 20 years per level of the caster. The following table gives typical results of 100 years of aging for various objects, arranged in order of descending severity:

Object	Result of Aging
diamond	none
silver	becomes tarnished
masonry	cracks and weakens
iron	rusts and corrodes
parchment	cracks, turns brittle
wood	rots, crumbles, turns to sawdust

The caster controls the extent of the aging; thus, he could age a book so its pages become yellowed and brittle but stop short of causing the book to crumble to dust. As a guideline, each additional 100 years of aging causes an increasingly severe reaction. Thus, after 200 years, parchment might become little more than powder, while iron might begin to flake away at a touch.

Many items (especially gems) show little reaction to age. The DM must adjudicate all effects.

The material components are a flask of seawater and a piece of coal.

The reverse of this spell, *youthful object*, returns an object ravaged by the effects of time to its original condition; thus, rusty iron becomes strong and shiny, crumbled masonry becomes firm, and rotten wood becomes solid. The age of matter can be reduced by 20 years per level of the caster.

The material components for *youthful object* are a piece of eggshell and a hair from the head of a human or humanoid infant.

Barrier of Retention (Abjuration)

Sphere: Wards
Range: Special
Components: V, S, M
Duration: 1 turn/level
Casting Time: 1 turn
Area of Effect: 10'-cube/level
Saving Throw: Neg.

This spell creates a one-way invisible force field around the area of effect. The spell creates one 10' × 10' × 10' cube for every level of the caster. These can be arranged into any rectangular shape the caster desires.

Intruders entering the protected area suffer no ill effects, but the *barrier of retention* prevents them from leaving. The spell affects all creatures who fail a saving throw vs. spell. The caster can pass in and out of the barrier freely.

Intruders trapped by the *barrier of retention* can cast spells out of the barrier and can use spells such as *teleport* to escape the protected area. Objects cannot be hurled out of the barrier but can be carried out by an escaping creature. *Dispel magic* and similar spells negate the *barrier*.

The material component is a small cage made of silver wire. The caster must walk around the perimeter of the area of effect when casting.

Blessed Abundance (Conjuration)

Sphere: Creation
Range: Touch
Components: V, S, M
Duration: Permanent
Casting Time: 1 round
Area of Effect: 1 cubic foot/level
Saving Throw: None

This spell allows a priest to duplicate a specified amount of animal or vegetable matter. Magical items and minerals (including rocks, metals, and gemstones) cannot be duplicated. Although organic materials (such as food or living plants) can be duplicated, living creatures cannot be copied by this spell.

The caster can create 1 cubic foot of material per his experience level. The material to be duplicated must be equal to or less than 1 cubic foot in size or volume. For example, a 9th-level priest can create up to 9 cubic feet of animal or vegetable matter. Using a loaf of bread 1 cubic foot in size, he can produce nine such loaves; using a bucket of apples totaling 1 cubic foot in volume, he can create nine such buckets.

The material component is the priest's holy symbol.

Champion's Strength (Alteration)

Sphere: Law
Range: 0
Components: V, S, M
Duration: Special
Casting Time: 2
Area of Effect: Special
Saving Throw: None

Champion's strength bestows one member of a group with attack and damage bonuses from the rest of the group. The recipient of the spell can then fight as the group's champion.

The spell draws bonuses from one person for every two levels of the priest. All characters involved must be within a 30'-radius of the priest. At the time of casting, the priest designates the recipient of the spell and the contributors. All characters who contribute to the spell must do so willingly.

When the spell is completed, the designated character (the group's champion) gains any non-magical bonuses to THAC0 and damage possessed by the characters who contributed to the spell. Characters without bonuses or with combat penalties could conceivably be included in the spell; such characters count against the maximum number of creatures that can be affected. Penalties are likewise applied to the champion; contributors to this spell must be chosen carefully.

The bonuses gained through this spell are added to the character's own bonuses (if any). The champion channels the energy of others through himself, improving his fighting ability.

The champion must be in the line of sight and within 30 feet of the characters aiding him. Characters who contribute their bonuses must concentrate on the champion for the duration of the spell. If this concentration is broken (by moving more than 10 feet per round, fighting, being struck, or losing sight of the champion), that character's contribution is immediately lost.

The spell expires when the last character contributing power to the champion ceases concentration.

A champion may benefit from only one *champion's strength* spell at one time. Contributors can aid only one champion at one time.

The material component is a chain of five gold links worth at least 1,000 gp.

Chaotic Commands (Enchantment/Charm)

Sphere: Chaos
Range: Touch
Components: V, S, M
Duration: 1 turn/level
Casting Time: 3
Area of Effect: One creature
Saving Throw: Special

Chaotic commands renders a creature immune to magical commands. *Taunt, forget, suggestion, domination, geas, demand, succor, command, enthrall, quest, exaction,* and other spells that place a direct verbal command upon a single individual automatically fail.

In addition, anyone casting one of these spells on a creature protected by *chaotic commands* must save vs. spell. Failure means that the caster must obey his own magic; the spell's effect has backfired on the caster.

The material component is a piece of eelskin.

Clear Path (Alteration)
Reversible

Sphere: Travelers
Range: 0
Components: V, S, M
Duration: 1 hour/level
Casting Time: 5
Area of Effect: Special
Saving Throw: None

This spell clears away weeds, stones, and other debris in a 10-foot-wide path extending 10 feet in front of the caster. The caster can create a continuous path for the duration of the spell, clearing a 10-foot-square ahead of him as long as he continues to move forward. The spell affects jungles, forests, rocky ground, and snow.

The result of the cleared path is that movement costs are reduced by half. This is reflected in a reduction of the penalty against movement in rough terrain. (See Table 74 of the *Dungeon Master Guide* for terrain costs for movement.) For example, if *clear path* is used in heavy jungle, the movement cost is reduced from 8 to 4. In no case can *clear path* reduce movement cost below 1.

Clear path has no effect on rivers, lakes, or other bodies of water, nor does it affect quicksand, lava, or similar natural obstacles. It also has no effect on magically-created terrain or manmade barricades.

A priest using the *clear path* spell can be tracked easily. Tracking proficiency is not required.

The material components are a knife blade and a straw from a broom.

The reverse, *clutter path,* causes weeds, small stones, and similar debris to litter a 10-foot path extending 10 feet behind the caster. This hides a trail, making tracking more difficult. The caster can create a continuous path for the duration of the spell. The chance to successfully track on a cluttered path is reduced by 50%.

The material components are a handful of pebbles and a handful of weeds.

Cloud of Purification (Evocation)

Sphere: Elemental Air, Water
Range: 30 yards
Components: V, S
Duration: 1 round/level
Casting Time: 5
Area of Effect: 20-foot cube
Saving Throw: None

This spell creates a billowy cloud of magical vapors that moves in the direction of the prevailing wind at a rate of 20 feet per round. A strong wind (greater than 15 miles per hour) breaks it up in 4 rounds, and a greater wind (25 MPH or more) prevents the use of the spell. Thick vegetation disperses the cloud in 2 rounds.

The *cloud of purification* transmutes organic filth, garbage, and vermin (mice, rats, rot grubs, and so on) into an equal quantity of pure water. For example, a nest of rot grubs caught in the cloud would "melt," becoming small puddles of clean water. If the spell is cast over a body of water, the cloud merges with a portion of the water equal to its own size, transmuting any filth, microbes, small fish, or other "impurities" into clean water.

The cloud's vapors are heavier than air, so they sink to the lowest level of the land (even down holes in the ground). Thus, this spell is perfect for cleansing a sewer or well.

This spell in no way affects magical creatures or creatures larger than a normal rat.

Consequence (Divination)

Sphere: Numbers, Divination
Range: 0
Components: V, S, M
Duration: Instantaneous
Casting Time: 1 round
Area of Effect: Special
Saving Throw: None

This spell allows the priest to determine how one recent event fits into the "grand scheme." By casting this spell, the priest can determine whether the sequence or situation that gave rise to the specific event is complete or whether it is ongoing; whether it was a significant or insignificant event in the larger picture; or whether it will continue to have repercussions for the participants.

Using his knowledge of circumstances, the DM communicates these facts to the caster's player. This "arcane message" is normally straightforward and easy to understand, but in the case of highly complex circumstances, the message might be cryptic. In any case, the message will always be truthful.

As an example, consider a priest and his party who are on a holy quest to retrieve an item of power. On the way to the location of this item, the party is ambushed by evil creatures from the Inner Planes but manages to defeat them. Concerned that these creatures might be outlying guards protecting the item of interest, the priest casts *consequence*, hoping for guidance. The DM knows that these creatures have nothing to do with the quest; the encounter was coincidental. However, the surviving monsters will soon be returning with reinforcements to avenge their dead. Therefore, the DM tells the priest's player, "To your goals these have no place, but still they can cause more woe."

Casting this spell "taints" subsequent castings of the same spell within a 24-hour span. A second attempt within this period always results in the same message as the first, regardless of the true situation. If a second priest casts the spell within 24 hours of another casting, he receives an accurate reading.

The material component is three special coins or dice made of platinum (total value of at least 1,000 gp), which the priest tosses in his hand while concentrating on the spell. The coins or dice are not consumed in the casting.

Disguise (Illusion/Phantasm)

Sphere: War
Range: 200 yards
Components: V, S, M
Duration: 1 turn/3 levels
Casting Time: 2 turns
Area of Effect: One unit up to 300 individuals
Saving Throw: None

This spell changes the appearance of a single unit so it resembles another unit. The *disguise* can cause the affected creatures to appear to be of another class, nationality, rank, race, alignment, or military affiliation (i.e., a unit from one army may appear wearing the armor and carrying the colors of another army). *Disguise* cannot change the size category of the unit's members. Thus, a unit of humans may appear to be a unit of elves, but may not appear as a unit of giants or halflings. The spell does not affect the size of the overall unit; a unit of 50 creatures will still appear to be a unit of 50 creatures.

The disguised unit may appear to be carrying any melee or personal missile weapons (e.g., axes, long swords, crossbows, etc.), and may appear to be wearing any type of armor. In combat, however, the unit attacks and defends with its real weapons and armor regardless of the gear they may appear to be carrying.

Disguise is most effective at long range. If another unit moves within 20 yards of a disguised unit, it automatically sees through the illusion.

The caster automatically sees through the illusion. Members of the subject unit see no change in their appearance. *True seeing* or similar magic is required for other individuals to see through the *disguise* (unless they move within 20 yards of the unit).

The material components are a fine silk veil and a length of woven platinum wire. The wire is consumed during the casting.

Easy March (Invocation)

Sphere: Travelers
Range: 50 feet
Components: V, S, M
Duration: 1 day/level
Casting Time: 1 turn
Area of Effect: One creature/level
Saving Throw: None

This spell enables a number of creatures equal to the caster's level to force march for a number of days equal to the caster's level. Creatures affected by *easy march* can travel $2^{1}/_{2}$ times their normal movement rate without any risk of fatigue; thus, they are not required to make a Constitution check at the end of the day.

All creatures affected by this spell suffer a -1 penalty to their attack rolls for the duration of the spell; this modifier is not cumulative (that is, a party experiencing its second day of *easy march* suffers only a -1 penalty). The modifier cannot be negated by resting.

Easy march has no effect on modifiers to movement due to terrain, fatigue, weather, or other normal factors. (Refer to Chapter 14 of the *Player's Handbook* for more about force marching.)

The material component is a piece of shoe leather.

Elemental Forbiddance (Abjuration)

Sphere: Wards, Elemental—Air, Earth, Fire, Water
Range: Special
Components: V, S, M
Duration: 1 turn/level
Casting Time: 1 turn
Area of Effect: 5'-cube/level
Saving Throw: None

This spell prevents the entry of all elementals into the area of effect. Further, elementals outside the area of effect cannot make physical attacks against those inside. Spells and missile attacks can be cast into the area by elementals.

The spell affects a cube whose sides equal the caster's level times 5 feet (a 12th-level priest could affect an area equal to a 60' × 60' × 60' cube).

Elemental forbiddance has no effect on elementals that are within the area of effect when the spell is cast. If such elementals leave the area of effect, they cannot reenter.

The material components are the priest's holy symbol and four glass beads, each of a different color (green, blue, red, and yellow). The priest must pace out the perimeter of the warded area at the time of casting.

Extradimensional Manipulation

(Alteration)

Sphere: Numbers
Range: 10 yards
Components: V, S, M
Duration: 2d12 rounds + 4 rounds/level
Casting Time: 5
Area of Effect: One extradimensional space up to 20 feet × 20 feet
Saving Throw: Special

This spell allows the priest to alter the characteristics of certain extradimensional spaces such as those created by *rope trick* and similar spells or those contained in items like *bags of holding* or *portable holes*.

Extradimensional manipulation can increase or reduce the size of a single extradimensional space. The amount of increase or decrease depends on the level of the caster:

Level	Multiplier
Up to 10	× 2
11 to 16	× 3
17 or above	× 4

This means that a 10th-level priest can double the capacity of a *bag of holding* or decrease it to half its normal size. A 15th-level priest can triple the capacity or reduce it to one-third capacity.

If the size and capacity of an extradimensional space is decreased, any contents of the space that exceed the current capacity are expelled (determined randomly). These contents are expelled from the space in the same way they originally entered it, if that path is still open. If the path is closed, as it would be if a *bag of holding* were tied shut or a *portable hole* were folded up, the "extra" contents are expelled into the Astral plane. Any items in an enlarged space when the spell duration expires suffer the same fate.

Placing an extradimensional space inside another such space, such as placing a *bag of holding* inside a *portable hole* (see the *DUNGEON MASTER Guide*), is a dangerous undertaking. *Extradimensional manipulation* may be cast for the purpose of removing this danger. When used in this manner, the size of the space cannot be affected. However, while this version is in effect, the affected extradimensional space can be placed within another such space (or another extradimensional space may be placed within the affected space) with no adverse consequences. If one space is within the other when the spell expires, the usual consequences ensue immediately.

If the space to be affected is being maintained by a spellcaster, as in the case of a *rope trick*, that spellcaster receives a saving throw to resist the *manipulation*. If the space is created by a magical item, however, no saving throw is allowed.

The material component is a strip of gold tissue worth at least 5 gp that is twisted into a Moebius strip. The strip is consumed in the casting.

Extradimensional Pocket (Alteration)

Sphere: Numbers
Range: Touch
Components: V, S, M
Duration: 1d12 rounds + 2 turns/level
Casting Time: 1 round
Area of Effect: Special
Saving Throw: None

This spell allows the priest to create a single extradimensional space or pocket like the one inside a *bag of holding*. The spell must be cast on a container such as a sack, bag, or backpack. Once under the influence of the spell, the container opens into a nondimensional space and is much larger inside than its outside dimensions. The container always weighs a fixed amount, regardless of what is put inside. This weight and the capacity of the extradimensional space depend on the level of the caster:

Level	Apparent Weight	Weight Cap.	Volume Cap.
9-13	15 lbs	250 lbs	30 cu.ft.
14-16	25 lbs	500 lbs	70 cu.ft.
17-19	35 lbs	750 lbs	100 cu.ft.
20 +	60 lbs	1,000 lbs	150 cu.ft.

If the container is overloaded or if it is pierced by a sharp object, the bag immediately ruptures and the contents are lost into the Astral plane. Any items within the bag when the spell duration ends are also lost in the Astral plane.

The material components, in addition to the container, are 200 gp worth of powdered diamond and a sheet of platinum worth 500 gp. The platinum sheet must be inscribed with a drawing of a Klein bottle (a paradoxical figure with only one surface—the three-dimensional analogue of the Moebius strip). The diamond dust is consumed during the casting—the platinum sheet is not.

Grounding (Abjuration)

Sphere: Wards
Range: 30 yards
Components: V, S, M
Duration: 1 turn/level
Casting Time: 1 turn
Area of Effect: 10-yard square/priest
Saving Throw: None

Grounding offers protection against normal and magical electrical attacks within the area of effect. The protected area and creatures within it suffer no damage from normal electrical attacks (such as those caused by lightning bolts in a thunderstorm and nonmagical creatures such as electric eels). Magical electrical attacks (including lightning bolt breath weapons) cause only 50% of their normal damage. Additionally, creatures within the area of effect receive a +2 bonus to saving throws made against electrical attacks, regardless of whether the attacks originate inside or outside the warded area.

The material components are the priest's holy symbol and a coil of silver wire.

Illusory Artillery (Enchantment/Charm)

Sphere: War
Range: 300 yards
Components: V, S, M
Duration: Instantaneous
Casting Time: 1 turn
Area of Effect: 30 yard × 30 yard square
Saving Throw: None

This spell creates a vivid illusion of incoming artillery fire (ballista bolts, catapult stones, etc.) at a target indicated by the caster. The illusion is complete, comprising both audial and visual elements. It is impossible for victims to determine where the missiles were fired from; creatures under attack notice the missiles only when they are about to strike.

The missiles never actually strike—they vanish inches above the victims' heads and do no damage. The illusion is so terrifying, however, that victims must immediately make a morale check. The first time a group or unit is the target of this spell, this morale check is made with no modifier. The second and subsequent times that the same unit is attacked with this spell, the unit receives a +1 bonus to its morale score (for checks against this effect only) *unless* the unit has been the target of *real* artillery fire in the interim. In this case, the bonus does not apply.

The material component is a small, empty cylinder made of brass.

Impeding Permission (Enchantment/Charm)

Sphere: Law
Range: 150 yards
Components: V, S
Duration: 1 turn/level
Casting Time: 3
Area of Effect: One creature
Saving Throw: Neg.

This spell may be cast only on creatures with Intelligence of 2 or greater and the ability to communicate with the caster. The spell interferes with the victim's ability to make decisions. It prevents the victim from performing any action without first gaining the permission of the caster or a character designated by the caster. The victim will heed only the person designated by the caster.

Before the victim undertakes any action, he must gain permission. He will not follow through with an action until he gains permission. If permission is denied, the victim cannot act until he thinks of an alternate action and gains permission for that action.

Every round, the victim must decide his action for that round; at the victim's initiative, he must ask permission to perform his action. If permission is denied, the victim can take no other action that round.

The only actions exempt from the need for permission are involuntary actions such as breathing.

Asking and gaining permission takes only a short amount of time in most cases. A simple request, such as asking for permission to swing a sword in the middle of combat, can be accomplished quickly. Complicated requests, such as getting permission to act on a complicated plan, will naturally take more time. The DM may consider adding a modifier to the victim's initiative roll in such cases.

Meld (Enchantment)

Sphere: Charm
Range: 10 yards
Components: V, S, M
Duration: 12 hours
Casting Time: 1 turn
Area of Effect: One priest
Saving Throw: Special

This cooperative spell requires only one priest to cast it, but can be cast only on another priest of the same faith. The recipient of the spell must voluntarily surrender himself to the spell. The recipient becomes a host for the caster. While the recipient does not lose his own persona or ability to act, the host can be dominated by the caster at any time. For the most part, this domination is complete.

For the duration of the spell, the caster is essentially detached from his own body. He can neither move nor act on his own. His mind is connected to the host's. He sees, hears, smells, tastes, and otherwise senses everything the host does. He can telepathically communicate with the host. Once the spell is completed, there is no limit to the range over which it can function. However, both the caster and host must remain on the same plane. Since the spell relies on telepathic communication, thin lead sheeting will effectively block the connection.

When desired, the caster can dominate the host. When this happens, the host's own mind is pushed to the background and the caster's personality dominates. The host's personality, memories, proficiencies, and spells are temporarily replaced by those of the caster. While occupying the host, the caster can cast any spell he himself has memorized, provided that the necessary components are on hand. These spells function exactly as if the priest had cast them from his own body.

The caster can return control to the host at any time, restoring the character's abilities and personality without harm.

The spell is not without limitations and risks. The domination must be voluntary. If the host resists the casting of the spell, it automatically fails. Once the spell is in effect, the host can attempt to resist the domination. He is then allowed a saving throw. If successful, the spell immediately ends.

Whenever the host suffers damage, the caster must make a saving throw vs. death to maintain the spell. If the save is failed, a wave of pain is transmitted to the priest, causing 1d6 points of damage and canceling the spell. If the host should die, the caster must make a system shock roll with the risk of suffering instant death.

The material component is a chalice worth no less than 1,000 gp. This chalice must be given as a gift to the host (who cannot return it to the donor for any reason).

Memory Wrack
(Alteration, Enchantment/Charm)

Sphere: Thought
Range: 10 yards
Components: V, S, M
Duration: 2 rounds/level
Casting Time: 1 round
Area of Effect: One creature
Saving Throw: Neg.

This nasty spell "disconnects" the subject's short-term and long-term memory. While the spell is in effect, the subject is incapable of storing information in long-term memory. Every moment is virtually an independent event for the subject; he or she can remember recent events, thoughts, and sensations for no more than a few seconds (the amount of time they remain in short-term memory).

Memories of events that happened before the onset of the spell are not affected at all; these are safely stored in long-term memory. This means that the subject can cast any spells memorized before the *memory wrack* took effect, but he is likely to have difficulty casting the spell as described below.

The subject of this spell has a limited ability to

act. He is restricted to one action at a time and must concentrate mightily to keep the situation and any planned actions in short-term memory. As long as the subject is able to maintain concentration, he may act normally within these limits.

If the subject is distracted (he is struck in combat, affected by a spell, startled, surprised, or a similar event occurs), he forgets everything that occurred from the onset of the spell to the moment of distraction. The subject must re-evaluate the situation as if it had just come to pass.

Consider the following example. The subject of the spell is a soldier assigned to guard the entrance to a building. The priest arrives and casts *memory wrack* on the guard. The guard has no problem remembering his orders, since he received them before the onset of the spell. He also remembers the arrival of the priest. The priest now tries to convince the guard that he is authorized to enter the building. The guard refuses him entry. The priest now picks up a rock and throws it at the guard, striking him and distracting him. The guard forgets everything that happened between the onset of the spell and the moment the rock struck. He forgets that the priest has already tried to con him and that he threw a rock at him. He must reevaluate the situation as though the priest had just arrived. The priest is free to make another attempt at entering the building.

When the spell expires, the subject remembers nothing that happened while the spell was in effect, possibly leading to amusing consequences ("By the gods, how did I get here?").

The material component is a ruby of at least 200 gp value, which is crushed during the casting.

Mindshatter (Enchantment/Charm)

Sphere: Thought
Range: 3 yards/level
Components: V, S, M
Duration: Special
Casting Time: 1 round
Area of Effect: One creature
Saving Throw: Neg.

This spell allows the priest to create one specific form of insanity in the subject. Five forms of insanity are possible through this spell.

Schizophrenia: This form of insanity is characterized by personality loss. The subject has no personality of his own, so he selects a role model and makes every possible attempt to behave like that character. The chosen role model will be as different from the subject as possible. (Thus, an insane wizard might begin to follow the habits of a warrior.) Obviously, a warrior who believes himself to be a wizard will be unable to cast spells (he might *think* that he's casting spells, or he might construct a sophisticated series of excuses explaining why he's "not in the mood for magic" at the moment). A character who emulates a member of another class does not gain any of the skills of that class and makes all attacks and saving throws as appropriate to his true class. Certain consequences might arise if the character's emulation causes him to break restrictions of his class. For example, a priest emulating a warrior might break his deity's prohibition against edged weapons, or a paladin might emulate a Neutral Evil thief. Both will suffer the appropriate consequences as if they had been compelled to violate their beliefs while *charmed.* Such characters will certainly have to atone for their actions once they return to normal.

Dementia praecox: The subject is totally uninterested in any undertaking. Nothing seems worthwhile, and the individual is lethargic and filled with tremendous feelings of boredom and dissatisfaction. No matter how important the situation, it is 50% likely that the subject will ignore it as meaningless.

Delusional insanity: The subject is convinced that he is a famous figure: a monarch, demi-god, or similar personage. Characters who fail to recognize the subject with the honor he deserves incur great hostility or disbelief. The subject acts appropriately to a station that he does not hold. He directs orders at real and imaginary creatures and draws upon resources that do not exist.

Paranoia: The subject is convinced that "they" (whoever *they* are) are spying on him and plotting against him. Everyone around the subject, even friends and allies, is part of the plot. If any other character acts in a way that the subject can interpret as reinforcing this delusion, the subject has a 20% chance of reacting with violence.

Hallucinatory insanity: The subject sees, hears, and otherwise senses things that do not exist. The more stressful the situation is to the subject, the more likely he will hallucinate. Although most hallucinations are external to the subject (that is, he perceives creatures, objects, and conditions that do not exist), there is a 10% chance that any hallucination will involve the subject's self-perception. For example, the subject might suddenly believe and act as if he had sprouted wings, grown to giant size, etc.

When this spell is cast by a priest of 13th level or lower, the DM chooses or randomly selects one of these forms of insanity (and should feel free to invent other interesting symptoms). If the priest is 14th level or higher, he can personally select the form of insanity to afflict the subject.

While under the effect of this spell, the subject can cast spells and use innate powers; the use of these abilities will be in accordance with the symptoms of the insanity, however. Player characters affected by this spell should be encouraged to role-play the appropriate effects to the limit.

The duration of this spell depends on the sum of the subject's Intelligence and Wisdom scores. A saving throw is allowed on a periodic basis depending on this total. The spell is broken if a successful saving throw is rolled. Refer to the table that follows.

Int + Wis	Time Between Checks
8 or less	1 month
9 to 18	3 weeks
19 to 24	2 weeks
25 to 30	1 week
31 to 35	3 days
36 or more	1 day

The effects of this spell can be removed by a *limited wish*, *wish* (or equally powerful magic), or by a *heal* spell cast for this specific purpose.

The material component is a small bust of a human head, about 3″ in height, made from fine, delicate china. The priest shatters this bust during the casting.

Repeat Action (Enchantment/Charm)

Sphere: Time
Range: 30 yards
Components: V, S
Duration: Special
Casting Time: 5
Area of Effect: One creature
Saving Throw: Neg.

This spell compels its victim to repeat the action of the previous round. The result of the repetition is always identical to the original result.

For example, if a character fired an arrow and inflicted 4 points of damage, a *repeat action* spell will cause him to fire a second arrow that will also inflict 4 points of damage. As long as the victim of the first arrow is within range, the subject affected by *repeat action* will adjust his aim and fire the second arrow at him. If the victim of the arrow moves out of range, the subject will fire his second arrow in the direction of the recipient. If the recipient is out of sight, the subject will fire in the direction of the recipient's original location.

The subject of a *repeat action* spell must be capable of performing the indicated action a second time. If a character has no arrows in his quiver, he cannot fire an arrow. If a wizard were ordered to repeat a spell, he would attempt the spell only if he had the spell memorized and had sufficient material components. If a subject discovered a gem during a given round, *repeat action* will only compel him to hunt again; he will not recover another gem unless a second gem is actually present.

An unwilling subject is allowed a saving throw vs. spell to resist the effects of *repeat action*.

The material components are two identical glass spheres, each an inch or less in diameter.

Shrieking Walls (Enchantment)

Sphere: Wards
Range: Touch
Components: V, S, M
Duration: 1 day/level
Casting Time: 1 turn
Area of Effect: 20′-cube
Saving Throw: None

This spell enchants any single room no larger than the area of effect. When any creature larger than a normal rat (larger than one-half cubic foot or weighing more than three pounds) enters the room, shrill shrieks begin to emanate from the walls. The shrieks persist for 2-5 (1d4 + 1) rounds. The walls do not undergo any physical change.

The shrieks can be heard only by creatures inside the room. Creatures hearing the shrieks experience no ill effects on the first round, allowing them time to leave the room or cover their ears. *Silence, 15′ radius* protects against the effects.

Creatures who remain in the room during the second or subsequent rounds of the shrieks who have not protected their hearing are penalized as follows:

• Creatures whose levels or Hit Dice are greater than the level of the caster are stunned for 2-8 (2d4) rounds.

• Creatures whose levels or Hit Dice are less than or equal to the level of the caster become deaf for 1-4 hours, suffering a −1 penalty to surprise; deafened spellcasters have a 20% chance of miscasting any spell with a verbal component.

The material components are a small golden bell and a bee's wing.

Thoughtwave (Divination)

Sphere: Divination
Range: 0
Components: V, S
Duration: Instantaneous
Casting Time: 1
Area of Effect: Special
Saving Throw: Special

This cooperative spell can be cast by either a single priest or a group of priests. *Thoughtwave* allows the priest to send a short but powerful message to one or more specific individuals, informing them of his situation and general location. The spell instantly generates a powerful mental impulse indicative of the caster's general mental state—anger, fear, pain, despair, etc.

The caster can designate as many as ten persons to receive this message, provided they can all be specifically named or grouped in a general category. Thus, the caster could designate a group of characters by name or could target "fellow priests," "superiors," "adventuring companions," "knights of Lord Harcourt," or "villagers of Dopp." If more than ten individuals are in the group, those closest to the source will receive the impulse.

There is no range limitation to the spell, although it cannot be projected outside the plane occupied by the caster.

Creatures receiving the impulse automatically know who sent it (even if they have never met the priest before) and gain a clear indication of the mood and situation of the caster. Recipients also intuitively know the general source of the spell, although they are unable to pinpoint rooms, dungeon levels, or landmarks. For example, a fighter could suddenly be struck by an image of Father Rastibon, who is injured and in great pain somewhere along the forest road. A priest might suddenly sense that his patriarch is being tortured in the dungeons of Castle Varrack.

The spell can also be cast by more than one priest, allowing them to either contact greater numbers of individuals or increase the intensity of the message. If greater numbers are desired, ten characters are contacted per priest involved in the casting.

Increasing the intensity of the message makes it more compelling. Doubling the intensity (requiring at least three priests) causes the message to act as a *suggestion*. In this case, the effect is limited to a single target. Tripling the intensity (requiring at least five priests) gives the spell the force of a *quest*. This effect is also limited to a single target. In both cases, the target is allowed a saving throw to avoid the effect of the *suggestion* or *quest*.

Time Pool (Divination)

Sphere: Time
Range: Touch
Components: V, S, M
Duration: 1 round/level
Casting Time: 1 round
Area of Effect: Special
Saving Throw: None

This spell allows the caster to cause a mirror, a pool of water, or any other reflective surface to reveal a specific event from the past. The image provides a perfectly clear picture with normal sounds, as if the caster were present at the scene. The image continues for the duration of the spell.

Time pool will not reveal images from other planes of existence.

The spell's success is not automatic. The caster must know the general nature of the event he wishes to view (i.e., "Show me the murder of King Thamak"). The caster's base chance of viewing the desired scene is 50%, modified as follows, to a maximum of 90%:

- Add 5% for each point of the caster's Wisdom above 15.
- Add 20% if the caster has successfully used *time pool* to observe the same event before.

Only one of the following may apply:
- Add 20% if the event is one in which the caster participated.
- Add 10% if the caster is well informed about the event.
- Add 5% if the caster is slightly informed about the event.

The caster cannot communicate or otherwise interact with the image. Spells cannot be cast into the *time pool*.

The material components are a suitable reflective surface and a pinch of powdered quartz.

Unceasing Vigilance of the Holy Sentinel (Alteration)

Sphere: Guardian
Range: 0
Components: V, S, M
Duration: 1 hour/level
Casting Time: 1 turn
Area of Effect: 5-foot-radius sphere
Saving Throw: None

This spell enhances a priest's ability to guard a person, place, or object. The spell's effect must be centered on a specific area, for it creates an invisible spherical boundary up to 10 feet in diameter. The effect is not mobile; it cannot move with a living creature.

While within the area of effect of this spell, the priest (and only the priest) gains several special abilities:

- His sense of sight is magically enhanced. He can see through normal darkness and can see invisible creatures and objects. He cannot see through solid objects, however, and the range of his magical sight is limited to 60 feet.
- The priest has no need for food, water, or rest. He does not feel fatigue and regenerates 1 hit point per hour spent within the circle. However, he does not actually rest and therefore cannot regain spells until he sleeps.
- He is totally immune to the effects of magical and natural fear, as well as *sleep* and *charm* spells.

If the priest leaves the circle, the spell is broken. When the spell ends, the priest must rest for 1 turn per hour (or portion thereof) spent in the circle. If the priest is forced into action (by being attacked, for example), he can move at only half his normal movement rate, has an Armor Class penalty of −2, an attack penalty of −2, and loses all Dexterity combat bonuses.

To cast this spell, the priest must trace a circle of sigils and runes 10 feet in diameter using a special ink containing the powder of a crushed sapphire (at least 1,000 gp value) and a drop of holy water. This procedure takes 1 turn to complete.

Undead Ward (Abjuration, Necromancy)

Sphere: Wards
Range: Special
Components: V, S, M
Duration: 1 turn/level
Casting Time: 2 turns
Area of Effect: 5-foot cube/level
Saving Throw: None

This spell prevents most types of undead creatures from entering the area of effect (a cube whose sides equal the caster's level times 5 feet—a 15th-level caster could affect a cube whose sides equal 75 feet).

When an undead creature attempts to enter the protected area, the creature is affected by the ward as if it were being turned by a priest two levels lower than the caster. The casting priest need not have the ability to turn undead himself. Thus, an *undead ward* created by a 10th-level priest would turn creatures as if by an 8th-level priest.

The results of the turning attempt are calculated normally. If a large number of undead assault the warded area, not all of them are turned by the spell, since the normal limitations apply. Undead who are unaffected by the turning attempt ignore the *undead ward* for its duration. Undead within the area of effect when the spell is cast are not affected. However, when such undead leave the area of effect, they are subject to the effects of the spell if they attempt to reenter.

The material component is the priest's holy symbol, which must be carried around the perimeter of the area to be warded.

Sixth-Level Spells

Age Creature (Alteration)
Reversible

Sphere: Time
Range: Touch
Components: V, S, M
Duration: Permanent
Casting Time: 1 round
Area of Effect: One creature
Saving Throw: Neg.

This spell ages the targeted creature one year per level of the caster. Unwilling subjects may attempt a saving throw to resist the spell. Subjects affected by *age creature* must make a successful system shock roll to survive the change.

Subjects cannot be aged beyond their natural life spans. If the priest's level indicates that a creature would be aged beyond this level, the creature is aged to one year short of his maximum age. The spell cannot cause a subject to die.

Human and humanoid characters affected by the spell experience changes in appearance associated with increased age, such as gray hair and wrinkles. More significantly, they suffer losses in Strength, Dexterity, and Constitution when they reach certain age levels. These are summarized in Table 12: Aging Effects in the *Player's Handbook.* The *Player's Handbook* also provides rules for determining a character's base age.

Nonmagical monsters can be affected by *age creature.* The DM determines a monster's current age and natural life span based on its description in the *MONSTROUS COMPENDIUM®* appendix or based on his own judgment. To determine the effects of aging on a monster, assume the following: a monster is middle-aged when it reaches half its natural life span; a monster reaches old age at two-thirds of its natural life span; a monster reaches venerable age in the last one-sixth of its years. A monster suffers the penalties which follow when it reaches these age levels. The penalties are *cumulative and permanent* (unless the affected monster becomes younger).

Age	Penalty
Middle Age	−1 to all saving throws
Old Age	−1 to all saving throws
	−1 to all attack rolls
Venerable	−1 to all saving throws
	−1 to all attack rolls

The material component is a pinch of powdered emerald.

The reverse of this spell, *restore youth,* permanently restores age that has been lost as a result of magic (such as an *age creature* spell). *Restore youth* reduces the age of the targeted creature by one year per level of the caster. The subject must make a successful system shock roll to survive the change. Subjects who become younger regain the lost ability scores described above. A subject cannot become younger than his actual age as a result of this spell.

The material component is a pinch of powdered ruby.

Crushing Walls (Enchantment)

Sphere: Wards
Range: Touch
Components: V, S, M
Duration: Permanent until activated
Casting Time: 1 turn
Area of Effect: Special
Saving Throw: None

This spell enables the caster to enchant a floor, ceiling, or single wall of a room to crush intruders. The enchanted surface can be no larger than a square whose sides equal the caster's level times 2 feet (a 13th-level priest could affect a 26′ × 26′ surface).

The spell activates 1d4 rounds after any creature other than the caster enters the room. The intruder must be larger than a normal rat (larger than one-half cubic foot or weighing more than three pounds). When activated, the enchanted surface moves toward the opposite surface at a rate of 3 feet per round. Unless the spell is canceled by the caster, the enchanted surface continues to move until one of the following events occurs:

• A creature with sufficient Strength (minimum score of 19) stops the enchanted surface from moving by succeeding a Strength check. Such a creature suffers no damage from the enchanted surface. If the creature prevents the enchanted surface from moving for three consecutive rounds, the wall returns to its original position and the spell is negated. If multiple creatures attempt to stop the wall, the highest strength score is used as a base score; one point is added to that score for every creature assisting. Thus, a creature with 16 Strength assisted by three creatures could attempt to stop the wall.

• A strong or heavy object made of stone, wood, or metal is placed in the path of the wall. If the item survives a saving throw vs. crushing blow, the object successfully braces the wall. If the object holds for three consecutive rounds, the surface returns to its original position and the spell is negated. The DM must use discretion in determining the types of objects that will brace the wall.

• *Dispel magic* or a similar spell or magical item is used to cancel the *crushing wall.*

Creatures can avoid being crushed by using a *potion of diminution, potion of gaseous form,* or other devices or spells that reduce size. The *crushing wall* almost never touches the opposite wall, usually being stopped by debris. A gap of two inches or more usually remains between the walls.

If the wall is not stopped, it causes crushing damage to everyone in the room. All creatures must make a saving throw vs. death. Those who fail are crushed to death. Those who save successfully suffer 5d10 points of damage. When the wall can move no farther, it returns to its original position and the spell is negated.

The material components are a 1-inch iron cube and a walnut shell.

Disbelief (Enchantment/Charm)

Sphere: Thought
Range: 0
Components: V, S
Duration: 1 round/level
Casting Time: 5
Area of Effect: Special
Saving Throw: Special

This spell allows the caster to temporarily convince himself that certain objects or as many as four creatures within the area of effect do not actually exist. While *disbelief* remains in effect, these objects or creatures cannot harm or hinder the caster. He can pass through them as if they did not exist and takes no damage from their attacks or actions. However, since these objects or creatures temporarily do not exist for the priest, he can take no action against them. If the creatures attack, the caster receives no Dexterity bonus to armor class (since this bonus represents dodging, and the priest is unable to dodge a creature that does not exist for him).

The caster can attempt to disbelieve as many as four creatures within 60 feet of his position at the time of casting. He disbelieves the same four creatures for the duration of the spell. Alternatively, the priest can disbelieve any or all inanimate objects of up to 20-cubic-yard volume (thus, he may

disbelieve a 12 foot by 15 foot area of 3-foot-thick wall). This volume must be centered on a point no more than 20 yards from the caster. These two options are mutually exclusive; the priest can disbelieve only creatures *or* objects, not a combination of both.

Disbelieving a creature includes all gear, equipment, or treasure carried or worn by that creature; it does not include other objects that come into contact with that creature, such as walls, doors, chairs, etc.

Disbelief is not automatic; it requires an extreme effort. To successfully disbelieve, the priest must make a saving throw vs. paralyzation. A *successful* save means the priest has disbelieved; an *unsuccessful* check means that the spell has failed and the priest has not convinced himself of the creatures' or objects' non-existence.

While this spell is in effect, the DM must record any damage suffered by the priest from disbelieved creatures. When the spell ends, the caster makes a saving throw vs. spell. If the saving throw is successful, the priest suffers only one-eighth of any damage inflicted by the creatures (round all fractions down); if the priest fails the saving throw, he suffers one-half of any damage inflicted (round fractions down).

Dragonbane (Abjuration)

Sphere: Wards
Range: 10 yards/level
Components: V, S, M
Duration: 1d4 rounds + 1 round/2 levels
Casting Time: 1 round
Area of Effect: 5'-cube/level
Saving Throw: Neg.

This spell prevents any dragon who fails its saving throw from entering the area of effect. The spell affects a cubic area whose sides equal the caster's level times 5 feet; thus, a 16th-level caster could affect a cube whose sides each equal 80 feet. The dragon can cast spells, blast breath weapon, or hurl missiles (if possible) into the area of effect.

Dragons within the area of effect when the spell is cast are not affected. If such dragons leave the area of effect, they must succeed a saving throw to reenter the area.

The material components are the priest's holy symbol and a dragon scale.

The spell's effectiveness can be greatly increased with the casting of a *focus* spell.

Gravity Variation (Alteration)

Sphere: War
Range: 10 yards/level
Components: V, S, M
Duration: 1 turn/3 levels
Casting Time: 2 turns
Area of Effect: 120-yard × 120-yard square
Saving Throw: None

This spell changes the characteristics of a square region of terrain. The area can be no more than 120 yards on a side. The priest can effectively turn a flat plain into a slope of any direction, or may flatten an existing slope. The spell does not allow the priest to alter the pull of gravity, however.

This spell lets the priest create or negate a height differential of as much as 20 feet (a 2″ slope in BATTLESYSTEM rules measurements) within the area of effect. This can have various consequences; the best way to discuss the effects is by example.

Example 1: Two units face each other on a flat plain. The priest can alter the slope of the terrain so that one unit is 2″ of elevation higher than the other. The unit that is upslope gains the combat benefits for higher ground, and the unit that is downslope must pay the movement cost for moving uphill if it wishes to approach the other unit.

Example 2: One unit is on flat terrain; another unit, 6″ away, is on a hill of 2″ elevation. Using this spell, the priest can effectively eliminate this difference in elevation (raising the low ground or lowering the high ground). All combat and movement involving these two units is then conducted as if there were no elevation difference (i.e., no movement penalty, no combat benefit for higher ground, etc.). Alternatively, the priest could *increase* the height differential by 2″. Combat and movement would now be conducted as if the total difference in elevation were 4″.

Example 3: A unit faces a hill of 3″ elevation. The priest casts *gravity variation*, decreasing the effective elevation of the hill to 1″. The unit pays a lower movement point cost to climb the hill. Alternatively, if the unit facing the hill were an enemy unit, the priest could increase the effective elevation to 5″.

The priest must specify the degree and direction of change at the moment of casting. These parameters cannot be changed while the spell remains in effect.

Gravity variation can have dramatic effects on siege engines and towers. Most siege engines can be moved only on the most gentle of slopes. By raising or lowering the effective elevation of siege engines by 2″, the priest can totally immobilize them by positioning them on a slope too steep to negotiate. In the case of siege towers, there is a 50% chance that the structures will topple over (totally destroying them).

The material component is a tiny plumb bob; the plumb line must be made of platinum wire while the bob itself must be a gem of at least 1,000 gp value. The device is consumed in the casting.

The Great Circle (Abjuration)
Reversible

Sphere: Sun
Range: 0
Components: V, S
Duration: 1 round
Casting Time: 6 turns
Area of Effect: Special
Saving Throw: Special

The great circle is a powerful cooperative spell that can be used only by four or more priests, each casting the spell simultaneously. Because of the nature of this spell and its casting time, it is often used to cleanse grounds in preparation for the construction of a temple or sanctuary.

When casting *the great circle*, the priests stand in a circle of no more than 20-foot diameter. Each faces inward; when the spell is completed, each priest faces outward, directing the energy of the spell.

When the casting is complete, the spell takes the form of a radiant halo of golden light 20 feet above the ground. This halo quickly expands in a shimmering wave. It can pass through objects, with small arcs of the halo disappearing momentarily and reappearing on the far side. As the halo moves, it generates a high-pitched hum that varies in pitch, almost like a chorus. The halo moves slowly at first, but builds speed, reaching its maximum range at the end of one round.

The radius of the golden halo is dependent on the number of priests casting the spell. Each priest adds 60 feet to the radius. Thus, four priests could generate a halo that extends 240 feet in all directions from the circle of priests. Theoretically, there is no limit to the number of priests who may contribute to this spell, but the need for the priests to be within a 20-foot diameter circle sets a practical limit of 20 casters.

The halo is pure energy tapped from the Positive Material plane. It causes harm to undead and evil beings within the area of effect. Undead creatures of 8 or fewer hit dice are instantly destroyed and are not allowed a saving throw to avoid the effect. More powerful undead suffer 1d8 points of damage per caster. A successful saving throw vs. death magic reduces this damage to half. Creatures of evil alignment suffer 1d6 points of damage per caster (a saving throw is allowed for half-damage).

The reverse of this spell, *the black circle,* creates a ring of shimmering black energy. Paladins and priests of good alignment suffer 1d10 points of damage per priest in the circle. All other good creatures suffer 1d4 points of damage per caster. Affected creatures are allowed a saving throw vs. death magic to reduce the damage to one-half.

Group Mind (Divination, Enchantment/Charm)

Sphere: Thought
Range: 0
Components: V, S
Duration: 1 turn + 1 round/level
Casting Time: 1 round
Area of Effect: 30-yard-diameter circle
Saving Throw: None

This spell is a deeper and more extensive version of *rapport,* in that it lets the priest communicate silently and instantly with several willing subjects. The number of subjects (in addition to the priest) depends on the caster's level:

Level	Number of participants
13 and below	2
14-16	4
17	6
18	7
19 +	8

As with *rapport,* the spell lets the participants share thoughts, emotions, and memories. Each participant sees, hears, and otherwise senses everything experienced by the other, although such "vicarious" experiences feel weak and cannot be mistaken for direct sensations. Participants can shut off these experiences at will if they find them confusing or distracting.

The participants can share such personal concepts as plans, hopes, and fears, although they cannot communicate complex or detailed information. It is impossible to communicate the procedure for casting a spell or picking a lock.

Communication through *group mind* is approximately 30 times faster than verbal communication. The priest can maintain only one *group mind* spell at any time; thus, he cannot communicate with multiple groups.

This spell cannot be used on unwilling subjects.

Land of Stability (Abjuration)

Sphere: Wards
Range: 10 yards/level
Components: V, S, M
Duration: 1 day/level
Casting Time: 6
Area of Effect: 10-foot-cube/level
Saving Throw: None

Land of stability protects the area of effect and all creatures and objects within it from the following natural disasters:

- Earthquakes—vibrations do not affect the warded area and fissures will not open beneath the warded area;
- Floods—the warded area remains dry, even if submerged;
- Windstorms—the warded area suffers no damage from strong winds and objects cannot be blown into the warded area;
- Lava and ash eruptions—lava and ash flow around the warded area; and
- Avalanches—stones and snow will not fall on the warded area.

Land of stability offers no protection against magically-generated disasters or spells that duplicate natural disasters. Disasters in progress in the area when the spell is cast are not affected.

This spell affects a cubic area whose sides equal the caster's level times 10 feet; thus, a 15th-level caster could affect a 150' × 150' × 150' cube.

The material components are the priest's holy symbol and a pinch of volcanic ash.

Legal Thoughts (Enchantment/Charm)

Sphere: Law
Range: 10 yards
Components: V, S
Duration: Permanent
Casting Time: 1 turn
Area of Effect: One creature
Saving Throw: Neg.

A priest casting this spell forces the victim of the spell to follow one specific law. The priest may choose any law prevalent in the area in which the priest and the victim currently reside.

Thus, if a city has no laws about murder, the priest cannot command the person not to kill.

The victim of the spell is forced to obey the letter of the law to the best of his ability. Thus, if a victim were commanded not to commit murder, he would go to any length to avoid murdering someone.

Since the essence of this spell is tied to legal (and not moral) interpretation, characters may find loopholes that will allow them to work around the law in specific cases or to ignore the law in light of extenuating circumstances.

When casting the spell, the priest must speak the law to the recipient in such a way that he can hear it. The victim is allowed a saving throw vs. spell to avoid the effect. If the save is failed, the victim will never willingly violate the stated law as long as the spell is in effect.

Legal thoughts can be negated by *dispel magic*. The victim of this spell never perceives anything wrong with adhering to the law, and therefore never seeks to have the spell removed.

Monster Mount (Enchantment/Charm)

Sphere: Travelers
Range: 30 yards
Components: V, S
Duration: 1 hour/level
Casting Time: 6
Area of Effect: 20-foot radius circle
Saving Throw: Neg.

This spell compels one or more living creatures to serve as mounts for the caster and his companions. The spell affects up to 10 Hit Dice or levels of creatures with Intelligence of 4 or lower. Creatures used as mounts must be of suitable size to carry at least one rider; smaller creatures can be used as pack animals.

Each intended mount receives a saving throw vs. spell. Creatures failing their rolls become docile and obedient, allowing riders to mount them, and moving at the speed and direction indicated by the caster.

To maintain the enchantment, the caster must remain within 10 yards of one of the affected creatures, and each affected creature must remain within 10 yards of another. The affected creatures will do nothing for the caster other than carrying riders and gear; they will not fight (although they will fight to defend themselves), nor will they intentionally endanger themselves. Any overtly hostile act by the caster or a rider against any mount breaks the enchantment for all the mounts.

When the enchantment ends or is broken, the creatures take no action for one round, then behave as their natural instincts direct.

Physical Mirror (Alteration)

Sphere: Numbers
Range: 30 yards
Components: V, S, M
Duration: 1d4 + 8 rounds
Casting Time: 6
Area of Effect: Special
Saving Throw: None

This spell causes a localized folding of space. The folded space takes the form of an invisible disk up to 20 feet in diameter. Any missile weapon or spell that intersects this disk is instantaneously reversed in direction. Melee factors such as speed, range, and damage are unaffected; the direction of the object or force is simply rotated through a 180° arc. The sender of the spell or missile finds himself the target of his own attack.

The *physical mirror* operates from only one direction; that is, only one side of the mirror reflects attacks. The caster of the mirror may direct spells and missile attacks normally through the space occupied by the mirror.

In the case of physical attacks, the attacker must roll to hit himself (without the armor class benefits of Dexterity or shield). Spells turned back may require the caster to make a saving throw vs. his own spell. In both of these cases, range is important. If the distance between the initiator of the attack and the *physical mirror* is more than twice the range of the attack, the attacker is safe; the attack has insufficient range to travel from the attacker to the mirror and back again.

When the priest casts the spell, he must specify the location and orientation of the *physical mirror* disk. Once it is created, the disk cannot be moved.

If two *physical mirror* disks touch or intersect, they destructively interact and both immediately vanish. The resulting "ripples" in the space-time continuum are exceedingly destructive and inflict 3d10 hit points of damage on any creature within 35 yards (a saving throw is allowed for half-damage). This always includes the casters of the physical mirror spells.

The material component is a tiny mirror of polished platinum, worth at least 500 gp.

Reverse Time (Alteration)

Sphere: Time
Range: 30 yards
Components: V, S, M
Duration: 1-4 rounds
Casting Time: 6
Area of Effect: One creature
Saving Throw: Neg.

This spell is similar to the 9th-level wizard spell *time stop*. When *reverse time* is cast, time stops within a 30-foot diameter of the subject. All creatures and items in the area of effect stand motionless, rivers stop running, and arrows hang suspended in the air. Any creature, person, or object entering the area of effect is likewise frozen in time. The caster is affected if he is within the area of effect, unless he is the subject of the spell.

An unwilling subject is allowed a saving throw vs. spell; if successful, the spell is immediately negated. Otherwise, the victim is forced to relive all the actions taken in the previous 1-4 rounds in reverse. Beginning with the most recent round, the subject moves backward, arrows fired by the subject return to his bow, and so on. All effects of these actions are negated. At the end of the spell's duration, normal time resumes and all creatures immediately continue their activities, picking up right where they had stopped.

Consider the following example. A party is battling a spellcasting red dragon. In the first round, the dragon breathes fire, roasting the party's wizard. The rest of the group attacks and injures the dragon. On the second round, the dragon bites and kills the group's thief. More damage is caused to the beast, but it is still alive in the third round, when it uses *magic missile* to kill the ranger. At this point, the priest casts *reverse time* on the beast. Fortunately, it fails its saving throw and is forced to reverse the last four rounds. While everyone else freezes, the dragon goes into reverse. The *magic missiles* zoom back to the dragon (and it regains the ability to cast that spell), it "unbites" the thief (removing that damage from the character), and then inhales its fiery breath (leaving the roasted wizard alive and uncooked). The dragon is then reversed through one more round—the round before it encounterd the party. The spell then ends and actions resume.

The dragon must now roll for surprise since it is encountering the party for the first time. The party is immune to surprise, since it was fighting the beast previously. All damage suffered by the dragon remains, since these actions were caused by the group and not the beast.

The material component is an etched silver arrow bent into a circle. The arrow must be no more than 3 inches long and worth no less than 500 gp. The arrow is destroyed in the casting.

Seclusion (Alteration)

Sphere: Numbers
Range: Touch
Components: V, S, M
Duration: 3d12 rounds +4 rounds/level
Casting Time: 6
Area of Effect: One creature
Saving Throw: Neg.

This spell encloses one individual in an extradimensional space. Creatures to be affected must be of size M or smaller. The space can contain only one creature, regardless of size. The priest may use the spell on himself or any creature he touches. Unwilling targets are allowed a saving throw vs. spell to avoid the entrapment.

While inside the space, the enclosed character is invisible and totally undetectable by any form of scrying. Powerful magic such as *contact other plane* will indicate that the character is "elsewhere," but will give no more information.

The creature within the extradimensional space can see and hear everything that occurs around him. However, he cannot cast spells, and no action of his can affect anyone or anything in the "real world."

While occupied, the extradimensional space is totally immobile. If the caster chooses to occupy the space, he can pass in and out of the space at will. Other creatures can leave or reenter the space only if the caster allows it. To an outside observer, an enclosed character who exits the space simply appears from nowhere.

If the space is occupied when the spell terminates, the occupant is immediately ejected back into the real world and suffers 1d6 hit points of damage in the process.

Any time the extradimensional space is empty, or when the occupant is someone other than the priest, the space follows the priest around. Thus, the priest may *seclude* a comrade in the extradimensional space, walk past some guards into a building, then release the comrade.

If any other form of extradimensional space (such as a *bag of holding*) is taken into the space created by *seclusion*, both spaces are ruptured and all contents are expelled onto the Astral plane. *Extradimensional manipulation* can temporarily prevent this.

The material components are a tiny crystal box of the finest workmanship (worth at least 1,500 gp) and a gem of at least 250 gp value. The gem is consumed in the casting; the box is not.

Skip Day (Invocation/Evocation)

Sphere: Time
Range: 0
Components: V, S
Duration: Instantaneous
Casting Time: 1 round
Area of Effect: 10-foot radius
Saving Throw: Neg.

When this spell is cast, all persons and intelligent creatures within 10 feet of the caster are instantly transported 24 hours into the future. Creatures outside the area of effect will believe that the affected characters have disappeared. Unwilling creatures can attempt a saving throw vs. spell to resist the effect of *skip day.*

No time passes for creatures affected by *skip day*; they are in the exact condition that they were in before the spell was cast. They are fatigued, have recovered no hit points, and carry the same spells. Wizards must wait for actual time to pass before they can memorize spells.

The affected creatures remain in the same location as they were before *skip day* was cast. Their immediate environment is likely to have changed; for instance, fires have burned out, enemies who were attacking have departed, and weather has changed for better or worse.

Although *skip day* is a possible substitute for *teleporting* out of a dangerous situation, it is not without risk; characters could reappear in a situation more threatening than the one they left behind (for instance, a forest fire may have started or a pack of hungry wolves may have arrived).

Sol's Searing Orb (Invocation)

Sphere: Sun
Range: 30 yards
Components: V, S, M
Duration: Instantaneous
Casting Time: 6
Area of Effect: One gem
Saving Throw: Special

This spell must be cast upon a topaz. When the spell is complete, the stone glows with an inner light. The gem must be immediately thrown at an opponent, for it quickly becomes too hot to hold. (The acts of casting and throwing occur in the same round.) It is not possible for the priest to give the stone to another character to throw.

The stone can be hurled up to 30 yards. The priest must roll normally to hit; he gains a +3 bonus to his attack roll and suffers no penalty for nonweapon proficiency. In addition, the glowing gem is considered a +3 weapon for determining whether a creature can be struck (creatures hit only by magical weapons, for example). There is no damage bonus, however.

When it hits, the gem bursts with a brilliant, searing flash that causes 6d6 points of fire damage to the target and blinds him for 1d6 rounds. The victim is allowed a saving throw vs. spell. If successful, only half damage is sustained and the target is not blinded. Undead creatures suffer 12d6 points of damage and are blinded for 2d6 rounds (if applicable) if their save is failed. They receive 6d6 points of damage and are blinded for 1d6 rounds if the save is successful.

If the gem misses its target, it explodes immediately, causing 3d6 points of damage (or 6d6 against undead) to all creatures within a 3' radius. It blinds them for 1d3 rounds (1d6 rounds vs. undead). All victims are allowed a saving throw vs. spell, with success indicating half damage and no blindness. The DM should use the rules for grenade-like missiles found in the *DUNGEON MASTER Guide* for determining where the stone hits.

The material component is a topaz gemstone worth at least 500 gp.

Spiritual Wrath (Invocation)

Sphere: Combat
Range: 300 yards
Components: V, S
Duration: Instantaneous
Casting Time: 1 turn
Area of Effect: Special
Saving Throw: 1/2

This powerful cooperative spell is rarely invoked since it requires the concerted effort of six or more high-level priests. The casting effort severely weakens the priests, discouraging casual use of this spell.

To cast the spell, six or more priests must be within a 15-foot radius. Each priest must cast *spiritual wrath* at the same time. Before beginning the spell, the priests must decide upon the area of effect. The spell causes 10d6 + 1d6 points of damage per priest casting the spell. (The minimum damage, therefore, is 16d6.) Creatures within the area of effect are allowed a saving throw vs. spell to reduce the damage to half.

The spell strikes as a great wave of force that descends from the sky. Small objects must save vs. crushing blow. Structures suffer damage as if hit by a heavy catapult (2d12). The force of this spell often raises a great cloud of dirt and dust, obscuring the area for 1d4 + 1 rounds.

The spell's area of effect is determined by the number of casters. Each priest contributes 10 feet to the radius of the spell. Six casters would create a spell with a radius of 60 feet. No more than twelve casters can cooperate to cast this spell (maximum of 22d6 damage and a 120-foot radius area of effect). This converts to an 8-inch circle in the BATTLESYSTEM rules ground scale.

The spell is difficult to cast, physically taxing the spellcasters so much that each caster suffers 3d10 points of damage from the effort. There is no saving throw allowed to avoid this damage.

Seventh-Level Spells

Age Dragon (Alteration)

Sphere: Time
Range: 30 yards
Components: V, S, M
Duration: 1 round/level
Casting Time: 1 round
Area of Effect: One dragon
Saving Throw: Neg.

This spell allows the caster to cause any dragon to temporarily gain or lose one age level per five levels of the caster. For instance, a 14th-level caster could cause a dragon to gain or lose two age levels; a mature adult dragon could be temporarily transformed into a young adult dragon or into a very old dragon. A dragon's age cannot be reduced below hatchling or increased beyond great wyrm.

Unwilling dragons are allowed a saving throw vs. spells with a −4 penalty to avoid the effect.

A dragon affected by *age dragon* temporarily acquires the armor class, hit points, spell abilities, combat modifiers, size, and other attributes of his new age level. The dragon retains his memories and personality. At the end of the spell's duration, the dragon returns to his normal age level.

If the dragon suffered damage while experiencing his modified age, these hit points remain lost when he resumes his normal age. If the dragon loses more hit points at his modified age than he has at his actual age, he dies when the spell expires. For example, a young adult bronze dragon with 110 hit points is aged to a mature adult with 120 hit points. The dragon suffers 115 hit points in combat. Unless the dragon is healed of 6 points of damage before the spell expires, the dragon dies at the end of the spell since his damage is greater than his actual hit points.

If a dragon is killed while under the effect of *age dragon*, he is dead at the end of the spell's duration.

The material component is a handful of dirt taken from a dragon's footprint.

Breath of Life (Necromantic)
Reversible

Sphere: Necromantic
Range: 0
Components: V, S, M
Duration: 1 hour/level
Casting Time: 1 turn
Area of Effect: Special
Saving Throw: None

This powerful spell enables the caster to cure many persons (even an entire community) who are afflicted with a nonmagical disease. The priest need not touch or even see the diseased people for the spell to be effective, although recipients must be within the area of effect.

This spell does not cure all diseases in the community at one time; the caster must specifically state which disease is to be eliminated (black plague or yellow fever, for example) with each casting of the spell.

When the spell is cast, the priest exhales a sweet-smelling breath. This forms into a breeze that radiates outward, forming a circle that expands in a 50-yard radius per hour. During this time, the caster must remain at the center of the area of effect. For example, after 12 hours, the *breath of life* would cover a circle 1200 yards in diameter (600-yard radius). The breath is of a magical nature rather than a physical nature; therefore, it is unaffected by prevailing winds.

The breeze blows through the community, instantly eliminating the specified disease from all afflicted citizens. The *breath of life* spell does not destroy parasitic monsters (such as green slime, rot grubs, and others), nor does it cure lycanthropy or other magical afflictions. The spell does not prevent recurrence of a disease if the recipients are again exposed.

The material components are the priest's holy symbol and a cone of incense that has been blessed by the highest priest of the character's religion.

The *breath of death*, which produces a foul-smelling wind, is the reverse of this spell. Victims who fail a saving throw vs. death magic are afflicted with a nonmagical, fatal disease. To determine the results of this spell, the DM should roll saving throws for major NPCs in the area of effect. The effect on the rest of the community can be calculated as a percentage, based on the saving throw.

Infected creatures do not heal hit points until the disease is cured. The disease is fatal within 1d6 weeks (the duration varies from person to person).

The material components are the priest's holy symbol and a handful of dust taken from a mummy's corpse.

Divine Inspiration

Sphere: Thought, Divination
Range: 0
Components: V, S, M
Duration: Instantaneous
Casting Time: 5
Area of Effect: The caster
Saving Throw: None

This spell is a more powerful version of the *genius* spell. The priest's player may ask the DM one question about the current situation or about events that will occur within the next five rounds. Questions about the future must relate to external events, such as "Will the guards respond to the sentry's yell?" Questions cannot refer to the outcome of combat, such as "Will we win the battle?" The priest's player is allowed to use this spell to ask the DM for advice. In this case, the spell is the equivalent of asking the gods, "Okay, how do we get out of this one?"

Like the *genius* spell, the DM must be careful in adjudicating this spell. The answer to the question is always relevant and correct, although not necessarily complete. The answer can also be cryptic, in the form of a riddle or rhyme, depending on the DM's assessment of the situation and how potentially unbalancing the answer might be. In general, the answer will be a short phrase of no more than eight to ten words.

The material component is a gem of at least 500 gp value. This spell can be cast only once in any 24-hour period.

Hovering Road (Conjuration/Summoning)

Sphere: Travelers
Range: 0
Components: V, S, M
Duration: 1 turn/level
Casting Time: 1 round
Area of Effect: Special
Saving Throw: None

This spell enables the caster to create a magical 10-foot-wide road extending 10 feet in front of him. The caster can create an unbroken road for the duration of the spell, creating a 10-foot area ahead of him as long as he continues to move forward.

The road is approximately one foot thick and hovers in the air. It has the texture and color of black granite. Characters and creatures can move on the *hovering road* at their normal movement rate, ignoring the effects of surrounding terrain.

The *hovering road* must originate from a solid surface. Once anchored, the caster controls the contour of the road, causing it to rise and fall as he wishes. The road can thus be used to traverse rivers (if the road is anchored on the shore), swamps, and similarly hostile terrain. The caster can cause the *hovering road* to rise over a jungle or cross a chasm.

The road has AC 0. It is impervious to non-magical weapons. If the road suffers 100 points of damage (from magical weapons or other magical forces), it dissipates in a black mist; all those on the road fall to the ground below.

Unless the road is destroyed, the entire *hovering road* remains intact from beginning to end for the duration of the spell, even if the caster is killed or incapacitated. At the end of the spell's duration, the entire road dissipates.

The material components are a chunk of black marble and a loop of gold wire.

Illusory Fortification (Illusion/Phantasm)

Sphere: War
Range: 240 yards
Components: V, S, M
Duration: Special
Casting Time: 10 turns
Area of Effect: Special
Saving Throw: None

The ritual required to cast this spell is time-consuming and extremely complex. As its name implies, *illusory fortification* creates an illusion of a wall of heavy stonework up to 30 feet tall and 160 yards long, topped with crenellations. The illusory wall can be of any color and apparent age, potentially allowing the caster to match the false wall with the real walls of an existing castle. The illusory wall must be continuous (it cannot form two or more shorter walls), but it can follow any corners or bends that the caster desires.

In addition to the wall, the spell creates the illusion of constant movement among the crenellations, as if defending troops were moving atop the wall. The formation of the crenellations makes it impossible for a distant observer to determine exactly how many and what types of defenders are present on the *illusory fortification*.

The illusory wall remains in existence for 2d12 hours unless the spell is terminated earlier.

The spell has one very significant limitation: it is strictly two-dimensional and is visible from only one side (the side that the caster deems to be the "outside"). When viewed from the outside, the wall appears real; when viewed from the end, from above, or from the "inside," the wall is totally invisible except for a faint outline of the shape of the wall. This means that friendly troops, concealed from enemy view by the illusory wall, can see their opponents clearly. The wall is most effective if friendly troops are informed of the wall's presence and are careful not to walk through the illusion. Such an occurrence does not end the spell, but it will probably advise the enemy of the nature of the wall.

Spells cast at the wall and shots fired at the *illusory fortification* by siege engines appear to strike the wall and inflict normal damage. In reality, the missiles or spells pass through the illusion, possibly striking troops or real fortifications beyond. Such "hits" do not disturb the illusion.

As soon as an enemy unit moves within 10 yards of the *illusory fortification*, the spell terminates and the wall vanishes.

There are two ways in which the spell can be terminated before it expires. First, the priest can terminate the spell at any time. Second, if a friendly unit makes an attack, whether melee or missile combat, through the illusory wall from the "inside" to the "outside," the spell terminates instantly.

Once the *illusory fortification* has been created, the priest does not need to concentrate on the wall. The spell remains in effect even if the casting priest is killed in the interim.

The material components are the priest's holy symbol, a handful of stones, powdered mortar, and a gem worth at least 3,000 gp. All components except the holy symbol are consumed in the casting.

Mind Tracker (Divination)

Sphere: Divination
Range: Special
Components: V, S, M
Duration: Special
Casting Time: 1 turn/3
Area of Effect: One creature
Saving Throw: Special

The mind tracker is a magically-created creature which exists only on the Ethereal plane. It is called into existence when the first portion of this spell is cast.

When seen (which is seldom), the mind tracker has an indistinct body. It seems to be a near-solid coalescence of the vaporous atmosphere of the Ethereal plane itself. It is a roughly elliptical body with three or more limbs protruding at seemingly random locations. The number and size of these appendages shifts slowly, however, as new ones appear from the mist and old ones disappear. The body of the creature averages 2 feet across and 3 feet long, though this, too, tends to vary from minute to minute. The mind tracker has no discernible eyes, ears, nose, or other organs. It cannot be engaged in combat; if attacked, it simply disappears, to reappear after the danger has passed, or somewhere else entirely if its quarry has moved on.

The ceremony which creates the mind tracker takes one turn to perform. Its material components are a whiff of the Ethereal plane's atmosphere and the brain of a lizard.

Once the tracker is manifested, it must be assigned a quarry within one hour. If no quarry is designated, the tracker dissipates and the spell is wasted.

To assign a quarry to the tracker, the priest must have the quarry within his sight. This includes magical sight such as true seeing, but not remote sighting devices such as crystal balls. With the quarry in sight, the priest mouths the final phrases of the spell. From that point on, the mind tracker is mentally tethered to the victim. It follows its quarry (staying always in the Ethereal plane) wherever it goes. It constantly relays information about the subject to the priest: what it is doing, where it is. The priest does not actually see an image of the quarry, he receives 'reports' from the mind tracker. These reports contain only such information as the tracker can gather by looking. It cannot identify people the quarry is talking to, but can describe them in great detail. Nor can it hear anything the quarry or anyone else says, or read writing, but it recognizes and can report the fact that speaking or reading is happening.

While the tracker is dogging its quarry, its presence can be felt as an eery, creepy sensation of being watched. If the victim makes an initial save vs. paralyzation, each of the following stages lasts three hours instead of two. For the first two hours, the quarry has a general feeling of ill ease. In the third and fourth hours, the victim is distracted and nervous, and suffers a -1 penalty on all saving throws. In the fifth and sixth hours, the victim is convinced someone or something is following him and suffers a -3 penalty on saving throws and a -2 (or -10%) penalty on all other dice rolls. After six hours the victim is near his breaking point. He is unable to concentrate to cast spells or use any of his class's special abilities. All die rolls have a -5 (or -25%) penalty. After eight hours, he must make a saving throw vs. paralyzation. If he fails, he collapses, fevered and delirious. This state persists until the

tracker ceases to exist.

The mind tracker continues to exist for as long as the priest remains conscious of its input. If the priest is knocked out or falls asleep, or simply dismisses his creation, the tracker dissipates.

Shadow Engines (Illusion/Phantasm)

Sphere: War
Range: 240 yards
Components: V, S, M
Duration: 8 turns
Casting Time: 3 turns
Area of Effect: 180-yard × 180-yard square
Saving Throw: None

This spell creates the illusion of as many as four siege engines. The casting priest may choose from ballistae, siege towers, catapults, rams, or any combination thereof. Like the creatures created by the spell *shadow monsters*, these illusory engines have at least a tenuous reality and can inflict damage on enemies.

Shadow engines are accompanied by illusory crews of the appropriate number and race. The engines can move at a rate of 20 yards per turn and are unaffected by terrain considerations. (The caster can choose to slow them when passing through rough terrain to aid the illusion of reality.)

Shadow engines cannot carry real troops. They can be fired at the same rate as real engines of the appropriate type, but a hit causes only one-half the damage normal for that type of engine (round fractions down).

A *shadow engine* remains in existence until the spell duration expires, until an enemy unit approaches within 10 yards, or until it suffers damage from an enemy missile attack. When any of these conditions occur, the engine vanishes. If a single spell has created multiple engines, only the engine struck vanishes; the others remain.

The crew associated with a *shadow engine* must remain with that engine; it cannot move more than 5 yards away from the engine itself.

Shadow engines can move independently of other engines created by the spell as long as they remain within the area of effect and remain within 240 yards of the caster. The caster must maintain concentration to control the *shadow engines*. He cannot cast any other spells, and he is limited to a movement rate of 6. If the caster is struck for damage, the *shadow engines* vanish.

The material component is a finely detailed miniature model of a siege engine (of any type), which is consumed during the casting.

Spacewarp (Alteration)

Sphere: Numbers
Range: 50 yards
Components: V, S, M
Duration: 1 round/level
Casting Time: 7
Area of Effect: 50-foot-diameter sphere
Saving Throw: None

According to one view of the universe, what we perceive as gravity is actually a localized warping of the fabric of space-time. The *spacewarp* spell creates a temporary but very intense warping in a limited area.

When the priest casts this spell, he selects a specific point to be the center of effect. This point may be anywhere within 50 yards of the caster, including in midair.

When the spell is completed, this center of effect gains a gravity field equal to the force felt at the surface of the earth. In other words, gravity is centered at this point; everything within 50 feet of this center that is not attached to something immovable will fall toward the selected point.

This localized gravity affects only loose objects and creatures capable of movement (i.e., not trees, whose roots are buried in the ground). It does not affect the ground itself—soil, plants, desert sand, lake water, etc. are immune to the effect.

An object falling toward the center of gravity gains speed exactly as it would if it were falling toward the ground. When the object reaches the center, it instantly ceases its movement. If objects are already at the center, newly arriving objects will slam into them, causing normal falling damage (1d6 per 10 feet) to the newly arriving objects. Objects previously at the center must save vs. paralyzation or suffer half that amount of damage.

Consider the following example. An orc is 10 feet away from the center of effect when the spell is cast. He falls 10 feet to the center and stops. His companion, a bandit, is 30 feet from the center. It takes him longer to fall to the center, so the orc is already there when he arrives, and the two characters collide forcefully. The bandit suffers 3d6 hit points of damage—the falling damage associated with a 30-foot fall. The orc must save vs. paralyzation or suffer half that amount.

Other things are caught in the effect as well. The bandit's horse was 50 feet away from the center of effect, so it arrives at the center after the orc and the bandit. It falls 50 feet, suffering 5d6 points of damage, and potentially inflicting half that amount on both the orc and the bandit.

The center of effect can be anywhere within 50 yards of the priest. Possibly one of the most destructive uses of this spell is to cast it directly on an enemy creature. Everyone and everything within 50 feet of that creature falls toward him and strikes him, inflicting damage.

When the spell terminates, gravity returns to normal. If the spell has lifted any characters or objects off the ground, they immediately fall back to the ground, suffering the appropriate amount of falling damage.

The material components are a lodestone and a sphere of obsidian, both of which are consumed in the casting.

Spirit of Power (Summoning, Invocation)

Sphere: Summoning
Range: 0
Components: V, S, M
Duration: 1 hour
Casting Time: 3 turns
Area of Effect: The casters
Saving Throw: None

This cooperative spell is rarely used or spoken of, since its requirements are strict and the outcome is uncertain. The spell must be cast by six priests of the same faith. All six must touch hands at the time of casting. At the completion of the spell, the priests fall into a trance. The life essences of the priests leave their bodies and merge at a point within 10 feet of the casters. The spirits of the priests meld together to form the avatar of the priests' deity.

In this manner, the six characters become a single being with all the powers and abilities allowed to that avatar. The only stipulation is that the priests' deity cannot have created all avatars allowed to it at that moment. If this has happened, the spell fails and the priests are drained as described below.

If the spell succeeds, the priests have completely given their wills over to their deity, essentially forming the vessel into which it funnels power. In becoming the avatar, the priests retain the ability to make most of their own decisions. (The six must work in harmony or allow one of their number to decide all actions.) However, the deity can assume direct control of the avatar at any time it desires—the avatar is, after all, an earthly manifestation of the deity.

Although the spell has a duration of one hour, the deity is not obliged to release the priests at that time. If the priests are not released at the end of the spell's duration, they instantly die. A deity can choose to sacrifice its priests in order to maintain its avatar on the Prime Material plane. Such a cruel and unjust action is almost never undertaken by good deities or those that have any respect for life, free will, or mercy. For dark and sinister gods, the question is much more uncertain. If a deity chooses to maintain the avatar longer than one hour, control of the avatar instantly and permanently passes to the DM. (Clearly, a DM should seldom if ever exercise this power.)

While the priests are formed into the avatar, their bodies remain in a death like trance. The priests have no idea what might be happening to their real bodies (unless the avatar can observe them). Any damage to a priest's body requires an instant system shock roll. If successful, the damage is recorded normally, but the damage does not take effect until the spell ends (at which point the priest will almost certainly die). If the system shock roll is failed, the character instantly dies and the spell ends. Characters who die in this manner cannot be raised, resurrected, or reincarnated. They have been taken to the ultimate reward (or punishment) for the service they have rendered. If the bodies are moved from their positions, the spell ends.

Even if the deity releases the priests, they are left severely drained. All spells memorized are lost until the priest can rest and perform his prayers once again. The physical drain leaves each priest with only 1 hit point upon awakening, regardless of the number of hit points the character had when the spell was cast. Since damage suffered during the spell takes effect instantly, any priest who is hurt dies immediately (although quick action by others might save him).

Each priest who survives the spell will be bound by a quest (a duty that must be completed in exchange for calling upon their god).

The material component is an offering appropriate to the deity. The DM determines the exact nature of this offering.

Tentacle Walls (Enchantment)

Sphere: Wards
Range: Touch
Components: V, S, M
Duration: Special
Casting Time: 1 round
Area of Effect: 50-foot cube
Saving Throw: None

Tentacle walls enables the caster to enchant a single room whose volume is less than or equal to the area of effect. The spell activates 1d4 rounds after any creature other than the caster enters the room. The intruder must be larger than a normal rat; that is, it must be larger than one-half cubic foot or weigh more than three pounds.

When the spell is activated, six black, leathery tentacles sprout inside the room; the tentacles are evenly divided among the room's surfaces (for instance, if the room is a cube, one tentacle sprouts from the floor, one sprouts from the ceiling, and one sprouts from each of the four walls).

The whip-like tentacles grow to the length of the room and swing wildly. Each round, a tentacle has a 30% chance of striking a random creature in the room, inflicting 1d6 points of damage (save vs. spell for half damage). Each tentacle has AC 0 and 25 hit points. When a tentacle is reduced to 0 hit points, it disappears in a puff of black smoke.

If all creatures are killed or withdraw from the room, the surviving tentacles withdraw, disappearing into the walls. If the spell is activated again, six tentacles reappear; new tentacles are created to replace any destroyed previously. As long as one tentacle survives an encounter, the tentacles will continue to be replaced. Only when all six tentacles are destroyed is the spell permanently negated.

The material component is the dried tentacle of an octopus.

Timelessness (Alteration)

Sphere: Numbers
Range: Touch
Components: V, S, M
Duration: 1 day/level
Casting Time: 7
Area of Effect: One creature
Saving Throw: Neg.

This spell totally stops the flow of time for a single individual. All signs of life stop and the subject is incapable of any movement or thought.

While the spell is in effect, the subject is totally immovable and cannot be affected by any physical or magical forces. Weapons simply bounce off the subject as they would bounce off the hardest stone. Spells, including *dispel magic*, are totally incapable of affecting the subject in any way. The subject does not age.

Aside from the fact that the subject remains visible, frozen in place like a statue, he is effectively no longer part of the universe. (DMs may rule that the most powerful of magics, such as *wishes*, and creatures of demigod or higher status can affect the subject.)

When the priest casts the spell, he or she states the duration for which the spell will remain in effect (the maximum is one full day per level of the caster). Once the spell is cast, this duration cannot be changed; the priest cannot terminate the spell before the stated time has elapsed.

If the subject is unwilling to be affected by the spell, the priest must touch the victim for the spell to take effect; the subject receives a normal saving throw to resist the effects. A willing subject need not make a saving throw.

The priest may cast this spell on himself if desired. This spell can provide a powerful defensive maneuver; while the spell is in effect, the subject is totally invulnerable. *Timelessness* is also an effective form of long-term imprisonment, as long as the priest is around to cast the spell again at the appropriate time.

This is an exceptionally powerful spell. Casting it puts a significant strain on the priest. Each time he casts *timelessness*, the priest must make a system shock roll. If the priest fails this throw, he or she permanently loses 1 point of Constitution.

The material components are a gem worth at least 1,000 gp and a small cylinder of obsidian. Both are crushed during the casting.

Uncontrolled Weather
(Conjuration/Summoning)

Sphere: Chaos
Range: 0
Components: V, S
Duration: 1 turn/level
Casting Time: 1 turn
Area of Effect: 4d4 square miles
Saving Throw: None

This spell allows the caster to summon weather that is either appropriate or inappropriate to the climate and season of the region. The summoned effects are always dramatic—cool breezes or light fog will not appear. Instead, torrential floods will assault a desert, a heat wave will rage in polar wastelands, and tornadoes and hurricanes will rip across gentle landscapes. A blizzard might spring up in summer or a tornado might materialize in the winter.

The spellcaster has no influence over the weather pattern that emerges. He cannot control the area of effect or the duration of the weather.

Four turns after the spell is cast, the trend of the weather will become apparent—a sudden chill, gust of wind, overcast sky, etc. The uncontrolled weather arrives on the fifth turn. Once the weather has arrived, it cannot be dispelled. If the spell is canceled by the caster before the beginning of the fifth turn, the weather slowly reverts to its original condition.

The effects of the spell are the decision of the DM. The effects should be grand and impressive. Following are suggested effects of the weather.

Torrential Rain/Blizzard: Visibility is reduced to 100 yards or less; travel is nearly impossible due to water or heavy snow on the ground.

Storm/Hurricanes: All flying creatures are driven from the skies; trees are uprooted; roofs are torn off; ships are endangered.

Heat Wave: Intense heat immediately causes ice bridges to melt; avalanches of snow and ice roll down mountains.

The DM determines the area of effect randomly. The maximum duration of the spell is one turn per level of the caster; however, the DM may cancel the effect after a shorter time.

Quest Spells

The quest spells that follow are designed to be used only in extraordinary circumstances as determined by the DM. Players and the DM should read the explanatory notes about quest spells in the introduction to this book before entering these spells into play.

Abundance (Alteration)

Sphere: Creation, Plant
Range: 0
Duration: Permanent
Casting Time: 1 turn
Area of Effect: Special
Saving Throw: None

By casting an *abundance* spell, the priest quickens the ripening of a harvest or the growth of woodland. Fields of crops in the affected area will grow, ripen, and be ready for harvest in a single day. Seed must be sown any time before the casting of the spell.

An area of woodland will grow as if it had grown for 25 years in one day plus five years per day for another three days. There must be soil capable of supporting the woodland for the growth to remain healthy.

The priest must stand anywhere within the area to be affected. The priest designates the exact size and shape of the area in the casting.

The area of effect is 10 square miles for ripening a harvest and 25 square miles for woodland growth. This spell does not create effects such as entanglement or enlargement of the flora within the area of effect.

Animal Horde (Conjuration/Summoning)

Sphere: Animal, Summoning
Range: 0
Duration: 1 day
Casting Time: 1 turn
Area of Effect: 10-mile radius
Saving Throw: None

This potent spell summons a number of animals to the priest. For each level of the priest, a number of animals totaling 10 hit dice appear.

The Power who grants the spell enables the priest to know exactly what types and numbers of animals are within the area of effect. The priest may specify the numbers of animals he wants; for instance, a 16th-level priest could summon 60 HD of wolves, 40 HD of bears, and 60 HD of

wolverines. The animals will begin arriving in one round and will be assembled at the priest's location at the end of three turns.

The animals will not fight among each other even if they are natural enemies. Monsters (dragons, gorgons, hell hounds, etc.) cannot be summoned with this spell.

The summoned animals will aid the priest in any means of which they are capable. They will enter battle, protect the priest and his companions, or perform a specified mission until the priest dismisses them or the spell expires. During this time, the priest can automatically communicate with his animals.

At the end of the spell, the animals instinctively return to their lairs. For the first three turns after the spell expires, the animals will not attack the caster, his companions, or other summoned animals. After this time, the animals will behave normally.

Circle of Sunmotes
(Alteration, Invocation/Evocation, Necromancy)

Sphere: Sun
Range: 200 yards
Duration: 3 turns
Casting Time: 1 round
Area of Effect: 60-foot-radius hemisphere
Saving Throw: None

By casting *circle of sunmotes*, the priest creates a hemispherical shell filled with sparkling, glowing motes of bright sunlight. A one-foot radius globe of sunlight appears at the height of the caster's head in the exact center of the circle.

Creatures within the area of effect who are friendly to the cleric experience the glowing motes as warm, invigorating, inspiring, and healing. They are healed for 1d6 hit points, gain the benefit of an *aid* spell for 1 turn after the *circle of sunmotes* is created, gain +1 bonuses to all attack and damage rolls, and gain a +2 bonus to morale.

Enemies of the priest experience the same sunmotes as blinding, burning, and damaging. They must save versus spell or be blinded for 1 turn after the sunmotes are created. Each enemy is struck by a small fiery mote causing 1d4+1 points of damage (no saving throw is allowed, but creatures with magical fire resistance suffer only half damage), and suffers a −2 penalty to morale.

Companions of the cleric who step within 10 feet of the glowing miniature sun at the center of the effect are healed of 1d8 + 2 hit points. This affects each creature only once during the spell's duration.

Enemies of the priest who come within 10 feet of the minisun are burned for 1d8 + 2 points of fire damage. No saving throw is allowed, but creatures possessing magical resistance against fire suffer only half damage.

Companions of the priest who are outside the area of effect view enemies within the circle as if they are affected by golden *faerie fire*. Creatures affected by the *faerie fire* suffer a −2 penalty to armor class from attacks by creatures outside the circle.

Enemies of the priest outside the circle view the priest's allies as if obscured by a blinding light and suffer a −2 penalty to missile attacks against them.

Conformance
(Conjuration/Summoning, Invocation)

Sphere: Law
Range: 0
Duration: 6 turns
Casting Time: 1 round
Area of Effect: 80-foot-diameter sphere
Saving Throw: None

The *conformance* spell has a simple principle with a profound effect: probable events always manifest.

In game terms, this means that events with a probability of 51% or better always occur. Thus, if a saving throw of 9 is required to avoid an effect, no roll is necessary; the save is automatically successful. If a warrior must roll 10 or better to hit an enemy, he automatically hits.

Conversely, improbable actions (those with less than a 50% chance) always fail. If a warrior must roll 12 or better to hit an enemy, he automatically fails. If a thief's chance to hide in shadows is 49%, he automatically fails.

There are two conditions that affect this spell. First, a *prayer* spell is continuously operative in the area of effect, shifting the balance of combat probabilities toward the favor of the priest who casts this spell and his companions. Second, probabilities of exactly 50% always shift in favor of the spellcasting priest. For example, if a roll of 11 or better is needed to save against a spell effect, this is a 50% chance for success. In such cases, the priest and his friends always make the save and enemies always fail.

This spell is particularly potent if *bless* and *chant* spells are cast in the area of effect.

Elemental Swarm (Conjuration/Summoning)

Sphere: Elemental, Summoning
Range: 240 yards
Duration: 6 turns
Casting Time: 3 turns
Area of Effect: Special
Saving Throw: None

This spell enables the caster to open a portal to one elemental plane of his choice (as appropriate for his patron Power). He can then summon elementals from that plane.

After the first turn of casting, 3d3 elementals of 12HD each appear; after the second turn, 2d3 elementals of 16HD each appear; after the third turn, 1d3 elementals of 20HD each appear. Each elemental has at least 5 hit points per hit die. The elementals remain for six turns from the time they first appear.

These elementals will obey the priest explicitly and cannot be turned against the caster. The priest does not need to concentrate to maintain control over the elementals. They cannot be dismissed with spells such as *dismissal*; the elementals remain for the duration of the spell.

Etherwalk (Alteration)

Sphere: Astral, Travelers
Range: Special
Duration: Special
Casting Time: 5 rounds
Area of Effect: Special
Saving Throw: Neg.

By casting this spell, the priest transports himself and as many as 50 followers (who must join hands at the time of casting) to the Border Ethereal. Unwilling creatures are allowed a saving throw at a −4 penalty to avoid transportation.

The spell then allows the priest and his party to make as many as three round-trip journeys to and from the Inner Planes. It then allows them to return to the Prime Material plane.

Travel rates in the Ethereal plane are at four times normal speed. Travel times for locating or searching along curtains are all at the minimum time possible. Encounters with monsters occur at one-fifth the normal frequency. The priest and his party are not affected by the ether cyclone.

The spell expires when the priest and his party return to the Border Ethereal from an inner plane for the third time. They are then instantly transported to the Prime Material plane.

Fear Contagion (Abjuration)

Sphere: Charm, War
Range: 240 yards
Duration: Special
Casting Time: 1 round
Area of Effect: Special
Saving Throw: Special

A priest casting *fear contagion* selects a single creature to be the focus of the spell. The creature is affected by magical fear and receives no saving throw to avoid the effect. All creatures within 10 yards of the target creature must make a saving throw versus spell with a −4 penalty; failure indicates that they are also affected by fear.

If BATTLESYSTEM rules are used, the spell forces the affected unit to make a Morale Check at a −6 penalty. If this roll fails, the unit automatically routs.

Creatures affected by fear will flee in a direction away from the spellcaster for as long as they are able to run (refer to Chapter 14 of the *Player's Handbook* for rules). Such creatures will then spend one full turn cowering after being forced to rest. During this time, affected creatures suffer −4 penalties to attack rolls, and all dexterity bonuses are negated.

When using BATTLESYSTEM rules, fear-struck creatures are permitted rally tests with a −3 penalty and must engage in rout movement until they rally. However, a rally test is not permitted until two turns of rout movement have been completed.

As creatures run in fear, their fear is contagious. Any creature that comes within 10 yards of a creature affected by this spell must make a saving throw (no penalties) or be forced to flee from the spellcaster. In BATTLESYSTEM rules, creatures make a standard Morale Check with a −3 penalty.

Creatures affected by fear no longer cause fear in others after they have passed one mile from the original center of the spell effect.

Health Blessing (Necromancy)

Sphere: Healing, Necromantic
Range: 100 yards
Duration: 1 day/level
Casting Time: 1 round
Area of Effect: 50 creatures
Saving Throw: None

Health blessing provides a number of human, demi-human, or humanoid creatures with protection against ill health; it also enables subjects to heal others.

Recipients of a *health blessing* are immune to nonmagical disease, gain a +4 bonus to saving throws versus poison and death magic, and can cast *cure light wounds* on themselves once per day for the duration of the spell. In addition, a recipient of *health blessing* can heal one other creature per day as a paladin does by laying hands. The healing conferred is 1 hit point per level or hit die of the healer.

Highway (Alteration, Evocation)

Sphere: Travelers
Range: 0
Duration: 1 day
Casting Time: 1 turn
Area of Effect: 1,000 square yards
Saving Throw: None

The *highway* spell creates a shimmering plane of force that acts as a magical conveyor for the priest. By standing at the forward edge of the 10 × 100 yard plane, the priest and as many followers as can fit onto the square can travel as outlined below.

The *highway* travels 30 miles per hour (MV 88) over all terrains. The priest sets the height of the *highway* in a range from 1 foot to 100 yards above ground level. The *highway* moves as the priest wills; if the priest wishes to fix a destination in his mind, the *highway* will take the shortest route to that destination until the priest changes the course in his mind.

The *highway* cannot be used offensively. It will automatically travel over or around obstacles such as buildings and large creatures. It protects creatures traveling on it from adverse effects of the elements (ice, rain, gales, etc.). The *highway* can hover in place, but hovering can be achieved only at a height of 12 inches above ground level.

When the spell expires or the destination is reached, the highway gently lowers the priest and his party to the ground. The priest may order the *highway* to drop off creatures and collect others at intermediate destinations, although the priest who cast the spell must remain on the *highway* or it will disappear.

Imago Interrogation
(Divination, Enchantment/Charm)

Sphere: Astral, Divination, Time
Range: 0
Duration: Special
Casting Time: 1 turn
Area of Effect: The caster
Saving Throw: None

The imago is a mental image—a form of mental magical body. After casting this spell (requiring 1 turn), the caster falls asleep. After 1d6 turns of sleep, the imago of the priest begins to travel. The imago is not subject to any forms of attack and has no effective attacks.

The imago may travel to as many as four different locations separated by any distance, even across the planes and/or backward in time. At these locations, the imago may interrogate the imagos of as many as 10 other sentient creatures (other than Powers), compelling them to reply truthfully to its questions. A maximum of 40 questions may be asked during the spell duration.

Asking one question and listening to the reply takes 4 rounds of time in the caster's world. Each planar/time jump lasts 3 turns in that world.

Imago communications are telepathic. The questions must be able to be answered in a sentence of reasonable length, or the interrogated creature becomes confused and cannot answer.

The imagos of interrogated creatures will have no recollection of their interrogations. As a result, history cannot be changed through backward time travel using this spell.

Implosion/Inversion (Invocation)

Sphere: Numbers, Combat
Range: 120 yards
Duration: Special
Casting Time: 1 round
Area of Effect: One or more creatures
Saving Throw: Neg.

By use of this spectacular spell, the priest rearranges the extradimensional and spatial geometries of the molecules of one or more creatures. The result is that the rearrangement of the target creature causes it to implode (collapse inward upon itself) or invert (its insides become its outsides and vice versa).

The result is usually inversion, unless the target would not be adversely affected by this process (e.g., a slime, ooze, golem, elemental, etc.). In this case, implosion takes place. In either case, the effect kills/destroys the target instantaneously unless it makes a successful saving throw versus death magic at a −4 penalty.

The priest can affect one creature per round with this spell. After each round, the priest must make a Constitution check. If this fails, the priest is overwhelmed with the effort of sustaining the spell, at which time the spell terminates, leaving the priest fatigued (the equivalent of being stunned) for 1d4 rounds. The maximum possible duration of the spell is 3 turns.

Interdiction (Abjuration)

Sphere: Chaos, Law, Wards
Range: 240 yards
Duration: 1 day
Casting Time: 2 turns
Area of Effect: 200-foot cube/level
Saving Throw: Special

This powerful spell affects all enemies of the spellcasting priest who enter the area of effect. The spell inflicts a −2 penalty on saving throws, a −1 penalty to armor class, and a −1 penalty to attack and damage rolls. Creatures friendly to the cleric gain corresponding bonuses—+2 to saving throws, +1 to attack and damage rolls, and a bonus of 1 to AC. Additional effects are possible, depending on the Power granting the spell; effects must correspond (or at least not conflict) with the spheres the priest normally uses. Multiple effects are possible.

The variation for the Sphere of Wards requires that each hostile creature entering the area of effect make a saving throw vs. spells with a −4 penalty or suffer 4d6 points of damage. An affected creature must then flee the area; it is unable to return. The creature must make a second saving throw vs. spell with a −4 penalty as it leaves the area or be blinded until magically cured.

The variation for the sphere of Law requires that a hostile creature make a saving throw every time it wishes to change an action. Thus, if a creature wishes to stop running and draw a weapon, a successful save is needed or the creature continues to run. Actions that cannot be continued (e.g., firing an arrow if the archer has no more arrows) are repeated as empty automatisms. In addition, creatures hostile to the priest automatically fail saving throws against Enchantment/Charm spells cast by the priest.

The variation for the Sphere of Chaos requires that hostile creatures make saving throws vs.

spells at −4 or be affected by *confusion* (as per the spell). Affected creatures have a 5% chance per round of suddenly being attacked by a *phantasmal killer.*

All creatures who enter the area of effect are subject to the effects of the spell. All effects except blindness cease 3 rounds after an affected creature leaves the area. Creatures reentering the area of effect must make new saving throws.

Mindnet (Divination, Enchantment/Charm)

Sphere: Thought
Range: 0
Duration: 12 turns
Casting Time: Special
Area of Effect: Special
Saving Throw: Special

The priest casting a *mindnet* spell establishes a telepathic link with as many as 10 other creatures who may be separated from each other by as much as 10 miles. Thus, a chain of creatures 100 miles long could be established.

The Power granting this spell has the final word on the individuals who may be included in the spell. Most commonly, the spell will be cast to include individuals familiar to the caster. However, depending on the purpose of the spell, the Power may allow a stranger known to the caster only by name to be included in the *mindnet.* Unwilling creatures must make a saving throw at a −4 penalty to avoid being included in the *mindnet.*

Casting the spell requires one round per two creatures in the *mindnet.* The spell's duration begins after all affected creatures have been linked. Characters of any class may take part in this linkage, benefiting from several effects.

First, each member of the *mindnet* benefits from Intelligence, Wisdom, and Dexterity bonuses. The bonuses are equal to the bonuses held by the member of the *mindnet* with the highest ability score. For example, if five creatures in a *mindnet* have Wisdom scores of 15, 15, 16, 17, and 18, each creature would make saving throws, ability checks, and the like as if he had a Wisdom score of 18. Bonus spells are not gained due to enhanced Wisdom, however.

Second, spells may be pooled among the spellcasters within the *mindnet.* Any priest may use a spell memorized by another priest with two conditions: the priest who has memorized the spell must allow its use; and a priest "borrowing" a spell may use only spells of levels he could nor-

mally cast. Such borrowing still causes the spell to be lost from the mind of the caster who memorized it. A caster may *not* borrow spells outside his normal class restrictions. Priests and wizards within a *mindnet* cannot mix their priestly and wizardly spells, nor can a specialist borrow a spell from an opposition school.

Third, each member of the *mindnet* is in constant mental communication. Each member knows what is happening at the locations of all other members.

Finally, twice per turn, the priest casting this spell can instantly teleport any person linked by the *mindnet* to any other person who is also a part of the spell. This massive effort results in a +4 penalty to any Constitution checks made by the priest.

The priest casting the spell cannot perform any other actions while the *mindnet* exists; if he does, the spell is canceled. The priest must make a Constitution check at the end of each turn in order to sustain the spell. A failed check cancels the *mindnet.* The spell can last a maximum of 12 turns.

Planar Quest (Alteration)

Sphere: Astral
Range: Touch
Duration: Special
Casting Time: 5 rounds
Area of Effect: Special
Saving Throw: Neg.

By joining hands with as many as 12 companions and casting this spell, the priest transports his party to any other plane of existence. The priest and his party may arrive at a specific location in a plane (if one is known) or at an unknown destination. Travel time to the destination, whether known or unknown, will always be at the minimum possible. In an inner plane, a friendly guide will always be available to the priest. Hostile encounters occur at one-fifth normal frequency.

Unwilling creatures are allowed a saving throw at a −4 penalty to avoid being transported.

In the inner planes, the party is magically protected in any means necessary for survival. The party does not need to eat, drink, or rest if conditions make these activities impossible. Party members are immune to fire in the elemental plane of fire, and similar immunities are granted by the Power in other planes as necessary. The party can move through any terrain (including the elemental plane of Earth) at its normal movement rate.

In the outer planes, similar immunities apply. The priest is also granted a *power compass* (described in *Manual of the Planes*). Hostile encounters in an outer plane occur only half as often as normal.

The duration of this spell is decided by the Power who grants it. Normally, it is sufficient to allow the priest and his party to undertake the quest that the Power has set forth. When the quest has been completed successfully or has failed beyond recovery, the priest and his party are returned to the Prime Material plane.

Preservation (Abjuration)

Sphere: Wards
Range: 480 yards
Duration: Special
Casting Time: 1 turn
Area of Effect: One structure
Saving Throw: None

This spell creates a powerful set of protective wards that operate on a single fortified building, temple complex, tower, or similar structure. These wards protect the physical integrity of the structure and prevent magical access.

A building protected by *preservation* suffers only 25% of normal structural damage from sources such as siege engines, earthquakes (both natural and magical), and powerful weather-affecting spells. Spells which directly affect the physical integrity of the structure (e.g., *passwall, stone shape, transmute rock to mud*) simply fail when cast on the protected building.

Preservation creates a permanent *protection from evil* spell on the affected building. Every surface of the building benefits from the effects of the spell.

Magical spells allowing access to the building fail. Thus, creatures attempting to *teleport* or *fly* into the building are stopped. Birds and creatures with natural flight may enter the building normally.

If the building is a temple (or other consecrated building) dedicated to the Power that granted the spell, all priests inside it gain the benefit of a *sanctuary* spell for the duration of the *preservation*.

The *preservation* spell expires if the building is destroyed or after 60 days have passed.

Revelation (Divination)

Sphere: Divination
Range: Special
Duration: 1 day
Casting Time: 1 turn
Area of Effect: Special
Saving Throw: None

The *revelation* spell grants the priest extraordinary divination powers. He gains the following abilities that are effective to a range of 240 yards.

- The priest gains *true seeing* as per the 5th-level priest spell.
- The priest can see and identify all priest spell effects in the area (assume a line of sight in a 60° arc).
- The priest is instantly aware of any creature's attempt to lie to him.
- The priest can communicate with animals, creatures, and monsters of all types. He can communicate with any number of creatures, but may converse with only one at a time.
- The priest can communicate telepathically with humanoids.
- The priest may use a suitable item as a *crystal ball* once per hour, as per the magical item described in the *DMG* (including range). He gains a +20% bonus to all rolls to determine success.

Reversion (Alteration, Invocation)

Sphere: Time
Range: 0
Duration: Instantaneous
Casting Time: 1
Area of Effect: 10-foot-radius sphere
Saving Throw: None

By casting this spell, the priest reverses certain recent events in the area of effect. The spell affects only creatures friendly to the priest. The magic takes effect immediately after the spell is completed rather than at the end of the round.

All damage suffered by the priest's allies during the previous turn is undone. This includes energy drains, poison, and all special attack forms *unless* these resulted in instantaneous death. Death from cumulative physical damage is undone, however. Any creature brought back to life by the *reversion* spell is not required to make a resurrection survival roll.

Any spells cast by the priest's allies during the previous turn are restored and may be used again. This does not apply to magical or spell-like effects from magical items or scrolls. Material components consumed in spellcasting during this time are also restored.

The *reversion* spell affects only creatures and characters. Equipment and magical items are not affected.

Casting this spell ages the priest one year.

Robe of Healing (Enchantment, Necromancy)

Sphere: Healing
Range: Touch
Duration: 1 hour
Casting Time: 1 round
Area of Effect: One robe
Saving Throw: None

This spell enchants the priest's robe or cloak, enabling him to walk among wounded creatures and heal them. By touching the robe, a wounded creature is cured of 1d4 + 4 hit points. As many creatures as can physically touch the robe within the spell duration can be healed. A reasonable maximum is 20 creatures per round, allowing a total of 1,200 creatures to be healed. A creature can be affected only once per week by the *robe of healing*.

Siege Wall (Alteration, Invocation)

Sphere: Creation, Guardian
Range: 480 yards
Duration: Special
Casting Time: 1 turn
Area of Effect: One building
Saving Throw: None

A *siege wall* uses magical energy to fortify all external areas of a fortified building, such as walls, battlements, drawbridges, and gates. External surfaces to be protected must be contiguous.

The protective effects of the *siege wall* are compatible with BATTLESYSTEM rules (see Chapter 7). Creatures assaulting the protected building have their movement rates reduced by half when trying to scale the exterior surfaces (scaling ladders, etc.). Attackers suffer a −2 penalty to damage rolls for missile fire.

Damage or AD caused by war machines is reduced by 2 die levels (if normal damage is 1d12, 1d8 is rolled instead; if damage is 1d10, 1d6 is rolled; ballista has AD8). Damage caused by crushing engines is rolled at −2 to the damage roll or ADs. Hits or hit points of crushing engines are reduced by half.

All enemies attacking a building protected by *siege wall* who enter an enclosed wall space are

out of command unless they are in the line of sight of their commander, regardless of his control diameter.

All exterior areas of the fortification have their hit points or Hits doubled (see *Hits of Building Features* in BATTLESYSTEM rules).

The siege wall expires if the building is destroyed; it lasts a maximum of 24 hours.

Shooting Stars (Conjuration, Invocation)

Sphere: Combat, Sun, Weather
Range: 120 yards
Duration: Instantaneous
Casting Time: 1 round
Area of Effect: 40-yard radius
Saving Throw: 1/2

A priest casting *shooting stars* creates a violent turbulence in the air above the area of effect, from which a number of fiery-orange, electrically-charged miniature fireballs erupt and shower onto the ground. Within the area of effect, all creatures suffer 6d10 points of combined fire and electrical damage. A successful saving throw at a −4 penalty indicates half damage.

In addition, four large shooting stars materialize within the area of effect. The priest can individually target these at specific creatures. If creatures are not specified, the targets are randomly selected. Each shooting star causes 48 points of damage on impact (no saving throw is allowed). Any creature within 10 feet of impact suffers 24 points of fire damage (half-damage if a saving throw at −4 is successful).

Sphere of Security (Abjuration)

Sphere: Protection
Range: 0
Duration: 6 turns
Casting Time: Special
Area of Effect: 10-foot-radius sphere
Saving Throw: None

Sphere of security protects the priest who casts the spell and his companions within the area of effect. Enemy creatures within the area are unaffected.

The sphere grants affected creatures a +2 bonus to armor class, a +2 bonus to all saving throws vs. magic, and 50% magic resistance. Casting this portion of the spell requires 1 round.

In addition, the priest can specify as many as four additional specific protection effects from the List of Protection Scrolls in Appendix 3 of the

DMG. Each additional protection lengthens casting time by 1 round. The priest may create one effect per 5 levels of his experience, to a maximum of four effects.

Spiral of Degeneration
(Enchantment/Charm, Invocation)

Sphere: Chaos, Thought
Range: 0
Duration: 6 turns
Casting Time: 1 round
Area of Effect: 50-foot-diameter sphere
Saving Throw: Special

This potent spell affects all creatures hostile to the priest within the area of effect. The Power granting the spell causes the spell's effects to manifest in one of two ways: the Chaos variation or the Thought variation.

In the Chaos variation, the fabric of reality is altered to change events. Magical items dysfunction because the fabric of magical reality is changed.

In the Thought variation, the thoughts of the victims of the spell are distorted and altered so that they find themselves unable to function coherently and effectively. Magical items dysfunction because the thoughts of their users are warped to either convince them that the items cannot function or block thought so that proper commands cannot be given.

The effects on the victims of the spell are the same for both variations. Each round, there is a 50% chance that a degeneration effect will occur in the area of effect. When this occurs, two events take place. First, spellcasters lose one spell from each level of spell currently memorized (e.g., a spellcaster who has memorized three spells each from levels 1 through 3 loses one spell from each level for a total of three). Lost spells may be regained normally through rest and memorization.

Second, magical items are affected in the following ways:

• Weapons and armor lose one level of enchantment (a *sword +3* becomes a *sword +2*, etc.).

• Magical items that carry charges (wands, rods, staves, etc.) are drained of 1d10 charges.

• Magical items without pluses or charges must make a saving throw versus spell (using the saving throw of their owner) or become nonmagical.

• Potions lose all magic and scrolls lose one randomly determined spell.

• Permanent magical items (swords, boots, armor, etc.) temporarily lose all effects until the spell expires or until the items leave the area of effect and for 1d10 rounds thereafter.

Single-use and charged items are permanently affected by this spell. A potion destroyed by this spell remains useless even after the spell ends.

Within the area of effect, magical communication is impossible due to thought blocks and chaotic effects. No communication magic (*ESP, sending,* etc.) will function; any spellcaster trying to cast such a spell will be stunned for 1 round per level of the spell he attempts to cast. A reverse of the *tongues* spell operates continuously in the area of effect. Telepathic communication (e.g., with a familiar) is also impossible.

In the Chaos variation of the spell, the center of the area of effect moves 10' per round. The direction is randomly determined using 1d8 roll and compass points (1 = N, 2 = NE, 3 = E, 4 = SE, 5 = S, 6 = SW, 7 = W, 8 = NW). The radius of the spell effect will never exclude the priest who cast the spell; re-roll any result that leads to this occurrence.

Stalker (Conjuration/Summoning)

Sphere: Creation, Guardian, Plant
Range: 30 yards
Duration: Special
Casting Time: 1 round
Area of Effect: Special
Saving Throw: None

A priest casting this spell conjures 1d4 + 2 plant creatures which have statistics identical to shambling mounds of 11HD. These creatures will aid the caster in combat or battle, perform a specific mission, or serve as bodyguards. The creatures remain with the priest for seven days unless he dismisses them. If the *stalkers* are summoned only for guard duty, however, the duration of the spell is seven months. In this case, the *stalkers* can only be ordered to guard a specific site or location.

The *stalkers* gain resistance to fire as per shambling mounds *only* if the terrain is suitable (marshy, close to a body of water, etc.).

Storm of Vengeance (**Evocation**)

Sphere: Elemental, War, Weather
Range: 400 yards
Duration: 1 turn
Casting Time: 1 turn
Area of Effect: 120-yard radius circle
Saving Throw: Special

This spell requires the priest to concentrate and cast the spell for the full duration of the spell. The casting time and duration are simultaneous; both activities occur in the same turn.

In the first round of casting, the priest summons an enormous black storm cloud over the area of effect. Lightning and crashing claps of thunder appear within the storm; creatures in the area of effect must make a saving throw or be deafened for 1d4 turns.

On the second round, acid rains down in the area, inflicting 1d4 + 1 points of damage. No saving throw is allowed.

On the third round, the caster calls six lightning bolts down from the cloud. Each is directed at a target by the priest (all may be directed at a single target or they may be directed at six separate targets). Each lightning bolt strike causes 8d8 points of damage (a successful saving throw indicates half damage).

On the fourth round, hailstones rain down in the area, causing 3d10 points of damage (no saving throw).

On the fifth through tenth (and final) rounds, violent rain and wind gusts reduce visibility to five feet. Movement is reduced 75%. Missile fire and spellcasting from within the area of effect are impossible.

The sequence of effects ceases immediately if the priest is disrupted from spellcasting during the 1 turn duration of the spell. The priest may opt to cancel the effects at any time.

Transformation
(**Alteration, Enchantment, Illusion**)

Sphere: Numbers
Range: 0
Duration: 3 turns
Casting Time: 1 round
Area of Effect: 100-yard-radius sphere
Saving Throw: None

The *transformation* spell allows the priest to alter extradimensional and relative geometries within the area of effect. This enables the priest and his companions to use extradimensional links to facilitate rapid movement as follows.

All allies of the priest are able to *blink* (as per the 3rd-level wizard spell) once per round, with the ability to select the direction of movement.

As many as 10 creatures (designated by the priest at the time of spellcasting) can use the *teleport without error* spell. They may teleport anywhere within the area of effect of the *transformation* spell once during the duration of the spell.

As many as 10 creatures (specified by the priest at the time of spellcasting) gain abilities as if wearing *boots of striding and springing* for the spell duration.

At any time during the spell, the priest and as many as 10 other creatures can be affected as per a *shadow walk* spell. Creatures to be affected must stand in a circle and touch hands. As soon as the priest who cast the *transformation* spell leaves the area of effect via the *shadow walk*, all other effects of the *transformation* are canceled.

Undead Plague (**Necromancy**)

Sphere: Necromantic
Range: 1 mile
Duration: Special
Casting Time: 2 rounds
Area of Effect: 100-yard square/level
Saving Throw: None

By means of this potent spell, the priest summons many ranks of skeletons to do his bidding. The skeletons are formed from any and all humanoid bones within the area of effect. The number of skeletons depends on the terrain in the area of effect; a battlesite or graveyard will yield 10 skeletons per 100 square yards; a long-inhabited area will yield three skeletons per 100 square yards; and wilderness will yield one skeleton per 100 square yards.

The spell's maximum area of effect is 10,000 square yards. Thus, no more than 1,000 skeletons can be summoned by this spell.

The skeletons created by this spell are turned as zombies and remain in existence until destroyed or willed out of existence by the priest who created them.

Warband Quest (Enchantment/Charm)

Sphere: Charm, War
Range: 240 yards
Duration: Special
Casting Time: 1 round
Area of Effect: 200 creatures
Saving Throw: Neg.

A priest may cast *warband quest* on any group of 200 creatures who are capable of understanding his commands. The creatures are then affected in a manner similar to the 5th-level priest spell, *quest.* Unwilling creatures are allowed a saving throw with a −4 penalty to avoid the effects.

The specified quest must be related to the reason that the Power granted this spell (perhaps a quest to slay or overcome a specified enemy).

Warband quest gives subjects of the spell a bonus of 2 hp per level of the caster (maximum 20 hp). Subjects also gain the effects of a *prayer* spell and have Morale of 18 while on the quest. These benefits last for the duration of the spell; the spell ends when the specified task is completed. A creature who abandons the quest is subject to the wrath of his deity.

Ward Matrix (Invocation/Evocation)

Sphere: Wards
Range: Special
Duration: 60 days
Casting Time: 6 turns
Area of Effect: Special
Saving Throw: None

The *ward matrix* spell links as many as six locations within the Prime Material plane. Only locations that have a functioning Wards spell may be linked. *Ward matrix* conjoins the different Wards spells so that each linked site gains the protection of all other wards in the network.

From the place where the *ward matrix* is cast, magical connections spread to the other designated sites. These can be seen with a *true seeing* or similar spell as tendrils of magical energy running through the air just above ground level. The connections target their destinations and move toward them at a rate of 40 miles per turn. They can evade barriers such as *anti-magic shell*s by moving above or around them. When the connections reach their destinations, they multiply and spread to connect all other locations in the network; this secondary linkage is established at a rate of 20 miles per turn.

The conjoining of Wards lasts for 60 days unless a linked area is destroyed or a Wards spell is dispelled. Any location that is destroyed or has its Wards spell dispelled is removed from the matrix; other connections remain intact for the duration.

Wolf Spirits
(Conjuration/Summoning, Invocation)

Sphere: Animal, Guardian, Summoning
Range: 30 yards
Duration: Special
Casting Time: 2 turns
Area of Effect: Special
Saving Throw: None

The priest casting this spell calls upon the "spirits" of wolves (or another animal, if appropriate). The notion of wolf spirits is akin to the Wild Hunt of Celtic mythology: a pack of enormous magical wolves led by a human master who range Celtic lands seeking to destroy evil. The *wolf spirits* spell summons 2d4+2 such entities to serve the priest as master.

Wolf spirits' statistics are as follows: AC −4; MV 36 Fl 36 (B); HD 5+5; #AT 1; Dmg 3d6; AL N; SZ M; ML 20; THAC0 14. They are immune to all forms of mind control, illusions, gases, paralyzation, and spells which affect only corporeal creatures. They cannot be harmed by weapons of less than +2 enchantment.

Wolf spirits can be instructed to perform a service in the manner of the *animal summoning* spells. In this variation in the Animal and Summoning spheres, the spell does not expire until the spirits have performed their commanded service, to a maximum duration of 14 days. In the Guardian variation of this spell, the spirits can only be commanded to keep watch over an area or creature. The spell lasts 100 days for this type of service.

Table 4: POTIONS AND OILS

D20 Roll	Item	XP Value
1-4	Aroma of Dreams	300
5-6	Curdled Death	750
7-12	Murdock's Insect Ward	200
13	Oils of Elemental Plane Invulnerability	5,000
14-15	Oil of Preservation	750
16-17	Potion of Elemental Control	600
18-20	Starella's Aphrodisiac	250

Table 5: RINGS

D20 Roll	Item	XP Value
1-3	Affliction	—
4-6	Armoring (W)	2,000
7-8	Bureaucratic Wizardry (W)	—
9-11	Elemental Metamorphosis	3,000
12-14	Fortitude	1,000
15-17	Randomness (P)	—
18-20	Resistance (W)	1,000

Table 6: RODS, STAVES, WANDS

D20 Roll	Item	XP Value
1-4	Rod of Distortion	5,000
5-6	Staff of the Elements (W)	10,000
7-12	Wand of Corridors	4,000
13-14	Wand of Element Transmogrification	2,000
15-17	Wand of Misplaced Objects	2,000
18-20	Wand of Prime Material Pocket	5,000

Table 7: MISCELLANEOUS MAGIC: Books, Librams, Manuals, Tomes

D20 Roll	Item	XP Value
1-7	Manual of Dogmatic Methods	—
8-16	Tome of Mystical Equations (P)	1,000
17-20	Trimia's Catalogue of Outer Plane Artifacts (W)	12,000

Table 8: MISCELLANEOUS MAGIC: Jewels, Jewelry, Phylacteries

D20 Roll	Item	XP Value
1-2	Amulet of Extension (W)	1,000
3-4	Amulet of Far Reaching (W)	1,000
5-6	Amulet of Leadership	5,000
7	Amulet of Magic Resistance	5,000
8	Amulet of Metaspell Influence (W)	3,000
9-10	Amulet of Perpetual Youth	2,000
11	Brooch of Number Numbing	4,000
12	Gem of Retaliation	2,000
13-14	Medallion of Spell Exchange (W)	3,000
15-16	Necklace of Memory Enhancement	1,000
17-18	Scarab of Uncertainty	1,000
19-20	Talisman of Memorization (W)	1,000

Table 9: MISCELLANEOUS MAGIC: Bracers, Gloves, Hats, Robes

D20 Roll	Item	XP Value
1-4	Bracers of Brandishing	3,000
5-8	Fur of Warmth	5,000
9-12	Reglar's Gloves of Freedom	3,000
13-16	Robe of Repetition (P,W)	6,000
17-20	School Cap (W)	2,000

Table 10: MISCELLANEOUS MAGIC: Bags, Bottles, Pouches, Containers

D20 Roll	Item	XP Value
1-3	Bag of Bones (P)	3,000
4-8	Flatbox	5,000
9-13	Jar of Preserving	500
14-15	Nefradina's Identifier (W)	1,000
16	Tenser's Portmanteau of Frugality (W)	6,000
17-20	Thought Bottle	1,000

Table 11: MISCELLANEOUS MAGIC: Candles, Dusts, Ointments, Stones

D20 Roll	Item	XP Value
1-3	Candle of Propitiousness	750
4-5	Dust of Mind Dulling	1,000
6-7	Powder of the Black Veil	1,000
8-9	Powder of Coagulation	500
10-11	Powder of the Hero's Heart	750
12-13	Powder of Magic Detection	1,000
14-15	Puchezma's Powder of Edible Objects	1,000
16-19	Salves of Far Seeing	1,000
20	Warp Marble	5,000

Items followed by a letter in parentheses are usable only by specific classes: P = Priest, W = Wizard, Wr = Warrior.

Table 12: MISCELLANEOUS MAGIC:
Household Items, Tools, Musical Instruments

D20 Roll	Item	XP Value
1	Crucible of Melting (W)	1,000
2-3	Everbountiful Soup Kettle	1,000
4	Forge of Metal Protection	10,000
5	Glass of Preserved Words	2,000
6	Horn of Valor	5,000
7	Hourglass of Fire and Ice (W)	2,000
8	Lens of Speed Reading	500
9-10	Lorloveim's Obsidian Mortar and Pestle	500
11	Mirror of Retention	1,200
12	Mirror of Simple Order	—
13	Mordom's Cauldron of Air	3,000
14	Philosopher's Egg (W)	1,000
15	Pick of Earth Parting	5,000
16-17	Skie's Locks and Bolts	1,000
18-19	Tapestry of Disease Warding	2,000
20	Zwann's Watering Can (P)	1,000

Table 13: MISCELLANEOUS MAGIC:
The Weird Stuff

D20 Roll	Item	XP Value
1	Air Spores	500
2	Bell's Palette of Identity	1,000
3	Claw of Magic Stealing (W)	3,500
4	Contracts of Nepthas	1,000
5	Crystal Parrot	1,500
6	Dimensional Mine	—
7	Disintegration Chamber	5,000
8	Elemental Compass	10,000
9	Globe of Purification (P)	500
10	Globe of Serenity (P)	500
11	Law's Banner (Wr)	5,000
12	Liquid Road	500
13	Mist Tent	2,000
14	Mouse Cart	3,500
15	Portable Canoe	2,000
16	Prism of Light Splitting	1,500
17	Quill of Law	7,000
18	Saddle of Flying	4,000
19	Teleportation Chamber	10,000
20	Time Bomb	1,000

Aromatic Oils

Aromatic oils are a special type of magical oil. Like perfumes, their power comes from the scent released. All aromatic oils are inert until worn by a living creature. Once applied, the aromatic oil gradually begins to react, and after 1d4 rounds have passed, the scent's stated effect begins. In all cases, the creature wearing the aromatic oil is not affected, but other creatures (both friends and foes) within a 5-foot radius of the wearer are subject to its effects. Note that only those creatures with a sense of smell can be affected by a magical fragrance.

These precious perfumes are commonly found in tiny stoppered vials made of glass, clay, metal, or wood. Only a small amount is required per use. Each vial contains enough aromatic oil for 1d10 + 10 applications.

Aroma of Dreams: All creatures who come within 5' of the wearer of this oil are put to sleep. Potential victims are allowed a saving throw vs. spell. If successful, the victim suffers no effect and may remain near the wearer without need of further saving throws. If the roll is failed, the creature slumps to the ground, the victim of a magical slumber that lasts 1d4 + 4 rounds.

When an application of the oil is worn, the scent is potent for 3d4 rounds. After this time, the perfume evaporates and another dose must be applied if the wearer wishes to renew the effect.

Curdled Death: Perhaps the most powerful of all aromatic oils, the smell of *curdled death* has the ability to slay all living creatures of 3 or fewer Hit Dice or experience levels who come within 5' of the wearer. Magical, undead, and extraplanar creatures are immune to this oil, as are all creatures of 4 or more Hit Dice or experience levels.

Upon smelling the oil, potential victims are allowed a saving throw vs. spell. If successful, a creature suffers no effect and may remain near the wearer without need of further saving throws. Those who fail the save drop dead in their tracks.

When a dose is worn, it remains potent enough to kill creatures for 1d3 rounds. After this time, the fragrance evaporates and another dose must be applied if the wearer wishes to renew the effect.

Murdock's Insect Ward: This fragrance is a boon to travelers, since it repels insectoid creatures (both normal and monstrous) that come within 5 feet of the wearer of this fragrance. Insectoid monsters with Intelligence scores of 5 or more are allowed a saving throw vs. spell. If successful, they suffer no effects and may remain near the wearer without need of further saving throws. If the save is failed, the creature cannot approach within 5 feet of the wearer. (Note that this still may be close enough to cause harm.) One dose is effective for 1d3 + 1 hours.

Starella's Aphrodisiac: Any creature of a similar race and opposite sex who approaches within 5 feet of the wearer becomes thoroughly enamored with the wearer as if under the effect of a powerful charm. Potential victims are allowed a saving throw vs. spell. If the roll is successful, the victim suffers no effects and may remain near the wearer without need of further saving throws.

If the save is failed, the creature is charmed as long as he or she remains within 5' of the wearer (as long as the aphrodisiac is still potent) plus 2d4 turns outside that area. An affected creature regards the wearer as a trusted friend, ally, and romantic interest to be heeded and protected. The charmed individual does not behave as if he were a mindless automaton, but any word or action of the wearer is viewed in the most favorable way. This attitude does not extend to others, and it is possible for the person so enamored to be overcome by jealousy, viewing all others (especially other victims) as potential rivals.

When a dose of *Starella's aphrodisiac* is worn, it remains potent for 3d4 turns. After this time, the perfume evaporates and another dose must be applied if the wearer wishes to renew the effect.

Potions

Potion of Elemental Control: When this potion is consumed, the imbiber can influence one or two elementals in a manner similar to a *charm monster* spell. The elementals must be within 60 feet of the imbiber and are allowed a saving throw vs. petrification to avoid the effect. If only one elemental is influenced, it is subject to a −4 penalty on its save. If two are influenced, their saving throws gain a +2 bonus because the effect of the potion is weakened.

If either elemental is controlled by another wizard, it gains a +2 bonus to its saving throw. Note that if the elemental was summoned by the 5th-level *conjure elemental* spell, the summoner has a 50% chance of dispelling the creature. Control lasts for 5d6 rounds.

The type of elemental subject to a particular potion is randomly determined.

D4 Roll	Elemental Type
1	Air
2	Earth
3	Fire
4	Water

Oil of Elemental Plane Invulnerability: These precious oils provide total invulnerability against the elemental forces on one inner plane, as well as offering the same protection as the *oil of elemental invulnerability.* Any character covered in the oil suffers no ill effects from the harsh environments of the elemental, para-elemental, and quasi-elemental planes. Attacks by elemental creatures are effective, but with a −1 penalty per die of damage.

A flask of oil contains enough oil to coat one man-sized creature six times or six individuals once. An application is effective for 24 hours.

The protection the oil offers is determined randomly with two die rolls. First, 1d4 is rolled to select a table below: 1 = Table A, 2 = Table B, 3 = Table C, 4 = Table D. Second, 1d4 is rolled on that table.

Table A		Table B	
D4 Roll	**Plane**	**D4 Roll**	**Plane**
1	Air	1	Smoke
2	Water	2	Ice
3	Earth	3	Ooze
4	Fire	4	Magma

Table C		Table D	
D4 Roll	**Plane**	**D4 Roll**	**Plane**
1	Lightning	1	Vacuum
2	Steam	2	Salt
3	Radiance	3	Ash
4	Minerals	4	Dust

Anyone covered in the oil can see, breathe, and move in the respective plane without difficulty. Just as a character can move through flames or water without difficulty when covered in the proper oil, a character doused in the oil of earth can pass through the stone of the elemental plane of Earth as if it were air.

Oil of Preservation: Any nonliving, non-magical object may be coated with a layer of *oil of preservation.* If every surface of the object is covered, it will suffer no ill effects from the passage of time. Thus, wood will not rot, metal will not rust, and masonry will not crumble. The oil provides pro-tection from both natural and magical aging.

One flask of *oil of preservation* will protect 1 cubic foot of surface area. The effects of the oil wear off after one century, at which time normal aging resumes.

Powders

Magical powders are usually stored in small paper packets, cloth pouches, or hollow blow tubes made of glass, wood, metal, or bone. A packet or pouch can be shaken out to cover the area all around the user to a radius of 5 feet. This action lasts an entire round. Note that powders used in this manner can affect the user.

Alternatively, powder in a tube can be blown outward in a ten-foot-long cone shape that is one foot wide at the apex and five feet wide at the end. Used in this manner, the powder has no chance of affecting the user (unless it rebounds on him due to wind or similar circumstances).

Powders may also be blown from the user's hand, but can only affect a single individual within five feet of the user.

Powder of the Black Veil: This sooty, black powder causes temporary magical blindness to all those in the area of effect. If a creature's saving throw is successful, he suffers no effects. If the roll fails, the creature is blinded and suffers a −4 penalty to attack rolls, a −4 penalty to Armor Class, and a +2 penalty to initiative rolls. Blindness persists each round until the victim succeeds at a saving throw vs. spell, at which time the effect is instantly negated. An entire packet or blow tube must be used for each application.

Powder of Coagulation: When placed on an open wound, a pinch of this yellow powder stops all bleeding and heals 1d6 hit points of damage. Each pouch or packet contains 4d4 pinches. A blow tube contains one use, but stops bleeding and heals 1d4 hit points for all creatures in the area of effect.

Powder of the Hero's Heart: When used, this dull red powder instills bravery in all creatures within the area of effect (both friends and enemies). It grants such creatures a morale bonus of +2 and negates the effects of magical fear. The effect lasts for 5d4 rounds. An entire packet, pouch, or blow tube must be used for each application.

Powder of Magic Detection: Under close inspection, this ordinary-looking powder can be seen for what it truly is—an extremely fine powder of minute, crystalline granules. When this powder contacts a magical object, the crystals spark and flash with a rainbow of colors. This effect does not reveal the nature or intensity of the enchantment—only that the item is magical.

A small pinch of powder is needed for each use, no matter how large or small the object. Each packet contains 1d10+10 pinches. Powder that is placed on a nonmagical item yields no effect and cannot be reused.

Rings

Ring of Affliction: When an *identify* spell is used on this cursed ring, it will appear to be a *ring of resistance*. The ring will function as such until the wearer makes a saving throw to any school in opposition to the school represented by the ring. The school of magic represented can be determined by rolling 1d8 on the table below.

D8 Roll	Represented School
1	Abjuration
2	Alteration
3	Conjuration/Summoning
4	Enchantment/Charm
5	Illusion/Phantasm
6	Invocation/Evocation
7	Lesser/Greater Divination
8	Necromancy

The first time the wearer of a *ring of affliction* makes a saving throw against any school in opposition to the school of the ring worn, the *ring of affliction's* true properties are revealed. The ring causes the wearer to suffer a −2 penalty on all saving throws vs. spells of the ring's opposing school or schools. Once this power is activated, the beneficial effects of the ring no longer operate. Once the curse has been activated, the wearer can remove the ring only through a *remove curse* spell.

Ring of Armoring: A wizard wearing this ring gains an additional +1 bonus to any AC bonus he receives from casting a spell upon himself. Thus, an *armor* spell grants the wizard AC 5 instead of AC 6, and a *shield* spell grants the wizard AC 1 versus hand-hurled missiles instead of AC 2. Restrictions that apply to a spell (for example, *armor* does not affect a character already wearing armor) are in no way altered through use of this ring.

Ring of Bureaucratic Wizardry: This cursed ring is indistinguishable from a *ring of wizardry*, but has one important difference. When a wizard casts any spell while wearing the ring, a sheaf of papers and a quill pen suddenly appear in his hand. The papers are forms that must be filled out in triplicate explaining the effects of the spell, why the wizard wishes to cast it, whether it is for business or pleasure, and so on. The forms must be filled out before the effects of the spell will occur. The higher the level of the spell cast, the more complicated the forms become. Filling out the forms requires one round per level of spell.

As soon as the papers are filled out, the forms and the pen disappear and the spell effects occur as the spellcaster desired.

The ring cannot be removed willingly. *Remove curse* or a similar spell must be cast upon the wearer in order to remove the ring.

Ring of Elemental Metamorphosis: There are four types of these rings, each corresponding to one of the four elements. When one of these rings is discovered, the type is determined randomly.

D4 Roll	Element
1	Air
2	Earth
3	Fire
4	Water

Each of these rings has the power to *polymorph* the wearer into an elemental of the appropriate type. When the transformation occurs, the subject's equipment is absorbed into his new form. The affected character retains his mental abilities, but cannot cast spells.

Characters who are not accustomed to the new form suffer a −2 penalty on attack rolls until they successfully strike an opponent in two consecutive combat rounds. After this occurs, it is assumed they have mastered their new shape.

The *polymorphed* character acquires the form and physical abilities of the appropriate elemental. This includes Armor Class (but the character is subject to attacks by weapons of less than +2 enchantment), movement rates, and attack routines (including special attacks). Hit points and saving throws are identical to those for the character's natural form.

Additionally, the character is immune to damage from exposure to the element he has become, and may move and breathe freely within the natural element. Thus, a character metamorphosed into a fire elemental could swim in a pool of nonmagical lava without risk of injury, but the same character could be damaged by magical fire, such as that from a *fireball* spell.

The ring may be used once per day for 1d4+1 turns, at which time the character reverts to his normal form. The wearer can end the metamorphosis at any time. When returning to his own form, the wearer regains 1d12 hit points.

If a successful *dispel magic* spell is cast upon the subject at any time while he is transformed, he is forced back into his normal form and must succeed at a system shock roll or die. The wearer returns to his own form when slain or when the effect is dispelled, but no hit points are restored in these cases.

Ring of Fortitude: When worn, the *ring of fortitude* grants the wearer a bonus of +4 to one randomly selected ability score (roll 1d12: 1-6 = Dexterity, 7-11 = Wisdom, 12 = Constitution) **for the purposes of spell resolution only.** It does not affect ability checks or other aspects of ability scores, except those as a direct result of spells or spell-like abilities.

For example, a character with a natural Constitution of 14 would have an enhanced score of 18 while wearing such a ring. He does not gain any extra hit points from wearing it, but his system shock for resolving the *polymorph other* spell is increased to 99%. With the Constitution-enhancing ring, the bonuses even apply to the *raise dead* and *resurrection* spells. All effects are lost when the wearer removes the ring.

Ring of Randomness: When an *identify* spell is cast on this cursed clerical ring, it radiates the aura of a beneficial ring to disguise its nature. The DM should roll 1d100 to determine the ring's power.

D100 Roll	Power
01-25	*protection from evil*
26-40	*continual light*
41-60	*bless*
61-70	*cure light wounds*
71-80	*remove fear*
81-90	*heat metal*
91-100	*cure blindness or deafness*

A ring can be used three times per day at the 12th level of ability. Each ring functions normally half the time, providing the indicated power. However, the ring's curse causes the *reverse* of the desired effect to manifest 50% of the time. The DM should roll secretly each time the ring is used

to determine whether the result is the desired effect or the reversed effect. Thus, a person casting *continual light* has a 50% chance of getting either light or darkness.

If the ring is used to cure blindness or deafness, a reversed result yields a special curse. Since *cause blindness* has no effect on a blind character, the ring further distorts the spell effect by shifting to *cause deafness*. Thus, a priest attempting to cast *cure blindness* whose ring indicated a reversed result would cause his victim to become deaf.

In addition, the priest runs the risk of his spells reversing every time he uses a reversible spell (even those cast normally).

The ring can be removed only with a successfully cast *dispel magic* spell.

Ring of Resistance: This ring grants a wizard a saving throw bonus identical to the bonus gained by a specialist in a particular school of magic. The magical school affected is randomly determined on the table below by rolling 1d8.

D8 Roll	Affected School
1	Abjuration
2	Alteration
3	Conjuration/Summoning
4	Enchantment/Charm
5	Illusion/Phantasm
6	Invocation/Evocation
7	Lesser/Greater Divination
8	Necromancy

When required to save against a spell from that school, the wearer gains a +1 bonus to his saving throw. When the wearer casts a spell from that school, his opponent suffers a −1 modifier to all saving throws. This ring does not allow a wizard to cast spells from a school in opposition to his own.

These modifiers are cumulative with all others, including those in effect for specialization.

Rod

Rod of Distortion: This unpredictable device is capable of affecting the operation of all rods, staves, and wands within a 20-foot radius for a single round. The wielder rolls 1d20. On a roll of 1-15, the *rod of distortion* does not influence other items. On a roll of 16-19, it acts as a *wand of negation* and rods, staves, and wands within 20 feet simply do not function during that round (but are otherwise unaffected). On a roll of 20, the *rod of distortion* completely disrupts the functioning of rods, staves, and wands. This distortion results in the backfiring of these devices, causing maximum damage to their users if the item is used during that round (e.g., a *wand of lightning* will fire a backward-directed bolt striking its user, a *rod of cancellation* will affect one random magical item possessed by its owner, and so on). Items used by the wielder of the rod are unaffected.

This rod cannot be recharged.

Staff

Staff of the Elements: This powerful item appears to be a *staff +2.* If it is grasped by an elementalist, however, its true powers become evident.

A *staff of the elements* is charged by the life-force of an elemental trapped within it. The staff has charges equal to the number of Hit Dice of the elemental multiplied by 2. Thus, a staff holding a 12 HD elemental has 24 charges. Every time two charges are expended, the elemental loses one Hit Die. When all charges are used, the elemental dies and the staff becomes dormant.

If a dormant staff is used to successfully strike an elemental, the creature must immediately attempt a saving throw vs. rods, staves, and wands. If the save is failed, the elemental is absorbed into the staff, thereby recharging the device. If the roll is successful, the creature avoids the effect, but suffers normal damage from the strike of the magical staff (1d6+2).

It is possible to absorb an elemental only if the staff is dormant. Only one elemental may be held in the staff at one time.

The staff holds the following powers that do not drain charges; each may be used once per day even if the staff does not hold an elemental:

- *affect normal fires*
- detect elementals within a 100' radius
- *fool's gold*
- *metamorphose liquids**
- *wall of fog*

An occupied staff has the following powers depending upon the type of elemental trapped within. For example, if a fire elemental is held in the staff, only those powers related to fire are available. Each requires the expenditure of one charge per use:

Air:	• *stinking cloud*
	• *wind wall*
Earth:	• *dig*
	• *Maximilian's stony grasp**
Fire:	• *fireball*
	• *pyrotechnics*
Water:	• *water breathing*
	• *watery double**

The following powers drain two charges per use:

Air:	• *cloudkill*
	• *solid fog*
Earth:	• *passwall*
	• *transmute rock to mud*
Fire:	• *fire shield*
	• *wall of fire*
Water:	• *airy water*
	• *wall of ice*

The most powerful abilities of the staff drain four charges per use:

Air:	• *airboat**
	• *suffocate**
Earth:	• *crystalbrittle*
	• *stone to flesh* (reversible)
Fire:	• *Forest's fiery constrictor**
	• *Malec-Keth's flame fist**
Water:	• *Abi-Dalzim's horrid wilting**
	• *transmute water to dust*

The powers of a *staff of the elements* may be used only by an elementalist. Note that elementalists are restricted against the use of spells and magical items of the element that directly opposes their element of specialty. Thus, an elementalist specializing in water cannot use the staff's powers if it contains a fire elemental.

Using a *staff of the elements* can be dangerous. Each time a power is used that requires the expenditure of one or more charges, there is a 5% chance that the trapped elemental bursts forth, destroying the staff in the process. A successful *dispel magic* spell cast on the staff automatically releases the creature. An escaped elemental will certainly seek revenge against its tormenter.

Powers marked with an asterisk (*) are new spells found in this book.

Wands

Wand of Corridors: This wand allows its user to clear short corridors through the plane of elemental Earth and the quasi-elemental plane of Minerals. It does not function on any other plane, although it radiates magic. It is especially useful on the plane of minerals since travelers need not contact the sharp edges of the minerals.

One charge clears a 10′ × 10′ × 50′ path. The corridor is completed in 1 turn. The wand has no effect on animals or living creatures. Thus, if the wand clears a path through a space occupied by an earth elemental, the creature is unharmed, but is alerted to persons in the corridor. The wand can be recharged.

Wand of Element Transmogrification: This wand changes a quantity of one element into an equal amount of another element (water into fire, earth into air, etc.). The element to be affected must be within 60 feet of the wielder, who merely points the wand at the element and speaks the command word. For every 10 cubic feet (or portion thereof) transformed, one charge is drained from the wand.

The transmogrification is permanent unless a successful *dispel magic* is cast on the element.

Elements created by this wand have special characteristics. Fire requires no fuel to burn. Water never evaporates. Air is absolutely pure, but unless contained, the air mingles with the atmosphere and is lost forever. Earth can appear as soil, sand, clay, or stone, at the wielder's option. It is not possible to create treasure such as valuable metals or gemstones with this wand.

This wand has no effect upon creatures of any kind, except those from the Elemental planes. By changing such creatures into their element of opposition (fire into water, air into earth, etc.), the creature is totally obliterated. Thus, transmuting a water elemental into fire disintegrates it.

A creature attacked by the wand is allowed a saving throw vs. rods, staves, and wands. If the save is failed, the elemental is destroyed. If the save is successful, the creature is not obliterated outright, but suffers 6d6 points of damage and retains its true form.

In attacking an elemental, the number of Hit Dice of the elemental determines the number of charges used: 1 charge for an 8 HD elemental, 2 charges for a 12 HD elemental, and 3 charges for a 16 HD elemental. It is not possible to use this wand to change an elemental into another type of elemental.

The wand may be used once per round. It may be recharged.

Wand of Misplaced Objects: This wand emits a multitude of golden orbs that rush toward a target creature. The orbs surround the victim and swirl around him wildly for 1 round. During this time the victim is confused and can take no action.

At the end of the round, the orbs vanish and the victim is free to act. He discovers, however, that all objects on his person have been moved. Some items are inconveniently located, while others are nowhere to be seen. A warrior might find his magical ring on one of his toes, his sword in his pants, his gold pieces in the sheath of his sword, and his breastplate on his head. The more possessions a victim owns, the more confused the situation becomes. The DM is encouraged to be devious.

Because of the chaotic placement of items, the victim suffers several penalties. Movement is reduced by half. Armor class of characters wearing armor is reduced by 2, since pieces are not worn properly. Attack rolls made by the victim are made at a −2 penalty. These penalties are eliminated if the victim devotes 2-5 rounds (1d4 + 1) to rearranging his gear.

A character requiring an item carried in a backpack, pouch, pocket, or other container must spend 2-12 (2d6) rounds searching for the item. This penalty is canceled if 3 turns are spent unpacking and repacking all gear.

The DM must define the locations of objects any time a character reaches for them or if they impair motion or sight. When deciding locations of objects, the DM should state the obvious effects of impaired sight and movement immediately, such as boots worn on hands or a cloak over the face.

Items held within a *bag of holding, Heward's handy haversack,* or other magical containers are unaffected. However, the containers themselves are subject to relocation.

The wand uses one charge per attack. It may be recharged.

Wand of Prime Material Pocket: This wand allows a spherical pocket to be created in any plane. The conditions within the pocket are similar to the environment of the wielder's Prime Material plane. The pocket typically contains ground, air, and a controlled temperature. The lower third of the sphere is usually occupied by land and water, while the upper portion of the sphere is usually occupied by atmosphere.

The surface of the pocket is semipermeable, allowing creatures to exit and enter the sphere, but keeps the elemental conditions of the pocket completely separate from the elemental plane.

One charge creates a sphere 10' in diameter. If the wielder wishes, multiple charges can be used to create larger spheres. Thus, a 30'-diameter sphere could be created using three charges.

The conditions inside the pocket are of the wielder's choosing, although they must be similar to an area that naturally exists on the Prime Material plane. The pocket cannot contain buildings or man-made items.

The pocket lasts 1d6+6 hours on any plane other than the plane of Fire, on which the pocket will last 1d6 hours. The wielder may choose to use the wand before the pocket dissipates to extend the life of the existing pocket. The pocket can be destroyed through the use of a *dispel magic* spell. The wand is not rechargeable.

Miscellaneous Magic

Air Spores: Rumors indicate that the famed wizard Mordom created these odd, pollenlike spores. Only a few mages know how to make them today. *Air spores* that still exist are usually sequestered as specimens of study in the labs of powerful wizards.

When *air spores* are ingested by a creature, the spores work their way into the creature's lungs. There they grow, reproduce, and die. While living out their lives, they create oxygen that the host body can use to breathe when deprived of oxygen from the environment. The spore colony can live for 2d4 days.

In a normal environment, the spores hinder the character's normal respiration, causing all Constitution checks to be made with a −4 penalty. Fortunately, 12 hours of breathing in a normal environment for each day the spores were used will clear the lungs of the colony.

Amulet of Extension: When desired by the caster, this amulet can be used to increase the duration of 1st- and 2nd-level spells by 50%, and the duration of 3rd- and 4th-level spells by 25%. Fractions of one-half and above are rounded up (e.g., a spell with duration of 1 round extended to 1½ rounds is rounded to 2 rounds). Fractions less than one-half are rounded down (e.g., a spell with 1 round duration extended to 1¼ rounds is rounded down to 1 round and thus gains no benefit from the amulet).

The amulet has no effect on spells with instantaneous or permanent durations. A maximum of 1d10+4 spell levels can be affected by the amulet each day. Each amulet has its own individual limit, secretly determined when it is found. If this limit is exceeded on any given day, the amulet shatters and is destroyed permanently.

Amulet of Far Reaching: When willed by the caster, this amulet increases the range of 1st-level spells by 30%, 2nd-level spells by 20%, and 3rd- and 4th-level spells by 10%. Fractions of one-half and greater are rounded up; all others are rounded down.

The amulet affects only range and does not alter a spell's area of effect. The amulet cannot affect spells with ranges of 0 or touch.

A maximum of 1d10+4 spell levels can be affected by the amulet each day. Each amulet has its own individual limit, secretly determined when it is found.

Amulet of Leadership: This pendant or brooch bestows a character of any level the ability of a 9th-level fighter to attract men-at-arms. The amulet does not attract additional men-at-arms to a fighter who has already gained his followers.

A fighter normally gains troops at 9th level because his name is so well known that he attracts the loyalty of other warriors. The amulet works in much the same way. When a stranger meets a character wearing the amulet, the stranger perceives the character to be a leader who is destined for greatness, regardless of the character's class. Just as the reputation of a 9th-level fighter spreads, so the reputation of the person wearing the amulet spreads. Roll on Table 16 of the *Players Handbook* to determine the followers.

If the amulet is lost or destroyed, the followers immediately lose faith in their leader. They gradually depart or desert. Once this occurs, the character's reputation is sullied such that he can never benefit from the amulet again. A fighter can, however, gain followers normally upon reaching 9th level.

Amulet of Magic Resistance: This powerful amulet grants the wearer a degree of magic resistance ranging from 5% to 30%. The level of magic resistance is determined when the amulet is found by rolling 1d6 and multiplying the result by 5. Any time the amulet is worn and a spell is cast at the wearer, the wearer is allowed a percentile roll to avoid the full effects of the spell.

Only 50% of all such amulets confer magic resistance against all spells. The remaining 50% extend magic resistance only to spells of 1st through 6th levels. Such amulets have no effect on spells more powerful than these. The DM should secretly determine this information when the ring is discovered.

All such amulets, regardless of the degree of resistance conferred, are delicate magical structures. If the wearer rolls for magic resistance at any time and the roll is 95-00, this fragile item has been disrupted and the amulet shatters into useless scrap.

Amulet of Metaspell Influence: This amulet does not appear to have any magical function (although it radiates magic if detected) until it is worn by someone using one of the *dilation, far-reaching,* or *extension* spells. When such a spell is cast, the amulet adds 50% to the functional effect of the spell. For example, if *extension I* is used to increase the duration of a 3rd-level spell by 50%, the wearer of this amulet can add one-half (50%) to that effect size, raising it to a 75% extension effect.

Amulet of Perpetual Youth: This amulet glows continuously with a faint, blue light. The wearer has temporary immunity to the effects of both natural and magical aging; the amulet grows older instead of the wearer. As the amulet ages, it gradually becomes dimmer. The amulet can absorb 5-30 (5d6) years of aging, at which time its light dims completely, its magic is negated, and the wearer resumes aging at his normal rate.

Bag of Bones: This item, usable only by priests, is a small, ordinary-looking leather pouch that contains a number of tiny bones. When these bones are scattered over a 40 by 20 yard area and the word of command is spoken, a unit of skeletons immediately springs from the ground. This unit comprises eight BATTLESYSTEM rules figures of skeletons (80 skeletons) armed with swords. (The statistics for this unit are: AD 6, AR 8, Hits 1, ML n/a, MV 12". Hits from piercing and slashing weapons are reduced by half.)

The unit unconditionally obeys the combat orders of the priest, never checking morale. The unit fights until totally destroyed or until the sun sets (at which time the remaining skeletons crumble into dust). Two out of three (1-66 on 1d100) of these bags are "one-shot" magical items: once the bones are used, they are gone forever. One out of three (67-100 on 1d100) bags magically replen-

ishes itself every sunset if the bones have been used.

A *bag of bones* will work only on a battlefield in the full heat of battle. (For the purposes of this definition, a "battlefield" is a place where units are in conflict and where *at least* 100 individuals per side are involved.) The unit will never split up, and will obey no orders other than to enter combat.

Certain war deities may frown upon the use of undead or conjured troops, believing them to be unworthy and cowardly. Priests worshipping these deities may suffer divine consequences if they choose to use a *bag of bones.*

Bell's Palette of Identity: This device offers protection against *polymorph* spells and other magical effects that change a person's physical appearance.

The item is an artist's palette covered with bright, mystical paints. To use the item, a person must paint a self-portrait. The painting does not need to be created with any expertise, but the painter must believe that the portrait is accurate.

Any time a character carries his self-portrait on his person, the portrait suffers the effects of unsuccessful saving throws for him when *massmorph, polymorph other, polymorph any object,* or *seeming* spells are cast on him. The portrait also suffers the effects if a character steps in front of a *mirror of simple order.*

The character's saving throw is made normally. If successful, the spell simply fails. If the saving throw is unsuccessful, the portrait is altered, reflecting the effect of the spell, but the character is unharmed. Once the portrait suffers these effects, it no longer can offer protection for the person it represents.

A person on the plane of Hades carrying a picture made from *Bell's palette of identity* is protected from the effects of fading on this plane. It is the picture that slowly fades to grey while the person retains all of his color. After two weeks in Hades, a character makes a saving throw against being trapped in Hades. If the saving throw is unsuccessful, the portrait becomes useless to the person who painted it.

There is always a risk that some denizen of Hades will discover a baneful use for a discarded painting. Travelers are wise not to leave such personal effects behind on this plane.

A single *Bell's palette of identity* can be used to paint 2-5 portraits.

Bracers of Brandishing: These unpredictable and bewildering items appear similar to other magical bracers, but their magic is revealed only when the character wearing them uses a charged rod, staff, or wand. When a charge is expended from such an item, the *bracers of brandishing* alter the charge expenditure and the local balance of magical forces in a chaotic manner. The drain on the charged rod, staff, or wand is actually in the range of 5 charges to −4 (i.e., the item is recharged). The number of charges used is 1d10 − 5 (with negative results indicating that charges are restored). If an item is reduced below zero charges by a drain, it crumbles into dust immediately.

Items that are not normally rechargeable can be recharged through the chaotic operation of these items except for the *rod of absorption*.

Brooch of Number Numbing: This silver or golden brooch (15% are set with jewels) is used to fasten a cloak or a cape. It magically clouds the mind of anyone conversing with the wearer of the brooch, with the confusion applying only to numbers.

The brooch must be in plain sight to have any effect. Anyone conversing with someone wearing the brooch is allowed a saving throw vs. spell to avoid the effects.

If the save is failed, the victim falls under the brooch's special enchantment. The victim forgets the relative value of numbers. He cannot remember if five is greater than three or if tens are smaller than hundreds. Further, the victim does not recognize his inability to remember the values of numbers. While under the influence of the brooch, the victim thinks that all numbers are pretty much the same. He will accept any claim pertaining to numbers and accept almost any financial deal set before him.

The victim remembers the relative values of coins (that gold pieces are worth more than silver pieces), but not their exact conversions. Thus, the victim is unable to remember whether two silver pieces or 100 silver pieces are equal to one gold piece.

The enchantment lasts only as long as the wearer is present and for 2d6 rounds thereafter. Once the effect wears off, the victim regains his normal understanding of numbers. Furthermore, he remembers exactly what he did and said while under the influence of the brooch, although he may not be aware of the cause.

Candle of Propitiousness: This candle enhances attacks against a particular enemy within a defined area. The user lights the candle while speaking the exact name of a single foe. If the exact name is not known, the user must precisely identify the foe; saying, "the evil warrior" isn't precise enough, but stating, "the evil warrior who rules the village of Fair Meadows and carries a golden shield" is sufficient.

All characters who remain within a 50-foot-radius of the lighted candle receive a +2 bonus to all attack rolls made against the stated foe, regardless of whether the foe is within 50 feet of the candle. Characters who venture outside the area of effect lose the bonus. When the stated foe is within the area of effect, he suffers a −1 penalty to all his attack rolls.

There can be no interposing surfaces such as walls or doors between the *candle of propitiousness* and characters whom it affects. The stated foe is not allowed a saving throw to resist the effects of the candle.

The *candle of propitiousness* burns for up to one hour. If it is moved after it has been lit, its magic is immediately and permanently negated. Likewise, if its flame is extinguished, its magic immediately ends. Any magical or natural force capable of extinguishing a normal flame, such as a *gust of wind* or a splash of water, can extinguish a *candle of propitiousness*.

A *candle of propitiousness* can be lit and used only once.

Claw of Magic Stealing: This peculiar item is usually fashioned in the form of a miniature silver hand or claw. An attempt to identify it will suggest that it is an item capable of casting the 2nd-level wizard spell *spectral hand* three times per day. The claw can indeed do this, but this is only its secondary function.

The claw's real purpose is to steal spells from other spellcasters. If the victim of the *spectral hand* spell is a wizard, he must make a saving throw versus spell. Failure to make this save means that a randomly selected spell is drained from his memory and its energy is transferred to the claw's owner. The owner of the claw may then use this magical energy to "power" a memorized spell of his own, provided it is of the same or lower level. Such a spell may be cast without being lost from the mind of the wizard possessing the claw.

The *claw of magic stealing* does not store magical energy in any way; either the owner of the claw uses the energy to "power" a spell on the next round, or the energy dissipates and is lost.

Contracts of Nepthas: These magical contracts are written in black ink on golden-brown vellum. The contracts are usually found in ivory tubes, each tube containing 1d6 contracts. The contracts are blank and can be filled in by the user. The contracts will radiate magic if detected, but carry no overt signs of their special nature.

The *contract of Nepthas* automatically places an enchantment upon any persons who sign it in order to insure that both parties hold to the agreement. Anyone who has signed a *contract of Nepthas* and breaks the contract is struck deaf, blind, and dumb. The effects of the punishment last until they are removed with a *remove curse.*

A person who is both deaf and blind suffers a −8 penalty to his attack rolls and his opponents gain a +8 bonus to their attack rolls. He loses all bonuses for Dexterity and suffers −2 penalties to saving throws versus spells, petrification/ polymorph, and rod, staff, or wand.

A contract involves two parties agreeing on a set of conditions. The conditions are usually very specific, but if they are not, they might be perverted in the same way that a *wish* spell might be misinterpreted. If a group of adventurers signs a contract with a king stating that they will slay a dragon in the Northern Hills by the eve of the new moon, slaying any dragon will fulfill the contract, although the king may have had a specific dragon in mind. If the king agrees to pay the adventurers upon the completion of the task, the king had better have the money when the party returns.

Contracts signed by persons under the influence of *charm* and similar spells are null and void. A forged contract is also void. If any person who signs a contract dies before its completion, that person's obligation is ended. Note, however, that if a group of adventurers signs a contract and one of their members dies, the survivors are still bound to the contract.

A deadline for both parties' responsibilities must be stated in the contract in order for it to be activated.

Crucible of Melting: A crucible is a small bowl, usually made of fired clay or porcelain, used for heating substances to extreme temperatures. The bowl is usually placed on a furnace. The *crucible of melting,* however, requires no furnace. It melts any metals placed within it when the command word is spoken. It takes one turn to bring the crucible to a sufficient temperature to melt metals placed within it. It has no effect on substances other than metals.

The average *crucible of melting* can hold up to one cubic foot of material. Note that magical items are allowed an item saving throw vs. magical fire to avoid destruction. *Crucibles of melting* are most often found (when found at all) in the laboratories of wizards, particularly enchanters who specialize in the construction of magical devices.

Whenever a *crucible of melting* is used, there is a 5% chance of a mishap resulting in an explosion that inflicts 3d10 points of damage to all creatures within 10 feet. A save vs. rod, staff, or wand is allowed, with success indicating half damage. The crucible is allowed an item saving throw vs. disintegration. If it fails, it is destroyed; otherwise, it is unharmed and may be used again.

Half of all crucibles remain hot for 3 turns. The rest remain hot until a command word is spoken to cancel the heat.

Crystal Parrot: This is a 12-inch-high statue of a parrot made of clear crystal that is useful in the detection of trespassers. The *crystal parrot* is typically placed high on a bookcase, shelf, or a similar location that gives the parrot an unobstructed view of the area it is to oversee.

To activate the parrot, the user speaks the command word, causing a soft red glow to appear behind the parrot's eyes. Unless the *crystal parrot* is destroyed, it remains active for 30 days. The user may also choose to deactivate it with a second command word, at which time the red glow in its eyes disappears. Once deactivated, it cannot be activated again until 30 additional days have passed.

The active *crystal parrot* "sees" everything in a 180-degree arc in front of it, to a distance of 50 feet. The *crystal parrot* can see no better than a normal parrot; that is, its vision can be obscured by normal or magical darkness, or by physical barriers.

The user must instruct the parrot as to what types of intruders it is to observe. The user may be specific ("Watch for a 7-foot human male with a bald head and a red coat") or general ("Watch for all humanoid and animal intruders").

At the time an intruder enters the parrot's field of vision, the user will hear a telepathic report about all intruders matching the description. The telepathic reports will be general in nature, seldom more than brief phrases ("Man with red coat enters" or "Two rats enter"). If the user was not specific as to what types of intruders to watch for, the *crystal parrot* will report only the number and type of intruders (such as "one woman enters" or "a dozen orcs enter"). The *crystal parrot* will not report the actions of intruders, merely their presence; it tells the user when the intruders enter and leave, but nothing else.

The telepathic reports can be transmitted over an unlimited distance, but cannot be communicated into other planes of existence. The telepathy is one-way; the user cannot communicate with the *crystal parrot*.

The *crystal parrot* has AC 3. It shatters and becomes permanently useless if it suffers 12 points of damage. The user is instantly aware of the parrot's destruction.

Dimensional Mine: This nasty device can take the form of any small item, but most often appears as a small figure carved of jet or other black stone, similar to a *figurine of wondrous power*. As soon as the mine is taken into an extradimensional space, such as that created by a *rope trick*, *extradimensional pocket*, or a *bag of holding*, it ruptures that space. Everything in the space, including the mine itself, is spewed into the Astral plane and is lost unless someone can retrieve it. If the extradimensional space was created by a magical item, such as a *bag of holding*, that item is destroyed.

Disintegration Chamber: These frightful devices range in size from a 1′×1′×1′ box to a 10′×10′×10′ room. They are always made of iron, with the interior walls covered with mirrored tiles. They are used to cause matter to vanish, as per the 6th-level *disintegrate* spell.

The amount of material to be affected is limited only by the size of the chamber. Each use drains the device of one charge. *Disintegration chambers* generally have 81-100 charges (1d20+80) and may be recharged.

The material to be obliterated is placed inside the chamber, the door is closed, and the activation button is depressed. The interior of the chamber and its doomed contents then begin to glow with a sickly green light, and the material vanishes, leaving only fine dust. Creatures and objects that successfully save vs. spell are not affected, but must attempt another saving throw every time the chamber is reactivated.

The size of any given chamber can be determined from the table below.

D6 Roll	Size
1	1′ cube
2	2′ × 2′ × 3′ box
3	3′ × 3′ × 6′ box
4	3′ × 5′ × 6′ box
5	5′ × 5′ × 10′ box
6	10′ × 10′ × 10′ box

In the larger sizes, these devices are most often installed permanently and cannot be carried away as part of treasure, unless arrangements are made to transport a small room or shack.

Dust of Mind Dulling: This harmless-looking dust is the bane of spellcasters. One pinch of this dust can be flung up to 30 feet from the user and will scatter to fill a 5-foot-radius sphere.

All spellcasters within the area must make a saving throw versus spell or find their minds dulled and their wits slowed. All casting times less than 1 round are increased by 2 as the wizards hesitate, trying to remember the procedures. Spells which normally require 1 round to cast now require 1 full round plus a casting time of 5 on the following round; spells which normally have a casting time of 2 rounds or longer now require 50% longer than normal to cast. The dust persists in the area for 1 turn unless somehow removed (e.g., a *gust of wind* spell). Those affected by the dust are impaired in their spellcasting for 1d4+1 turns thereafter.

Elemental Compass: This device aids travelers seeking the elemental planes of Fire, Air, Water, or Earth. The compass, a small urn carved of stone and containing hollow pockets, works only in the Ethereal plane, an inner plane, or the Prime Material plane.

To make the compass work, a representative sample of material from the plane sought must be placed in the urn and the lid sealed. Thus, to find the elemental plane of Fire, a small, burning fire must be place in the urn. Once sealed, the fire will burn until the lid is opened (just as water will not evaporate from the urn as long as the lid is sealed).

When used on an inner plane or the Ethereal plane, the urn glows yellow when the characters are heading in the direction of a portal of the elemental plane they seek. On an inner plane, the compass leads to the para- or quasi-elemental planar border that exists between planes. In the Ethereal plane, the urn leads to the Ethereal curtain of the desired plane. There are no range restrictions on the inner or Ethereal planes.

On the Prime Material plane, the compass glows when the characters are headed for elemental vortices of the correct element, provided the vortex is within range. The range on the Prime Material plane is 300 miles.

Everbountiful Soup Kettle: When this two-gallon metal kettle is filled with water, the liquid is transformed into steaming, nutritious vegetable soup. One full kettle is sufficient to provide a single meal for up to six normal appetites. No ingredients are required for the soup, nor is heat necessary. Any nonmagical, nonpoisonous liquid can be used in place of water. The *everbountiful soup kettle* can be used once per day.

Flatbox: A practical example of hypergeometry and hypermathematics, the *flatbox* appears to be a wooden box about 3' long, 2' wide, and two inches deep. It weighs eight pounds. The top of the box is a hinged lid.

When the lid is opened, the interior of the box is filled with impenetrable darkness. This darkness cannot be dispelled by any form of magic; it is a characteristic of the hypergeometrical topography of the box.

Although from the outside the *flatbox* appears to be only two inches deep, it actually has the internal volume of a box six feet deep. (Thus, it has a volume of 36 cubic feet.) The maximum weight that can be loaded into a *flatbox* is 500 pounds. No matter how much of its volume is filled, the *flatbox* still weighs only eight pounds.

Since the inside of the box is completely dark, the only way to retrieve a specific item is to feel around within the box. Finding an object this way takes 1d4 rounds.

There is a significant danger associated with the *flatbox*. If it is taken into an extradimensional space (such as within a *portable hole*), if it is *teleported*, *gated*, or transported via *dimensional folding* or any analogous method, or if it ever suffers 15 hit points of damage, the *flatbox* explodes violently. This explosion destroys all contents of the box and inflicts 4d10 hit points of damage on any creature within 20 feet (save vs. spell for half damage).

Forge of Metal Protection: The first of these heavy (1,000 lb.) forges was created an unknown number of centuries ago. Because of the specific magical properties involved, it is believed that a wizard, assisted by a number of dwarves (all of whom were interested in planar research), constructed the device. Although the secret of the construction has since spread, the forge is an extremely rare magical item.

The forge is a furnace made up of enchanted rocks held together with a network of steel rods. When metal armor and weapons are placed within the furnace and heated to glowing red, the ar-

mor becomes immune to the effects of heat on the inner planes. All metal items tempered in this manner suffer no ill effects from heat on any of the inner planes, but suffer the effects of heat normally on the Prime Material plane.

The effect of the magical protection lasts 12 to 30 days (2d10 + 10). Magical armor or weapons that are placed in the forge take on the protection from heat, but temporarily lose their other magical properties. Thus, a *sword* +2 placed in the forge will not melt on the plane of Fire, but it ceases to functions as a *sword* +2 until the enchantment wears off. A weapon with an ego retains its ego, but loses all of its other magical properties.

Fur of Warmth: These large, white furs (5' by 8') are reportedly taken from the skins of creatures native to the para-elemental plane of Ice. A person wearing the fur still feels cold in a cold environment (such as the para-elemental plane of ice), but does not suffer damage from exposure.

Anyone wrapped in the fur is immune to the natural effects of cold, including the environments of the inner planes. Anyone wearing the fur takes half-damage from coldbased attacks. The wearer need not be covered completely by the fur to receive the enchanted protection; the fur must simply be draped over him like a cape. If the fur is cut into more than one piece, it loses its magical property.

If the fur is worn in pleasant or hot weather, it affects the wearer as any other large fur would.

Gem of Retaliation: The holder of this gem gains a special protection against Evocation spells directed at him. The owner of the gem gains a +4 bonus to any saving throw made against such a spell, and also acquires a base save of 18 (but not the +4 bonus) against any Evocation spell which normally does not allow a saving throw (such as *ice storm*). All standard modifiers (*ring of protection*, Dexterity, etc.) apply.

Additionally, if the saving throw is successful, the incoming spell is converted into outgoing *magic missiles*. The number of missiles is equal to one-half the level of the spell negated, rounding fractions up. The *magic missiles* then streak back to strike the person or creature who cast the spell at the owner of the gem. Maximum range for this strike is 160 yards.

Spell-like effects created from magical items are not affected by the *gem of retaliation* (thus, a *wand of magic missiles* will function normally against someone using this gem).

An individual holding a *gem of retaliation* who comes under attack by an area spell (*fireball, ice storm,* etc.) gains the advantages as described above. Other persons in the area of effect suffer all effects normally. Even if the gem's owner saves successfully, the area-effect Evocation is *not* transformed into *magic missiles* as described previously.

Glass of Preserved Words: This magical magnifying glass has a band of silver around the lens and an ivory handle. The glass has the ability to make illegible written words readable. Words that were carved into stone but worn away through time, inked letters blurred due to moisture, messages clouded by magic, and magical and normal writings all become clear when read through the glass.

The actual words remain illegible; they are not altered in any way. Only a character looking at them through the glass can read them clearly.

The glass does not protect the reader from any harmful effects as a result of a cursed scroll or trapped writings, nor does it make cryptically worded or coded messages understandable.

Globe of Purification: These enchanted glass spheres, 6 inches in diameter, contain the swirling blue-grey essence of a *cloud of purification* spell. When the globe is broken, the cloud billows forth, acting exactly as if the spell had been cast by a 12th-level priest. These devices are often given to a city's sanitation crews, who descend upon the streets and sewers during the wee hours of the morning.

Globe of Serenity: These glass orbs look very much like crystal balls. However, a *globe of serenity* emits a continuous, inaudible tone that affects all living creatures within 50 feet who fail a saving throw vs. spell. While in the area of effect, affected creatures feel the utmost serenity and self-control. Strong emotions such as joy, love, and hatred are totally subdued.

Creatures affected by the globe gain a +3 saving throw bonus to resist spells and special attacks that affect emotions (such as *charm, fear,* or *emotion*). At the same time, they suffer a −2 to all Intelligence checks, the spark of insight also repressed.

The globe also affects morale, raising the spirits of some while quelling the fires of fanaticism in others. All affected creatures have morale of 10, regardless of their training or skill. If a morale check is called for and failed, the affected creature does not rout or flee, but stays in place, taking no action until rallied.

Globes of serenity are best suited for lawful communities where open displays of emotion are frowned upon. Although crime and violence would be greatly reduced in these communities, citizens would also lack a sense of spirit. The people would go about their daily routines like emotionless automatons.

Horn of Valor: This golden horn is indistinguishable from any other magical horn until it is sounded. When sounded, each unit hearing it who is allied with or loyal to the character sounding the horn gains the following benefits. First, the unit gains a +2 bonus to its morale for 1d4 BATTLESYSTEM rules turns. Second, any routed friendly unit who hears it immediately makes a rally check with a bonus of 2 to its morale (for that check only). (This check is made when the horn is sounded—during the magic phase—rather than in the rally phase. If this additional check is failed, the unit is entitled to a second check in the rally phase, as normal.)

Enemy units who hear the horn are also affected: they suffer a −1 penalty to morale for 1d2 BATTLESYSTEM rules turns.

Under normal conditions, the sound of the horn can be heard at a range of 24″. Unusual conditions, such as a raging storm, can decrease this range, but the horn can *always* be heard at a range of 9″ (unless the character blowing the horn is within an area of magical *silence,* of course).

The *horn of valor* can be sounded only once per BATTLESYSTEM Rules turn, and no more than three times in any 12 hour period. If blown a fourth time within this period, it becomes totally nonmagical for 1d6 days, and any effects remaining from earlier soundings immediately terminate. Effects from multiple soundings are not cumulative. (Instantaneous effects such as the automatic rally check for friendly units take place each time the horn is sounded.)

Hourglass of Fire and Ice: This small, wooden-framed hourglass looks quite ordinary, but radiates invocation/evocation magic if detected. Half these hourglasses contain red sand and half contain blue sand.

An hourglass containing red sand in the lower portion enables a spellcaster to cast fire-based spells with increased potency: +1 per die of damage. Further, victims suffer a −1 penalty to all saves against such spells, and even saving throws against illusions of fire are made at −1.

When the hourglass is tilted, the red sand flows slowly through the aperture, turning blue as it does so. The hourglass takes 6 turns to fill with blue sand. When the hourglass has filled with blue sand, all cold-based spells cast by the owner of the houglass have +1 per die of damage. Victims also suffer a −1 penalty to saving throws against cold-based spells, including saves against illusions of cold.

The hourglass may be inverted to re-create the red sand, with a corresponding flip in the effects after 6 turns.

The hourglass may be inverted up to three times per day. However, with every inversion of the hourglass there is a 1% chance that it will break, spilling its sands and losing its magic forever.

Jar of Preserving: This piece of magical glassware is able to hold up to one cubic foot of material. The round jar is equipped with a glass lid that screws into place.

Any animal or vegetable matter placed in a *jar of preserving* enters a form of suspended animation. A rosebud never wilts, for example, and a small animal never ages and does not require food, water, or air. Spell components placed in the jar never lose potency.

Law's Banner: This blazing red standard has the magical ability to raise the morale of troops when held at the front of a lawful army. The banner inspires any soldier in the army who is within a quarter-mile of the banner and can see the flag. Troops inspired in this manner receive a +2 modifier to their base morale as per BATTLESYSTEM rules. In order for an army to be considered lawful, at least 90% of the troops must be of lawful alignment and no more than 1% can be chaotic.

If the banner falls, the effects are lost immediately. If the banner is raised within 1 turn, the effect returns. If the banner is not raised within 1 turn, the inspired troops become filled with dread, feeling that the battle has clearly gone against their cause. The same troops now suffer a −2 morale penalty for the duration of the battle. The standard may be raised any number of times, but will improve or impair morale only once per day.

Lens of Speed Reading: While looking through this lens, the user can read any book, document, or other written material at three times his normal speed with full comprehension. When used in conjunction with *read magic*, the *lens of speed reading* enables the user to quickly scan scrolls and magical tomes to learn their contents, but it has no effect on the time required to cast spells. The lens will not decipher codes, improve illegible writing, or allow magic to be read without the proper spells.

Liquid Road: When sprinkled on water, swampland, quicksand, or a similar surface, *liquid road* causes the terrain to harden to the density of granite, enabling easy passage. *Liquid road* is also effective in negating the effects of spells such as *transmute rock to mud*. The *liquid road* stays hard for one hour, after which the terrain returns to its original state. One flask of *liquid road* can harden a 5' × 5' surface (for example, a path 25' long and 1' wide).

Lorloveim's Obsidian Mortar and Pestle: This magical tool allows the wielder to grind even the hardest materials into a fine powder. Rocks, metals, and even gemstones of all types may be ground to dust in as little as 1d4 rounds.

Magical items pounded beneath the pestle are allowed a saving throw vs. disintegration. If the save is successful, the enchanted item cannot be destroyed in this fashion. If the saving throw fails, the item is reduced to nonmagical powder.

The obsidian mortar is commonly used by wizards in the preparation of spell components and ingredients for magical items. Neither the mortar nor the pestle is effective without the other.

Manual of Dogmatic Methods: This silver-bound book, studded with jewels, appears to be a tome of considerable value. The book is actually cursed, although this is not immediately obvious.

The manual has the power to provide advice on any action that its owner might consider taking. The owner need only open to any page in the book, and there before him will be a list of actions, most of them ritualistic in nature, to insure the success of any project he undertakes.

The first time the book is used, the owner is suddenly struck with the idea that he now owns a source of information that can give him valuable advice on any matter. It becomes a guide for his whole life. He will not share the book or let anyone take it away from him. If anyone tries to remove it, he will fight to keep the book.

Following the first use of the book, the owner cannot do anything without first checking the book. The information in the manual is completely worthless, but the owner of the book does not realize this. The pages in the manual change constantly, offering its owner an obscure (and usually ridiculous) ritual to perform before doing anything. Thus, if a character is about to go into battle, he might check the book and find several exercises he should undertake to loosen his muscles. If he is going to speak to a duke, he might find instructions for the color of his clothing according to the day of the year and the time of day of the meeting. If he is going to pray to his god for a spell, he might find six pages of cleansing rituals that should be performed first.

The manual's instructions are almost never harmful, but they might delay the owner's actions at a crucial moment.

Whenever a character is in a situation that requires hasty action (for example, he is attacked), the book will delay its owner by 1d8 rounds. If the owner is preparing for a lengthy activity (a long trip, for example), he will be busy for 1d4 days getting ready for the event. The DM should be creative in detailing the tasks the owner must perform before he can comfortably commit himself to his goal.

The compulsion to follow the manual's instructions can be ended with a *remove curse* spell. Following this, the next person to open the book becomes its new owner. If an owner should die, the book becomes the property of the next person to open its cover.

If possible, the DM should hint that the character is actually gaining bonuses for using the book, while allowing the other characters in the group to figure out the effects for themselves.

Medallion of Spell Exchange: This medallion allows the spellcaster to exchange one memorized spell of up to 6th level for others of lower levels, rather in the manner of *Mordenkainen's lucubration.* The wizard loses the sacrificed spell and recalls one or more spells from those he had memorized and cast within the past 24 hours. The total levels of these spells must be one less in sum than the spell sacrificed. For example, by sacrificing a 5th-level spell, a wizard could recall one 1st- and one 3rd-level spell, two 2nd-level spells, four 1st-level spells, and so on. The medallion can function only once per day. The wizard must have available any spell components required for exchanged spells.

Mirror of Retention: This appears to be an ordinary round silver mirror, about 12 inches in diameter. When the *mirror of retention* is hung in a 50 foot × 50 foot or smaller room and the command word is spoken, the mirror records all events occurring in the room for 24 hours. During this time, the *mirror of retention* appears to be a normal mirror.

When the command word is spoken again, the mirror replays all the events it recorded. The events appear as a series of silent images in the surface of the mirror. By rotating the mirror clockwise, the images can be accelerated, appearing as much as 10 times as fast as they occurred. Rotating the mirror counter-clockwise causes the images to appear in reverse. If the mirror is held parallel to the floor, the image freezes. Thus, by rotating the mirror and freezing the images, the user can scan for events, review previously viewed images, or freeze selected images for closer study.

When the command word is spoken a third time, the *mirror of retention* is cleared of all images and is ready to record new images for another 24 hours.

Mirror of Simple Order: When a character steps in front of this mirror, he sees a strangely distorted image of himself. The reflection moves as he does, but the face reflected in the mirror is the image of an ordinary face. There are eyes, a mouth, and a nose, but all lack character. Although the figure moves as the character does, it is shorter or taller than he is, adjusted in whatever direction approaches the average height of the character's race. Any clothing worn by the character is altered as well. Bright colors will be muted, appearing to be shades of grey. Any ornamental work on armor, weapons, or clothing will be gone.

If the character stands in front of the mirror for more than two rounds, he is instantly *polymorphed* into the image in the mirror. The *polymorphed* character must succeed on a system shock roll to survive the change.

Like the *polymorph other* spell, there is a chance that the subject's personality and mentality change into that of the new form. In this case, each of his ability scores becomes 11 and his hit points become the average for his Hit Dice at his level. He retains his level and class, but is not as exceptional as he might have been. He is bland and boring. The character's alignment changes to lawful neutral, and he becomes interested in little else other than setting order to the world. He passionlessly travels to wipe out chaos wherever he finds it.

All effects of the mirror can be removed through a *dispel magic* spell. Until the effects are removed, however, the character is unaware that any change has occured.

Mist Tent: A *mist tent* is contained in a small glass flask. Removing the stopper causes a stream of white mist to pour from the flask. One round later, the mist shapes itself into the form of a 10′ × 12′ tent with a single, open flap in the front. The stopper must be replaced in the flask as soon as the *mist tent* takes shape, or the tent will dissipate as described below.

The *mist tent* has the density of a cloud when unoccupied. When one or more characters enter the *mist tent*, the flap can be closed; from the inside, the flap has the density of canvas. From the inside, the walls and ceiling of the *mist tent* appear as opaque white mist, and the floor is transparent. Despite its appearance, the entire *mist tent* has the density of canvas once the flap is closed. When the flap is closed, the following effects occur:

• The *mist tent* and all occupants and items inside become invisible to all creatures outside the tent. A *detect invisibility* spell cast by a creature outside the tent reveals the *mist tent*.

• The *mist tent* rises 10 feet off the ground; it continues to hover in place as long as the flap remains closed. The transparent floor allows occupants of the tent to clearly see the surrounding area. The floor of the *mist tent* can support 1,000 pounds without rupturing.

If the flap is opened, the *mist tent*'s walls, floor, and ceiling instantly become visible to outsiders, appearing as a thin, white mist. Additionally, the *mist tent* slowly descends, landing gently on the ground. If the stopper is removed from the flask, the tent dissipates, returning to the flask in a stream of white mist; if the bottle is not stoppered immediately, the mist will pour from the flask to form the *mist tent* again.

The *mist tent* is unharmed by all types of fire, but does not offer such protection to its occupants. The tent is susceptible to other forms of damage. It provides no more protection to its occupants than a normal canvas tent.

The *mist tent* has AC 10. If the *mist tent* sustains 10 points of damage, it dissipates in a shower of light and is permanently negated. If this occurs while the *mist tent* is hovering, all occupants plummet to the ground. If the *mist tent* sustains less than 10 points of damage, it can be returned to its flask, then re-released; all damage will be repaired.

Mordom's Cauldron of Air: *Mordom's cauldron of air* is a round pot about two feet in diameter, weighing 60 pounds. There are two handles on either side of the pot and a compartment built like a small shelf under the cauldron. The compartment can be filled with wood or coal to heat the cauldron.

Although the device is heavy and bulky, the cauldron is valuable for characters planning an expedition to a place with little or no air. The cauldron functions as an air generator. To operate the device, the cauldron is filled with water and a fire is lit in the compartment. When the water boils, vapor is released. The air from the vapor creates a bubble of breathable air 10 feet in radius centered on the cauldron.

The water must not be allowed to spill out of the cauldron and the fire must be kept burning. As long as these conditions are met, the cauldron will provide air continuously.

The air produced is the same temperature as the surrounding environment. The device needs a minimum of one gallon of water per hour.

Mouse Cart: A *mouse cart* resembles a miniature wooden cart with two wooden wheels and a tiny leather harness. When a normal mouse is secured in the harness, the cart expands to the size of a normal cart (roughly 5 square feet). The mouse retains its normal size, but becomes enchanted, acquiring the ability to pull the cart plus 250 pounds of cargo at a movement rate of 12.

As long as the mouse remains in the harness, it is compelled to obey all oral commands from the person who put him in the harness. The mouse will run forward, stop, turn, and obey all similar commands; it will not attack or take any action that a mouse is normally incapable of performing. No other creature attached to the *mouse cart* will activate the device's magical properties. A character or other creature *polymorphed* or otherwise transformed into a mouse can activate the cart's magic.

Necklace of Memory Enhancement: The wearer of this brass necklace receives two benefits.

• The wearer is immune to all memory loss, from both natural and magical causes (such as a *forget* spell). The necklace has no effect on a wizard's spell memorization.

• The wearer can recall with absolute clarity any sight or conversation he experienced or any book he read within the previous seven days. Memories prior to seven days ago are recalled with only normal clarity. The necklace affects only events that occurred while the necklace was worn by the user.

Nefradina's Identifier: This highly valued item is a magical test kit used to identify potions, powders, and other alchemical substances. It consists of a wooden box (typically measuring 1' × 1' × 3') containing an assortment of vials, flasks, and beakers in small, padded compartments. Also in the box is a copy of a text called *Nefradina's Codex*. This book instructs the owner on how to use the test kit.

When the owner wishes to identify a potion, powder, oil, perfume, or similar liquid or powdered magical item, he looks up the substance's characteristics (odor, color, consistency, and so on) in the codex and follows the directions given to create a test mixture by combining a number of ingredients found in the kit. He then adds a drop of the test mixture to the substance he wishes to identify. The resulting effects (changes in color, sparks, smoke, bizarre odors, small explosions, and so forth) are looked up in the codex and the substance is identified through a process of elimination.

The DM secretly rolls 1d100 to determine the actual results:

01-20: The test kit is missing a vital chemical and can never identify that particular substance.

21-50: The user comes to a false conclusion and believes the substance to be something it is not (DM's choice).

51-100: The user successfully identifies the substance.

The DM should modify the roll by +2% per level of experience of the character using the test kit.

The time required to perform a single test is 1d4 + 1 turns. A typical kit may be used 1d10 + 40 times before it becomes useless.

Philosopher's Egg: This item is an enchanted retort: a long-necked piece of glassware in which substances are distilled. It is a highly prized addition to a wizard's laboratory, for it has two very important uses.

The first use of the *philosopher's egg* is in the creation of any magical or mundane fluid. The time required to create such a fluid is cut in half through use of the *philosopher's egg*.

The *egg's* second use is as a required component for creating the substance that turns lead into gold—the legendary philosopher's stone. Thus, it is sometimes said by wizards that "the stone hatches from the egg."

Pick of Earth Parting: This enchanted pick allows its wielder to cut through elemental earth quickly. The wielder of the pick must have strength of 17 or better. By repeatedly swinging the pick at elemental earth, the wielder can carve out a 10' × 10' × 60' tunnel per round. The pick's magical properties create a smooth, clean surface regardless of the mining skill of the user. All rubble from the excavation magically disappears, leaving a clear passage.

Portable Canoe: This ordinary, canvas-covered canoe is capable of comfortably holding two passengers. The canoe includes two wooden paddles. The *portable canoe* can be folded into a 6-inch-square packet, about an inch thick, weighing just under a pound. With the exception of the paddles, the *portable canoe* must be emptied of all other objects before it can be folded. Folding the canoe requires 5 rounds; unfolding requires 2 rounds.

Prism of Light Splitting: This useful device refracts light into the three primary colors of light—red, blue, and green. The user can choose the color of light that is emitted by the prism.

When creating a magical fluid or powder, the wizard casts the *enchant an item* spell. Following this, the wizard may use the *prism of light splitting* to shine a blue, red, or green beam of light on the mixture. The light must shine on the substance for one full day. At the end of this time, the material gains an additional magical property, depending upon the color of the beam employed.

Red: The potion, powder, or aromatic oil is stronger than normal; targets of its effects suffer a −2 saving throw penalty.

Blue: The duration of the magical potion, powder, or fragrance's effect is doubled.

Green: The amount of liquid or powder is doubled; the wizard now has enough for two potions, powders, or aromatic oils.

Puchezma's Powder of Edible Objects: An inveterate traveler who was notoriously cheap, Puchezma could never bring himself to spend money on decent provisions or hire a quality chef for his long wilderness excursions. In his efforts to create a seasoning that would make the bland dishes of his second-rate cooks more palatable, Puchezma stumbled on a formula for the *powder of edible objects*.

This powder, which resembles normal salt, causes any normally indigestible material to become edible, nutritious food. The material must be nonliving and nonmagical, and must be in a form the consumer can swallow; for instance, dirt and cotton cloth are acceptable (the diner could chew up and swallow these materials), but large stones and planks of hard wood are not (these objects would have to be broken up into small pieces before they could be swallowed). All poisonous and otherwise harmful properties (such as sharp edges) are negated by the powder. One pinch of *powder of edible objects* is sufficient to treat one cubic foot of material. The powder is normally found in small bags containing 10 to 100 pinches.

Quill of Law: This magical pen is used by despots and good rulers alike to ensure that their laws and proclamations are obeyed. Anyone reading a posted proclamation or law that was written with the pen must obey the law, regardless of whether it is a good law.

This effect applies only to persons who actually see the written message. If a person knows about the law but has not read a notice written with the quill, he still has the option to obey or break the law. Once he has read it, however, he must obey it.

The magical effect is limited in that only the three most recent laws written with the quill maintain this power. Laws written prior to the most recent three can still be the law, but citizens are not compelled to obey them.

Creatures with 15 or greater Intelligence and 12 or more Hit Dice or levels are entitled to a saving throw vs. spell when viewing the proclamation. If the saving throw is successful, the effect is negated and the person is left to his own moral decisions.

Reglar's Gloves of Freedom: These gloves appear to be thick, leather, combat gloves. Silvered pearls are sewn along the stitching.

A character under the influence of a *charm* spell or similar enchantment can be freed of the enchantment by shaking hands with the wearer of the gloves. This item frees only characters who are enchanted against their will. Those who have willingly submitted to a charm (such as a *quest*) are not affected by the gloves. The former victim retains all memories of his enchantment.

The gloves do not protect or release the wearer from such spells.

Robe of Repetition: This ordinary-looking robe radiates strong alteration magic if magic is detect-

ed. The wearer of this robe acquires a unique and powerful augmentation to his magic. After casting a spell, there is a percentage chance that a mnemonic/harmonic effect occurs so that the magical energies liberated in spellcasting are amplified and retained briefly. The wizard is then able to cast the same spell a second time. This must be done on the succeeding round or the bonus spell is lost.

Once the spell has been cast a second time, the energy is completely liberated. There is no possibility of a third casting. In all cases, the spell is lost from the wizard's memory until the wizard memorizes it again.

The chance of a spell being available for a second casting varies according to spell level:

1st Level	50%
2nd Level	40%
3rd Level	30%
4th Level	20%
5th Level	10%

Energy from spells of 6th level and above are not retained within the robe's magical weave. Furthermore, a maximum of 24 spell levels per day can be reused with the benefit of this robe. If the wizard opts not to use a spell which is made available for a second use, this counts toward the maximum limit.

If a wizard removes the robe, spells cast while the robe is off do not count toward the spell limit. For example, if a wizard casts 15 spell levels that count against the robe's daily limit and he then removes the robe, subsequent spells do not count against the robe's limit. If the wizard then puts on the robe during the same day and casts more spells, the robe retains the 15 spell levels that counted against it and all spells cast subsequently also count against the robe.

Only one wizard may use the robe's magic in a single day; if a second wizard puts on the robe, it does not function.

Saddle of Flying: This saddle resembles a normal leather saddle with a small, silver buckle near the pommel. When the saddle is secured to a horse or any other nonmagical mount and the silver buckle is fastened, the mount sprouts wings and acquires the ability to fly at its normal movement rate (Maneuverability Class D). The flying mount can carry its normal encumbrance.

The *saddle of flying* functions for only one hour per day. When the silver buckle is unfastened or the duration expires, the wings disap-

pear and all flying ability is immediately lost, regardless of whether the mount is airborne or on the ground.

Salves of Far Seeing: These salves allow a character who puts a drop of the salve into each of his eyes to see as well as he would on a brightly lit day on his Prime Material plane. The proper salve also serves as a protection against blindness on planes where protection is necessary. Several types of salves exist for the different elemental, para-elemental, and quasi-elemental planes. The salves have no effect on normal or magical blindness.

The salves are found in small metal containers made of precious metals. A container contains 4d12 drops of salve. One drop in each eye bestows the magical property for one day. A drop must be placed in every usable eye for the magic to work.

A different salve exists for each of the planes where such a salve is required, and each has a distinct look and feel. The following table lists the planes that limit sight and the color and texture of each respective salve. The salves function only on their respective planes.

Plane	Color	Texture
Water	Blue	Smooth
Earth	Black	Grainy, Thick
Positive	White	Opaque Liquid
Negative	Clear	Liquid
Smoke	Ashen	Liquid
Ice	Bluish-white	Thick
Ooze	Gray	Rubbery
Magma	Copper	Thick
Steam	Gray	Liquid
Salt	White	Grainy
Radiance	Golden	Smooth
Ash	Gray	Grainy
Minerals	Silver	Grainy
Dust	Black	Dry

Scarab of Uncertainty: This scarab has a specific and potentially powerful effect. If the wearer is within range of a *monster summoning* or similar spell (*invisible stalker, conjure animals,* etc.) when cast by another creature or character, the summoned creatures make a saving throw versus spell the instant they appear. If the summoned creatures fail this saving throw, they mistakenly believe that the wearer of the scarab is the individual who summoned them and will then serve the scarab wearer as best they can, rather than the caster of the spell.

School Cap: The wearer of this cap gains a +2 bonus to saving throws against spells of one particular school of magic. In addition, specialists of the designated school do not inflict a −1 penalty on a wearer's saving throws against their specialist spells. The nature of the *school cap* is determined using a 1d8 roll.

D8 Roll	Affected School
1	Abjuration
2	Conjuration/Summoning
3	Greater Divination
4	Enchantment/Charm
5	Illusion
6	Invocation/Evocation
7	Necromancy
8	Alteration

Of these caps, 10% are mixed blessings since they have a cursed side-effect: The wearer suffers a −1 penalty to saving throws against spells of the opposition school(s). The curse takes effect the first time the wearer is subjected to a spell from the opposition school(s). Once the curse has been engaged, the cap cannot be removed except through a *remove curse* spell.

Skie's Locks and Bolts: This device looks like a small, ornate lock with a tiny silver key. When the key is turned clockwise, all doors, windows and other portals within 50 feet of the item slam shut and become *wizard locked.* For purposes of opening them, the *wizard locks* are the equivalent of those cast by a 12th-level wizard. The effect lasts until the key is twisted counterclockwise or the device is transported more than 50 feet away.

Skie's locks and bolts are sometimes found in the homes of wealthy merchants and secretive wizards.

Talisman of Memorization: This talisman allows a wizard to memorize spells in half the normal time (i.e., 5 minutes per spell level). Half of these amulets (1-5 on 1d10) affect memorization of spells only of levels 1-5. The remaining half affect memorization of spells of levels 1-8. Spells of 9th level are never affected by this talisman.

Tapestry of Disease Warding: This is a 3-foot-square cotton tapestry bearing the image of a rainbow. When hung in a house or other building (10,000 square feet or less), it protects the occupants from nonmagical diseases. It has no effect on persons already suffering from diseases, but protects healthy characters from contracting contagious diseases ranging from common colds to deadly plagues. The tapestry offers no protection against any disease caused by magic or of a magical nature.

The *tapestry of disease warding* is subject to rips, fire, and other damage that could be sustained by a normal tapestry, although it is allowed a saving throw. Its magic is permanent only as long as it remains intact. The tapestry may be moved to a new location, but has no effect outdoors.

Teleportation Chamber: These devices are used to teleport matter (as per the 5th-level *teleport* spell) and vary in size from a 1' × 1' × 1' box to a 10' × 10' × 10' room. They are usually made of ornate wood, but can be fashioned of stone or metal. In any case, the interior walls are always covered with mirrored tiles much like *disintegration chambers*. A small, green sphere is fastened to the outside of the chamber near the door, and another sphere is positioned on an inside wall.

To activate the device, a creature must touch one of the spheres while concentrating on a mental image of the destination. The chance of error is exactly the same as that described in the *Player's Handbook* for casting the 5th-level *teleport* spell, with one exception. If the contents of the chamber are being sent to another teleportation chamber, the chance of a mishap is 0%.

The number of people or objects that may be teleported is limited only by the size of the chamber. The size of any given chamber can be determined from the table below.

D6 Roll	Chamber Size
1	1' cube
2	2' × 2' × 3' box
3	3' × 3' × 6' box
4	3' × 5' × 6' box
5	5' × 5' × 10' box
6	10' × 10' × 10' box

All travelers and materials in the chamber arrive at the same destination, which is determined by the activator. Distance is not a factor, but interplanar travel is not possible by means of this magical machine. Each use drains the device of one charge. *Teleportation chambers* generally have between 81-100 charges (1d20 + 80) and may be recharged.

Tenser's Portmanteau of Frugality: This moderately large, black leather traveling case contains a bewildering number of small instruments—tweezers, measuring beakers, small ceramic jars, and the like. It can be used to extract the greatest possible benefit from certain single-use magical items by partly diluting or admixing them. All potions, oils, dusts, incenses, glues, solvents, and *Nolzur's marvelous pigments* can be affected by *Tenser's portmanteau.*

For every two potions, applications of dust, or similar substances that are treated by the portmanteau, a third active dose or use can be extracted. Any such item may be affected only once by the power of the portmanteau. Single doses (a single potion, etc.) do not provide sufficient magic for treatment by the portmanteau.

The process of extracting the magic is not a simple task. The work takes 2d6 hours to complete. At the end of this time, the wizard must make an Intelligence check. If successful, the third dose is created. If failed, the third dose fails and only enough remains of the original materials for a single dose of the magical substance.

If *Alamir's fundamental breakdown* is cast during the process, the wizard gains a +2 to his Intelligence check. In this situation, the spell does not consume the magical items on which it is cast.

Each use of the portmanteau consumes some of the special agents required for the process. When discovered, the case holds enough materials to attempt 4d10 duplications.

Thought Bottle: This item usually takes the form of a metal flask similar in appearance to an *efreeti bottle.* Bottle and stopper are usually engraved with intricate runes. The bottle can be used to store and protect important memories and thoughts, and is often used by powerful characters as a way of managing their (potentially cluttered) memories.

To use the bottle, a character concentrates on the thought or memory to be stored. He then uncorks the bottle and speaks the word of command. The thought or memory is then transferred from the character's brain into the bottle. All details of the thought or memory are held within the bottle. The caster remembers the general nature of the thought ("Oh, that was my thought on the design of an efreeti-powered steam engine") but need not worry about forgetting specific details, since these are trapped in the *thought bottle*.

To retrieve a thought, a character uncorks the bottle and speaks another word of command. The thought or memory is then transferred directly into the user's brain.

Thought bottles are sometimes used to protect vital information. A messenger carrying vital plans through enemy territory where there is a significant chance of capture and subsequent interrogation might carry all sensitive plans in one or more bottles. The messenger does not know the contents or the command word and therefore cannot reveal the contents of the bottles. Likewise, a spy could gain secret information, transfer it to a thought bottle, then use *forget* or *modify memory* to wipe this information from his mind. After this, regardless of the methods used, the spy is incapable of revealing the sensitive information.

Thought bottles are sometimes used as "memory archives," where characters can save memories that are "cluttering up" their minds. (This would be more of a problem for long-lived races such as elves, since the sheer volume of memories recorded over several centuries could be overwhelming.)

Thought bottles will function (in both storage and retrieval) for any intelligent creature.

When discovered, 75% of all *thought bottles* can hold only a single thought or memory. The remaining 25% have a capacity of 2d4 separate thoughts or memories. There is a separate word of command for each "thought slot."

Time Bomb: A *time bomb* resembles a small hourglass without sand. To set the bomb, the user removes one base from the hourglass and fills one end with an amount of sand of the user's choice (ranging from one minute's worth of sand to one hour's worth). When the hourglass is set on a flat surface so that the sand begins to trickle from one end to the other, the *time bomb* is activated.

When all the sand has trickled to the bottom of the hourglass, it explodes in a ball of flame equal to a *fireball* spell cast at 5th level, delivering 5d6 points of damage and filling a 20-foot radius. Victims within this area who make a successful saving throw vs. spell suffer only half damage.

If an activated *time bomb* is shattered, tipped over, or otherwise disturbed before it detonates, its magic is permanently negated; it cannot be reactivated. From that time on, however, it can be used as a normal hourglass.

Tome of Mystical Equations: This book is indistinguishable from other magical tomes. It contains charts and equations relating to several of the spells belonging to the sphere of Numbers. It can be used as the material component for the spells *personal reading*, *telethaumaturgy*, and *addition*. If it is used in this manner, the casting time for the spell is halved, and any saving throw that the subject of the spell might be entitled to suffers a −2 penalty.

Trimia's Catalogue of Outer Plane Artifacts: This magical device is a large book bound in heavy wooden covers that do not reveal the title or nature of the work. Upon opening to the first page, the owner finds the title of the book along with a table of contents listing the various outer planes.

Upon opening the book to the desired page, the owner finds either a blank page (25% chance) or a description of a magical device (75% chance) that provides transportation to that particular plane. Along with the description of the device is a price ranging from 1,000 to 20,000 gp (1d20 × 1,000). If the appropriate sum is laid on the open book and a *vanish* spell is subsequently cast on the coins, the transport device shown appears in place of the cash. The page then immediately goes blank and the catalogue disappears, teleported to a random location on the Prime Material plane.

The transport device can deliver characters to the outer planes and can return them to their point of departure on the Prime Material plane. Each transport device brings a person or persons to the upper layer of an outer plane. The point of arrival in the plane is left to the DM and usually changes each time the device is used.

Each device has a command word which is always the name of the plane associated with the device. Unless otherwise noted, anyone touching the device or touching the person who holds the device is transported to the upper plane of the outer plane named.

Each transport device can be used once per day. With each use, there is a 5% chance the device will malfunction, sending the characters to the desired plane, but with the device itself disappearing.

Nirvana: The device used to transport to the plane of Nirvana is a small pocket watch, a device of unspeakable rarity. The watch keeps perfect time according to the yearly cycle of the sun and never needs winding. The watch is solid gold and has two long, thin gold chains that run through a metal loop at the top of the watch.

Arcadia: Arcadia's transportation device is a palm-sized metal sculpture representing the outlines of geometrical shapes. The largest shape is a six-sided cubic cage made of 12 silver rods. Within this cube is a four-sided pyramid, also made of silver rods. Inside the pyramid is a circle of silver.

Seven Heavens: A featureless sphere of gold is used to travel to the Seven Heavens. The sphere is three inches in diameter and would appear to be nothing more than a valuable bauble if not for the golden glow it always radiates. The glow has the properties of a *continual light* spell.

Twin Paradises: This device appears to be a featureless cube of silver measuring three inches on a side. If it is carefully examined, four small, nearly invisible buttons will be visible. If the four buttons are pressed in the correct order, the cube splits in half. (The correct order can be determined through the use of *legend lore* and similar spells.) The device will teleport to the Twin Paradises when half the cube is held in each hand and the command word is spoken. The travelers arrive in Dothion, considered the topmost plane. The two halves of the cube must be reassembled before it can once again be used to teleport.

Elysium: The device used to reach this plane is a sturdy currach, a primitive vessel made from thick hide stretched over a wood-and-wicker frame. This device functions as a normal ship, with a seaworthiness rating of 95%. If anyone touches the ship's mast and speaks the word Elysium, the boat, its passengers and crew, and all cargo are transported to the Oceanus River in the plane of Amoria.

Happy Hunting Grounds: A leaf sculpted of gold is the device used to arrive in the Happy Hunting Grounds. The leaf is about two inches long and is wrought in fine detail.

Olympus: The device used to reach the plane of Olympus is a silver chariot. The chariot can comfortably hold four passengers and their gear or eight passengers without equipment. A team of four horses must be attached to the chariot; when the chariot is in motion and the command word is spoken, the horses, chariot, passengers, and gear are transported to Olympus. The chariot arrives in the plane in motion.

Gladsheim: The device used to reach Gladsheim is a prism approximately three inches in length. To operate the device, the prism must be used outdoors to create a rainbow on the ground. When the command word is spoken, the rainbow grows out of the ground and rises up into the sky. The rainbow lasts for 1 turn. Anyone who steps onto the rainbow is whisked up the colored path and into the plane of Asgard.

Limbo: Limbo is reached through the use of a magical mirror. When a person stands before the mirror, he sees his own image reflected normally. The reflected world behind him, however, is in utter chaos—the bricks from the wall behind him float in the air, flames drift across the room, gold and silver pieces break apart and wander aimlessly. If the command word is spoken as a character looks into the mirror, he is transported to any of the planes of Limbo. The mirror does not travel to Limbo. Another means of returning to the Prime Material plane must be found.

Pandemonium: This device is a jar perpetually filled with black pitch. When the pitch is spread on a stone wall and the command word spoken, a portal forms in the wall, leading to a cavern in Pandesmos. The pitch evaporates after 5 rounds and magically reappears in the jar.

Abyss: Pazunia, the uppermost layer of the innumerable layers of the Abyss, can be reached through the use of a circular black cloth that looks like a *portable hole.* The cloth is three feet in diameter and can be folded to fit inside a pocket. When the cloth is spread on the ground and the command word is spoken, the cloth becomes a pit that leads to the plane. The cloth exists as a pit for 1 turn, then returns to its state as a piece of cloth. It does not follow travelers to the Abyss.

Tarterus: This device is a necklace of dull, reddish pearls. A character who wears the necklace and speaks the command word will be transported (along with anyone touching him) to Othrys, the topmost layer of the plane.

Hades: The device used to reach Hades is an iron keelboat. When any character on the boat speaks the command word, the keelboat and all it passengers are transported to the river Styx in Oinos, the uppermost layer of Hades.

Gehenna: Characters who wish to travel to Gehenna must gather in a small, enclosed room with this magical urn of silver and bronze. A flame must be lit within the urn using materials that cause a great deal of smoke. When the room is so choked with smoke that breathing is almost impossible, the command word may be spoken. This transports everyone and everything in the room, including the urn, to Khala, the uppermost layer of Gehenna.

Nine Hells: The Nine Hells can be reached by using special pieces of blood-red coal. When one of these coals is lit or dropped into a flame, a ball of fire flares out from the coal. It does no damage, but transports all creatures and objects within 20 feet to Avernus. No command word is needed for the effect to take place.

Acheron: The device used to reach Aceheron is a two-inch cube of black onyx. The cube always appears as a puzzle inside a black sack. The puzzle is made up of 43 small pieces, which must be fit together to form the cube. When complete, the command word must be spoken.

Solving the puzzle require an Intelligence check at half a creature's Intelligence score. Each attempt to solve the puzzle requires 1d6 turns. Once the cube has been used to teleport, it falls to pieces. The pieces all reappear in the sack, wherever it might be. To use the device again, the pieces must be reassembled.

Warp Marble: This item is a small (1/2-inch diameter) sphere of fine crystal, often appearing with a rich blue or aquamarine hue. Each marble has three words of command associated with it.

The first command triggers the marble to create an extradimensional space large enough to contain a single large-sized creature. When this word is spoken, the closest creature to the marble is instantly transported to and imprisoned within this space. Similar to the *seclusion* spell, the inhabitant of this space can see and hear events in the "real world," but can do nothing to affect anything outside the prison. Spellcasting and use of psionics are impossible while within the prison. If the prison is already occupied, this first word of command will have no effect.

The second command word releases the occupant of the extradimensional space. The occupant is immediately returned to the "real world," appearing within three feet of the marble (wherever it might be). Note that this word of release can be spoken and will be effective from within the prison. Thus, the possessor of the marble can use it as a sanctuary to escape from harm.

The third word of command sets the marble as a trap. After this word is spoken, the first creature of large size or smaller to touch the marble is immediately imprisoned within the extradimensional space. If the first creature to touch the marble is larger than size L, the magic is not triggered; if a size L or smaller creature subsequently touches the item, the magic takes effect.

Once one creature has been imprisoned, other creatures can touch the marble with no adverse effects. A creature trapped in this method can be freed only through the use of the word of release from outside the marble.

A marble trapped in this manner can be thrown at another creature in an attempt to trap the creature. If an attack roll is successful, the target creature is allowed a saving throw versus spell. Success indicates that the creature suffers no effect. Failure indicates that the creature is trapped in the *warp marble.*

If a marble is taken into an extradimensional space (such as within a *portable hole*), if it is *teleported, gated,* or transported via *dimensional folding* or any analogous method, or if it is shifted to another plane of existence, any occupant of the extradimensional space is immediately expelled into the Astral plane.

Zwann's Watering Can: Invented by the noted botanist Salerno Zwann, this otherwise ordinary watering can is activated when the user fills it with two gallons of water and lets it stand undisturbed for 30 days. At the end of that period, the user may sprinkle the water from *Zwann's watering can* over a patch of tilled soil no larger than a 25-foot square. Seeds subsequently planted in this treated soil grow normally, but are permanently immune to disease, drought (the plants never need to be watered again), insects, bad weather (such as hailstorms and early frost) and all other forms of nonmagical trauma. The plants can be harvested normally by the planter.

Water from *Zwann's watering can* has no effect on already maturing plants. It cannot revive withered, diseased, or insect-infested plants.

The patch of soil retains its effectiveness for one year, after which time it must be watered again for the effect to be renewed.

Boldfaced spells are described in the *Tome of Magic* rule book. The remainder are found in the AD&D® 2nd Edition *Player's Handbook*.
Italicized spells are reversible. The reverse name follows the slash.
An asterisk (*) indicates a Wild Magic spell.

Abjuration

Alarm (1st)
Cantrip (1st)
Protection From Evil/Protection From Good (1st)
Chaos Shield* (2nd)
Nahal's Nonsensical Nullifier* (2nd)
Protection From Cantrips (2nd)
Protection From Paralysis (2nd)
Dispel Magic (3rd)
Non-Detection (3rd)
Protection From Evil, 10' Radius/Protection From Good, 10' Radius (3rd)
Protection From Normal Missiles (3rd)
Fire Trap (4th)
Minor Globe of Invulnerability (4th)
Minor Spell Turning (4th)
Remove Curse/Bestow Curse (4th)
Avoidance/Attraction (5th)
Dismissal (5th)
Lower Resistance (5th)
Safeguarding (5th)
Von Gasik's Refusal (5th)
Anti-Magic Shell (6th)
Globe of Invulnerability (6th)
Repulsion (6th)
Banishment (7th)
Sequester (7th)
Spell Turning (7th)
Hornung's Random Dispatcher* (8th)
Mind Blank (8th)
Serten's Spell Immunity (8th)
Elemental Aura (9th)
Imprisonment/Freedom (9th)
Prismatic Sphere (9th)
Stabilize* (9th)

Alteration

Affect Normal Fires (1st)
Burning Hands (1st)
Cantrip (1st)
Color Spray (1st)
Comprehend Languages/Confuse Languages (1st)
Dancing Lights (1st)
Enlarge/Reduce (1st)
Erase (1st)
Feather Fall (1st)
Fire Burst (1st)
Fist of Stone (1st)
Gaze Reflection (1st)
Hold Portal (1st)
Jump (1st)
Lasting Breath (1st)
Light (1st)
Mending (1st)
Message (1st)
Metamorphose Liquids (1st)
Murdock's Feathery Flyer (1st)
Shocking Grasp (1st)

Spider Climb (1st)
Wizard Mark (1st)
Alter Self (2nd)
Continual Light (2nd)
Darkness, 15' Radius (2nd)
Deeppockets (2nd)
Fog Cloud (2nd)
Fool's Gold (2nd)
Irritation (2nd)
Knock/Lock (2nd)
Levitate (2nd)
Magic Mouth (2nd)
Maximilian's Earthen Grasp (2nd)
Pyrotechnics (2nd)
Ride the Wind (2nd)
Rope Trick (2nd)
Sense Shifting (2nd)
Shatter (2nd)
Strength (2nd)
Whispering Wind (2nd)
Wizard Lock (2nd)
Alacrity (3rd)
Alternate Reality* (3rd)
Blink (3rd)
Delude (3rd)
Explosive Runes (3rd)
Far Reaching I (3rd)
Fireflow* (3rd)
Fool's Speech* (3rd)
Fly (3rd)
Gust of Wind (3rd)
Haste (3rd)
Infravision (3rd)
Item (3rd)
Leomund's Tiny Hut (3rd)
Maximilian's Stony Grasp (3rd)
Melf's Minute Meteors (3rd)
Secret Page (3rd)
Slow (3rd)
Squaring the Circle (3rd)
Tongues/Babble (3rd)
Water Breathing/Air Breathing (3rd)
Wind Wall (3rd)
Wraithform (3rd)
Dilation I (4th)
Dimension Door (4th)
Extension I (4th)
Far Reaching II (4th)
Fire Shield (4th)
Leomund's Secure Shelter (4th)
Massmorph (4th)
Mordenkainen's Celerity (4th)
Otiluke's Resilient Sphere (4th)
Plant Growth (4th)
Polymorph Other (4th)
Polymorph Self (4th)
Rainbow Pattern (4th)
Rary's Mnemonic Enhancer (4th)
Solid Fog (4th)
Stoneskin (4th)
Turn Pebble to Boulder/Turn Boulder to Pebble (4th)
Vacancy (4th)
Wizard Eye (4th)
Airy Water (5th)
Animal Growth/Shrink Animal (5th)
Avoidance/Attraction (5th)
Distance Distortion (5th)
Extension II (5th)
Fabricate (5th)
Far Reaching III (5th)

Leomund's Secret Chest (5th)
Lower Resistance (5th)
Passwall (5th)
Stone Shape (5th)
Telekinesis (5th)
Teleport (5th)
Transmute Rock to Mud/Transmute Mud to Rock (5th)
Waveform* (5th)
Claws of the Umber Hulk (6th)
Control Weather (6th)
Death Fog (6th)
Dilation II (6th)
Disintegrate (6th)
Extension III (6th)
Glassee (6th)
Guards and Wards (6th)
Lower Water/Raise Water (6th)
Mirage Arcana (6th)
Mordenkainen's Lucubration (6th)
Move Earth (6th)
Otiluke's Freezing Sphere (6th)
Part Water (6th)
Project Image (6th)
Stone to Flesh/Flesh to Stone (6th)
Tenser's Transformation (6th)
Transmute Water to Dust/Improved Create Water (6th)
Wildshield* (6th)
Duo-Dimension (7th)
Hatch the Stone From the Egg (7th)
Hornung's Surge Selector* (7th)
Mordenkainen's Magnificent Mansion (7th)
Phase Door (7th)
Reverse Gravity (7th)
Spell Shape* (7th)
Statue (7th)
Suffocate (7th)
Teleport Without Error (7th)
Vanish (7th)
Abi-Dalzim's Horrid Wilting (8th)
Airboat (8th)
Glassteel (8th)
Incendiary Cloud (8th)
Otiluke's Telekinetic Sphere (8th)
Permanency (8th)
Polymorph Any Object (8th)
Sink (8th)
Crystalbrittle (9th)
Estate Transference (9th)
Glorious Transmutation (9th)
Mordenkainen's Disjunction (9th)
Shape Change (9th)
Succor/Call (9th)
Temporal Stasis/Temporal Reinstatement (9th)
Time Stop (9th)

Conjuration/Summoning

Armor (1st)
Cantrip (1st)
Conjure Spell Component (1st)
Find Familiar (1st)
Grease (1st)
Mount (1st)
Unseen Servant (1st)
Glitterdust (2nd)
Melf's Acid Arrow (2nd)
Summon Swarm (2nd)

Flame Arrow (3rd)
Monster Summoning I (3rd)
Phantom Steed (3rd)
Sepia Snake Sigil (3rd)
Watery Double (3rd)
Evard's Black Tentacles (4th)
Monster Summoning II (4th)
Summon Lycanthrope (4th)
Conjure Elemental (5th)
Khazid's Procurement (5th)
Leomund's Secret Chest (5th)
Monster Summoning III (5th)
Mordenkainen's Faithful Hound (5th)
Summon Shadow (5th)
Conjure Animals (6th)
Ensnarement (6th)
Forest's Fiery Constrictor (6th)
Invisible Stalker (6th)
Monster Summoning IV (6th)
Wildstrike* (6th)
Drawmij's Instant Summons (7th)
Intensify Summoning (7th)
Limited Wish (7th)
Monster Summoning V (7th)
Mordenkainen's Magnificent Mansion (7th)
Power Word, Stun (7th)
Prismatic Spray (7th)
Maze (8th)
Monster Summoning VI (8th)
Power Word, Blind (8th)
Prismatic Wall (8th)
Symbol (8th)
Trap the Soul (8th)
Wildzone* (8th)
Gate (9th)
Monster Summoning VII (9th)
Power Word, Kill (9th)
Prismatic Sphere (9th)
Wildwind* (9th)
Wish (9th)

Enchantment/Charm

Cantrip (1st)
Charm Person (1st)
Friends (1st)
Hypnotism (1st)
Sleep (1st)
Taunt (1st)
Bind (2nd)
Deeppockets (2nd)
Forget (2nd)
Insatiable Thirst (2nd)
Ray of Enfeeblement (2nd)
Scare (2nd)
Tasha's Uncontrollable Hideous Laughter (2nd)
Hold Person (3rd)
Minor Malison (3rd)
Suggestion (3rd)
Watery Double (3rd)
Charm Monster (4th)
Confusion (4th)
Emotion (4th)
Enchanted Weapon (4th)
Fire Charm (4th)
Fumble (4th)
Greater Malison (4th)
Leomund's Secure Shelter (4th)
Magic Mirror (4th)

Chaos (5th)
Domination (5th)
Fabricate (5th)
Feeblemind (5th)
Hold Monster (5th)
Leomund's Lamentable Belaborment (5th)
Magic Staff (5th)
Mind Fog (5th)
Enchant an Item (6th)
Eyebite (6th)
Geas (6th)
Guards and Wards (6th)
Mass Suggestion (6th)
Charm Plants (7th)
Hatch the Stone from the Egg (7th)
Shadow Walk (7th)
Steal Enchantment (7th)
Antipathy-Sympathy (8th)
Airboat (8th)
Binding (8th)
Demand (8th)
Mass Charm (8th)
Otto's Irresistible Dance (8th)
Sink (8th)
Mordenkainen's Disjunction (9th)
Succor/Call (9th)

Illusion/Phantasm

Audible Glamer (1st)
Cantrip (1st)
Change Self (1st)
Nystul's Magic Aura (1st)
Phantasmal Force (1st)
Spook (1st)
Ventriloquism (1st)
Blindness (2nd)
Blur (2nd)
Deafness (2nd)
Fools' Gold (2nd)
Hypnotic Pattern (2nd)
Improved Phantasmal Force (2nd)
Invisibility (2nd)
Leomund's Trap (2nd)
Mirror Image (2nd)
Misdirection (2nd)
Whispering Wind (2nd)
Illusionary Script (3rd)
Invisibility, 10' Radius (3rd)
Lorloveim's Creeping Shadow (3rd)
Phantom Steed (3rd)
Spectral Force (3rd)
Wraithform (3rd)
Fear (4th)
Hallucinatory Terrain (4th)
Illusionary Wall (4th)
Improved Invisibility (4th)
Minor Creation (4th)
Phantasmal Killer (4th)
Rainbow Pattern (4th)
Shadow Monsters (4th)
Vacancy (4th)
Advanced Illusion (5th)
Demi-Shadow Monsters (5th)
Dream/Nightmare (5th)
Major Creation (5th)
Seeming (5th)
Shadow Door (5th)
Shadow Magic (5th)
Demi-Shadow Magic (6th)

Eyebite (6th)
Lorloveim's Shadowy Transformation (6th)
Mirage Arcana (6th)
Mislead (6th)
Permanent Illusion (6th)
Programmed Illusion (6th)
Project Image (6th)
Shades (6th)
Veil (6th)
Mass Invisibility (7th)
Sequester (7th)
Shadowcat (7th)
Shadow Walk (7th)
Simulacrum (7th)
Screen (8th)
Weird (9th)

Invocation/Evocation

Alarm (1st)
Cantrip (1st)
Fire Burst (1st)
Magic Missile (1st)
Nahal's Reckless Dweomer* (1st)
Shield (1st)
Tenser's Floating Disc (1st)
Wall of Fog (1st)
Flaming Sphere (2nd)
Hornung's Baneful Deflector* (2nd)
Stinking Cloud (2nd)
Web (2nd)
Augmentation I (3rd)
Fireball (3rd)
Lightning Bolt (3rd)
Melf's Minute Meteors (3rd)
Dig (4th)
Divination Enhancement (4th)
Fire Shield (4th)
Fire Trap (4th)
Ice Storm (4th)
Mordenkainen's Celerity (4th)
Otiluke's Resilient Sphere (4th)
Shout (4th)
There/Not There* (4th)
Thunder Staff (4th)
Unluck* (4th)
Wall of Fire (4th)
Wall of Ice (4th)
Bigby's Interposing Hand (5th)
Cloudkill (5th)
Cone of Cold (5th)
Dream (5th)
Leomund's Lamentable Belaborment (5th)
Sending (5th)
Vortex* (5th)
Wall of Force (5th)
Wall of Iron (5th)
Wall of Stone (5th)
Augmentation II (6th)
Bigby's Forceful Hand (6th)
Chain Lightning (6th)
Contingency (6th)
Death Fog (6th)
Enchant an Item (6th)
Guards and Wards (6th)
Otiluke's Freezing Sphere (6th)
Tenser's Transformation (6th)
Acid Storm (7th)
Bigby's Grasping Hand (7th)

Delayed Blast Fireball (7th)
Forcecage (7th)
Hatch the Stone from the Egg (7th)
Limited Wish (7th)
Malec-Keth's Flame Fist (7th)
Mordenkainen's Sword (7th)
Bigby's Clenched Fist (8th)
Binding (8th)
Demand (8th)
Gunther's Kaleidoscopic Strike (8th)
Homunculus Shield (8th)
Incendiary Cloud (8th)
Otiluke's Telekinetic Sphere (8th)
Astral Spell (9th)
Bigby's Crushing Hand (9th)
Chain Contingency (9th)
Elemental Aura (9th)
Energy Drain (9th)
Meteor Swarm (9th)
Wildfire* (9th)

Divination

Cantrip (1st)
Detect Magic (1st)
Detect Undead (1st)
Hornung's Guess* (1st)
Identify (1st)
Patternweave* (1st)
Read Magic (1st)
Detect Evil/Detect Good (2nd)
Detect Invisibility (2nd)
ESP (2nd)
Know Alignment/Undetectable Alignment (2nd)
Locate Object/Obscure Object (2nd)
Past Life (2nd)
Alamir's Fundamental Breakdown (3rd)
Clairaudience (3rd)
Clairvoyance (3rd)
Wizard Sight (3rd)
Detect Scrying (4th)
Locate Creature (4th)
Magic Mirror (4th)
Contact Other Plane (5th)
False Vision (5th)
Khazid's Procurement (5th)
Legend Lore (6th)
True Seeing (6th)
Vision (7th)
Screen (8th)
Foresight (9th)

Necromancy

Cantrip (1st)
Chill Touch (1st)
Detect Undead (1st)
Spectral Hand (2nd)
Feign Death (3rd)
Hold Undead (3rd)
Spirit Armor (3rd)
Vampiric Touch (3rd)
Contagion (4th)
Enervation (4th)
Mask of Death (4th)
Animate Dead (5th)
Magic Jar (5th)
Summon Shadow (5th)
Bloodstone's Spectral Steed (6th)
Death Spell (6th)

Reincarnation (6th)
Bloodstone's Frightful Joining (7th)
Control Undead (7th)
Finger of Death (7th)
Intensify Summoning (7th)
Suffocate (7th)
Abi-Dalzim's Horrid Wilting (8th)
Clone (8th)
Homunculus Shield (8th)
Energy Drain (9th)
Wail of the Banshee (9th)

Wild Magic

Hornung's Guess* (1st)
Nahal's Reckless Dweomer* (1st)
Patternweave* (1st)
Chaos Shield* (2nd)
Hornung's Baneful Deflector* (2nd)
Nahal's Nonsensical Nullifier* (2nd)
Alternate Reality* (3rd)
Fireflow* (3rd)
Fool's Speech* (3rd)
There/Not There* (4th)
Unluck* (4th)
Vortex* (5th)
Waveform* (5th)
Wildshield* (6th)
Wildstrike* (6th)
Hornung's Surge Selector* (7th)
Spell Shape* (7th)
Hornung's Random Dispatcher* (8th)
Wildzone* (8th)
Stablize* (9th)
Wildfire* (9th)
Wildwind* (9th)

Elemental Air

Feather Fall (1st)
Lasting Breath (1st)
Wall of Fog (1st)
Fog Cloud (2nd)
Ride the Wind (2nd)
Stinking Cloud (2nd)
Whispering Wind (2nd)
Alamir's Fundamental Breakdown (3rd)
Gust of Wind (3rd)
Water Breathing (3rd)
Wind Wall (3rd)
Solid Fog (4th)
Airy Water (5th)
Cloudkill (5th)
Conjure Elemental (5th)
Control Weather (6th)
Death Fog (6th)
Suffocate (7th)
Airboat (8th)
Incendiary Cloud (8th)
Elemental Aura (9th)

Elemental Earth

Fist of Stone (1st)
Fool's Gold (2nd)
Maximilian's Earthen Grasp (2nd)
Alamir's Fundamental Breakdown (3rd)
Maximilian's Stony Grasp (3rd)
Dig (4th)
Stoneskin (4th)

Turn Pebble to Boulder (4th)
Conjure Elemental (5th)
Distance Distortion (5th)
Passwall (5th)
Stone Shape (5th)
Transmute Rock to Mud (5th)
Wall of Iron (5th)
Wall of Stone (5th)
Glassee (6th)
Move Earth (6th)
Stone to Flesh (6th)
Transmute Water to Dust (6th)
Hatch the Stone From the Egg (7th)
Statue (7th)
Glassteel (8th)
Sink (8th)
Crystalbrittle (9th)
Elemental Aura (9th)

Elemental Fire

Affect Normal Fires (1st)
Burning Hands (1st)
Dancing Lights (1st)
Fire Burst (1st)
Flaming Sphere (2nd)
Pyrotechnics (2nd)
Alamir's Fundamental Breakdown (3rd)
Fireball (3rd)
Flame Arrow (3rd)
Melf's Minute Meteors (3rd)
Fire Charm (4th)
Fire Shield (4th)
Fire Trap (4th)
Wall of Fire (4th)
Conjure Elemental (5th)
Forest's Fiery Constrictor (6th)
Delayed Blast Fireball (7th)
Malec-Keth's Flame Fist (7th)
Incendiary Cloud (8th)
Meteor Swarm (9th)
Elemental Aura (9th)

Elemental Water

Metamorphose Liquids (1st)
Insatiable Thirst (2nd)
Alamir's Fundamental Breakdown (3rd)
Water Breathing (3rd)
Watery Double (3rd)
Ice Storm (4th)
Wall of Ice (4th)
Airy Water (5th)
Cone of Cold (5th)
Conjure Elemental (5th)
Transmute Rock to Mud (5th)
Lower Water (6th)
Otiluke's Freezing Sphere (6th)
Part Water (6th)
Transmute Water to Dust (6th)
Acid Storm (7th)
Abi-Dalzim's Horrid Wilting (8th)
Elemental Aura (9th)

Boldfaced spells are described in the *Tome of Magic* rulebook. The remaining spells are found in the 2nd Edition *Player's Handbook*. *Italicized* spells are reversible. The reverse name follows the slash. An asterisk (*) indicates a cooperative magic spell.

All

Bless/Curse (1st)
Combine* (1st)
Detect Evil/Detect Good (1st)
Purify Food & Drink/Putrefy Food & Drink (1st)
*Sanctify/Defile*** (2nd)
Focus* (4th)
Uplift* (4th)
Atonement (5th)

Animal

Animal Friendship (1st)
Invisibility to Animals (1st)
Locate Animals or Plants (1st)
Charm Person or Mammal (2nd)
Messenger (2nd)
Snake Charm (2nd)
Speak With Animals (2nd)
Hold Animal (3rd)
Summon Insects (3rd)
Animal Summoning I (4th)
Call Woodland Beings (4th)
Giant Insects/Shrink Insect (4th)
Repel Insects (4th)
Animal Growth/Animal Reduction (5th)
Animal Summoning II (5th)
Animal Summoning III (6th)
Anti-Animal Shell (6th)
Creeping Doom (7th)

Astral

Speak With Astral Traveler (1st)
Astral Window (3rd)
Join With Astral Traveler (4th)
Plane Shift (5th)
Astral Spell (7th)

Chaos

Mistaken Missive (1st)
Dissension's Feast (2nd)
Miscast Magic (3rd)
Random Casualty (3rd)
Chaotic Combat (4th)
Chaotic Sleep (4th)
Inverted Ethics (4th)

Chaotic Commands (5th)
Uncontrolled Weather (7th)

Charm

Command (1st)
Remove Fear/Cause Fear (1st)
Enthrall (2nd)
Hold Person (2nd)
Music of the Spheres (2nd)
Mystic Transfer* (2nd)
Emotion Control (3rd)
Cloak of Bravery/Cloak of Fear (4th)
Free Action (4th)
Imbue With Spell Ability (4th)
Meld* (5th)
Quest (5th)
Confusion (7th)
Exaction (7th)

Combat

Magical Stone (1st)
Shillelagh (1st)
Chant (2nd)
Spiritual Hammer (2nd)
Prayer (3rd)
Unearthly Choir* (3rd)
Flame Strike (5th)
Insect Plague (5th)
Spiritual Wrath* (6th)
Holy Word/Unholy Word (7th)

Creation

Create Holy Symbol (2nd)
Create Food & Water (3rd)
Addition (4th)
Blessed Abundance (5th)
Animate Object (6th)
Blade Barrier (6th)
Heroes' Feast (6th)
Wall of Thorns (6th)
Changestaff (7th)
Chariot of Sustarre (7th)

Divination

Analyze Balance (1st)
Detect Magic (1st)
Detect Poison (1st)
Detect Snares & Pits (1st)
Locate Animals or Plants (1st)
Augury (2nd)
Detect Charm/Undetectable Charm (2nd)
Find Traps (2nd)
Know Alignment/Undetectable Alignment (2nd)
Speak With Animals (2nd)

Extradimensional Detection (3rd)
Locate Object/Obscure Object (3rd)
Speak With Dead (3rd)
Detect Lie/Undetectable Lie (4th)
Divination (4th)
Reflecting Pool (4th)
Tongues/Babble (4th)
Commune (5th)
Commune With Nature (5th)
Consequence (5th)
Magic Font (5th)
Thoughtwave* (5th)
True Seeing/False Seeing (5th)
Find the Path/Lose the Path (6th)
Speak With Monsters (6th)
Stone Tell (6th)
Divine Inspiration (7th)
Mind Tracker (7th)

Elemental

Create Water/Destroy Water (1st)
Log of Everburning (1st)
Dust Devil (2nd)
Fire Trap (2nd)
Flame Blade (2nd)
Heat Metal/Chill Metal (2nd)
Produce Flame (2nd)
Flame Walk (3rd)
Meld Into Stone (3rd)
Protection From Fire (3rd)
Pyrotechnics (3rd)
Stone Shape (3rd)
Water Breathing/Air Breathing (3rd)
Water Walk (3rd)
Lower Water/Raise Water (4th)
Produce Fire/Quench Fire (4th)
Air Walk (5th)
Cloud of Purification (5th)
Elemental Forbiddance (5th)
Spike Stones (5th)
Transmute Rock to Mud/Transmute Mud to Rock (5th)
Wall of Fire (5th)
Conjure Fire Elemental/Dismiss Fire Elemental (6th)
Fire Seeds (6th)
Part Water (6th)
Stone Tell (6th)
Transmute Water to Dust/Improved Create Water (6th)
Animate Rock (7th)
Chariot of Sustarre (7th)
Conjure Earth Elemental/Dismiss Earth Elemental (7th)
Earthquake (7th)
Fire Storm/Fire Quench (7th)
Transmute Metal to Wood (7th)
Wind Walk (7th)

Elemental Air

Dust Devil (2nd)
Water Breathing/Air Breathing (3rd)
Air Walk (5th)
Elemental Forbiddance (5th)
Cloud of Purification (5th)
Wind Walk (7th)

Elemental Earth

Meld Into Stone (3rd)
Stone Shape (3rd)
Elemental Forbiddance (5th)
Spike Stones (5th)
Transmute Rock to Mud/ Transmute Mud to Rock (5th)
Stone Tell (6th)
Transmute Water to Dust/ Improved Create Water (6th)
Animate Rock (7th)
Conjure Earth Elemental/Dismiss Earth Elemental (7th)
Earthquake (7th)
Transmute Metal to Wood (7th)

Elemental Fire

Log of Everburning (1st)
Fire Trap (2nd)
Flame Blade (2nd)
Heat Metal/Chill Metal (2nd)
Produce Flame (2nd)
Flame Walk (3rd)
Protection From Fire (3rd)
Pyrotechnics (3rd)
Produce Fire/Quench Fire (4th)
Elemental Forbiddance (5th)
Wall of Fire (5th)
Conjure Fire Elemental/Dismiss Fire Elemental (6th)
Fire Seeds (6th)
Chariot of Sustarre (7th)
Fire Storm/Fire Quench (7th)

Elemental Water

Create Water/Destroy Water (1st)
Water Breathing/Air Breathing (3rd)
Water Walk (3rd)
Lower Water/Raise Water (4th)
Elemental Forbiddance (5th)
Transmute Rock to Mud/ Transmute Mud to Rock (5th)
Part Water (6th)
Transmute Water to Dust/ Improved Create Water (6th)

Guardian

Sacred Guardian (1st)
Silence, 15′ Radius (2nd)
Wyvern Watch (2nd)
Glyph of Warding (3rd)
Unceasing Vigilance of the Holy Sentinel (5th)
Blade Barrier (6th)
Symbol (7th)

Healing

Cure Light Wounds/Cause Light Wounds (1st)
Slow Poison (2nd)
Cure Serious Wounds/Cause Serious Wounds (4th)
Fortify* (4th)
Neutralize Poison/Poison (4th)
Cure Critical Wounds/Cause Critical Wounds (5th)
Heal/Harm (6th)

Law

Command (1st)
Calm Chaos (2nd)
Enthrall (2nd)
Hold Person (2nd)
Rigid Thinking (3rd)
Strength of One (3rd)
Compulsive Order (4th)
Defensive Harmony (4th)
Champion's Strength (5th)
Impeding Permission (5th)
Legal Thoughts (6th)
Control Weather (7th)

Necromantic

Invisibility to Undead (1st)
Aid (2nd)
Animate Dead (3rd)
Cure Blindness or Deafness/Cause Blindness or Deafness (3rd)
Cure Disease/Cause Disease (3rd)
Feign Death (3rd)
Negative Plane Protection (3rd)
Raise Dead/Slay Living (5th)
Breath of Life/Breath of Death (7th)
Regenerate/Wither (7th)
Reincarnate (7th)
Restoration/Energy Drain (7th)
Resurrection/Destruction (7th)

Numbers

Analyze Balance (1st)
Personal Reading (1st)
Moment (2nd)
Music of the Spheres (2nd)
Extradimensional Detection (3rd)
Moment Reading (3rd)
Telethaumaturgy (3rd)
Addition (4th)
Dimensional Folding (4th)
Probability Control (4th)
Consequence (5th)
Extradimensional Manipulation (5th)
Extradimensional Pocket (5th)
Physical Mirror (6th)
Seclusion (6th)
Spacewarp (7th)
Timelessness (7th)

Plant

Entangle (1st)
Locate Animals or Plants (1st)
Log of Everburning (1st)
Pass Without Trace (1st)
Shillelagh (1st)
Barkskin (2nd)
Goodberry/Badberry (2nd)
Trip (2nd)
Warp Wood/Straighten Wood (2nd)
Plant Growth (3rd)
Slow Rot (3rd)
Snare (3rd)
Spike Growth (3rd)
Tree (3rd)
Hallucinatory Forest/Revealed Wood (4th)
Hold Plant (4th)
Plant Door (4th)
Speak With Plants (4th)
Sticks to Snakes/Snakes to Sticks (4th)
Anti-Plant Shell (5th)
Pass Plant (5th)
Liveoak (6th)
Transport Via Plants (6th)
Turn Wood (6th)
Wall of Thorns (6th)
Changestaff (7th)

Protection

Endure Cold/Endure Head (1st)
Protection From Evil/Protection From Good (1st)
Ring of Hands/Ring of Woe* (1st)
Sanctuary (1st)

Barkskin (2nd)
Resist Fire/Resist Cold (2nd)
Withdraw (2nd)
Dispel Magic (3rd)
*Line of Protection/Line of Destruction** (3rd)
Magical Vestment (3rd)
Negative Plane Protection (3rd)
Protection From Fire (3rd)
Remove Curse/Bestow Curse (3rd)
Remove Paralysis (3rd)
Protection From Evil, 10' Radius/ Protection From Good, 10' Radius (4th)
Protection From Lightning (4th)
Repel Insects (4th)
Spell Immunity (4th)
Anti-Plant Shell (5th)
Dispel Evil/Dispel Good (5th)
Anti-Animal Shell (6th)
Forbiddance (6th)

Summoning

Call Upon Faith (1st)
Draw Upon Holy Might (2nd)
Summon Insects (3rd)
Abjure (4th)
Animal Summoning I (4th)
Call Woodland Beings (4th)
Animal Summoning II (5th)
Dispel Evil/Dispel Good (5th)
Aerial Servant (6th)
Animal Summoning III (6th)
Animate Object (6th)
Conjure Animals (6th)
Conjure Fire Elemental/Dismiss Fire Elemental (6th)
Wall of Thorns (6th)
Weather Summoning (6th)
Word of Recall (6th)
Conjure Earth Elemental/Dismiss Earth Elemental (7th)
Creeping Doom (7th)
Exaction (7th)
Gate (7th)
Spirit of Power* (7th)
Succor/Call (7th)

Sun

Light/Darkness (1st)
Continual Light/Continual Darkness (3rd)
Starshine (3rd)
Blessed Warmth (4th)
Moonbeam (5th)
Rainbow (5th)

The Great Circle/The Black Circle*
(6th)
Sol's Searing Orb (6th)
Sunray (7th)

Thought

Emotion Read (1st)
Thought Capture (1st)
Idea (2nd)
Mind Read (2nd)
Emotion Control (3rd)
Memory Read (3rd)
Telepathy (3rd)
Genius (4th)
Mental Domination (4th)
Rapport (4th)
Solipsism (4th)
Thought Broadcast (4th)
Memory Wrack (5th)
Mindshatter (5th)
Disbelief (6th)
Group Mind (6th)
Divine Inspiration (7th)
Mind Tracker (7th)

Time

Know Age (1st)
Know Time (1st)
Hesitation (2nd)
Nap (2nd)
Accelerate Healing (3rd)
Choose Future (3rd)
Age Plant (4th)
Body Clock (4th)
Modify Memory (4th)
Age Object/Youthful Object (5th)
Repeat Action (5th)
Time Pool (5th)
Age Creature/Restore Youth (6th)
Reverse Time (6th)
Skip Day (6th)
Age Dragon (7th)

Travelers

Know Direction (1st)
Aura of Comfort (2nd)
Lighten Load (2nd)
Create Campsite/Break Camp (3rd)
Helping Hand (3rd)
Know Customs (3rd)
Circle of Privacy (4th)
Tree Steed (4th)
Clear Path/Clutter Path (5th)
Easy March (5th)
Monster Mount (6th)
Hovering Road (7th)

War

Courage (1st)
Morale (1st)
Emotion Perception (2nd)
Rally (2nd)
Adaptation (3rd)
Caltrops (3rd)
Leadership/Doubt (4th)
Tanglefoot/Selective Passage (4th)
Disguise (5th)
Illusory Artillery (5th)
Gravity Variation (6th)
Illusory Fortification (7th)
Shadow Engines (7th)

Wards

Anti-Vermin Barrier (1st)
Weighty Chest (1st)
Frisky Chest (2nd)
Zone of Truth (2nd)
Efficacious Monster Ward (3rd)
Invisibiity Purge (3rd)
Squeaking Floors (3rd)
Thief's Lament (3rd)
Zone of Sweet Air (3rd)
Fire Purge (4th)
Weather Stasis (4th)
Barrier of Retention (5th)
Elemental Forbiddance (5th)
Grounding (5th)
Shrieking Walls (5th)
Undead Ward (5th)
Crushing Walls (6th)
Dragonbane (6th)
Land of Stability (6th)
Tentacle Walls (7th)

Weather

Faerie Fire (1st)
Obscurement (2nd)
Call Lightning (3rd)
Control Temperature, 10' Radius (4th)
Protection From Lightning (4th)
Weather Stasis (4th)
Control Winds (5th)
Rainbow (5th)
Weather Summoning (6th)
Control Weather (7th)

BIRTHRIGHT™ Campaign

Experience the thrill of playing rulers of legend who command mighty armies and wield the power of kingdoms! The Birthright Campaign setting for the AD&D® game makes this possible as never before. Role-play warriors, wizards, priests, and thieves descended from royal bloodlines, command imperial powers, and control the destinies of far-reaching lands. But be prepared to battle enemies who are equally as powerful, as well as millennia-old monstrous abominations that will stop at nothing to steal your kingly power - your birthright.

FORGOTTEN REALMS® Campaign

Well met, and welcome to the most popular, most detailed fantasy campaign world ever created! Here gods walk the earth, and fantastic armies clash. Visitors explore a vast frontier filled with fascinating folk, from bold heroes and whimsical characters to shadowy villains and clandestine societies. This is the home of Elminster the sage and Drizzt the dark elf—two heroes featured in TSR's best-selling FORGOTTEN REALMS novel line. No setting can match the grand scope of the FORGOTTEN REALMS campaign world.

RAVENLOFT® Campaign

Whether you journey to Ravenloft for an evening of terror or an extended nightmare, the experience will haunt you forever. The RAVENLOFT campaign is a horrific realm of dread and desire, rooted in the Gothic tradition. The misty fingers of this world can reach into any other campaign setting to draw unsuspecting travelers into its midst. Once it holds them in its icy embrace, it may never let them go. In a shadowy world filled with vampires, werewolves, and ghosts, only the strong of heart may survive!

DARK SUN® Campaign

The DARK SUN world is the AD&D® game's most savage game setting—a desert realm scorched by a relentless sun, blasted by the destructive magic of generations of evil wizards. It is a land of evil sorceror-kings and powerful psionicists who command astounding mental powers. In this wild and brutal landscape, a single adventurer can alter the course of history and forever change the world. One of those heroes could be yours!

PLANESCAPE™ Campaign

Until now, only the most powerful wizards could peek into the magnificent wealth of the multiverse, but no longer! Now every adventurer can enter the mighty planes—but surviving them is another matter entirely. Infinite universes of infinite variety and danger lie beyond the portal, beginning with Sigil, the City of Doors, where all worlds in existence meet.

DRAGONLANCE® Saga Campaign

Enter Krynn, a world of romance and high adventure. Discover tinker gnomes, gully dwarves, gleeful kender, nefarious villains, noble heroes . . . and dark, deadly dragons. Draconian thugs patrol the streets, evil red dragons fill the skies, and beautiful dragons of gold and silver do battle on the side of good. This world struggles to regain its lost honor and glory, and unlikely adventurers can become legendary heroes!